Jenna Blum is the *New York Times* and number one international bestselling author of the novels *Those Who Save Us* and *The Stormchasers*. She was also voted one of the favourite contemporary women writers by Oprah.com readers. Jenna is based in Boston, where she earned her MA from Boston University and has taught fiction and novel workshops for Grub Street Writers for twenty years.

'Jenna Blum plumbs the depths of loss and love in this exquisite page-turner'
People Magazine

'The perfect encapsulation of the changing times and turbulence of mid- and late-20th-century America'
Publishers Weekly

'An unsentimental, richly detailed study of loss and its legacy'
Kirkus Reviews

'Jenna Blum shines a powerful light on how the past swings back and how we must face it. *The Lost Family* is an extraordinary read, the kind of book that makes you sob and smile, the kind that gives you hope ... It is compassionate, masterful and disturbingly contemporary'
Tatiana de Rosnay, bestselling author of *Sarah's Key*

'This is a dazzling novel of great compassion, honestly reckoning with the time-and-place-spanning ripple effect of great pain as well as love'
Laura Moriarty, *New York Times* bestselling author of *The Chaperone*

'Deftly executed, deeply moving and full of heart, Jenna Blum's *The Lost Family* is an evocative look at the legacy of war and how it impacts one memorable family'
Jami Attenberg, bestselling author of *The Middlesteins*

ALSO BY JENNA BLUM

The Lucky One in Grand Central
The Stormchasers
Those Who Save Us

THE
LOST FAMILY

Jenna Blum

B
BLACKFRIARS

BLACKFRIARS

First published in the United States in 2018 by Harper,
an imprint of HarperCollins Publishers

First published in Great Britain in 2018 by Blackfriars

1 3 5 7 9 10 8 6 4 2

ISBN 978-0-349-13463-5

Printed and bound in Great Britain by
Clays Ltd, Elcograf S.p.A.

Book design by Leah Carlson-Stanisic

Papers used by Blackfriars are from well-managed forests
and other responsible sources.

This imprint has no connection with The Order of Preachers (Dominicans)

Blackfriars
An imprint of
Little, Brown Book Group
Carmelite House
50 Victoria Embankment
London EC4Y 0DZ

An Hachette UK Company
www.hachette.co.uk

www.littlebrown.co.uk

To my parents and their New York

Directory to Dining

Masha's, 1705 Second Avenue, REgent 4–1143. Menu items memorialize the owner/chef's wife, who died in Europe during WW2. If you aren't plotzing over the story, come for schmaltz: the sumptuously decadent Continental and Jewish dishes, including Brisket Wellington and chocolate "Masha Torte," will make even jaded diners weep. Entrees from $7.95. Cocktails and wine. Lunch and dinner; closed Monday. Reservations recommended.

—Craig Claiborne, *New York Times*, September 1964

Masha's Fall 1965

Appetizers

Warm Brussels Sprout Salad with Toasted Pecans, Bleu Cheese,
Lardons & Black Truffle Mustard Vinaigrette

Cream of Mushroom Soup with House-Made Croutons,
Crème Fraîche, Brandy & Chives

CHICKEN IN A BLANKET:
Chicken Liver Pâté en Croute, Served with Mustard &
Horseradish Crème Fraîche Dipping Sauces

Blue Point Oysters Baked in Crème Sauce with
Bread-Crumb & Butter Crust

"LITTLE POLISH DOVES":
Miniature Cabbage Rolls with Mustard & Sweet & Sour Dipping Sauces

Entrees

Breast of Duck with Kirsch-Flambéed Cherries and Oranges in a Nest of
Sautéed Cabbage, Accompanied by Pommes Frites

Brisket Wellington, Accompanied by
Horseradish Mashed Potatoes & Vegetable du Jour

Pan-Fried Flounder with Parmesan & Bread-Crumb Crust,
Accompanied by Roast Fingerling Potatoes & Green Beans Amandine

Stuffed Roast Chicken with Beach Plum & Cranberry Conserve,
Accompanied by Diner's Choice of Tzimmes or
Mashed Potatoes & Brussels Sprouts

HAMBURGER WALTER:
Ground Chuck au Poivre & Flambéed in Brandy, Accompanied by
Pommes Frites & No Vegetables At All

Sides

Mushrooms in Burgundy Sauce

Green Beans Amandine

Creamed Spinach with a Garlic & Parmesan Crust

Roast Fingerling Potatoes

Pommes Frites (French Fried Potatoes)

Latkes (Potato Pancakes with Applesauce)

Tzimmes (Casserole of Sweet Potato, Citrus Zests, & Currants)

Pickled Beets with Horseradish Crème Fraîche

Dish of House-Made Pickles

Spätzle

Just Desserts

Honeycrisp Apple Crumble with Brown-Sugar Crust & Vanilla Ice Cream

MASHA TORTE:
Inside-Out German Chocolate Cake with Cherries Flambé

Plum Tart with Roasted Walnut Crust & Kirsch-Infused Whipped Cream

"LITTLE CLOUDS":
Cream Puffs Filled with Vanilla Ice Cream, Accompanied by
Mini Chocolate Fondue for Dipping

Pumpkin, Honey, and Vanilla Ice Cream in Chocolate Cups (Available as
Trio or Individual)

Assortment of Chocolate, Walnut-Currant, & Apricot Rugelach

1705 2ND AVE. NEW YORK, NY 10128 / RE 4—1143

* RESERVATIONS IF YOU PLEASE!

I

PETER, 1965

Well, what if Peter hadn't caught the wolf? What then, eh?

—SERGEI PROKOFIEV

1

MASHA'S

The first time Peter saw the girl was during the dinner seating at Masha's. She was sitting at the center table beneath the chandelier, her face spangled with light. It was what Peter's staff called the death seat because of what would happen to whoever was unfortunate enough to be occupying it if the chandelier, a two-hundred-pound fountain of dripping Venetian crystal, ever decided to fall. The girl—the young woman—was looking around the restaurant as if bored by her dining companion, a silver-haired fellow with thick horn-rimmed glasses and a head as square as a sugar cube, who was at least twice her age and was, at the moment Peter first noticed her, leaning in to whisper something in her ear. The girl wrinkled her nose and pushed her suitor, if that was what he was, away—and then, upon spying Peter, grinned in a way that was completely transformative, changing her expression from the somewhat sulky ennui of the New York girl-about-town, been there, done that already, into something altogether more sunny and sweet. Peter raised his eyebrows in return. The girl's light hair was short as a boy's—not a style Peter was fond of; she wore a white shift with fur at the collar and cuffs and red high-heeled boots whose tops disappeared beneath the tablecloth. Her eyes were outlined in thick curls of black. Peter was not, as a rule, a fan of these new fashion trends—although like every other man in Manhattan, he would have thanked God, had he believed in Him, for the miniskirt. Yet this girl held Peter transfixed.

He went about the business of making the rounds, as he did once a seating, clapping a shoulder here, lighting a woman's cigarette there. There was always a preponderance of pretty women at Masha's—more so during lunch, when tables were almost completely occupied by wistful bachelorettes and their determined mothers. This had been the case since the *Times* review came out the year before. The ladies praised the salads, but they were there for the single owner with the sad story. The dinner crowd consisted more of regulars, residents of this Upper East Side neighborhood on their way down to, or returning from, the city's events, theater and orchestra and opera and ballet. Still, there were enough romantic hopefuls mixed in that Peter had become wary and immune. Or so he had thought. Why this particular young woman had caught his interest now, he wasn't sure. He stole glances at her as he made conversation with the Lynns, who had concluded their evening with nightcaps at Masha's ever since it had opened; as he ignored the way old Mrs. Allison, holding court at Table 14, kept slipping her palsied hand beneath the table to feed scraps to her poodle, Lucius, who the staff routinely pretended wasn't there. Peter wasn't playing the game again—was he? Looking for people who were long gone? A fruitless exercise, he reminded himself severely. And cruel. And yet . . . The young woman in the death seat looked to be younger than forty, the age Masha would have been, and older than twenty—not by much, but enough.

Peter was about to make his way over and give the girl a special welcome to Masha's when there was the discreet stir at tables nearest the front door that meant Mr. Cronkite had arrived, that the hostess was taking his trench coat and leading him to his habitual table, the second banquette with its high red leather walls. Mr. Cronkite was alone, as he usually was when he dined at Masha's—en route from the CBS studio to his apartment on East Ninety-Fourth Street, on a night when his wife, Betty, wasn't there to share a meal with him. Peter held up one finger at Maurice, the waiter on Mr. Cronkite's station, to indicate he would bring the newscaster's bourbon over himself.

"How are you this evening, Mr. Cronkite?" he asked, setting the drink down—it always startled Peter, no matter how he thought he had grown used to it, to see how blue the man's eyes were, since on the television screen they appeared gray.

"Very well, and you, Mr. Rashkin?" said Mr. Cronkite.

"I can't complain," said Peter.

Mr. Cronkite favored Peter with the famous twinkle. "That makes you quite unlike much of our viewing audience," he said. "Tumultuous times, Mr. Rashkin. Tumultuous times. But we are no stranger to those, are we?" He toasted Peter with his highball glass. "A salute," he said.

"To your health," Peter responded. "May I bring you a menu? Or your favorite?"

"How could I pass up a Hamburger Walter?" said Mr. Cronkite, of the dish Peter had invented specially for him—ground chuck seasoned au poivre and cooked in brandy, with, as the menu said, No Vegetables At All. Mr. Cronkite gave Peter a wink. "One of the small sorry perks of bachelorhood, eh, Mr. Rashkin? Don't have to eat the peas."

"Indeed," said Peter. It was a little joke between them, the long and happily married Mr. Cronkite not being a bachelor and Peter being considered one of the city's more eligible—much to his dismay.

"I'll have Maurice bring that right out for you," he said to Mr. Cronkite and knocked a knuckle against the tablecloth in farewell.

Having ascertained that everything front of house was running

exactly as it should, Peter headed toward the kitchen to supervise
the plating of that evening's special, a Cornish hen served with
horseradish mashed potatoes and cherries flambé—Peter had not
been surprised that his customers loved food being set on fire ta-
bleside, since Americans tended to be pleased by potentially explo-
sive things, but he had been startled to find how much he himself
enjoyed it. He glanced again at the center table, the death seat.
What was it about this young woman? Did she remind him of
someone after all? Perhaps Twiggy; yes, with her close-cropped
ashy blond hair, her almost skeletal slenderness, she did resemble the British model who sometimes came in with her entourage.
This girl, too, was probably a model—her dinner, the warm Brussels sprout salad with Roquefort, was untouched. Perhaps Peter
had seen her face in the subway, sliding past on a wall. The girl's
dining companion had his arm around her now; he had hitched his
chair closer, and as Peter watched, he offered her a sip of his Rusty
Nail, holding his highball glass up toward the girl's mouth. Once
again Peter considered going over, introducing himself, perhaps
offering a complimentary dessert—but wasn't one suitor twice her
age enough for the poor girl? She didn't need another. And Peter
wasn't looking for entanglement. He stepped through the port-
holed door to his kitchen.

*

The kitchen at Masha's was tiny, not much bigger than a sailboat's
galley, its cramped confines made all the more so by its inhabitants:
Peter's sauté/grill chef, his prep chef, his sous-chef Lena, the dishwasher. In the early mornings, the pastry chef was sometimes there
as well. Tonight the air was thick with the smells of poultry, fish,
cabbage, potatoes, and the sounds of sizzling, running water, roaring ovens, the dishwasher churning, and the cooks yelling shorthand
to each other—"Flounder up! Twelve needs potatoes. Eighty-six
the chicken. Already? Fuck me." It was Peter's favorite place in the

world. All his life he had felt safest in kitchens. He was the owner of Masha's, a restaurateur as well as a chef, yet it might have surprised his patrons and even some of his staff to know how hard it was for him to play the role—what an effort to circulate among the tables in his suit, making small talk. It was precisely because this didn't come easily to Peter that he was good at it; as his childhood speech tutor in Berlin had scolded him, *Peter, you must project!* He did—except now, instead of his voice, he amplified his personality. Still, it was a joy to him, the moment he looked forward to above all others, when he could exchange his suit for chef's whites and fall into the rhythm of chopping, sautéing, assembling, and sending food he had prepared, dishes he had created, out into the world.

So it was a surprise to Peter that tonight, as he hung his suit coat on the back of his office door, pulled on his white jacket, and took his usual spot next to Lena, he felt something was amiss. It was the light—the good overhead fluorescents, strong white bulbs in ceiling ice-cube-tray grids, seemed dim. Peter felt himself start to sweat. He blotted his forehead with a towel from the top of his stack and unrolled the satchel containing his knife. The prep chef had already set out Peter's *mise en place*; little bowls of shallots and parsley and garlic confit and lemon zest and kosher salt ringed his cutting board. But why was Peter having a hard time seeing them?

"Catch me up," he said to Lena.

"Twenty-two covers done," said Lena, breathing like a vacuum cleaner—she was a large lady, taller than Peter's six feet and wider than the stove; a refugee, like Peter, but from Leningrad. "Chicken is finished. Mushroom Burgundy kaput. Flounder is moving. Five hen left."

"Thanks," said Peter. "What's open?" he called.

"Eight tickets, boss!"

Peter squinted toward the slips of paper hanging from the magnetized rail. Was it his imagination, or was the room growing darker still?

"Lena," he started to say, "take charge, I'm not well—"

But she shouted over him, "Who fuck with fuse box? Is darker than Stalin's *zhopa* in here!" and Peter realized, with relief, that it wasn't just him—Lena was having trouble seeing too, and the rest of his staff were exclaiming perplexities in the coffee-colored air.

Lena turned on Rodrigo, the dishwasher. "I know you do this, *toshchiy blyudok,*" she said. "I see you in storage closet earlier."

The dishwasher responded in rapid Spanish. Peter's English and German, even his Russian, were better than his Spanish, but after thirty years of kitchen work he knew Lena had called Rodrigo a skinny little bastard and the dishwasher had called her a sow.

"Lena," Peter said, "stop. Rodrigo, turn up your radio, please."

Everybody strained to listen except the sauté chef, who kept prodding and flipping now-invisible meat. Over a murmur from the dining room and the hiss of the grill, they could hear the battery-powered radio, tuned to 1010 WINS: *"The electrical blackout is citywide, although the full scope has yet to be determined. Mayor Wagner has asked all New Yorkers to stay inside. The subways are not operational, but extra buses . . ."*

"Somebody fuck with whole city's fuse box," said Lena, not without satisfaction. "Will be looting. Fires. Probably killings too."

"That will do, thank you," said Peter—although that had been his first instinct as well. He was all too familiar with what happened to civility when a city's lights went out.

He organized his thoughts, then issued a stream of orders. Get flashlights for the kitchen and extra candles for the dining room. Tell the headwaiter to lock the front door and open it only to let people leave—nobody in. The kitchen staff would close out their tickets and take no more orders. Peter would comp the patrons a round of drinks. To himself he added a footnote to give Mrs. Allison an extra meal in her doggie bag; that way, if the power remained out the next day, she would have something to eat. A waiter should escort her home, as well.

"And for God's sake open the walk-in as little as possible," he finished. "I'll go make an announcement."

He stepped to the door of the dining room again—tonight his patrons would have the unusual experience of seeing him in his whites. Many of them were gathered at the front window, peering out, trying to ascertain what was happening. The waiters and hostess were lighting extra candles on every table, setting the red-lacquered walls aglow and sparking the crystal chandelier to life. Mr. Cronkite, Peter saw, was gone—probably back to the newsroom, in case the power returned and CBS could address the crisis on air. The square-headed silver-haired man was still at the center table, scowling into his half-empty drink. But the young woman? Peter scanned the room, the knot of people at the window. She was nowhere to be seen.

He walked to the bar and tinked a spoon against a wineglass.

"Ladies and gentlemen," he said, "your attention please."

❉

After everyone had left—after the patrons had been let out, old Mrs. Allison escorted by the headwaiter; after he had locked the night's receipts in the safe, to be gone over in the morning, when there was more light; after he had dismissed his staff—Peter poured himself a brandy and began his rounds. He did this every night after closing, ensuring that Masha's was secure; the only difference tonight was that he was using a flashlight. The beam was weak, after so much exercise in the kitchen earlier, but it was sufficient for Peter to sweep around the coat closet, the dining room, the kitchen, the walk-in refrigerator, his office, and the cellar—now even more dungeon-like without the illumination of the ceiling bulb. He checked the wine racks, the dry-storage bins and barrels, and the rat traps, thankful that the latter were empty. He made inventory notes in the little spiral-bound notepad he always carried in his back pocket: "onions, olive oil, paprika, matchbooks.

New rubber mat for kitch." He went back upstairs, set his brandy down, and went to check the restrooms.

He had long since turned the radio off—he preferred silence, and if he hadn't thought the staff would mutiny, he would have banned music in the kitchen—but he was mindful of the news he'd heard earlier. Lena's predictions had been right: in addition to reports of long lines of people at phone booths, ferries, and buses, desperate to escape the stricken city, there were lootings and fires, some as close as Harlem. Since Masha's wasn't very far south, between Eighty-Ninth and Ninetieth Streets on Second Avenue, Peter wondered whether he should take extra precautions. Sleep in his office, perhaps. It wouldn't be the first time. In 1955, when Masha's opened, Peter had practically lived at the restaurant, returning to his apartment on East Ninety-Sixth Street only to shower and change clothes. He gave the men's room a scan and made a notation to order more paper towels—he'd ask Sol, his cousin and partner, whether they could try a cheaper service Peter had found in the Bronx or whether they had to keep using Sol's supplier. The flashlight went out.

Peter cursed. He knocked the metal cylinder against his palm, trying to jar the beam back on, but nothing happened. Peter navigated his way from the bathroom by touch, amazed as always by how walls, corners, doorways seemed to move once you couldn't see them. It was a lesson forgotten until now but familiar, learned during air raids, in basements, on U-Bahn platforms, in closets, and, of course, in the bunks. The smell of strangers' wool coats, unwashed hair, bodily secretions, breath—hunger in particular created a dead-mouse odor. The shuffling that might be feet, limbs shifting in very little space, or vermin. The unidentified movement inches from one's face. At least in the aboveground shelters there was usually some ambient light, a precious match lit to check a watch or tend a sick child, the outline of a night sky around a windowshade. But here in the hallway at Masha's, the lack of light reminded Peter of subterranean hideouts, of his narrow bed slot in Block 14 when the SS ordered the camp blacked out due to bombing raids. The dark in those cases assumed an unpleasant solidity, a gelid quality that made it impossible for Peter to see his palm when he touched his nose with it—assuming he was able to lift his arm from among the four other men to do so.

Peter sighed and felt along the hallway wall until he reached the dining room, where he groped for and lit a candle. He was drenched with perspiration beneath his chef's whites, his body crawling with it, a sensation he hated. He felt impatient with himself. It was all very well, even understandable, that the blackout had caused him to remember things he'd worked so hard to forget. That was how the body ticked, perhaps. But he had to exercise more control over his mind. He would not, could not, go back to the insanity he'd lived through right after he'd come to this country, when apropos of nothing—he could be applying butter to toast, petting a dog, walking through a park—time would suddenly seesaw and slide him back into Auschwitz. Or Theresienstadt. Or Berlin. He would not do it. He would not indulge these memories. "I refuse," said Peter to the dark.

As if in answer, there was a sound from back in the hallway, like the mewl of a cat. "Hello?" Peter called. The noise came again—*myooou?*—sounding as though it were coming from the ladies' room, which, Peter remembered now, he hadn't yet checked. It probably was a stray—he hoped. Sometimes the patrons or staff opened the window as far as it would go, three inches, and God knew what could have come in through the bars. Peter wouldn't put anything past this city. His neighbor at East Ninety-Sixth had once lifted the lid of his toilet to find a boa constrictor. And one morning Peter had come in before dawn to make stock and demi-glace only to find, waddling happily around the floor of his office, a skunk.

He lifted the candle and walked back down the hallway, feeling absurdly like the miser Peter had read about in his nighttime

English-language classes, Ebenezer Scrooge. All he lacked was
the nightgown and cap. "Hello?" he said again, opening the ladies' room door. "Is anybody here?" He shone the flame around
the little pink-tiled room. It was flickering—the window was
indeed open—but he didn't need its uncertain light to see the
door to the second stall open and from it emerge, her hair rumpled and makeup mussed, the girl. The young woman from the
center table.

*

Peter got her settled at the bar, gathering and lighting candles from
nearby tables and pouring them both drinks—although he then
realized the girl hadn't asked for one. She looked at it, sitting on
the zinc bar amid a glittering semicircle of tea lights, which reflected in the mirror behind the liquor bottles and sent infinite
glimmers into the dark.

"It's only brandy," said Peter. "I may pretend to wizardry in the
kitchen, but I'm a poor bartender."

"As long as it's brown and strong," said the girl, "I don't mind
what it is."

She tossed it back in a businesslike fashion and with a horselike
huff. This accomplished, she banged the glass down and tapped its
rim with a white-nailed finger.

"Hit me again," she said, and Peter did, taking a moment to
translate the command. It had been a long time since he had stumbled over an idiom; this blackout had done something to him,
uncoupled hard-earned language and opened unwelcome doors in
his mind. He hoped the lights would come back on soon, though
in a way that was irrelevant; it was disconcerting to discover how
easily one's defenses were still undone.

This girl took her second brandy with more decorum, arcing
her long neck down to the snifter in a way that put Peter in mind
of a giraffe he had recently seen at a fund-raiser in the Central

Park Zoo, delicately lipping leaves off a tree. Peter handed her his handkerchief.

"What's this for?" she asked. Peter pointed to his own face, smiling. The girl swung on her stool and confronted her reflection in the mirror.

"Oh God," she said and dipped Peter's handkerchief in her brandy to wipe her streaked makeup from her cheeks. She turned to him questioningly, and he nodded.

"You missed a spot, just there," he said and almost but not quite touched her left temple.

The girl leaned forward to take care of it. "Thank you," she said and started to pass Peter's handkerchief back. He shook his head, and her neck above her white fur collar mottled in a blush that could be embarrassment, or heat from the candles, or both.

"Oh, of course you wouldn't want it back this way," she said. "I'll have it dry-cleaned and sent to you."

"That won't be necessary," said Peter. You could return it yourself, he was about to say, when the girl let out a gusty sigh and ran her hands through her very short blond hair. Divested of her fashionable heavy makeup, she looked like a child—her lashes pale, her extraordinary high cheekbones lightly freckled—and, Peter thought, even more fetching this way.

"You must think I'm an awful baby," she said.

"Hardly," he said, "although you do appear quite young."

She smiled, the expression transforming her face with a sweetness that reminded Peter of everything American: sugary cereal, Crest toothpaste, fabric softener, milk.

"Go on," she said. "I'm twenty-five. Practically an old maid."

"An infant," said Peter. "If you stay out much longer, I shall have to call your governess."

Now she laughed and toasted him. "Cin cin."

"Prost," said Peter automatically. He winced and drained his brandy.

The girl watched him curiously over the rim of her snifter. "I'm sorry about all that hysteria in the ladies' room."

"I don't see why," said Peter. "If one must weep, the ladies' lounge seems the ideal place for it."

"I don't want you to think I'm a crybaby."

"Of course not," said Peter. "I'm sure you're usually tough as nails."

"I am," she agreed and finished off her drink. She pushed the glass toward Peter, who obligingly refilled it. "It was just a hell of a night."

"Your . . . gentleman friend?" Peter asked, hoping to be told he was a cousin—or uncle.

"No, it wasn't him," she said, and Peter was examining his feeling of deflation when she added, "He was a creep, but garden-variety. You know the type, the kind of guy who thinks just because he takes a girl out for drinks she owes him a roll in the hay. I wouldn't've even bothered with him—he was a blind date—but my friend Dominique said he was some bigwig producer with CBS, with contacts to Hollywood. Turns out he was just a lousy writer." She wrinkled her nose.

"I'm sorry to hear that," said Peter gravely. He wanted to laugh.

"Yes, well, around drink three or so he started putting the moves on me—he was a real smoothie, ol' Allen or Alfred or whatever his name was. First he did the yawn and stretch to drape his arm over my shoulder and cop a feel. Next thing you know he dropped his lighter and had to fish around under the table for it—and up my skirt. I swear he jammed his hand up there as if it were a cigarette machine or something."

"Good Lord," said Peter. "If I'd known, I would have done something about it."

"Would you?" The girl looked at him sideways, her first coquettish gesture of the night, Peter thought. "What would you have done?"

"There are plenty of cleavers back there," said Peter, indicating the kitchen. She laughed. "Or if you prefer a less dramatic solution, I could always have thrown the bum out."

The girl smiled. "I believe you would. You strike me as a perfect gentleman."

"Sadly, yes," said Peter. "So you were crying over this bum, Albert or Alfred? That hardly strikes me as being tough as nails."

"Oh, God, no," she said. "Not him. I did what I always do with creeps—told him I was going to the ladies' room, then stayed in there long enough so he'd leave. Only I must've had a highball too many, because I fell asleep—you know, you could use a chaise in there or something."

"I'll look into it."

"And when I woke up," she said, "everyone was gone and it was dark. As in pitch dark, as in I couldn't tell where the door was, as in I couldn't see my hand in front of my face. I dropped my lighter, and I couldn't find it, and I just . . ." She shrugged, which turned into a shudder. "Ugh, the dark," she said. "I've hated it since I was a little girl. My mom locked me in a rut cellar once and forgot me in there. She said it was for my own good, that there was a bad storm coming, and that it wasn't as long as I thought. But I know she forgot. And it was hours in that total darkness. Hours." She rubbed her arms, which were, like her legs, almost preternaturally long and white. "The dark still gives me the meemies."

"I know what you mean," said Peter.

"Do you?"

"I do."

The girl's eyes, wide and silver-blue, scanned Peter's face. "I believe you."

"I am unclear on one thing, however," said Peter. "What is a rut cellar?"

"What?" the girl said, then laughed. "Oh, sorry, *root*. 'Rut' is the way they say it where I come from."

"And where would that be? This place where mothers lock little girls in cellars?"

"Minnesota," the girl said. "Land of a Thousand Lakes."

"And rut cellars," said Peter, exaggerating the foreign word. He thought he knew what she meant now; his family's cook, Hilde, had kept a similar storeroom on the Charlottenburg estate where Peter had grown up, a dank underground space lined with hundreds of jars of rotkraut, Spargel—white asparagus—with dill, and pickles. The decades of preserves had been smashed in a single night's bombing, but they were the reason Peter still canned his own for Masha's.

The girl held out her empty snifter, and Peter replenished it and his. "To escaping the dark," he said, and they clinked glasses.

"Where are you from?" she said. "I'm guessing not the Bronx."

"I'm from long ago and far away," said Peter. The girl raised a half-moon eyebrow at him. He sighed. "Europe," he said.

"Not France, either. Are you from—"

"Germany."

The girl sat up a little straighter. "From before or after the war?"

"After. Just."

"I thought so. Your accent . . ."

"And here I thought I'd done such a good job erasing it."

"Oh, you have," she assured him. "It's very slight. But it's also something about the way you carry yourself. A little more formal."

"Like a headwaiter?" Peter said.

"Like the guy in that movie," she said, "you know the one . . ." She cast about, snapping her fingers in frustration. "The guy with all the kids and the whistle? You must know what I mean."

Peter shook his head.

"I think I've drunk more than I thought," she said. "Anyway. Do you ever . . . go back? Do you miss it?"

Only an American, thought Peter, and only a young American,

could ask such a question. Did he miss Germany? Had they taught no history in her American school?

"I have not gone back," he said carefully, and then, "And you? Do you miss being in your land of lakes?"

To his astonishment, the girl's chin started to quiver, and then she began to cry. She unfurled one of her long arms down across the bar and dropped her head onto it and sobbed.

"No," she wept. "Not at all. Not—at—all! I got out of there as soon as I could—so I wouldn't turn into every other woman there. They all get married right out of high school, if they even finish, and by the time they're my age they have middle-aged spread and perms and six kids! I spent my whole life trying to avoid that!"

By which you mean your whole twenty-odd years, Peter thought. The girl's back heaved; she was so slender he could see the knobs of her spine through the white fabric of her dress, beneath its tracery of silver brocade. Her boy's haircut came to a tiny elfin comma on the nape of her neck. He reached his hand out to comfort her, then pulled it away.

"But here you are," he said reasonably. "Safe, all the way in New York."

She turned her face partially toward him, her cheeks and eyes swollen and streaming. "But that's just it," she cried, "I'm not safe at all. Now that Twiggy's here . . . ," and she released a fresh torrent of tears. "That's why they made me cut my hair like this," she said, yanking at it, "so I could compete with the British Invasion. It's not enough to be pretty anymore, or to show up early for every shoot, or to weigh ninety-nine pounds in your shoes—you have to be exotic, too. That's the new look! And I can't! I'm not! I can't compete with horrible scary Peggy Moffitt or beautiful Negresses like Donyale Luna. I had three bookings canceled this week. I'm going to get sent home to marry some farmer!" and she cried and cried.

Peter waited, and finally he did rest a palm on her back. He could feel the living warmth of it, and her vertebrae, too. She was so thin. He felt two things: first, exasperation that any woman should deliberately starve herself so, even for the sake of a career. He remembered, against his will, other women with equally short hair—though less artfully shorn—their bones protruding the same way; one, in the DP camp Peter had shared with her in Bremerhaven, died from eating a chocolate bar a well-meaning American soldier had given her too soon. How Peter should like to shake this girl, to remind her of what was important, to feed her crème brulée, foie gras, Brie *en croute* . . . Yet he admired her, too, for having the tenacity to leave her home at such a tender age and come to a hard city where she knew no one, to make her fortune; unlike Peter, she had done so by choice rather than necessity. If it had been a long time since Peter had touched a woman, aside from bumping elbows in the kitchen or a hasty coupling with a stranger no more meaningful than a sneeze and just as imperative, so too had it been ages since Peter had encountered any woman with an ambition beyond securing a handsome and well-situated husband.

I will someday be the first female chef in Berlin, in my very own restaurant, said a voice in his head. *Oh, Petel, do you think it's possible?*

Peter took his hand off the girl. It was slightly damp.

"Now listen here," he said. "I have met this Twiggy, and she is a fire in the pan, believe me. She won't last more than a few months."

The girl turned her face sideways and blinked. "Oh, you mean a flash in the pan."

"Yes, that's it. She is merely a trend, whereas you, your looks are timeless."

"You're too sweet," the girl said automatically. Slowly she sat up, wiping her face with the heels of her palms. "You've really met Twiggy? Wh-where?" she hiccupped.

"Why, here, of course. She and her friends descend on Masha's like a plague of locusts, order everything on the menu, and eat nothing of it. A colossal waste of food. Right before closing time as well."

The girl laughed. "Of course she wouldn't eat anything. She cuh-can't," she hiccoughed. "Occupational huh-hazard."

"She is quite louche," Peter said firmly. "You have nothing to fear from her." He held out his hand. "Don't talk for a moment. Stay still."

He ran a glass of water behind the bar, shook out a napkin over it like a magician performing a trick, and pushed it toward her. "Drink it," he said. "All of it. Through the cloth."

"Whu—"

"Please," he said, and the girl drank, watching him over the glass. Her long lovely throat worked above her fur collar. When she was done, Peter applauded.

"There, you see?" he said.

"No—," she said, then put a hand to her throat. "Oh, I do! They're gone. The hiccups. How did you know to do that?"

"My . . . somebody I knew long ago taught me," said Peter.

"Well, thank whoever it was for me," said the girl. "It's a neat trick."

She looked at her watch and slid from her stool. "It's so late," she said. "I have an eight o'clock booking. I really have to go."

She had made it almost all the way to the door before Peter, startled by her abrupt exodus, recovered himself and caught up with her.

"Wait," he said. "You can't leave."

She gave him a suspicious look. Although Peter stood six feet in his socks, her eyes were almost level with his. "And why not?"

"Your coat," he said.

She laughed. "Oh. Right."

Peter retrieved her jacket, the only one left in the cloakroom; it was a collection of blond fur that looked like a litter of stitched-together Pomeranians. He stood behind her as she slipped her arms into it; the garment was longer than her minidress, so once she had fastened it, it looked as though she were wearing only the coat and high boots. The illusion was bewitching, impossible to look away from. The girl stood by the door, waiting.

Peter felt in his pocket for his handkerchief, but the girl had left it on the bar. He reached past her to unfasten the lock; she smelled of cigarettes and Chanel No. 5 and, beneath those, something like fresh salted butter. Her carefully contrived sideburns came to little points in front of each ear.

"I don't think I can let you go," he said.

"Excuse me?"

"Not by yourself," Peter clarified. "I don't want to alarm you, but the news was full of warnings earlier—lootings, possible assaults. It's not safe for you to be out in the blackout by yourself."

"I'll be fine."

"I insist."

She turned fully, and Peter felt her breath, warm and brandy-scented, on his face. "You wouldn't be trying to put the make on a girl, would you?"

"Certainly not," said Peter. "Perhaps a little."

She grinned.

"I'll wait," she said.

She stood demurely while Peter extinguished the candles and got his own overcoat and ring of keys—he could return early to deal with the mess on the bar. He took her furry arm, and they stepped out onto the sidewalk together. Peter realized with surprise that he could see her without artificial light: although every shop and storefront along Second Avenue was as dark as Masha's, there was a full moon floating over the stricken city, a huge white thing like a prop from a Broadway musical.

Peter pulled the metal grate down over Masha's and locked it. "Now then, how shall we get you home?"

"I'll get a cab."

"I don't think so," said Peter. The longer they stood outside, the stranger the night became: there were no cars on the street, no taxis or buses or bicycles or beggars, the only movement a band of pedestrians hurrying northward carrying candles, like pilgrims. The November air smelled of cold, subway soot, and—faintly, from Harlem—fires.

"I'll walk you," Peter offered.

The girl laughed. "Don't be silly. I live all the way down in the Village."

"Even so."

"No way," she said. "I can't let you do that."

"Let me escort you to the St. Regis, then. There will be taxis there."

"All right," she said. "Or how about the Plaza? I'll get a horse and carriage!"

"Now you're talking," said Peter.

He offered her his arm again, but just then a taxi did come around the corner, a Checker cab with, like everything else in the city, its lights off. The girl jumped into the street nonetheless and windmilled her arms, a movement that caused her dress and coat to ride up and expose garters and a flash of panties that looked lavender. The cab screeched to a stop.

Peter held the door for her as she folded herself in. She grinned up at him. "Thank you again for everything."

"What's your name?" he asked.

"June. June Bouquet."

"Aw, come on," said the cabbie from the depths of the front seat.

"What?" said June Bouquet indignantly. "It's true! It's pronounced 'Bucket' where I come from."

"It suits you," said Peter. "June Bouquet. Lovely as spring."

He tapped the roof of the cab, and it slid away. Peter stayed where he was, watching until it turned a corner. He was struck by a number of peculiarities: the stillness, the blackened buildings standing silent like the surviving walls of air raids; the lack of streetlights, color, people, and noise; the enormous full moon.

June herself, a bouquet of contradictions. Charming and fey, brash and fearful, young and ambitious, a model who drank like a sailor. Could that possibly be her real name? Had she been fibbing to Peter; was it a professional sobriquet? It didn't matter. The oddest thing of all about this night was that for the first time in a long time, much further back than he allowed himself to remember, Peter felt regretful about having let someone go.

2

CARNEGIE HALL

That Saturday night, after the city had been restored to its usual bustle and glitter, Peter had what he considered a command performance to join his cousin Sol and Sol's wife, Ruth, at Carnegie Hall for a concert. Peter had explained to Sol time and time again that Saturday night was prime time at the restaurant, the busiest slot on the schedule, but Sol was not only a Gold Circle Patron of Carnegie Hall, he was Peter's patron too, Masha's sole investor and Peter's partner. So Peter worked the first dinner seating, then went back to his office and emerged in what Lena called his penguin suit. "You are going to zoo?" she yelled over the sizzle of that night's special, pan-fried flounder, as Peter tried to sneak out the back door. "What other costume you have in office? Clown outfit? Pilot uniform?" Peter raised a hand in acknowledgment of his staff's catcalls and wolf whistles; they loved it whenever they caught him making the transition to the other side of what they called his double life.

Peter was only a little late; there was still quite a crowd milling about in front of the hall, smoking, ambling toward the doors, greeting each other with breath that steamed with smoke and the

November chill. In Sol's case, it was a Cuban cigar. "What took you so long?" he said as Peter climbed from his cab.

"Very few taxis," said Peter. "Saturday-evening rush."

"Euh," said Sol, "you gotta be more aggressive," and he stomped off to mash his cigar out in the gutter.

"Bubbie," cried Sol's wife, Ruth, "let me look at you!" She seized Peter's hands in her tiny, surprisingly strong ones and held them out to either side, all the better to inspect Peter as if she hadn't seen him in decades instead of the previous weekend.

"Sha," she said, "handsome as ever. My Peter, the movie star," and she beckoned Peter down for a kiss. Ruth was a lesson in mathematics: she'd been under five feet tall to begin with, and early osteoporosis subtracted perhaps an inch, but her hair, teased into a permanent maroon soufflé, added it back and then some. She gave Peter a hearty smack on the cheek, then licked her thumb to swipe at the mark she'd left. "I got you all schmutzed up," she said. "Look who's here with us: Art and Sylvia."

"Hello, Arthur," said Peter, who also saw Sol's partner Arthur Rabinowitz—called Choppers, Peter assumed in reference to his very large and very white dentures—and his wife, Sylvia, at least twice a month.

"How ya doin', kid!" boomed Choppers, putting out his liver-spotted hand to shake, which was a little like handling a large, flexible baseball mitt. Choppers had decided during Peter's first year in America, when Peter lived with Sol and Ruth, that Peter was deaf rather than learning a new language—an impression the subsequent decades seemed not to have erased.

"How's life in the apron?" shouted Choppers, and laughed heartily at his own joke. Choppers was the kind of man—as was Sol, and as Peter's own father, Avram, had been—who thought being a cook was women's work, though that didn't prevent him from stopping by Masha's with Sol for free food. "How's business?" he bawled. "Stealing any recipes from that French broad?"

"*Stop* it, Art," purred Sylvia, "you'll em*barr*ass him." But Peter put on his best Julia Child falsetto and said, "You simply must use an awful lot of rum!" and they all laughed.

"I forgot you were *funny*," said Sylvia to Peter. She was swathed in fur from head to calf, including a fox coat and a matching turban that retained the animal's small, snarling face, just over Sylvia's left ear. She withdrew a cigarette from a crocodile clutch, screwed it into a gold holder, and waited for Peter to light it. "*Thank* you, darling boy," she said, shooting out smoke. "*Where* have you been *hiding* from Sylvia? In that *bistro* of yours, I suppose," and she pursed pomegranate-colored lips and narrowed her eyes at him. "Very *naughty*. I think you need a *spanking*."

"And look who else is here!" said Ruth brightly, inserting herself between Peter and Sylvia to usher forth a young lady in a cream-colored wool cape and matching pillbox hat. "Peter, this is Art and Sylvia's niece, Rebecca Dannett."

Another niece? thought Peter as he took Miss Rebecca's gloved hand. Either the Rabinowitz siblings were extremely prolific, or they needed a more creative cover story. They presented Peter with a new niece, with Ruth's enthusiastic collusion, every few months.

"Charmed," said Peter.

"How do you do," said Miss Rebecca, or at least Peter assumed she did; her lips moved, at any rate. If she looked startlingly like the slain president's young widow Jacqueline Kennedy in dress, feature, and coloring, her manner of speaking was much more Miss Monroe, a breathy murmur that Peter had to tilt forward to hear.

"Pardon?" he said, cupping his ear.

"I said, you look just like the actor Christopher Plummer," whispered Miss Rebecca, darting a glance up at Peter from beneath spiky lashes. "I hope you don't think it's terribly forward of me to say."

"Not at all," said Peter, and indeed, ever since the musical film *The Sound of Music* had been released that fall, not a day had passed that he hadn't heard the comparison. Perhaps that was the fellow in the movie June Bouquet had referred to during the blackout. *The guy with all the kids and the whistle.*

"He *does, doesn't* he," said Sylvia. She gripped Peter's right arm; he could feel her nails through his overcoat. "Just a *dead ringer. Maybe* somebody should put him in a *captain's* uniform." She shivered dramatically.

"Maybe we should go in now." Ruth let go of Peter's other arm and nudged him toward Miss Rebecca, to whom Peter offered it. Miss Rebecca laid her kid-gloved hand lightly atop the crook of Peter's elbow, and thus, Sylvia on one side of Peter and her purported niece on the other, the trio made their slow six-legged way toward the entrance, Sol, Ruth, and Choppers trailing in their wake.

"Excuse me?" Peter said to Miss Rebecca, who had murmured something else.

"I said," she breathed as they entered the hall's lobby, "have you seen it? The film? *The Sound of Music?*"

"Ah. No, I haven't." Everyone had told Peter he must. He supposed he should. He had no intention of doing so.

"You must," whispered Miss Rebecca. "It's positively magical. So inspiring."

"So I've heard," said Peter, helping her off with her cape as they queued for the coat check.

"They say it's based on a true story," murmured Miss Rebecca, and now she did turn her almond-shaped eyes fully on Peter. She put her hand on her bosom, which Peter had to admit looked impressive beneath a sweet pink evening gown—like mounds of sculpted strawberry pavlova. For some reason this made him think again of June Bouquet, although she'd had no cleavage to speak of.

Miss Rebecca tipped her dark head to unpin her hat and glanced at Peter sideways. "Escaping from the Nazis through the mountains— I can't imagine such courage! But of course, *you* can."

"You're very kind," said Peter, handing his and Miss Rebecca's outerwear through the coat check window and pocketing the chit.

He wished he could tug at his collar; it was very warm in the lobby, all the smoke and perfume and body heat. Damn Ruth! he thought, but without much vigor; Miss Rebecca might just as well have found out about Peter's own time in Nazi Germany, the tragic loss of his wife, not from Ruth but from the profile in the *New York Times*. Then again, that was Ruth's fault as well; she had relayed the story to a new friend at a fund-raiser who turned out to be the gossip columnist Liz Sutton, whose story piqued the interest of Mr. Craig Claiborne, the restaurant critic, who then visited Masha's. "Me and my big mouth," Ruth had said. "I didn't mean anything by it! Who knew that nice girl worked for a newspaper?" Peter had been furious at the wholesale marketing of his past, but he supposed in a way he should thank Ruth. Mr. Claiborne's profile had included a review and Peter's recipes for brisket Wellington and tzimmes; the verdict had been favorable, and Masha's hadn't had an empty reservation book since.

The lights dimmed three times. "Let's go, people, move along here," said Sol impatiently, pushing through the other concertgoers schooling toward the hall like fish. Sol was pugilistic in every way, from his short boxer's build to his manner; he was so like Peter's dead father that they could have been brothers instead of cousins, which Peter found either irritating or comforting, depending on his mood. "Move it," Sol repeated. As he passed Peter, he said, "I got a fund-raiser needs catering next month—Young Zionists."

"Fine," said Peter. He had long ago tired of explaining what catering events gratis did to the restaurant's bottom line. Sol only told Peter to quit kvetching and cut food costs, and Peter paid no attention, and the arrangement, which suited no one, had become status quo.

"I'll have my girl call you with the details," said Sol as they followed the usher to their row.

"You two kids sit together," said Ruth, "I insist." She smiled at Peter and Miss Rebecca. Ruth was wearing one of her habitual caftans, this one floor-length silver lamé, with layers and layers of polished stone beads. Peter let Miss Rebecca slide in first and then stood between her and Ruth until all the ladies were seated. Their placement was excellent as usual, fifth row center. Looking idly about as the audience settled itself, all excited coughing and chatter, Peter saw a young blond woman in the front row, her hair cropped short, her white columnar dress exposing her long, pale neck and shoulders. Peter craned forward, although something told him June Bouquet would have been more likely to attend folk singer Bob Dylan in this hall than Sviatoslav Richter.

Miss Rebecca touched his sleeve and said something, and Peter sat with some reluctance. "Pardon?" he said.

"I said, have you seen Mr. Richter perform before? He's an utter genius."

"I have, in fact," said Peter. "We had the privilege of seeing Mr. Richter make his American debut here in May."

Miss Rebecca smiled at him. Really, she was very pretty; with her strawberry-fondant-colored gown and very white teeth, she was like a human petit four. "I'm so envious," she whispered. "I wish I could have been here. I don't hear half as much classical music as I'd like. It's so hard to find cultured men who appreciate it as I do."

Sylvia leaned past Ruth to tap Peter on the knee with her program. "I heard Richter's hands span an *octave* and a *half*," she said.

"Bet that comes in handy," said Choppers and laughed uproariously. "'Specially with the ladies."

"I heard he's a feygele," said Sol.

"Shhh," said somebody else behind them, and someone else said "Really," and then the lights dimmed and Miss Rebecca smiled at Peter, her teeth a glimmer in the dark, and the audience applauded wildly as the pianist walked out of the left wing and headed in a very businesslike fashion to his Steinway at the center of the stage.

*

As soon as Richter began to play, Peter knew something was wrong. At first he thought it was the pianist: although Peter knew Richter was Russian and that he too had suffered tremendous losses during the war, the very spare planes of Richter's face—a skull-like appearance emphasized by the stage's spotlight—reminded Peter of a certain SS sergeant named Stultz. . . . But Peter's discomfort was caused by more than the maestro; it was the music picking and plucking and running along his nerves, the jangling discordancy, the chords like a piece of furniture falling down a staircase. It wasn't the piece Peter dreaded above all others, the one he absolutely could not tolerate, but still—

"Is this Prokofiev?" he whispered to Miss Rebecca, tugging at his collar.

"Pardon?" she murmured.

"I thought tonight was Rachmaninov, not Prokofiev."

"What?" said Miss Rebecca.

"Shhhh!" somebody said behind them. Peter raised a hand in apology and pointed to the program in Miss Rebecca's lap. He was drenched in sweat; it felt as though ants were creeping all over him. Peter had been here with Sol and Ruth for Richter's debut concert in May when the hall staff turned off the air conditioning to ensure the audience would hear every nuance of the pianist's performance; that had been a sauna, but it hadn't been half so bad as this.

Miss Rebecca handed Peter her program, which confirmed Richter was performing Prokofiev's Sonata No. 2. Peter gripped his armrests. "Are you all right?" Miss Rebecca asked, her prettily manicured hand descending on Peter's.

"Forgive me, I must get some air." Peter stood and sidled in a half-crouch past the others in his row, trying to be mindful of knees and toes, hating his rudeness but desperate. Finally he reached the aisle and walked toward the exit door as quickly as he could without drawing more notice from the performance.

In the lobby he ripped loose his tie, unbuttoned his collar, and released a tremendous breath of relief. An usher hurried over. "Are you unwell, sir?" he asked.

Peter waved him off. "I will be fine, thank you." He headed for the bar. He asked first for a glass of water, which he drank down without stopping, and then a double brandy, which he carried to the men's lounge with him. The attendant flicked a glance at Peter's highball glass but otherwise remained impassive.

Peter removed his tuxedo jacket, folded it, and laid it on the counter; as he had suspected, his shirt was transparent with perspiration, sticking to his skin in gray patches and clearly showing the undershirt beneath. Peter undid his cuffs, put the gold links—emblazoned with an *M*—in his pocket, and took off the top shirt. He blotted himself as dry as he could with several paper towels. His undershirt was still drenched, and he pulled it away from his torso, fanning himself with it. That would have to be enough; he would never remove it in public. Peter swallowed half his brandy and doused his face in cold water; arms braced on the countertop, he surveyed his pale, dripping reflection with dispassion. It was always a surprise for Peter to look in any mirror and see this strong-jawed, even-featured matinée idol fellow with his waves of golden hair—"My very own film star," Masha had used to tease him, mussing it; "my pet Buster Crabbe, my Van Johnson!" It was a ridiculous disparity, a joke: if Peter's insides had matched his outsides, he would have looked like a Picasso. Like *Guernica*. He was shaking out his tuxedo shirt to put it back on when he heard approaching voices and the tramp of feet and knew it must be intermission. Not wanting to risk encountering Sol or Choppers or any other mutual acquaintance who might hinder an easy departure, Peter carried his clothes and brandy into the far stall.

He hung his shirt and jacket on the back of the door, lowered the ring, and sat waiting as his brethren did their business. The bathroom rang with voices, with the sounds of running water and zippers being undone and done and flushing and other noises Peter had gotten very adept, during his enforced years of communal living, at tuning out. He kept an eye on his watch and drank his Courvoisier—really, it was an insult to good brandy to drink it in such a place, but it was better than tending obligations he had no desire to fulfill. Such as Miss Rebecca, sweet as she might be. Or enduring Prokofiev . . . But that was his own fault. Peter should have been more vigilant; he should have called the hall for the program beforehand, as he usually did. He had never liked the modern composers, even before; it had been Masha who loved them. "You stodgy burgher," she'd said, laughing over Peter's preference for Bach and Brahms, "next you'll be telling me you don't like jazz!"

Peter leaned his head back against the cold metal stall and employed the technique that served better than most to blot out unwelcome thoughts: he took inventory, cataloging what the restaurant had in its storeroom and what he would have to order come Monday. A bushel of onions. Two of shallots. Three of potatoes—fingerlings were mostly done for the season, but maybe Peter could find some Kennebec at that farm in Patchogue? If he went out to Long Island, he might as well go all the way to Montauk for blues and bass. And squash; Peter was not a fan of pumpkin, which he found mealy and bland, but he could perhaps do some variation on his regular tzimmes using acorn, even butternut—

"Hey, pal, you fall asleep in there?" somebody said, rattling Peter's door.

"Sorry," said Peter, "I'm not well," and he sipped his brandy.

He had finished planning the week's menu—he would also offer a beach plum and cranberry torte—by the time the intermission bathroom tide had receded. He was reaching for his shirt when he did hear, over the pump of paper towel dispenser, Sol talking to somebody, probably Choppers, at the sinks.

"I'll give you he's got chutzpah with the technique," Sol was saying. "But I don't see what the big deal's all about."

"Dontcha?" said Choppers—it was definitely Choppers. "I think the guy's a giant."

"If you gotta have a Russki, I'll take Horowitz any day," said Sol. "Now there's an interpreter," and then, presumably to the attendant, "Hey, you, got any more towels over here?"

"I'm sorry, sir," said the attendant.

"Great," said Sol, "I'll just drip on my shirt like a schmuck. By the way," he said as their voices moved off, "nice niece you brought tonight."

"Yeah? You like her? You can have her—I don't think the kid was too impressed."

"You know I don't play around," said Sol, "but if I did—hotcha! She's some dish. As for my little cousin, don't take it personally. He only shtups shiksas."

"Yeah, so I heard," said Choppers, "but Ruth said I should keep trying. What is it with him?"

"He's always been that way," said Sol philosophically. "It's like a disease with some guys. You know his wife was goyish too. Looked like one of those Nazi propaganda posters, with the braids and everything."

"Oh yeah, the one the Nazis killed," said Choppers. "That's a sad story. But you'd think maybe he'd want to try a different flavor this time. . . . Here you go, pal, here's a dollar, don't spend it all in one place."

The attendant thanked him, and there was the whoosh of the outer door opening, and then Choppers asked as if he'd just thought of it, his voice growing ever fainter, "Hey, where'd he go, anyway?"

Peter ran through the meat delivery one more time as he finished buttoning his shirt—thirty young chickens, forty pounds of bottom round for the brisket, and had George at Primo's remembered to set aside the Moulard magrets for him? Peter put his jacket on over his shirt, which was damp but tolerable, as if a too-enthusiastic laundress had overspritzed it while ironing, and walked out of the stall. The men's lounge was empty again, except for the attendant. Sol and Choppers and the dozens of other men might never have been there. Sol wasn't right about everything—in fact, in Peter's opinion, he was wrong about a great many—but he was correct about two: Horowitz was the Russian pianist of more colorful interpretation. And although Peter had sex only when it was necessary, and then quickly, in the dark or clothed, preferably standing up, with stewardesses, waitresses—not his—and other pretty strangers he would likewise never see again, it always seemed to be with non-Jewish women, though this was by coincidence or subliminal inclination rather than design.

This made Peter think of June Bouquet again—which was very unlike him, or maybe unlike her, to keep appearing in his thoughts this way. He handed the attendant a five from his money clip, then held up one finger and retrieved his empty glass from the sink. This too the attendant received without change in expression.

"Thank you, sir," he said. "Enjoy your evening."

"You as well," said Peter. He shot his cuffs and went out—and there, in the lobby, leaning against one wall in her confectionary evening gown, Miss Rebecca was waiting for him.

*

"I hope you don't mind," she said. "I wanted to make sure you're all right."

"That's very thoughtful," said Peter, "and unnecessary. I just have a headache. Please, go back in. You'll miss the second half of the program."

He started to open the door for her, but Miss Rebecca put her hand over his on the brass handle.

"I think I understand," she said, twinkling up at him from beneath her dual lines of lashes. "I don't care for Prokofiev myself. It's so discordant. Jangly. It gets on my nerves."

"I think it's supposed to."

"Now, why would anybody want that," said Miss Rebecca, inching closer, "when they could have Brahms? Or Beethoven? Why would you want to be disturbed when you could listen to something romantic?"

"I have no idea," said Peter. He resisted the urge to check his watch. "But I believe the second half of the program is Ravel—"

"I'll tell you something else I don't like," Miss Rebecca murmured. "Setups."

Peter smiled. For the first time, he felt a genuine fondness toward her.

"I had a suspicion you were not really Arthur's niece," he said.

"I'm his dental hygienist," said Miss Rebecca.

"Ah," said Peter. That explained the excellent teeth.

"I don't usually agree to this sort of situation," she said.

"I don't imagine you have to."

She smiled up at him. "Thank you," she breathed, "you're very sweet. Just like Ruth said. And I thought you must be from the *Times* article. I remember it from the day it came out . . ."

You and every other hopeful young lady in the greater New York area, Peter thought.

"It's not what you think," whispered Miss Rebecca. "I'm not like all the other girls, just looking for a successful husband—although I'd love to see your restaurant, Pasha's?"

"Masha's."

"Oooh, like the Russian Tea Room? That's one of my favorites."

Peter hid a grimace. The Tea Room was a permanent thorn between his toes, his biggest competitor in everything except the nationality of the cuisine. "Something like that," he said.

"I'm sure your restaurant is infinitely more charming. And I admire what you did with it, dedicating it to . . . somebody you love who was lost."

"Thank you," said Peter. He was starting to perspire again. "Really, Miss Dannett—"

"Rebecca," she corrected him. She tilted up her square little chin so she could look directly at him.

"I was engaged to be married," she said, her breathy voice a bit more forceful than usual; "did Ruth tell you?"

"She didn't," said Peter.

Miss Rebecca nodded. "Yes. My high school sweetheart. We were all set to be married at the Briar Rose Club last fall when there was an accident. He was driving, and another motorist who had been drinking swerved into him on the Post Road. So."

Peter bowed his head. "I'm so sorry," he said. And he was, if even in the abstract way of feeling sympathy for a stranger. There were so many hurting people in the world.

"Thank you," said Miss Rebecca. She bravely threw her shoulders back. Her eyes glistened. "So you see, although you must meet an awful lot of nieces, I have more in common with you than most. I understand what it's like to lose the person you love. But I think sometimes you just have to take a leap of faith. Try again."

She pushed herself up on tiptoes and kissed Peter's cheek, and then, while he was digesting the surprise of this, she moved to his mouth. Peter tried not to sigh into Miss Rebecca's lips as she pressed them insistently against his—he meant no disrespect to her, but all he could taste was the wax of her lipstick. It wasn't that she wasn't attractive, or intelligent, or cultured or pleasant or deep-feeling or nice—she certainly seemed to be all of these things, and Peter gave her credit for boldness as well. But he had spent the last twenty years avoiding precisely this sort of situation, one that would lead to entanglement, negotiation, obligation. A wedding at the Briar Rose Country Club. A house in Mamaroneck or Rye, visiting Sol and Ruth each weekend. And, of course, children.

Peter broke the kiss and drew away. Miss Rebecca looked sadly up at him. "Too fast?" she asked.

Peter put his hands on her shoulders. "Look," he said. "You

seem to be a perfectly lovely young woman. And I'm truly sorry for your loss. But this isn't for me."

Miss Rebecca nodded. "Are you . . . ," she whispered and made a delicate flipping gesture with her wrist. "I won't tell."

Peter smiled. He had sometimes contemplated just letting people think he was a homosexual—working in a kitchen, a woman's job, would help the charade. But it would break Ruth's heart.

"That's not it," Peter said. "And it isn't you. I just can't . . ."

Miss Rebecca looked confused—but suddenly her face cleared. "Oh!" she said, putting her hand over her mouth. "The war?" She glanced at Peter's tuxedo trousers.

"Pardon?" said Peter.

Miss Rebecca stood on her toes again to kiss his cheek. "Don't say another word, I read *The Sun Also Rises*. Saw the film, too." She gave Peter a look of immense sympathy. "You poor, poor man. Don't worry. Your secret's safe with me." Then, with a last glimmering glance, she was through the door into the concert chamber.

Peter stood where he was for a few moments, letting this sink in. Then he couldn't help laughing. "Well!" he said. He hoped Miss Rebecca would keep her promise and not share her misunderstanding—he had no wish to be known as an impotent gelding—but it was a relief to be off the hook for the evening.

Peter retrieved his overcoat from the coat check, leaving the chit with a scribbled description of Miss Rebecca so she could get her own, and left the hall. He was thinking of what Miss Rebecca had said, and Ruth too, in the early days when she had caught Peter pretending to comprehend much less of his dates' English than he did. "Bubbie," she'd said, "I understand. Healing takes time, nu? But meanwhile—you have to live a little."

For whatever reason, this advice was now coming back to Peter in a new way. He headed west on Fifty-Seventh Street and turned left onto Seventh Avenue, striding along with his coat unbuttoned and breathing deeply of the frigid air that smelled of metal grates and steam—it was invigorating. He saw a bank of pay phones and beyond it the Carnegie Deli. He would stop in for a pastrami on rye after he made his call, Peter decided. He was suddenly famished.

He stepped into the nearest free cubicle and took out his wallet, plugging a dime into the slot and dialing a number off a scrap of paper he had been carrying around since the day after the blackout, when he had called the Ford Agency as soon as the power was restored. Miss Bouquet was on a shoot, he had been told, and they didn't give out their girls' information. But when Peter had dropped his name and mentioned he was considering using June for a new full-scale advertising campaign, the receptionist had provided him with a number: SPI118–7, a Greenwich Village exchange. So this June Bouquet was indeed something of a bohemian, the free spirit she had seemed to be. Peter smiled and tapped his foot between rings until, on the other end of the line, somebody picked up.

"Hello?" June said.

LARCHMONT, 1965

When Peter left the restaurant, June was waiting for him on the sidewalk, smoking. He held up the shopping bag— brown paper, with handles, and "Masha's" written on its side, the carrier he'd designed himself for all patrons who wanted to take food home.

"Dessert," he said, "and bread and cheeses. Let's go before there is some crisis or I change my mind."

"Done," said June. She extinguished her cigarette beneath the toe of one platform boot—today, like her fur-cuffed leather jacket, they were oxblood, in homage to the fall holiday, Peter assumed. It was a beautiful morning, cold but sunny, and their breath plumed and mingled as Peter hailed a cab.

Traffic was slow to Grand Central, snarled because of the parade. Above the park, giant inflatable balloons in the shapes of cartoon dogs and mice waited to be cheered throughout the city. So American, Peter thought; only in this bizarre, exuberant, childish country would people celebrate having enough to eat this way. Today he felt like one of them—almost. He was like a schoolboy playing truant, abandoning the restaurant to the care of his sous-chef for the first time in a decade. Today Lena would oversee the preparation and serving of the special menu: pheasant and caramelized yams, Brussels sprouts with slivered almonds, oyster stuffing, apple and pear tortes. June put her head on his shoulder and yawned—they had been out late at El Morocco, which she called ElMo, the night before, and today Peter was taking her to Sol and Ruth's house for Thanksgiving dinner.

Beyond Peter's window, June's face, twelve feet high, sprayed silver and encased within an astronaut helmet, slid past on the side of a bus. He squeezed her knee.

"Look, there you are again," he said. "You are ubiquitous."

June lifted her head to look. "Oh, that shoot. I had that shiny makeup in my hair for days. I felt like the Tin Man."

She reached for the Masha's bag, from which a ficelle, a baguette nearly as slender as June herself, protruded. "May I?"

"Certainly—though why didn't you eat at the restaurant, goose?"

"I wasn't hungry then," said June. "Plus I wanted to get out of there before that Lena fileted me. She always looks at me as if she wants to make me into soup."

"Don't be silly," said Peter, though it was true Lena had no fond feelings for June, muttering things like *blyad* and *tupa shlyukha*—whore and stupid whore, respectively—and, whenever June was in the restaurant, standing in the doorway and sharpening her knife more dramatically than necessary. Peter handed the bread to June, who nibbled the end of it. Peter looked away again, June's otherworldly face having now been replaced by a cab, from which a very old Negro woman stared at him stoically as an oracle. Peter knew June had to eat very little to stay slim for her work, but still it bothered him.

June handed the ficelle back to Peter. "I'm nervous. Should I be nervous?"

Definitely, thought Peter. "Of course not," he said.

"Will they like me, do you think?"

"What's not to like?"

"What about my outfit?" June unbuttoned her leather coat and held it open. Beneath, she wore a gold brocade dress, higher-necked and a little longer than her usual minidresses—this one was mid-thigh.

Peter slid his hand up her knee. "With legs like this, who cares what anyone thinks."

He leaned over and kissed her, her breath tasting of bread, smoke, and the alcohol of the night before. June put her hands on either side of Peter's face and pulled him closer. She bent her back like that newfangled wire toy—a Slinky. She was the most flexible woman Peter had ever met, and he wondered whether it was her job—her body a maneuverable object—or June being June. Whichever it was, he was grateful.

"Break it up, kids," said the cabbie. "Here's your stop."

In Grand Central terminal, Peter bought tickets and consulted the board: they had fifteen minutes before the next train to Larchmont. Somebody somewhere was playing Vivaldi on a violin. White sunlight slanted in through the high windows, and Peter experienced a moment of such well-being it could almost be called bliss. He was unprepared for it. It had been years. He shut his eyes and turned his face into the light.

"I used to work here," he said to June.

"You didn't. As what? A ticket taker?"

"No, goose," he said, "there," and he nodded to the Oyster Bar.

"Ugh, oysters," said June, "slimy." She shuddered.

June herself tasted like an oyster fresh from the Sound, Peter thought, Blue Points or Peconic Pearls. "That means you've had only bad ones," he said. "When we get back to Masha's, I'll change that."

"I've never actually had one," she said, and Peter laughed.

"Then how do you know you don't like them?"

"I can just tell," said June.

She took his elbow and they strolled across the concourse. "How long did you work here?" she asked.

"Not very long," said Peter truthfully. "It was my first job when I came to this country, after . . ."

He trailed off. Their footsteps echoed with everyone else's in this vaulted space, along with the flap of trapped birds' wings and stir of voices, but for a moment Peter fancied that the special acoustics of the terminal allowed for time preservation as well, that every soul and moment that had ever been through here was collected and preserved under the high roof, where they mixed and mingled. The boy he had been then—in his mid-twenties, barely speaking English, waking every morning at Sol and Ruth's and remembering where he was and wishing he were dead; that boy who had spurned Sol's offer, more like a demand, to work in the law firm and instead took the first job he saw off the train, a busboy at the Oyster Bar; the boy who had then been fired because the tattoo on his forearm, the small line of crooked greenish numbers his shirt had slid up to reveal, had upset the prosperous diners— that boy was gone. Peter had left him twenty years behind. He had worked very hard to. Still, for a moment Peter could feel him—his fathomless terror, the hopelessness and bleakness of those days.

"What happened?" said June. "You didn't like it?"

"I got a better job. Traveled a little, from here to there and back. It doesn't matter. It was a long time ago."

Peter took her face in his hands and kissed her, other travelers eddying around them and the coo and burble of pigeons overhead.

"Today is what matters," he said.

"Speaking of which, I need hostess flowers," said June and dragged him over to a newsstand, in front of which was a white bucket full of cellophane-wrapped blooms. She deliberated among clusters of mums, seeming not to notice dozens of replicas of her face, lips pursed coyly around a peppermint stick, gazing from the December issue of *McCall's*. Peter had asked her once, Did she really not see herself? Goodness, no, June had said; she couldn't look at newsstands at all. Spotting her competition on other covers, Jean Shrimpton or Peggy Moffitt, made her crazy. Sometimes she literally shielded her eyes, with a hat or her hand, when they walked by kiosks. "I'll take . . . this one," she said, selecting a rust-colored bunch, and then they had to sprint for the train.

They were lucky and got two seats together; the train wasn't as crowded as it normally was with commuters, rows and rows of men in hats, but there were still plenty of people in transit for the holiday. Peter offered June the window and she nestled in, seemingly unaware of the looks she drew from men and women alike. To Peter it was still a novelty, the reflected celebrity of her presence. The few dates he had been on in this country had been with pretty girls, some actually quite lovely. But none in the same category as June, with her height and boyish blond hair; her startlingly exquisite white face; her miniskirts and collection of thigh-high platform boots in every color. She was, as the chefs at Masha's called her, some dish. The train began to move forward, producing vertigo in Peter at first when, compared to the cars next to them, they seemed to be sliding backward. Then they were in the tunnel, picking up speed. Peter thought as he always did that if one were cognizant of the moment right before one's death, it might be like this: rushing through dark space at a speed that made one's ears pop, suspended between one place and another.

They emerged to the clustered projects of the Bronx, the city reappearing in miniature on Peter's right. June leaned across his lap to watch it go by. "I never get tired of that skyline," she said, and hummed a little—*If I can make it there, I'll make it anywhere*—before she sat back and took out her Marlboros.

"Sometimes it all still seems like a dream," she said.

"I know what you mean," said Peter, lighting her cigarette.

She smoked ruminatively. "Every night I wake up knowing it's all going to pop like a soap bubble. Realistically, I've got a year at most, maybe two, before I have to go back to Minnesota."

"Yes, to your farmer husband, your six children, and your permanent wave."

June shot Peter a sideways glance. "Tell me again," she said. Already they had a catechism.

"You'll never have to do that," said Peter.

"Ever?"

"Never."

"Even when I'm saggy and baggy and sit around eating bonbons all day?" said June.

"Especially then," said Peter. "I'll make sure of it."

"Oh," said June, "you are the sweetest man," and she snuffed her cigarette in the ashtray and hooked one leg over Peter's and took his face in her hands and kissed him for so long that it was the throat-clearing of the conductor, moving through the car taking tickets, who stopped them.

"Hi there," said June. She rearranged herself and handed over her ticket. "'Scuse me, I'm going to go reapply my lipstick, which this guy here messed up." She slid out of her seat and swayed up the length of the car, everyone—the conductor and Peter included—watching her go.

"Lucky man," said the conductor.

"I am," said Peter.

He looked out the window as bars of sunlight and shadow alternated over his face. The tangle of highways, the seemingly thousands of cars, the three- and four-story brick buildings with their graffiti and advertisements at every stop: CUTTY SARK, LUCKY STRIKE, BAN THE BOMB, CHEVY, COCA-COLA, FUCK 'NAM! Peter thought how different they were from the posters of his youth: EIN VOLK, EIN REICH, EIN FÜHRER!, for example, or DER JUDE: KRIEGSANSTIFTER, KRIEGSVERLÄNGERER—war agitator, war prolonger. Neither had there been, in Berlin, any of this disorderly scribbling on walls. In fact, little about the American travel system with its litter and anarchic epithets resembled the U-Bahn and S-Bahn of Peter's native city, not to mention the later trains, the ones on which one had no choice of where to sit, the ones in which there were no seats or even windows but instead rough walls against which one stood, pressed, with hundreds of other people, unable to sit or move or scratch one's nose, stinking and waiting in the dark. For a moment Peter thought of a child's hand winking in the sunlight: "Papa! Over here!" Then it was gone.

He got up and made his way through the car, past a family sharing lunch, a woman in rollers and kerchief smoking, a fat man scowling at his newspaper. One of the bathroom doors stood open. The other was closed. Peter tapped on it.

"June? Are you all right?"

The door rolled open an inch on its track, and one of June's blue eyes peered through.

"I need help with my zipper," she said.

Peter stepped into the tiny compartment and shut the door. "Are you . . . changing outfits?" he asked with some confusion—he hadn't seen her bring any other bags along—and then she was grabbing him, her hands around his neck, sucking on his lower lip. Peter caught on; without removing his mouth from hers, he hitched her legs up around his waist and swung her so she was perched on the tiny sink. He reached under her skirt; she was wearing garters but no underwear. She planted her boots on the opposite wall as Peter unzipped his fly. "Oh!" she said and her head knocked back against the mirror as he entered her.

She pushed against him, her muscles flexing. Peter gripped her buttocks with one hand and braced the other against the wall. Water sloshed in the commode; the lights went off and on again, the rails went *ka-chk ka-chk, ka-chk ka-chk* beneath them and the whole room rocked. Somebody tapped on the door; "Just a minute!" June and Peter yelled in unison, and then they looked at each other and tried not to laugh. Peter began moving again, and June bit her lip and put her head back and presented him with her long white throat. Above it, in the mirror, Peter saw himself reflected: he still had his hat on, his coat. Good. The more layers he had on, the better. For nearly a month they had been enjoying just this kind of vigorous entanglement, and June had yet to see him without a shirt or in full daylight. Just the way Peter liked it. It was a lot of work but worth it. June was worth it. The train slowed for a stop, and Peter slid as far as he could into her, into the welcome oblivion of pure sensation. He buried his face in her neck and closed his eyes.

*

They took a cab from the Larchmont station, passing the White Stag Country Club, which did not admit Jews, and the Briar Rose, which did. June twisted in her seat, taking in the stone walls, the vast lawns, the houses set so far back from the road that only glimpses of them were available. "These places are mansions," she said.

"Do you think so? They are just houses," Peter said mildly.

June extracted a cigarette for Peter to light as the driver followed a narrow lane into a cul-de-sac. Here the land ended; more houses, tucked among two-story boulders of schist and towering old trees, surveyed the Long Island Sound. "Is that *theirs*?" June asked, craning forward.

"No," said Peter, "that one," and he pointed to a half-stone, half-timbered house perched on a cliff.

"Jeez, Pete," said June, "you might have warned me."

"Warned you of what?" said Peter. "Sol is a lawyer, a partner in his own firm. I told you that. He does well. He likes to play golf."

He was starting to sweat. He took out his handkerchief and patted his forehead as the cabbie wended up the long drive, between rock faces furred with moss and glittering with mica. "Thank you," Peter said, pulling out his billfold to pay. He helped June out of the taxi, and they stood in the motor court looking up at the house as the cab drove away.

June stamped out her cigarette and looked around for somewhere to put the butt. "Never mind," Peter said, "Yoshi will get it." He added, "The gardener."

"Remind me, who are these people again? Your cousins?"

"Not strictly. Sol was my father's cousin. Ruth is his wife. They're the only family I have."

"Oh," said June.

Peter put his arm around her.

"Listen," he said. "They will absolutely adore you. I do—so how could they not?"

"Well," said June. But she started to smile.

Peter tugged her gently toward the steps, which were carved straight into the rock upon which the house sat. As they ascended, they passed through Ruth's stepladdered gardens—barren this time of year, but with enough Japanese maples and evergreens planted in them that they weren't totally devoid of color. A waterfall chattered down one rock wall. When they reached the terrace, Peter turned June around to take in the grounds: the yard beneath them a grassy bowl ringed by oaks, in which a kidney-shaped swimming pool gleamed in summer but was currently shrouded in canvas; the wild reeds separating the property from the marsh; the Sound beyond that. Boats bobbed on the horizon.

"Wow," said June again. She clung to Peter's arm. "It's amazing."

"You're amazing, June Bouquet," said Peter, and was kissing her when the door to the kitchen opened and Ruth came out.

"Bubbie!" she crowed.

She gave Peter a smack on the cheek and lick-wiped the lipstick off. She was wearing a special caftan today in honor of the occasion, patterned with thousands of tiny brown and orange feathers; she looked like a little maroon-crested pheasant. In the folds of her clothes Peter smelled Shalimar, mothballs, and gravy. She turned to June.

"And this must be the mysterious June I've been hearing about?" she asked.

"Indeed, this is she," Peter said. "My lady friend June Bouquet. June, this is Ruth."

"June Bouquet!" said Ruth, looking from June to Peter with an expectant smile as if waiting for somebody to let her in on the joke; when nobody did, she said, "How nice!"

"How do you do," said June, "these are for you," and she handed Ruth the mums.

Ruth clucked. "A bouquet from a bouquet? That's extra special."

She tipped her head back to look at June, like a tourist trying to see the top of a skyscraper.

"Hoo, you're a tall one," she said. "And so skinny! Peter, aren't you feeding this girl?" She took June's elbow. "Let me guess, you're a picky eater, but we'll fix that. Wait'll you see the spread we've got today."

She led June inside, June making a comical wide-eyed face over her shoulder at Peter. He blew her a kiss and followed them into the kitchen, where the maid was struggling with something at the sink.

"Here, let me," said Peter and took from her one of Ruth's prized copper molds. He ran a few inches of warm water in the sink and dropped it in. "How are you, Maria?"

"Fine, Mr. Peter," said Maria—whom Ruth called her girl although Peter guessed Maria was in her mid-fifties. Peter had grown up with servants, in fact had felt more comfortable with them than his own parents, but it still surprised him a little to find the class system alive and well in America. Wasn't this supposed to be the land of equal opportunity, of egalitarianism? Of course, one had only to watch Negroes in the South marching for their rights and being attacked with dogs and hoses for their trouble to know that wasn't quite true, but—among Jewish people, too, this sense of others as destined to serve? Peter didn't subscribe to it. In his profession, most of the best-skilled workers had brown skin of one shade or another.

"How are Hector and Victor?" he asked Maria of her sons.

"Trouble," she said and pushed at her hair, gray and white in its net.

"If Victor wants a job when he's released, send him to me."

"You a good man, Mr. Peter," said Maria. Her smile exposed a gold tooth. "That lady who come through with Missus Ruth, she your girlfriend?"

"She is," said Peter, smiling.

"Ay!" said Maria, "tall," and she canted her body back to look at the ceiling in illustration.

"She is indeed," said Peter. He lifted the mold from the sink, inverted it onto a waiting platter, gave it a gentle tap, and a ring of jellied cranberry embedded with walnuts slid out. Peter had never eaten Thanksgiving dinner here, but he knew what else Ruth had in store for them because every year she called him to consult about the unvarying menu: turkey—of course; sweet potatoes, oyster stuffing, vegetables from her garden. Peter was half dreading, half anticipating the food parade: he knew he would spend the meal mentally cataloging what he would have done differently, but one could always learn something new from someone else's recipes, too. He patted Maria on the shoulder of her gray uniform, unwrapped the cheese to breathe, slotted the tortes from Masha's into the already overflowing refrigerator, and went in search of June and Ruth.

They were in the living room, where a fire crackled behind the brass grate. At the bar Peter fixed himself a vodka tonic—it was past noon, after all. "June?" he said, "may I get you something?" but she already held a glass of white wine, her hangover apparently having fled. There was a run in her right stocking from their escapade on the train.

"So delicate," she was saying of Ruth's Venetian glass collection; "like sea creatures. And all the colors!"

"Handblown," said Ruth with satisfaction. She took June by the hand, tugging her around the room. "And look at this," she said, "and this, and this . . ." Peter smiled into his drink. He had lived in this house for two years when he first arrived in this country, and there were rooms into which he now did not go—the guest room with its slanted-eye deer, for instance. And Sol and Ruth's master suite. But the living room was a neutral and luxurious space, a warehouse of what Ruth called her tchotchkes—the treasures she and Sol had imported from their many overseas trips. Oriental rugs so thick footsteps were noiseless; jade figurines; Japanese scrolls and screens; china bowls filled with potpourri. A waist-high gold Buddha sat cross-legged and serene on a stand before the picture window, admiring the view of the Sound. There was a Steinway nobody played; a Picasso, a Kandinsky, and a Klee—Sol was a great collector of art.

June stooped to peer into the lighted display case containing Sol and Ruth's Judaic memorabilia: Torah, tallith, kiddush cup, dreidels. Ruth had identified them all for Peter when he'd first arrived, aghast at his lack of knowledge. *Your parents taught you nothing? Such a shame.*

"What a pretty candelabra," June said.

"Darling," said Ruth, "that's a menorah. You've never seen one before?"

"No," said June, "but it's very clever, isn't it? I bet it gives beautiful light when all the candles are lit at once."

"Oy," said Ruth, patting her face in dismay. She was starting to explain when Sol came in.

"What does a man have to do to get a kiss and a drink around here?" he said.

"Darling!" said Ruth. "How was golf?"

"Lousy," said Sol. "Too windy," and indeed his black-and-gray hair, normally slicked down into thousands of tiny waves, had exploded so it looked like the brand-new hairstyle Peter sometimes saw on Negroes in the city, the Afro. "Who's this?" Sol asked of June.

"This is my lady friend," said Peter, "June Bouquet."

Sol's face creased in a smile. "Aren't you some hot ticket."

"Thank you," said June. "I think."

"Didn't think you had it in you," said Sol to Peter and stumped over to the bar, where he poured himself a Scotch—far from his first, Peter surmised. Sol's eyes were watering and his nose reddened in a way that couldn't be completely attributed to the wind on the eighteenth hole.

"Let's get dinner on the table," Sol announced. "I'm starved."

*

Although there was a formal dining room in the Larchmont house, complete with mahogany dining set, Peter had never once seen it used. Today's meal, like all others, was served in the solarium—the glass box Sol had appended to one wing of the house for Ruth's sixtieth birthday. It was a bit of a horror architecturally, matching nothing, but it was an excellent environment for Ruth's indoor garden, cacti and ferns and flowering plants that ringed the room on floating shelves and hung from the skylights. From floor to ceiling the walls were glass, giving the impression of eating outside among the giant boulders, the lawn and open sky.

Peter held Ruth's chair, then June's. The table had been laid for the holiday with Belgian linens, Ruth's Wedgwood china, and Tiffany silver. There were salt and pepper cellars at each place setting. There was a bowl of purple grapes with its own scissors for cutting the stems, which gave Peter a pang whenever he saw it; his mother had had one as well. In the center, a wicker cornucopia overflowed with gourds from Ruth's own garden.

Maria came in with the breadbasket, into which she had sliced

Peter's ficelle and a loaf of challah. She lit candles, poured water and wine.

"Thank you, Maria," said Ruth. "Are you sure the bird's cooked enough? I don't want we should all get worms."

"Why don't I look," Peter offered, but then Sol came in with a fresh Scotch.

"Siddown," he commanded. "In my house men don't work in the kitchen. That's what the girl is for. Maria!"

"Yes, Mr. Sol?"

"Bring the bird and my carving knife."

"Yes, Mr. Sol."

Peter nudged his foot against June's under the table. He raised his eyebrows—*All right?*—and she smiled. They sipped their wine as Maria ferried in the side dishes: string beans and squash; sweet potatoes with pineapple and—abomination!—marshmallows; the cranberry mold and stuffing. The turkey came last, a leathery brown giant on a silver tray. "Twenty-seven pounds," said Ruth proudly, "from the kosher butcher in Mamaroneck!" They all applauded except Maria, who got to her knees to plug Sol's electric knife into a socket.

Peter made one last attempt. "Are you sure you don't want me to carve? I do it twenty times a day—"

"I said I've got it," said Sol.

He took the knife to the turkey and switched it on. The blade whirred, then shuddered as it cut through the skin into the breast. Little shreds of turkey flew everywhere. Peter couldn't watch. He couldn't look at June, either, who was kicking him; he knew they would both burst out laughing. There was a squeal as the knife hit the bone.

"Goddamned thing," Sol said.

Finally the butchering was done and Sol sat back, breathing hard. "Isn't that lovely," said Ruth.

"Everybody eat," said Sol.

The plates went around the table clockwise: turkey first, then the sides. The table brightened and darkened as the sun winked in and out, clouds moving in on the previously sunny sky. June took a full portion of each dish, though Peter knew she would only rearrange it artfully on her plate to make it look as though she'd eaten.

"This looks delicious, Mr. and Mrs. Rashkin," she said. "Thanks for inviting me."

"Please, it's Ruth and Sol," said Ruth. "Do you know, you're the first girl this one has brought home in twenty years? It must be bashert."

June smiled at Peter. "Is that good?"

"It means 'meant to be,'" Peter explained.

"And of course he brings a shiksa," said Sol around a mouthful of squash. "Just like the last one. His wife."

"My former wife," Peter emphasized quickly to June, who nodded—by this time she knew about Masha.

Ruth grasped Peter's hand in her small, chilly, corded one. "Well, I for one am thrilled," she announced. "Peter is a son to me, the only one I ever had." She gave his hand a resounding kiss and set it back on the tablecloth. "And now, he's yours," she said to June. "Such a beauty, *shayne punim*. And so tall! You should be a model."

June smiled. "Actually, I am a model."

"I told you that, Ruth," said Peter.

"Did you?" said Ruth. "Maybe you did. Maybe you didn't. My blood pressure medication—I get forgetful."

Sol stabbed through the turkey on the platter. "Where's the tuches?" he demanded. "You know I always like the tuches."

"How should I know?" Ruth raised her hands. "You're the one who cut it."

"Euh," said Sol and contented himself with a drumstick. "What kind of outfit you work for?" he said to June, chewing. "Catalogs, department stores?"

June crinkled her nose at Peter, who knew she was trying not to laugh.

"Because if you wanna get into stores," said Sol, "I know a guy. He owns Bamberger's—you familiar with Bamberger's?"

Peter dropped his forehead into his hand in mock anguish. "Sol," he said, "June works for Ford. The Ford Agency."

"You model cars?" said Ruth.

Peter pantomimed banging his head on the table.

"Sometimes," said June. "Among other products. I mostly do runway and covers."

"Oh," said Ruth. "Well, what do you know about that?" She lifted her hands and smiled around as if she'd arranged the whole thing. "Who wants seconds?"

The food carousel resumed, counterclockwise this time. Peter took more turkey, though his first portion had been stringy and dry. Sol took more yams and Scotch.

"Where are your people from?" he said to June. "You're not from around here."

"No," said June. "Minnesota."

Sol grunted. "Good trout there."

"Where in Minnesota?" Ruth asked hopefully. "Minneapolis?"

"A little farm town, near the border of Iowa," said June. "New Heidelberg?"

"Never heard of it," said Ruth.

"I'm not surprised," said June, "not many people have," and she cut a polite sliver of quivering cranberry mold.

"Not many Jews there, I'm guessing," said Ruth.

"Not many," agreed June cheerfully. "In fact I never met a person of the Jewish persuasion until I came to New York."

"Is that so," said Ruth. She fanned herself with her napkin.

"In New Heidelberg," said June, "you're one of two stripes: Catholic or Lutheran."

"And which . . . stripe are you?" Ruth asked faintly.

"Lutheran," said June.

"And your people are . . ."

June waited, bewildered, until Sol said, "What she means is, are they Krauts."

"Oh," said June. "No, we're Norwegian, not German, don't worry." She looked to Peter in confusion, mouthing, *No offense*. Peter smiled tiredly. It was complicated.

"Well," said Ruth. She seemed to be gathering herself to offer a third round of food when Sol said, "Norwegian, German, doesn't matter—they're all anti-Semites."

Everyone looked at him. "Who?" said Ruth.

"Lutherans," said Sol. He swiveled to pour himself another drink from the sideboard. "Their whole religion is founded on driving Jews into the sea. Martin Luther was the king anti-Semite of them all."

"Oh, I don't know about that," said Peter, as June said, "I never heard—"

"Of course you haven't," said Sol. "They're not going to teach that at your church in the sticks, are they? But it's true. Luther made Hitler look like a piker."

Peter bristled. "I think that is hardly apt—"

Sol smashed his highball glass onto the table. "Are you calling me a liar in my own house?" he thundered.

There was a silence, broken only by the clink of an ice cube moving in Sol's tumbler.

Peter stood. June appeared to be studying her barely touched plate. When she finally glanced up, he sent her a reassuring smile.

"I've had enough," he said. "Who would like some coffee?"

*

After coffee—dessert, it was decided, would be reserved for later, when everyone had had time to digest—the men adjourned to discuss business and Ruth whisked June off on a house-and-grounds tour. Peter barely had time to embrace June, to whisper "How are you holding up?" and she to reply "Fine" before Ruth took her

away. Peter wondered whether Ruth would show June her prize:
the secret garden tucked amid the reeds of the marsh, where, Ruth
swore, the mucky, sulfuric soil contributed to the gargantuan size
of her vegetables. The dampness, she said, or maybe all the crushed
shells. Revealing the garden would be Ruth's ultimate sign of trust
and approval, and Peter made a mental note to ask June on the
way back to the city if she'd seen it—without disclosing its impor-
tance, of course, if she hadn't.

Meanwhile, Sol and Peter sequestered themselves in Sol's study,
where Sol went over the monthly figures Peter had imported in
the Masha's shopping bag and Peter placed a call to the restaurant
to ensure everything was fine. It was: only one small fire, easily
extinguished, and the prep chef had cut himself, but not into the
Brussels sprouts nor badly enough to warrant a hospital run. "He
barely need stitches," said Lena, "I sew up myself." Otherwise, they
had done eighty covers and were on track for twenty more, if the
reservations were fulfilled. Obviously, not everyone in Manhattan wanted a home-cooked family meal for Thanksgiving, Peter
thought. He was thankful for that.

He told Lena he would be in early the next morning and hung
up, wandering around the study to inspect Sol's latest acquisi-
tions. The little room, whose picture window overlooked the motor court, oaks, and the Sound, contained a leather couch and
hassock, a fine library of first-edition books Peter doubted Sol
had ever read, and Sol's newest art purchases, which would be lived
with for a while and carefully considered before they were hung.
Aside from a small Miro and an Egon Schiele—a colored pencil
rendering of a woman's torso, her face blotted out—Sol seemed
to be branching out into photography. They were black-and-white
portraits of street people, mostly, taken by—Peter peered at the
signatures—Diane Arbus, Lisette Model. Peter had just started to
hear of some of the names, floating around Masha's dining room
in conjunction with exhibits, and he had no doubt they were quite

good—though whether Sol purchased them because he liked them and the artists or for their financial value was another matter. They disturbed Peter, however. The subjects were unhappy, homeless, missing limbs, obese, isolated in their frames, and although that very grotesquerie was something Peter was drawn to look at over and over—thereby, he supposed, qualifying the images as art—they were nothing he would ever hang on his walls.

"I like this one," he said, of a very large lady in a black swimming suit, laughing and slapping her legs at the shore while the ocean crashed around her.

"Quiet," said Sol, who was breathing heavily as he trawled a mechanical pencil down the numbers in Peter's ledger—but then he relented and said, "Very talented girl. Good investment."

He held out his tumbler—for Sol, coffee translated to more Scotch. Peter refilled it from Sol's bookshelf bar and poured a Grand Marnier for himself. He sat on the couch to wait, warming the glass in his hands.

Finally Sol swiveled in his chair, tossed the ledger back toward Peter, and said, "Not so good. Better cut back."

Peter nodded because this was what Sol always said, although Masha's was in the black, a rarity among New York restaurants of which he was justifiably proud. He said, "Cut back on what?"

Sol shrugged. "You're the boss, you figure it out."

Peter sighed. "I've been meaning to talk to you about our paper supplier. Linens too; the laundry is eating us alive. Can't we switch? There's a supplier in New Jersey—"

"Forget it," said Sol. He swirled the remaining cubes in his glass, lifted it, crunched them. "We're sticking with my guys."

Peter ran his free hand through his hair, frustrated. "But they're charging us twice as much. Your laundry man, three times. If you're concerned about the bottom line—"

"No changes," said Sol. "They're like family. You gotta cut back on the food."

"I can't do that," Peter said. He wanted to stand and pace in his frustration but stayed seated; he didn't want to show his belly, as Sol would say.

"We've talked about this," he said. "The food is what makes Masha's what it is. Eighty-five percent of restaurants go out of business in New York in the first year, and we've been up and running for ten. The success isn't in the linens or napkins, I assure you—"

"No, it's that sob story Ruth told the papers," said Sol with satisfaction. He went to the bar to fix another drink.

Peter stared at Sol's back, broad and a little humped. Sol meant the story behind the menu: how Peter had based it on the dishes he and Masha once discussed as they lay on the mattress on the floor of their fifth-story, one-room cold-water flat in Berlin. "Wouldn't it be lovely, Petel," Masha had said one night, rolling over on her elbow, "if we could own a place together! It would be all our favorite recipes, yours and mine, the things we loved best in childhood. Little Polish doves—miniature cabbage rolls—and roast chicken and duck. And profiteroles! What my mutti called 'little clouds,'" and she had gotten so excited she'd begun bouncing on the bed, her hair falling over Peter's face in a white curtain. Peter had been barely twenty then, Masha not out of her teens.

"Did you have something to do with Ruth telling that story to that gossip columnist?" Peter asked Sol now. "Did you invite her to that fund-raiser on purpose?"

"I invited her because it's good business," said Sol.

"You did," said Peter. "How could you?"

Sol shrugged. "Don't look at me. Ruth knew the story, and she has a big mouth."

He stumped back to his desk chair and sat down with a grunt. "You oughta thank her. You think they're coming to you for that hotsy-totsy French dreck you serve? They come to get a look at you—for the sad story."

"It's not *French*," said Peter through clenched teeth. "It's Continental."

He stood and went to the window and drank his Grand Marnier in one gulp. It burned going down. The sky was now completely gray, and there was no sign of June's bright head or Ruth's maroon one anywhere—they must be either down in the garden or somewhere in the house. How Peter wished he could run Masha's on his own, without Sol's help! But owning a restaurant was an expensive venture. Peter had not saved a nest egg nor gotten a bank loan to open Masha's—not that he probably would have received one had he applied. He was working at the place as a sous-chef when he inherited it. Giuseppe, the previous owner, had taken a liking to him from the time Peter walked in the front door, freshly returned from a year of traveling the American West and the South, working as a busboy and short-order cook. Peter was roaming the city then, without any real plan, and had come to Giuseppe's—as Masha's was called then—because he was asking every restaurant he passed whether they needed kitchen help, and also because he was hungry. He had ordered espresso and a cannolo, then asked to see the chef because he wanted to know how the little pastry had been made. Giuseppe—Guy—had given Peter a job as a prep chef, dicing herbs and vegetables for *mise en place*, deboning veal and chicken, making stock. "Not bad," Guy said in his raspy voice, watching Peter's knife skills, "for a Yid," and he'd given the back of Peter's head an affectionate cuff. One night Guy found Peter in the kitchen with zucchini he'd pilfered from Ruth's garden, testing a side in which the squash had been spiral-cut to resemble noodles. Guy sampled it and said, "What'm I tasting here, kid, lemon zest?" and Peter said "No, Chef, lemon thyme," and from then on the men were friends—better than that, equals. When Guy died of throat cancer, he left Giuseppe's to Peter, who would have had to close the doors without backing. So Peter had gone to Sol.

There was no way, Peter realized in those early days, that he could run Masha's without Sol's help. When Sol said, "Beats me why you want a woman's job, but if it's kitchen work you want, kitchen work you'll get," Peter took full advantage. He had a fantasy now of replacing Sol's money with that of another investor, a patron—Mr. Cronkite?—or a bank, but it would mean a major shake-up in the restaurant's finances. So here he was, beholden to a man who could have cared less about food, who was illiterate about it, to whom Peter could have served dog excrement and said it was pâté and who would not have known the difference—nor cared, it if was cheaper to procure.

". . . I don't know why you gotta serve all that fancy shit any-way," Sol was saying, as if to prove Peter's point. "Wild veal this, flaky crust that. I keep telling you, give people something tasty, a little nosh, they're fine. You gotta go simpler. Scale back."

I doubt Craig Claiborne would agree with you, thought Peter, but Sol wouldn't know the food critic for the *New York Times* if Mr. Claiborne bit Sol on the tuchus. "I'll look into it," he said.

"Good," said Sol. "Oh, before I forget, that olive oil importer I mentioned? From Israel? I want you to use him. Top-quality stuff." He handed Peter a card, which Peter slipped into his pocket. Sol stood up and started tucking his shirt back into his golf pants.

"That's quite a hot ticket you picked up there," he said. "Where'd you meet her?"

But Peter had no time to answer—not that he had any intention of discussing June with Sol—because the ladies' voices could be heard in the hall outside the study, approaching, and there was a tap on the door.

"Yeah," said Sol, "come in, we're done here."

The door opened, and June and Ruth stood there. June was in her leather jacket, and her face was red—with November cold, Peter assumed at first. But then he saw that her eyes were pink as well, mascara smeared beneath them, and as June came into the room and threw herself into Peter's arms, he knew something had gone wrong.

*

"Why didn't you tell me?" June asked.

They were walking to the Sound—not on the reedy, marshy path past Ruth's vegetable garden, which Ruth had said she thought would ruin June's boots, but through the neighborhood; Peter knew a way to a public landing. They walked along the side of the road, beneath the great trees and between rock faces. The day had turned blustery and overcast, and the wind brought the smell of fireplaces. In the houses they passed, here a colonial mansion, there a contemporary tumble of glass boxes, Peter glimpsed families eating their own Thanksgiving dinners, heads bent over tables in lamplit windows.

He felt numb. He was holding June's hand, had made a point of taking it as soon as they left the house, but he could barely feel it. She squeezed his fingers, to get his attention or out of solicitude; it was a distant sensation, having little to do with him.

"How could you not tell me?" June asked.

She bent her head forward to peer into his face. He was aware of her anxiousness, her perfume, the creak of her leather jacket, but he kept his gaze straight ahead.

"It's horrible about your wife," June went on. "It's such a sad story, Peter. Just awful. And I'm so sorry. But why didn't you tell me about your little girls?"

Peter felt he was shriveling within his own skin. He wanted to lash out. He kept walking, looking for landmarks. On their left was an open field—the MacGregors' estate, where they kept a stable and horses as if they were landed gentry and not a banker who worked in the city and his wife. On the other side, trees, a rock wall, more houses. Eventually they came to a street sign that announced Slippery Elm Lane.

"This way," said Peter.

They turned left onto an even narrower lane, beneath a canopy of branches. Peter could feel June staring at his face. He wished she would fucking stop that.

"Please understand," he said. "It's not you. I won't discuss them with anybody."

"But why?"

"I can't."

"But why?"

"I just can't."

Peter crunched through the dead leaves, smelling the dampness in the bottom layer as they started to rot. He looked for a white boulder stenciled IOI, and when he saw it he lifted the chain attached to it. A sign swung from the chain: PRIVATE PROPERTY, it said, NO TRESPASSING.

June hesitated as Peter put out his hand to help her over the chain. "Won't the owners be mad?"

"It's all right. They know me. They know Sol."

They walked down a long driveway, over gravel and oyster shells. At the end of it, the trees opened up to a vast lawn that sloped down to the Sound. On their left was the garage, a structure disguised as an English cottage that could have housed a family of ten; on their right, the house, a colossal version of the garage, sat on a rocky outcropping, surveying the sea.

"Sol keeps a boat near here," said Peter. "He likes to bring some of his catch to these people—the Reinholdts. And in return they let him fish off their shore."

Between the lawn and water was another low stone wall. They climbed up three steps to the top of it and onto a dock. June's boot heels clopped along the boards like a horse's hooves, and Peter suddenly remembered Vivi galloping along the Ku'damm in wooden-soled shoes, calling, "Mutti! Papa! I'm a pony!" while Ginger, ever shyer, held back and stared at the streetcars and clung to Peter and Masha's hands.

Peter sat down on the bench on the platform at the end of the dock. He felt weak and a bit nauseous. He passed a palm over his face. It came away damp. Gulls cawed and buoys clanged out in the Sound.

"I'm sorry you had to find out in such a way," he said. "It must have been a shock."

"Yes," June agreed. "Ruth showed me their picture. It's the only picture left, she said. She thought I might want to know what they looked like."

Peter made a little noise as if somebody had punched him in the stomach.

"Please don't be mad at her, Pete," said June. "I genuinely think she thought I knew."

Peter snorted. "I doubt that. She knows I never discuss them."

"Well, maybe," June said tartly, "Ruth thought we were serious enough for you to have told me."

She lit a cigarette without waiting for Peter's lighter, the sulphur smell of the match sharp in the wind. Peter got up and walked to the railing, his fists balled in his pockets. He looked at the shoreline opposite, the houses there with their own docks and boats; at the line, gray upon gray, where the Sound emptied into the open ocean.

"June," he said, "please understand. It has nothing to do with serious or not serious. I do care for you, very much. But I don't discuss them with anyone."

"Yes, I'm starting to get that message," said June. After a moment she said, "They were beautiful. Twins?"

"Yes."

Vivian and Ginger, Peter thought, and would have told her, but speaking their names aloud hurt too much. His double miracle, his pair of golden coins; his daughters. Vivi and Gigi. Named by Masha, of course; she with her unquenchable penchant for films and their stars, so pronounced that on a couple of occasions she had almost lost her job over it, had quite forgotten herself and snuck into the Adlon's dining room to peer at some of the more famous patrons from behind the mirrored columns. "Petel, it was Clark Gable! Nobody else is as dashing—except you. I could tell it was Clark by the mustache and the smile—what a rascal! And do you know, they say he has false teeth?" Or: "Marlene Dietrich—I swear it was her, Petel, what other woman wears a tuxedo? And those eyebrows!" Masha, who never bought clothes, whose dresses had holes in them and whose soles flapped right off her shoes, but who saved every pfennig for matinees—at least until the signs appeared: *Juden Verboten!* Then she would no longer attend the theater, in solidarity with Peter, although with her perfect Aryan lineage she certainly could have. "Magazines are good enough for me," she said with a sniff, "and it's so stupid—ironic. Keeping you out, and you're the one who looks like a movie star!" Masha, with her long Modigliani face and straw-white hair, no pretensions toward vanity herself but obsessed with Vivien Leigh's cat-slanted eyes and Ginger Rogers's dazzling long legs—*gams*, Masha called them, pronouncing the slang with a careful American accent. Hence the names of their girls, born into the dark year 1940, a total surprise and terror to their young parents, who were barely into their twenties themselves.

"Look, June," Peter said. "There is one thing you must know about me if we are to continue." He heard how clipped his accent had grown, in his upset, but he couldn't help it. "I will not talk about them," he said.

June finished her cigarette without answering, and when she was done she stamped out the butt, then put it in her leather jacket pocket rather than cast it into the water or onto the owners' property. She joined Peter at the railing, all red and gold in the gray afternoon. Masha, he thought, might have been awed by her. The wind streaked water from the corner of June's eye, or maybe a tear, back toward her temple. Ordinarily Peter might have lifted his thumb to brush it away.

"I won't," he repeated. "Do you understand?"

June nodded. She heaved a sigh. "Peter, I'm kind of scared to say this, but I'm going to anyway. I really like you. In fact, I think I'm falling for you. But I think"—and here she mocked his formal cadence, giving Peter a little smile—"if we are to continue, you should see somebody professional. An analyst. I'd be nervous to get more involved otherwise. Do you know what I mean?"

Peter looked down at the dark water, at the flotsam bobbing and swirling around the pilings: seaweed, foam, Styrofoam, murk.

"I do," he said.

"Then will you go see one?"

Peter sighed. It was such an American idea—not analysis itself, for which the Austrian Freud had been responsible, but this optimism, the idea that lying on a couch fifty minutes a week and talking about one's dreams and troubles would solve anything. Peter had tried therapy during his second year in America. When the sleepwalking had begun. When he wandered about Sol and Ruth's house every night, waking in odd places like on the piano bench, or in the basement, without any idea of how he'd gotten there—on a couple of occasions, more disconcertingly, without knowing who he was. He had literally forgotten his own name. Sol's doctor had said these episodes would conclude on their own, once Peter had recovered from malnourishment and shock and moved further away in time from the war. But when Peter had been found standing chest-deep in the pool one morning, terrifying Ruth when she looked out the window, Sol had the doctor recommend a guy. "That's all he is," he said, "a guy. Just go and see him." And indeed, the guy was just a guy, a middle-aged gentleman with wire spectacles and a mole on his nose that very much bothered Peter—but that he didn't mention because he was sure this would say something damning about his psyche. Peter had lain on the scratchy orange sofa in the analyst's office, beneath a black-and-purple reproduction Rothko, listening to the traffic outside on Fifty-Seventh Street and the suck and burble of the analyst's pipe, and he waited for the analyst to say something and the analyst waited for Peter to say something until one day, in the middle of their fourth session, Peter heard a snore, and realized the analyst was fast asleep. He had gotten up and walked out.

But here was June, and if Peter had told the truth when he had said he would not talk about his daughters, he had also been honest about his feelings for her. And so, forgiving himself in advance for the lie, he said, "If that is what it takes to keep you, June Bouquet, I will see an analyst."

"Oh, good," she said, "thank you," and she kissed him.

They kissed for a long time, and embraced, Peter sliding his hands into June's jacket and then lifting the hem of her dress, her bare skin breaking into goose bumps when the wind reached it, her mouth in contrast very warm. Peter drew away.

"Come," he said, "I want to show you something."

"What?"

"Come," Peter said.

June rolled her eyes, then followed him down the metal ladder to the strip of sand beneath the dock. "Here?" she said doubtfully. "In that?" And she eyed the dinghy, half rotted out and with its green paint curling off, that butted up against the pilings.

Peter laughed. "No, sex fiend. Though we can if you like—after."

"After what?"

Peter beckoned her over and showed her the hundreds of dark-blue shells clinging to the underside of the dock, like butterflies with their wings closed. He pulled one off the splintered wood and opened it with his thumbs, exposing the soft innards, the pearl of flesh at the top.

"Sweetest creature in the world," he said, "except for you."

June crinkled her nose. "I'll take your word for it."

But she helped him extract the mussels from the pilings, from the sea wall and rocks and nests of seaweed, making a quickly growing pile in the sand to take back to Masha's; she even offered her own scarf when the plastic bag Peter had in his pocket grew full. Watching her as the afternoon grayed further and the tide started to come in, June clambering long-legged up and down the beach, as artless and focused as a child, Peter thought: Why would I need an analyst? I'm happy now. I have you.

4

CHRISTMAS 1965

Two nights before Christmas, Peter took June to the Rainbow Room. June had cocktails at Masha's while Peter worked the first dinner seating; then he changed, and they made their way to Rockefeller Center. The city had the feverish feel it always did during this season, New Yorkers shoving through intersections and trying to snatch cabs from tourists who clogged the sidewalks, craning up at the buildings, boggling at department-store displays. Peter was both mildly amused by all the hoopla—this was not his holiday; he had no holidays—and irritable because he was away more than usual from the restaurant, at such a highly trafficked time of year. Several times a day he felt he had forgotten something, and he was patting his pockets or checking his notebook before he remembered, guiltily: Ah. Masha's. For the first time in two decades, he was not spending every waking hour there.

But tonight he would make a special effort: June was leaving for Minnesota the next day, to spend Christmas with her mother, and therefore Peter found himself doing everything visitors to New York did and that he, as an inhabitant, had never done himself. They admired the holiday tableaux in Macy's windows—June pointing out the mannequins with her face, which had been made, she explained, from a mold. "I had to lie on my stomach breathing through straws up my nose while the plaster hardened," she said, and Peter tsked sadly and said, "And people think the life of a model is glamourous." At Rockefeller Center they waited in line at the skating rink and ate chestnuts from a cart. Down on the ice June skated figure eights, giggling when Peter's ankles bowed inward, and coaxed him off the encircling wall by gliding backward and holding his hands. Afterward, thawing, they had hot chocolate, and then they waited amid a crush of fur and wool in the Rockefeller Center lobby, where finally an elevator whisked them to the sixty-fifth floor.

Peter had made arrangements, and they were seated at a window-side two-top with the Empire State Building as their candle. The city sprawled vertiginously at their elbows. They had martinis, and June ordered shrimp cocktail and Caesar salad, Peter a lobster Thermidor that he knew he would assess for industrial flavor—the Rainbow Room, unlike Masha's, was a massive brigade kitchen, an assembly line serving hundreds and hundreds of people a day. Peter wished the executive chef no ill will, but he hoped he would be able to taste the butane of the warming tray his entrée had been kept in, discern the slightly chewy texture of a dish broiled under the sala-mander. He lit June's cigarette and smiled at her as she surveyed the room: the red-clothed candlelit tables clustered around the dance floor, the massive chandelier suspended from the round ceiling fa-mously aglow with rainbow hues; more shimmering prisms shoot-ing from floor lights at the room's periphery, and all Manhattan glittering beneath their feet.

"You were right," Peter said as the orchestra began a medley from *The Nutcracker*, "this is festive."

"You should have seen it during the Mod Ball last month," June said. "It was crammed! Duke Ellington was playing."

"Ah," said Peter, who, aside from his cooks' transistor radio and the mandatory concerts at Carnegie, tried not to listen to music at all.

"Who is that?" he asked, as June waved merrily to a man on the other side of the room, a bearded fellow in a turtleneck and candy-striped trousers.

"That's Roger, one of the photographers I work with."

"Ah," said Peter again. He watched June blow smoke rings toward this Roger, visible signatures of her lips on the air. Was it Peter's imagination, or was June drifting a bit? He didn't have any fact to hang the feeling on; when she wasn't working, she was always available to him, in fact a little too available for Peter's schedule, ceaselessly cajoling him to places he never would have sought on his own: ElMo, the Copa, the Factory to see Mr. Warhol. Her attention wandered more to gossip and future plans, other clubs and cities they would visit, than to other men. But Peter was sharply aware that the women in her circle dated tycoons or sporting figures; he had experienced some rueful amusement at being, as a restauranteur, one of the lower totems on the pole. Surely he was jealous, and that was a good sign, wasn't it? He couldn't locate the source of his unease, and he feared it was that at the prospect of losing June, along with the dismal sense of having woken from a wonderful dream, there was another slight one of relief.

He tried to shake this off—after all, one couldn't ask for a more charming companion. "You are especially dazzling tonight," he told June, "like the Snow Queen." Indeed June was all in white, her dress a sparkling sheath that brushed the tops of her thigh-high silver boots, around her head a white turban fastened by a diamond snowflake.

"Thank you," said June. She swayed confessionally toward Peter. "I'm not wearing any underwear."

So much for drift. Peter raised his eyebrows. "Happy Christmas to me."

"I thought you didn't celebrate Christmas," June said.

"I do now," said Peter.

He took her hands across the table and considered bringing out the velvet jeweler's box, but then their food arrived. It was just as well, Peter thought; the gift would be better presented over dessert—a Floating Island Peter had preordered, hoping June would eat at least a few bites of low-calorie meringue.

The orchestra segued into "Moon River." June tucked the croutons of her salad beneath the romaine, then lifted a lettuce leaf to her mouth and nibbled the edges. She did the same to another, and a third; then she sat back and rubbed her nonexistent stomach. "I'm stuffed," she said. Her shrimp glistened untouched, clinging like inverted commas to the rim of their frosted silver dish.

"But you barely ate a thing," Peter said. It made June happy when he said this, and Peter had thought he had gotten used to her eating so little—but now, quite unbidden, there came to his mind the recollection of standing next to a man in the Auschwitz kitchen, and the man sneaking a bit of potato peeling into his mouth, and then the peeling dropping out of it, half chewed, when the man was shot in the head. His blood had spattered on Peter's pile of potatoes, so that Peter had been punished too. The man's name had been Merckel. Merckel's family had once owned a chain of beer halls in Munich. This memory shrapnel was surfacing more and more for Peter lately; it was beyond disturbing. Peter stuck his fork in the mottled flesh of his lobster and pushed it away.

The orchestra went on intermission; their waiter cleared their plates. "Was the food not to your liking, sir?"

"Quite the contrary," said Peter, "my compliments to the chef."

"He will be pleased, Mr. Rashkin," said the waiter and cleaned their tablecloth with a silver crumb-catcher. "May I bring coffee? Cordials?"

"I'm impressed," said June, when Peter had ordered a port for himself, a White Russian for June. "You're famous!"

Peter waggled his eyebrows. "Shtick with me, kid," he said in his best Humphrey Bogart accent. Being recognized wasn't really a remarkable achievement; most of Manhattan's chefs of a certain level knew of each other. Nonetheless, Peter was pleased; it was always nice to receive another chef's salute, and their dessert would probably be comped as well.

June extracted another cigarette, and Peter lit it. "Are you excited about your trip?" he asked.

"No," she said.

"No?"

"Oh, I suppose," she said. "It's always good to see my mom. But the place—blech," and she made a face. "It'll be all one color this time of year, hip-deep in snow, and all anyone'll talk about is their husbands and kids and what brand of laundry detergent works best."

"That sounds . . . restful," said Peter carefully.

"You mean stultifying."

"Well, yes," he admitted, and June snorted smoke through her nose like a dragon.

"There must be something festive about it," Peter said. "What will you do for your Christmas?"

"Go to church. Eat dinner. My mom is a terrible cook, she lives mostly out of cans, but every year on Christmas Eve she and her friends make about a thousand cookies and serve all the traditional Norwegian foods. Lefse, rommegrot—"

"Grout?" said Peter doubtfully. "You eat wall paste?"

June laughed. "Now that I think of it, that's probably why they named it that," she said. "It has exactly the same consistency. No, it's a flour and milk pudding. The legend is the Norwegian farm wives used to give birth, eat a bowl of rommegrot, and go back to work in the fields. And if that isn't fortifying enough for you, there's always lutefisk," and she made a gagging noise.

"And what is this? Is it like gefilte fish?"

"I have no idea," said June, "but I'm sure lutefisk is more repulsive. It's cod boiled in lye—it stinks to high heaven, and it's like eating an eyeball."

"Lye," said Peter thoughtfully. "I supposed it must originally have been a method of preservation . . ."

He took out his notebook to jot this down and looked up to find June watching him with a mixture of, he thought, fondness and exasperation. "Only you could find lutefisk interesting," she said and ground out her cigarette. "Of course, you could always come with me and sample it for yourself."

"I wish I could," Peter said mildly. He picked up her nearest hand and kissed it. The orchestra had reassembled and was playing "Silent Night" with a swing tempo. *Stille Nacht, heilige Nacht*, sang a small voice in Peter's head.

"I don't *have* to go," said June, squeezing his fingers. "I could visit at Easter instead, and you could come with me. But meanwhile, I could stay here with you."

"Nothing would please me more," said Peter, "but I fear you would be bored to tears. I'll be so busy with the New Year's Eve gala, you see—oh, did I tell you?" He lowered his voice and stage-whispered, from behind his palm, "I hired an ice sculptor. There will be statues at Masha's! The Russian Tea Room's owner will turn green with jealousy."

June withdrew her hand from Peter's and sat back. "That's nice," she said, gazing out over the dancing couples. Her dress had ridden up to nearly the tops of her thighs, and Peter couldn't help noticing the interested glances in her direction.

"What is it?" he said.

"Nothing," said June.

"It is my experience," said Peter, "that when a woman says this, she means quite the opposite."

June shook out another cigarette. "I just wish you were a little more . . ."

"What, June?"

"I don't know," she said. "Into it?"

"Into . . . ," said Peter. He struggled with the phrase. "Into what?"

June exhaled with frustration. "It means enthusiastic."

"I am enthusiastic," said Peter. "This is how I am when enthusiastic."

"Okay, that's nice," said June. "I know not everybody makes a big song and dance out of everything. But I just wish . . ."

"What?" said Peter again. He was trying to modulate his irritation—it was like having a conversation with the caterpillar from *Alice's Adventures in Wonderland*.

"That we'd be together for New Year's, for instance. That we'd made plans."

"But that's the biggest night of the year for the restaurant," said Peter, "and you'll be in—"

"Paris. I know."

"A work assignment you accepted," said Peter. "I don't understand the problem."

"The problem is, I invited you to come with me—on the magazine's dime—and you won't. Not even for a weekend."

"June, I am a businessman. I cannot completely abandon Masha's. Lena can run it for only so long."

"That doesn't really wash," said June. "I've never known a chef to turn down the chance to go to Paris."

Peter grappled with his temper. He had not told her—he had not told anyone—that he would never, ever set foot on the European continent again. Why should he have to? Anybody with an ounce of sensitivity would see it was self-explanatory.

"Well, you know one now," he said. "And was I upset that you have chosen to go to France with *Mademoiselle* rather than stay with me? We both love our work, June. We are both career people. New Year's Eve is just a night, a square on a calendar. Was I angry when you went to Lisbon for Halloween?"

He lowered his head bullishly and smiled up from beneath his brows, meaning to make a joke out of it, but June sighed.

"No," she said. "That's just it. You weren't angry at all."

She set her cigarette in the ashtray and stood up.

"I think I should go," she said.

"What?" said Peter. "Before dessert?"

He rose as well, automatically, and the waiter, who was bringing forth their Floating Island, backpedaled in some confusion. June kissed her fingers and touched Peter's cheek.

"I'll be in touch," she said. "Happy Christmas."

Off she floated through the whirling couples—the band was playing a Strauss waltz. Peter watched June thread between the tables and the dancers. He held up one finger at their waiter—*Wait, please*—and caught up with June at the hallway coat check. She was digging through her silver clutch, and Peter took their chit out of his wallet.

"Is this what you're looking for?" he asked.

June held out her hand. "Please," she said.

Peter closed his fingers over the chit. "Not until I wish you Happy Christmas."

"Go ahead."

Peter took the jeweler's box from his pocket. "Happy Christmas," he said.

June eyed the box but made no move to take it. Her face was very still except for a tiny muscle that jumped like a minnow near her left eye.

"What is this," said June finally, "a bribe?"

"I suppose that depends upon whether you like it."

Peter gave the box a little shake. The coat check girl peeked from behind her curtain.

"Go on," said Peter, "it won't bite you. What do you think will pop out, a jack-in-the-box?"

"More like something from a Cracker Jack box," said June.

But she took the box and flipped open the lid. Her expression shifted—Peter couldn't quite read it in the dim red light of the hall: Surprise? Disappointment? The coat check girl nearly broke her stomach in half leaning over the counter to see.

June lifted the necklace out of its satin nest. "It's beautiful," she said, in what Peter thought was a curiously toneless voice. What had he done wrong now?

"I hope you like it," he said. "Because if not I'll have a devil of a time finding some other June to give it to."

June said nothing, but she presented the back of her neck to Peter, who took this as a signal to fasten the necklace around it. Once he had secured the clasp, he kissed her nape, where the point of her hair was just visible beneath the white turban. June turned and touched her collarbone, where on silver mesh tiny diamonds spelled out her name.

"There," said Peter. "Happy Christmas, love. Now let's have dessert."

"What did you say?" June said.

"Dessert," said Peter, "a Floating Island—"

"Not that. You called me 'love.'"

Peter inclined his head. He hadn't intended to say this, it had slipped out of its own accord, but he found he didn't want to re-scind it, either. "If the name fits," he said.

June put her hands on either side of his face and kissed him.

"I love you, too," she said. "Now prove it, mister. Dance with me."

"Dance!" said Peter in mock horror. "Have you forgotten my ice-skating disaster? Wait until you see me on the dance floor."

"I have," said June. "At the Copa, the Factory . . . Not a pretty sight."

She smiled at the coat check girl, who withdrew into her window like a cuckoo into a clock. They returned to the dining room. The orchestra was in full swing, the bandleader singing Bing Crosby: "Iiiiiii'm dreaming of a whiiiiiiiiiite Christmas . . ." June led Peter, mock-protesting, onto the parquet floor. People smiled at Peter snapping his fingers and stomping out of rhythm. "Like this?" he said. "Can you help me?" June put her arms around his neck and told him no, he was hopeless. They stood in place, swaying.

*

"You know, you really could use a decorator in here," June said.

They were in the living room of Peter's apartment, sitting on the floor on either side of a wok full of scrambled eggs. The sun was just coming up over the East River; the room was filling with gold. It was Christmas Eve morning and June had an early flight to Minnesota; she wouldn't let Peter accompany her to Teterboro. No, too much trouble, she said, and didn't he have to work? But Peter had gotten up with her and made some breakfast. It was the least he could do, even if she wouldn't eat it.

He looked around his living room and said, "You don't like my minimalist style?"

June jabbed the air with her chopsticks, which she preferred to regular cutlery because, she said, they helped her eat less.

"It's very Breakfast at Peter's," she said, referencing one of her favorite films. "It would be charming if you were Audrey Hepburn. As it is, it just screams bachelor."

Peter put his hand over his heart. "Guilty as charged . . . until now."

June leaned over the wok and kissed him, then unfolded her long limbs to prowl the room. She was wearing only one of Peter's white button-down shirts, and he watched her with pleasure. She ran her fingers over the dark-green leather couch, the Steinway grand piano—the only furniture, besides his bed, that Peter had accumulated in fifteen years. Even these were donations from Sol, castoffs from the estate of a client who'd had to leave the country, Sol had said, rather quickly.

June lifted the lid of the piano and peeked beneath it at the keys. "I've never heard you play anything."

"No coincidence. I don't play."

June laughed. "Then why do you have it?"

"Because it's beautiful," Peter said.

"Doesn't it bother you, to live with so little?"

Peter thought of his parents' home in Charlottenburg, crammed to the rafters with cherished items that had belonged not only to them but to four previous generations. The walnut dining table, capable of seating twenty. His grandmother's silver that the scullery maid, Berte, polished every week. The Belgian lace tablecloths;

the sheets hand-stitched by French nuns. His mother's Oriental rugs. His father's prized humidor and five antique Daimlers. What good had any of those things done them? Where were they now?

"I like to travel light," he said.

He would have added that he was rarely here, that before June he had spent all his time at Masha's, but he didn't want to resuscitate the previous night's discussion about his work habits. Instead he said, "You should talk—that garret you live in, with the bathtub in the kitchen. With a roommate, yet!"

June made a face. "That's not a home. It's more like a bus station. I can't wait to have my own place someday."

She beckoned for her cigarettes and Peter got up, stiffly—one difference between forty-five and twenty-five was that twenty-five didn't ache from sitting on the floor. He took her cigarettes from the mantel and shot the pack to her across the bare floor.

"You need at least a few rugs," said June. "And some lamps, maybe a pair in the foyer, on a demilune table?" She frowned, hands on hips. "A mirror on that far wall would amplify that spectacular view of the river . . . Did you know I wanted to be a decorator when I was little?"

"Not a farm wife with six children, like all the other girls?" Peter teased.

"Please. I killed every baby doll I ever had."

"And not a world-famous supermodel?"

"I would have liked that better, but I wouldn't've dreamed it'd happen in a million years. I was eight feet tall by the time I was six, and so skinny—my mother thought I had a tapeworm, and all the boys called me Stilts."

Peter smiled. It was a sign of June's youth that she didn't think she wanted marriage and children—all women did, eventually; it was tucked into their biology. Perhaps June just hadn't reached that stage yet. Peter pictured her as a girl, all elbows and knees and braids sticking out at awkward angles, scowling as she rearranged a dollhouse.

"I'm sure you were adorable," he said.

"Only to a discerning eye," said June absently. She held her hands up in a square, framing the east window. "All I ever wanted was to make things beautiful."

"Which you do," said Peter, "simply by existing."

She flashed him a quick grin. "Thanks, you're a doll," she said in her girl-about-town voice. "But really, I don't want to just be decorative—I want to create decorative settings. Beauty doesn't last forever. Beautiful places do."

Peter could have told her otherwise, that nothing on earth was exempt from its own demise, not a king, clerk, bird, or tree; no matter if it were a modern skyscraper, a stolid row of burghers' apartments, a castle that had stood for a millennium—all could be reduced in a flash to stones. But why spoil her Christmas Eve–morning reverie? "Well, Stilts," he said, "how about this: when you get back from Minnesota, you can decorate this place."

June looked at him. "Really?"

"Really and truly."

She came to him and threw her arms around him. "Thank you! That's the best Christmas gift I've ever had!"

"You mean besides the necklace?" said Peter.

June touched it, the diamonds glittering on her clavicle; last night, when they'd come back from the Rainbow Room, it was the only thing she'd worn. "Of course."

Peter kissed her. "It's getting late. Why don't I take a quick shower, and then we'll get you a cab."

He walked down the hall to his bathroom, whistling "Silver Bells," and shaved while he waited for the water to run hot. He would miss June, he thought with relief as he stepped into the shower. Five days seemed suddenly too long. Maybe he would surprise her by meeting her return plane—

"Hey, got room in there for me?"

Peter jumped and reached for his robe, but it was not in its usual place on the back of the door. "I'm just about to get out," he said, "if you'd hand me a towel—"

But he was too late: the curtain rattled back on its metal rings, and then she was in there with him, naked. At least Peter assumed she was, from the warm length of her pressed behind him. The water poured over them. It would have been erotic, if only—

"You don't have to hide your scars, you know," said June. "I've seen them."

Peter stood dumbly. "When?" he asked finally.

"Just glimpses here and there," said June. "But I've felt them all along."

Peter sighed. And he had been so careful! He never came to bed without pajamas. He never swam without a shirt. And he never left the bathroom door unlocked when he bathed. Happiness, today, had made him careless. But he should have suspected June would have felt them. They were thick, raised, the size of ropes. They would be tactile even through a layer of cloth.

"I'm sorry," he said. "They're grotesque."

"Oh, Peter! Please, don't apologize. They're just . . . How did you get them?"

"From an SS sergeant," Peter said, "at Auschwitz, with a whip and a bad temper."

"Jesus," said June.

"No," said Peter. "Just a fat man named Stultz."

He got out of the shower and pulled on his robe—there it was, the traitorous thing, on the lid of the hamper. He started combing his hair, automatically, with no real idea what he was doing. So now June had seen them—the braille of Peter's humiliation and helplessness. Next she would want to know what it had been like. Americans always wanted to know—they were like children that way, well-meaning, insatiably curious. What was it like? What was it like, Ruth had demanded the first months Peter had lived in Larchmont, following him around with *Life* and *Time*, their lurid covers proclaiming, NEW

NAZI HORROR DISCOVERED! THOUSANDS OF CORPSES UNEARTHED IN PIT!
"Did you see anything like this? Or this? What about this? My poor, poor Bubbie! How did you get through it? What was it like?" There had been no way to tell her, even if Peter had wanted to. About the perversity of luck, for instance, so that the whipping Stultz gave Peter on the Appellplatz for no reason one icy January day had laid Peter's back open to the bone, which was why Peter had passed out and been taken to the infirmary, which was where he had in his delirium called out recipes for sauerbraten and schnitzel, which was why when he came out of it he had been reassigned, was no longer on pickup detail, on which Peter had loaded corpses no heavier than box kites on the crematorium wagon, but on kitchen duty, which was where he was working two months later when the Allies liberated the camp. So really, the whipping Stultz had given him was what had saved him. There was no way to tell anyone who hadn't been there any of that, how your very concept of luck turned inside out and upside down, so that when you found yourself alive at the end of it, you were no longer sure whether that was a good thing.

Peter watched June in the mirror as she emerged from the shower, her admirable but too-thin body glistening. She wrapped herself in a towel and came up behind him, and Peter waited for her to ask: What was it like? Instead, she said, "What happened to him? Was he hanged at Nuremberg?"

"Who, Stultz?" said Peter, and June nodded. "No, he was a pretty small fish."

"I wish we could find him," said June. "I'd kill him."

"Would you now?" said Peter. "How would you do that?"

"I'd shoot him."

"Ah. You have a license to kill, like 007?"

"I'd push him out the window," said June. Her eyes were red, but she was starting to smile.

"And I'd hold it open for you," said Peter. He looked at his watch, which covered his other set of scars—this one he would bet the restaurant June didn't know about. Nobody did, not Sol and Ruth, not his staff. Peter never, ever removed his watch; one of the best days of his life had been when the Swiss Army had offered their waterproof timepiece for sale.

"We have to get you into a cab," he said. "You're going to miss your plane."

"All right," June agreed, but she didn't move, and Peter didn't know why until she asked, "Can you really not feel that?" and he realized she was running her hands over his back.

"No," he said, "I have no sensation there." That was true, and it was the blessing of scars: the deeper they were, the more you couldn't feel anything in them at all.

*

After Peter put June in a cab, he decided to walk to Masha's. It was only a few blocks, and it was still early; the sun had risen into milky clouds, but the temperature was fairly mild. After the previous evening's holiday throngs, Peter relished the empty sidewalks. The only people out at this hour were returning from a night of revelry or walking dogs; in neither case did they want to make conversation, which suited Peter fine. He bought a cup of coffee from a corner grocery on Ninety-Second and First, again wrapped in a queer feeling of well-being. How could this be, when June was gone, soaring somewhere in the sky above? But Peter was heartened by that morning's conversation; he had never disclosed so much to any woman, and she had handled it well. He glanced at the ladies' wear boutiques he passed and smiled when he realized he was looking for the mannequins with June's face.

He stopped to admire a mechanical Christmas tableau, a family, mother, and father and two children opening presents with painted-on smiles and jerky movements—and suddenly found himself thinking of the last time he had observed the holiday. Peter's last Christmas had been in 1942, when Vivi and Gigi were toddlers; they were growing quickly then, out of their baby round-belliedness into long-legged little girls, and it seemed they could never get enough to eat, particularly Vivi, who loved anything Peter set in front of her. Their ration cards were a joke; if not for the scraps Masha brought home from the Adlon, the girls would have starved. Their growth would have been stunted; Peter was home with them full time by then, his work permit having been revoked, and he deliberately kept from Masha the tales he had heard from mothers in the building's stairwells, about children grown slow and fretful, about their developing sores or their adult teeth not coming in for lack of milk.

That Christmas there were no presents, although they did manage to have a tree, a pathetic little foundling Peter had salvaged from a scrap heap. Their specimen was barely two meters, and it listed to the side on which it also had no needles. But Peter had propped it on their kitchen table and wrapped its trunk in a tea towel, and he had spent several nights while the girls were asleep punching holes in tin cans with a screwdriver; when he inserted candle stubs in them and put them on the tree, he thought, it would look quite festive. Not quite the magnificent firs of his childhood, ablaze with tapers—Peter's family, quite assimilated, celebrated Christmas just as Masha's had. But it would do for a surprise.

Masha came home from the Adlon long after midnight, having had to close out the hotel's Christmas Eve buffet. Peter had been watching for her through the window and saw her bundled figure drop off the tram as it rattled past the flat, clattering the plates on the shelves. The girls slept on; city children, they woke only when it was too quiet.

By the time Masha had climbed the six flights of stairs, Peter had the candles lit in the tin cans, which he had inserted among the few branches that would hold them. "Happy Christmas, Mashi," he whispered.

"Happy Christmas, Petel," said Masha. They kissed. Masha's pale face was nearly translucent with exhaustion but for the very red tip of her nose. She unwrapped her scarf and took off her coat;

Peter smelled roast bird wafting from her whites, and his stomach growled.

"Goose?" he whispered.

Masha nodded. "And duck," she whispered back; "I had the carving station," and she held up her lunch pail.

Peter didn't bother with utensils; he sat at the table and shredded meat with his fingers, careful to set aside the bulk of it for the twins. Vivi twitched at the odor of food but didn't wake, merely put her hand on her sister's cheek in the room's double bed.

"This is delicious," said Peter, "thank you."

Masha sat across from him and started removing her hairpins with such emphatic movements, some of them flew into the corners. "Why that girl," his mother had asked, "out of all the eligible young ladies we've introduced you to? She's not only common, she's homely." It was true; Masha's face was long and bony, her coloring too anemic for beauty. She barely had any eyelashes. But Peter had been in awe of Masha since the first moment he became aware of her: in the Adlon kitchen, Peter's second day as a *commis*. Chef had stopped the entire staff to watch Peter dice an onion, making an example of Peter's clumsiness, his utter incompetence. "Look at this," he had screamed in Peter's ear, seizing a handful of ragged slices and flinging them into Peter's face, "my grandmother could chop onions better using her dentures! You will not stop, nobody will cook, until you do it right," and he had dumped a basket of yellow onions onto Peter's chopping block, some of the orbs bouncing off to the floor and rolling away. There was no sound but for the sizzling and bubbling of ignored food on various burners, Chef's enraged huffing, and Peter's snuffling as he chopped and chopped, blindly, eyes burning with tears, lacking even the burned match one usually held between one's teeth to prevent weeping during this task. Until finally he felt his knife taken from him. "Watch," said a soft voice near his shoulder, and when Peter's stinging tears had subsided, he saw an even younger and smaller apprentice making quick work of his latest onion, Peter's knife moving so fast he couldn't see it, like a hummingbird's wings. "Like this," said the small *commis*, "put your finger on top of the blade to guide it, you see?" and Peter nodded. Chef, who had been hulking behind them both, flicked at the pile of tiny dense cubes on Peter's cutting board and said, "Ach . . . Back to work!" and as if the Adlon kitchen staff had been frozen by enchantment and were now released by his bawl, they sprang back to life. All except the little *commis*, who patted Peter's shoulder, retreated to the sink near the walk-in, and took off her white cap to dash water on her forehead—for it was a woman, Peter saw, with amazement, a tiny one with white-blond braids, which she tucked back up into her cap before she resumed work at her own station, stretching strudel dough as though nothing had happened. And that was Masha.

Now she started to giggle. "That tree is . . ." She covered her mouth with her hand to block the sound but laughed all the harder; soon she was quaking with it.

"The tree is what?" said Peter, feigning indignation. "Magnificent? A masterpiece? Worthy of *The Nutcracker?*"

"Yes," said Masha, "exactly, that's what I was trying to say."

She wiped her wet eyes and nose and put her face in her hands.

"I'm so tired," she said, "and I'm sorry, Petel, but I couldn't get any chocolate for the girls. Chef had it practically under lock and key."

"That's all right," said Peter. "The tree is the present—don't you dare," he warned her as she snickered again. "The girls will think it's a marvel, you wait and see."

"I'm sure they will," said Masha. Peter patted his lap, and Masha came to sit there. Peter could smell the grease in her hair, cooking lard and oil.

"Our being together is the gift," he said.

"Petel," she said, picking up his hand and playing with his fingers. "About that . . ."

"Not this again," said Peter.

"Dieter says he can get three ID cards," said Masha. "It'll cost us, but isn't that why we saved your mother's earrings?"

Peter looked down at her small hand with the scars and burns earned by any chef. Her whole left palm was a shiny lineless pink from when she'd grabbed a saucepan without a rag. She was toying with his wedding ring, spinning it around and around.

"I want to save the earrings," said Peter. "For an emergency."

"Petel, this is an emergency."

Peter scoffed. He gestured toward the window, where the snow fell silently on the streetcar tracks, covering the sidewalk. "Does that look like an emergency to you?"

"I've started to hear things. About how there will be a roundup—"

"Horseshit," said Peter, "propaganda."

Masha sat up on his lap, eyes blazing. "That doesn't even make sense. Why would the Nazis spread rumors about a roundup? That'd give people time to leave!"

"Scare tactics," said Peter. "That's been their game all along. To cow people into doing what they want."

"Well, it's working, isn't it?" said Masha.

She got up and went to the window, where she stood gripping her elbows and shivering—the pane was cracked, and the room was cold.

"Come away from there," Peter said, "you'll catch your death of pneumonia."

"And what will your death be? Theirs?"

Masha nodded to the twins, asleep like a heap of rags in the bed.

"Keep your voice down," said Peter. "Stop being so dramatic, Lana Turner."

He'd hoped the reference to one of Masha's idols would cheer her, but she just stared at him.

"Hasn't everything I've said come true so far? Haven't things gotten worse and worse? Look what happened to your father, your mother. You can't even work!"

"But you can, your work pass is still good," said Peter. "My father was a troublemaker, and my mother— Lots of people caught that flu. You act as though the Nazis gave it to her! Look, we're fine here, we're safe and warm and fed. As long as you can work, we'll be fine."

"For how long?" said Masha. "People know. They know you and the girls are here. How long before some Jew-catching *Greifer* gives us up? For money, or a travel permit, or to save their own skins?"

"I think you underestimate our friends, Mashi."

"I think you overestimate how many friends we have, Petel." Masha shook her head, her long hair falling like a curtain around her face. Impatiently she pushed it back.

"You're here all day," she said, "with the girls. You don't know what's going on out there. You don't see."

"Yes," said Peter with a bitterness that surprised him, "you're right, I'm like a recluse, or a man in a cell."

He regretted it the moment he said it, for Masha was then in front of him, crouching on her clogs, seizing his hands in her cold ones.

"That's just it. You are. You're a prisoner here in our flat. And it's only going to get worse. The roundup—"

"Just rumors."

"—I heard it'll be in spring, as early as February. We don't have much time—"

"No," Peter said.

His voice was loud enough that it woke Gigi, who started to cry. He went to her and lifted her from the bed, her body warm and heavy with sleep.

"Shhh, you'll wake your sister. Everything is all right; Mama's here, see?"

Masha waggled her fingers. "Hi, sweet love," she said.

Gigi buried her face sleepily in Peter's shoulder.

"How," Peter whispered, "do you expect me to take them God-knows-where—to America or England or whatever outlandish destination you have in mind? They're so little. They tire so easily. They'll talk."

"There are ways," Masha said. "Sleeping syrups—"

"And what about you?"

"I'll be fine. I'm Aryan."

"I'm not leaving you."

"After the war—"

"I'm not breaking up our family," he hissed. "I will not."

Gigi lifted her head from his shoulder and put her hand on his cheek.

"Papa angry?" she asked.

Peter kissed her palm.

"No, sugarplum," he said and turned her toward the tree. "Do you like the lights? See how they glow?"

Gigi stared at the candle stubs in their perforated tin cans.

"Vivi sleeping," she said with satisfaction and corked her mouth with her thumb. She put her head back on Peter's shoulder, and he inhaled the unwashed scent of her hair—white like her mother's, stringy without a bath since the previous week.

Masha was breathing hard—furious or on the verge of tears or both.

"Petel, I'm begging you to be reasonable. These people will stop at nothing. You must see—"

"Reasonably," said Peter, "things are bound to get better. It's always darkest just before dawn—right, Gigi?" She nodded. "We're almost to a new year. How about this: by spring, when it's warmer and easier to travel—I'll consider it. Consider it," he repeated.

Masha looked at her daughter, stroking the child's hair over and over.

"They are half Jewish," she said. "Have you considered what will happen to them if—"

"But you are their mother, and you are Aryan."

She chewed her lip. "By spring I might be able to get a fourth *Ausweis* as well."

"You see?" Peter said. "It will all work out." He put out his free arm and drew his wife to his side.

"By next Christmas, we will probably all be in London," he added.

*

"Hey, buddy, would you mind stepping aside?"

Peter looked over; the man who owned the shop he was standing in front of waved for Peter to move so the man could unlock the grate.

"Apologies," said Peter.

"Don't worry about it. It's Christmas. Or almost." The man was gnomic and bald except for tufts of black hair sticking out of his ears. "You window-shopping, handsome?" he said, unlocking the grate. "You wanna come in, pick up something for your wife or sweetheart? I got some great haberdashery."

"Thank you, no," said Peter.

He touched the brim of his hat and started walking, then realized he was heading north and needed to go south. He corrected his course. He removed his overcoat despite the chilly air and slung it over one arm—he had perspired through his shirt. His coffee had gone cold; God knew how long he had been standing there. Peter would have been embarrassed if it hadn't been New York, where people were accustomed to much stranger sights. He took one deep breath, then another. The air smelled of the hot sooty wind from the subway grates, hot dogs from a nearby cart. Peter pitched his coffee into a garbage can. He was in New York and it was 1965 and there wasn't a bit of snow on the ground. The sun was shining fully now. Peter glanced at his watch; it was almost nine. He would need to truss partridges, make sure the chestnuts were roasted for stuffing and hard sauce had been made for the plum pudding.

He quickened his step down the glittering, gum-spattered sidewalk, then changed his mind at the last minute and hailed a cab. He gave the driver, a turbaned Oriental fellow, an address and sat back. The sitar music spiraling out of the radio reminded Peter of his days as a younger man wandering the city: ashamed of having lost the job at the Oyster Bar but using the freedom, and the wages he had saved, to sample every food he had never had before. Potstickers. Saag paneer and gulab jamun. Chicken in mole sauce. Roti. Shawarma. His favorite had been dim sum in Chinatown, where he could sit at a counter and point at whatever rolled past him on a cart. He remembered his astonishment at being served, in this manner, a broiled, breaded chicken foot.

The cab stopped at the southeast corner of Fifth and Fifty-Seventh, and Peter hopped out. He did have to fight crowds again now—tourists and last-minute shoppers, men who had forgotten to have their secretaries buy gifts for their wives. Peter went through the famous brass doors. Enough was enough. He had to put a stop to this . . . invasion of the past. It was June, he felt quite sure, June was the ticket, with her optimist's innocence, her lack of appreciation of how bad things could get, her charm and youthful vigor—she was the quintessence of Peter's adopted country, his fresh American start. Peter had waited long enough; it was time to take a confident step toward the future. Maybe this would do it. He stood looking around Tiffany's until he identified where the rings were, and then he walked to the glass counter. An associate in a Savile Row suit stepped over.

"May I help you, sir?" he said.

Masha's Spring 1966

Appetizers

Nova-Wrapped Hearts of Palm Salad on a Bed of Spring Lettuces,
with Truffle Vinaigrette Dressing

Spring Pea Soup with House-Made Croutons, Crème Fraîche, & Fresh Mint

CHICKEN IN A SPRING BLANKET:
Chicken Liver Pâté–Filled Blintzes with Mustard &
Horseradish Dipping Sauces

WALDORF SALAD:
Bibb Lettuce, Grapes, Green Apple, Radishes, Bleu Cheese,
Roasted Walnuts, Hand-Creamed Mayo, & Pickled Beets

Baby Asparagus en Croute with Mini-Fondue Dipping Sauce

Entrees

Lamb Wellington Accompanied by Mashed Potatoes & Baby Asparagus

Poached Bluefish with Dill Sauce, Roast Fingerling Potatoes,
& Green Beans Amandine

Rabbit Stew on a Bed of Garlic Mashed Potatoes & Sautéed Spring Peas

Chicken Kiev with Herbed Rice & Vegetable du Jour

HAMBURGER WALTER:
Ground Chuck au Poivre & Flambéed in Brandy,
Accompanied by Pommes Frites & No Vegetables At All

Sides

Spring Peas with Fresh Mint

Creamed Spinach with a Garlic Parmesan Crust

Roast Fingerling Potatoes

Mashed Garlic or Horseradish Potatoes

Pommes Frites (French Fried Potatoes)

Latkes (Potato Pancakes with Applesauce)

Tzimmes (Casserole of Sweet Potato, Citrus Zests, & Currants)

Pickled Beets with Horseradish Crème Fraîche

Dish of House-Made Pickles

Spätzle

Just Desserts

Rhubarb Pudding with Brown Sugar–Vanilla Ice Cream
& Candied Rosemary

Rum-Soaked Apple
Cake Masha with Crème Anglaise

MASHA TORTE:
Inside-Out German Chocolate Cake with Cherries Flambé

"LITTLE CLOUDS":
Cream Puffs Filled with Vanilla Ice Cream, Accompanied by
Mini Chocolate Fondue for Dipping

Strawberry, Raspberry, and Blueberry Ice Cream in Chocolate Cups
(Available as Trio or Individual)

Assortment of Chocolate, Walnut-Currant, & Raspberry Rugelach

1705 2ND AVE. NEW YORK, NY 10128 / RE 4–1143

* RESERVATIONS IF YOU PLEASE!

5

THE BUBKES

On a sunny Monday morning in mid-April 1966, Peter was helping Ruth put in her garden. First he had turned over the soil himself, although Yoshi the gardener would have been happy to do it, Ruth said; moreover, he should—it was his job. What else were they paying him for? But Peter liked the spade's weight, its splintery wooden handle; he relished wearing an old pair of trousers and jacket and the feeling of being bareheaded in the sweet chilly air. He welcomed perspiring from exertion rather than some bad dream or memory. He even enjoyed his muscles complaining, ones in his back and shoulders that he used differently from in the kitchen. He would be sore tomorrow, but tonight he would have a hot bath with a glass of whiskey. The best soaks of his life were after he helped Ruth put her garden to bed and, in spring, woke it up again.

There. He had done it. He sank the spade in the dirt at the plot's edge. It was black and wet and smelled of sulfur, minerals from the nearby Sound. Every so often Peter's spading had turned up a whole mussel or clamshell, dropped into the garden by a traveling seagull, and white shards salted the soil. Sometimes he found wampum—coins of smooth bright purple that, Peter had learned in his American history book when he first arrived in this country, served the Indians who had settled New England as currency. Peter had been entranced by this wampum. It was all quite unlike the gardens of Peter's youth—which he had not been allowed to dig in anyway, for his mother, Rivka, had feared and loathed dirt; those had been exquisitely manicured beds of roses, tulips, topiary. But Peter had on occasion been allowed to accompany the cook, Hilde, back to her country home in Boitzenburger Land, where she had shown him how to dig holes twice as big as root balls, to put crushed eggshells and coffee grounds around the tomato plants, to make mounds over melons to protect them. Peter remembered Hilde, a somber woman with orthopedic shoes and a coronet of gray braids, throwing her head back and laughing at Peter's expression the first time he ate a radish straight from the dirt. That was the moment he made the connection between the seeds he and Hilde had pushed into the ground with their thumbs and what he was putting in his mouth. Peter still marveled at the miraculous alchemy of food growing from earth; it was something he never quite got used to.

He turned to look at Ruth, who was kneeling on a foam pad she had carried down from the garage, wearing a conical straw hat that she had brought back one year from Thailand. With her head bowed over her work, she looked a little like the Vietnamese women Peter saw on the news. It was disconcerting to see Ruth's hat against a backdrop of marsh reeds and pale blue sky instead of flaming jungle, helicopters strafing villages and dropping clouds of Agent Orange. Peter wondered if Ruth had put on the hat with any sense of irony or protest. He doubted it. He himself, as much as he thought the war in Vietnam a shame and a waste, was grateful to be able to spend some time in this privileged enclave, to live where nothing was on fire.

"Hoo!" said Ruth and clapped her gloves to free them of dirt. "That's finished."

"Let's have a look," said Peter and walked over to her, his shoes sinking satisfyingly in the dirt. Ruth had planted all the herbs Peter would need for Masha's: dill, mint, rosemary, oregano, thyme—lemon and Greek; chives, chervil, basil, parsley, garlic, fennel, bay leaves, and lavender, which Ruth used for sachet and Peter's pastry chef for shortbread.

"Beautiful," said Peter, and meant it.

Ruth looked up at him with a smile no less lovely for her dentures. She had put on lipstick for today's work, bright fuchsia, and clip-on earrings like golden snails. She held out her hand.

"Help an old lady up, would you?" she asked.

Peter did, firmly but gently, mindful that despite her enthusiasm for cooking, gardening, theater, matchmaking, opera, bridge, travel, and mah-jongg, Ruth was in her sixties—the same age Peter's mother would have been.

"I know you're just hustling me," he said as Ruth groaned to her feet. "How about you put in the green beans."

"Oy," said Ruth and walked stiffly to the lawn chair Peter had carried down for her, a lightweight folding contraption of aluminum and mesh strips, and set on the path next to the garden. She lowered herself into it. "I'll just rest a minute, Bubbie, and watch."

"You do that," said Peter and turned to the flats of seedlings he had hand-selected from various Long Island farms. These vegetables were the staples of Masha's spring menu, and he thanked them silently as he tapped them from their black plastic containers, untangled their roots, and set each plant in the soil. The salad greens—Bibb and Boston lettuce and arugula—should be ready by mid-May, along with radishes, and about a week later, spring peas, onions, and leeks. The others would ripen in summer: Big Boy and yellow cherry tomatoes; beets, fingerlings, sweet potatoes, cabbage, Brussels sprouts, squash, cucumbers, string beans. Peter checked each type of plant off the list on his notepad once it was in the ground. Again he thought of Hilde as he unfurled chicken-wire fencing along the rows of vegetables that needed to climb; it was she who had taught him to lift the leaves of green-bean plants to look for the pods. "Find one and you will find many," she said; "see how they grow in clusters? They are the most sociable vegetables," and Peter, who had been six or seven then, had so loved that idea—companionable beans!—that he had laughed until he had wet his pants, a little.

"You want iced coffee, Bubbie?" said Ruth from her chair and held up her thermos. "You shouldn't get dehydrated. No? All right."

She drank as Peter pounded in stakes for the fencing. "How is your lady friend? The model?"

"She's in Rome," said Peter, "on a shoot for Dior."

"Fancy," said Ruth and clucked her tongue. Peter smiled over at her. Ruth had her prescription sunglasses on now beneath the hat, although a thin layer of fish-scale clouds was starting to fill the sky.

"She says it's not all that glamorous," said Peter. "It's her job."

"Nice work if you can get it," said Ruth. "You didn't want to go with? Or maybe she didn't invite you?"

Peter sighed inwardly. How many times had he explained, resisted, refused Ruth's well-meaning invitations for overseas cruises, flights, guided tours? *Not even to Israel? That's nowhere near Europe.* "I can't, Ruth," he said patiently. "I've got work."

"Work, schmerk. That Russian terror of yours could keep your place running like a gulag for months."

"True," said Peter, "but then who would you have to kick around?"

Ruth waved her hands at this, and Peter stood back to admire his efforts. Was the fencing straight? It didn't really matter, the vegetables would grow either way, but he preferred it if it was. He pulled one of the stakes out of the dirt, readjusted the line.

"So," said Ruth. "How serious is it? Do I hear wedding bells?"

Peter whacked the stake into the ground with his mallet.

"You hear wedding bells every time I look at a woman," he said.

"And this is so terrible?" said Ruth. "Look at me, I'm almost too old to dig in the dirt. By the time I have grandchildren, I'll be under it."

Peter knelt to sink the chicken wire into the dirt next to the seedlings and wrestled with the urge to say, *Mind your business, Ruth.* It was an old and ineffective strategy. Instead, he said, "You could always adopt."

"Ha ha," said Ruth, "always a comedian." She tapped her gloved fingers on her thermos. "I thought you really liked this one— June."

"I thought you really didn't," said Peter.

"Bubbie!" Ruth sounded shocked. She pulled her sunglasses down to peer at him. "Why would you think that?"

"Because she's a shiksa." Peter got up and surveyed the orderly lines of tiny green shoots in the black dirt. "There," he said, "what do you think?"

But Ruth was shaking her head. "I'm ashamed my own flesh and blood would think I'm so prejudiced."

Peter laughed. "Come on. Every single woman you've tried to set me up with over the past two decades has been Jewish."

"And is that so bad?" Ruth asked again. "Of course I want you to marry a nice Jewish girl. We lost so many . . ."

She teared up and looked away, down the path of mud and crushed reeds that led back to the house.

"I'm sorry," she said. She withdrew a Kleenex from the sleeve of her quilted jacket and daubed her eyes. "I know you don't like to talk about it. But yes, I want you to carry on our traditions. A nice Jewish girl would be just the ticket."

She smiled at him, eyes watering, as she tucked the tissue away.

"But Jewish, not Jewish, I don't care," she said. "If you really love this girl, why not marry her? You can still raise the kids Jewish. I don't care, Bubbie. I just want grandkids before I'm too old. And I want to see you happy."

Peter looked at his workboots, sunk in the black dirt. He was a little surprised to find his throat felt thick. He remembered, unwillingly, the first time Masha had come to his parents' home, how his mother had thought from Masha's headscarf and pallor, her rabbity red nose and worn cloth coat, that she was a servant and directed her to the rear door. How his father, Avram, as Peter stood gripping Masha's hand on the Turkish carpet in Avram's study, had not even glanced up from the papers on his desk as he said, "You marry her, don't come back."

He cleared his throat. "Thank you, Ruth. I appreciate that."

Ruth smiled at him and slid her sunglasses back on. "So?" she said, "this girl? She's the one?"

Peter looked out across the acres of waving marsh reeds between the garden and the Sound. They were tall, but he was taller, so when the wind bent them he could see the water glinting navy in the sun. He slid his hands into the pockets of his old trousers. In the left pocket was the ring. It was foolish to be carrying around something so expensive—but after all, it was insured. And Peter wanted to be prepared in case the right moment for a proposal presented itself. He somehow had not managed to find it yet. On New Year's Eve, Peter had been at Masha's, June in Paris. Valentine's Day he had likewise been at the restaurant, for February 14 was the second-biggest moneymaker after December 31; Peter had seated June in the corner banquette, the best seat in the house, and sent her champagne and chocolate truffles, but the night had been too hectic, not to mention a cliché. So what other occasion had there been? Presidents' weekend? Tax day? Peter thought perhaps June's birthday—June 10. That was what he was aiming for now.

"If I pop the question," he said, "you'll be the first to know. How's that?"

Ruth shook her head. "Bubbie," she began again, but then Sol came crunching down the path over the reeds, preceded by the sound of ice cubes rattling in the highball glass he was carrying.

He was wearing a yellow windbreaker and khaki pants and his fishing hat, covered in lures.

"You ready?" he said to Peter. They were going out on Sol's boat to catch whatever was biting, which would become the week's seafood special at Masha's. Peter was hoping for flounder, early spring blues.

"C'mon," Sol said, "brush the dirt off your pants and let's go. The fish won't wait all day."

*

Sol's new boat was called the *Bubkes*—it was a twenty-five-foot fiberglass Bertram, he told Peter on the way to the Brewer Post Road Boat Yard. Peter tried to look suitably impressed, though the information meant nothing to him. To Peter, a boat was a vessel in which you set out to sea and sometimes caught fish. To Sol and his friend Dutch, Sol's skipper, it was a fanaticism—the only difference between them being that Sol was a weekend fisherman and Dutch ran fishing charters on their boats year-round, as long as the weather permitted.

"How ya doin', kid?" said Dutch as Peter climbed onto the deck. Dutch was a wizened little man with a head like a walnut and a cigarette permanently notched in one side of his mouth. Dutch wasn't his real name—Peter had no idea what it was. All of Sol's friends had these nicknames, based on peculiarities of appearance or character. Like Choppers, Sol's partner, for instance; then there was Pickles, another attorney, who liked kosher dills; Dr. Gorgeous, Pinky, and—Peter's favorite—Hoo-Hoo, so called because he hollered the phrase at every woman between eighteen and eighty. Like many of Sol's friends, Dutch, who worked at the shipyard, didn't seem to be the kind of fellow Sol would naturally cross paths with at his Madison Avenue law firm, but when Peter asked how Sol had met them, Sol had said, "We came up together," and that was that. Peter understood nicknames as a mark of affection. His own, at the Adlon, had been Tarzan, because he looked so much like Buster Crabbe, the film actor who played the Jungle King. At the Oyster Bar he had been Pretty Boy; at Giuseppe's, Dreamboat; at Auschwitz he had been known as Chef, even before his transfer to the kitchens. It was why Peter forbade his staff to call him that now, instead permitting Boss or Chief.

After greeting Peter, Dutch began navigating the *Bubkes* out of the harbor, he and Sol speaking in fisherman-ese. Peter stood at the bow, enjoying the speed—Sol had told him the *Bubkes* had not one but two engines—and the fresh salt wind in his face. He tried to imagine June next to him, wearing a big sweater, but she seemed far away. Instead Peter found himself contemplating what he would do with today's catch: marinate the bluefish in mustard and dill, grill it; make leftovers into a dip for appetizers. . . . Then they slowed and stopped in some indeterminate location. The smell of chum grew strong, and the *Bubkes* rocked with the swells. Peter started to feel nauseated. He focused on the horizon, which he'd heard sometimes helped. It didn't.

"Dutch," he said, "is there a place I might lie down?"

"Sure, there's a bench in the hold. Why, wassamatter, kid?"

"I'm feeling a little seasick."

"Oh for God's sake," said Sol, who was sitting in a swiveling chair with a rod planted between his knees.

Peter excused himself and went to the hold, a dark, sloshing space. He dry-swallowed the Dramamine he always brought on these excursions and lay back on the bench, using a lifejacket as a pillow. He focused on a pinpoint of light near the hatch. It was probably the conversation with Ruth as much as the rough seas that had upset him. He hated it when she brought up marriage; it dragged him back. The only time he had ever raised his voice to her was during his first year here, when she said to him, "But Bubbie, don't you want to try again? What happened to her—to those poor little girls—was so terrible, but it wasn't your fault," and he had yelled, had actually shouted, "Shut up, Ruth! I won't discuss it!" This had been in the solarium, over breakfast. Ruth had slowly gotten up and walked out, and for the rest of the day Peter had been unable to shake the terrible shame, not of speaking sharply to Ruth—although that was bad enough—but because she was wrong. It had been his fault. Completely.

*

The roundup happened just as Masha had warned—in February of 1943—but it was on a Saturday, the twenty-seventh, and nobody had expected that. Masha had told Peter to be extra careful that week; she had heard from one of the Adlon's delivery drivers that the Gestapo had requested that Jewish community leaders, doctors, and nurses be on standby. Standby for what? Peter had asked. "Nobody knows," said Masha. "But it can't be good. Just stay indoors today, would you? And if anything happens, I'll find you in the safe space." And off she had gone to work.

Peter had tried, really he had. But the girls were restless and fretful, and Vivi had developed a terrible cough that sounded like croup, a seal-pup bark, so how safe would they be in hiding, anyway? He didn't dare ask any of the women in the building for medicine; Masha had convinced him that anyone at this juncture, when ration cards were so precious, could be a *Greifer* who would turn them in. But Peter had to do something. He locked the girls in the apartment and hurried out to see if he could get some brandy, schnapps—anything to soothe Vivi's cough.

There was a fellow Peter knew from his own Adlon days who now worked on the black market, selling stolen bottles of liquor from the restaurant he worked at on nearby Rosenstrasse. Peter went to the rear door of the kitchen and asked for him. The price of the bottle was his mother's earrings. At this point, there was no choice. Peter stashed the brandy in the lining of his coat and hastened back toward the flat, his cap pulled low.

He started to see signs of the roundup when he reached the Oranienburger Strasse: trucks, with German guards and Gestapo encouraging Jews to climb in—young women, old women, men, children, anyone wearing the Star. Some went with resignation. Some helped others climb up into the vehicles. Some implored the uniformed men to let them back into the buildings; their little boy, their sick husband, their children, were still in there! In the bedroom with pneumonia! Too young to walk by himself! In the communal bathroom! Please! Please! These people were assisted into the trucks not by their fellow Jews but by the Gestapo, who used their batons and pistol handles as encouragement. Peter wanted to run. He dared not. It would call too much attention. He strolled along as nonchalantly as he could, the taste of copper and cotton in his mouth, keeping his eyes down like any good Aryan burgher, until he reached his street.

There was a truck in front of their building as well—37 Kinderstrasse.

Peter tried to backpedal around the corner so he could go in through the alley. He would grab the girls and bring them to the safe space, the room he and Masha had created within the ceiling of the cellar. There none of them would be able to stand, or even sit up, but they would lie side-by-side until Masha let them know the roundup was over.

But it was too late. One of the Gestapo had seen him.

"Peter Albert Rashkin?" he said, consulting a clipboard.

Peter pretended not to hear. He made a show of digging in his pocket as though he had forgotten something, then turned. The guard grabbed him by the shoulder. He was blond, brown-eyed, not much taller than Peter himself and much younger. He couldn't have been older than nineteen.

"You've forgotten where you're going?" he said.

Peter tried to smile. "I forgot rolling papers, for my cigarettes."

He was hoping this could be construed as a bribe—he'd heard

you could sometimes trade tobacco for a few minutes' freedom, just enough time to look the other way. But the guard said, "You won't need your cigarettes. Papers."

Peter handed over his identity card. The guard checked it against the list on the clipboard he held.

"Get in the truck," he said.

Peter started to shake.

"Sir—"

"In the truck," the guard said and casually swung his baton. It hit Peter a careless blow on the chin, and his teeth clacked together on his tongue. His mouth filled with blood.

"Please, sir," he said, trying not to drool. "I'm exempt. I'm *Geltungsjude*—married to an Aryan. Margarete Rashkin, née Stusskopf. Our daughters are Aryan. You see, it's stamped right on my papers?"

"Did you say daughters?" The guard consulted his list. "Vivian and Ginger Rashkin?"

"Yes," said Peter, "their mother is Margarete Stusskopf Rashkin, full-blooded—"

"Where are they now?"

"Upstairs, sir. Margarete is at work—"

"Get them," said the guard.

"Sir?"

"Get. Them."

Peter ran upstairs, shaking. He spat as he went, but still the girls squealed like piglets when they saw his bloody mouth. "Shhh," he said and gathered them up. He stared frantically around the room for their prepacked valise, for their coats and hoods, but something seemed to have happened to his mind; he couldn't spot the satchel anywhere. He felt slow and stupid, time speeding past as he stood with a girl on each hip. The cellar or the truck? The truck or the cellar? If they went down the fire escape to the safe space, perhaps the guards would grow bored with waiting and move on—or maybe they would be caught and shot . . . But maybe if they complied, they could stay together—

"What number is he?" he heard one of the guards say on the stairs.

"Seven."

"Unlucky for him."

"And for you, Klaus, since you get to climb all the way up to fetch him."

Laughter. Peter snatched up the closest thing at hand, the blanket on the bed, and darted from the room. Gigi coughed in his ear. Her face was hot against his cheek. Vivi was crying indignantly.

"Slower, Papa," she said.

"Shh," said Peter. He opened the door to the back stairwell, where the window to the fire escape was. The young guard was on the landing.

"I'll give you ten seconds to get in the truck," he said.

There was nowhere to sit. Peter stood sandwiched in with the girls, one on each hip, the blanket slung over their shoulders. Gigi dozed. Vivi stared around. An old lady in a fur-trimmed hat and coat, the Star on her lapel, made faces at her—grinning, then wiping her hand across her face to reveal a grimace. Vivian buried her head in Peter's neck.

"Beautiful girls," said the woman sadly. "Twins?"

"Yes," said Peter. He didn't want to talk. He was trying to figure out from the distances and rights and lefts where they were going.

"How old?"

"Three."

"May God keep them," said the old woman.

"Please, Mother," said another man whose breath had the dog-shit smell of malnutrition, "be quiet."

"Where are they taking us?" asked Peter.

"I heard to a Russian POW camp," said the man from the side of his mouth, "an empty one, in Wuensdorf."

"I heard the East," somebody else murmured.

"The East?" Somebody laughed. "Where, the Orient?"

"Wherever it is, it can't be good."

"You don't know that."

"Quiet!"

The truck ground to a stop, and the rear door was thrown open. The guards started pulling them out by the ankles, the legs, the arms, whatever they could reach. Was this really necessary? Peter wanted to ask. They would all come peaceably if given a chance. He was shoved forward. "Hold tight to my neck, girls," he said, struggling to jump down from the truck without losing his grip on them.

Once out of the truck he stood for a few seconds, trying to make sense of what he was seeing. They were in a square—outside the Clou Concert Hall. It was jammed with people. Hats, heads, coats, children riding on parents' shoulders, a group in hospital gowns? It was like a pointillist painting—Peter had to blink to make them all into individuals. Otherwise it was a solid mass of people. There must have been more than four thousand. The Gestapo and guards were driving them toward the hall. An announcement droned over and over: "Move forward. You will be processed inside. You will receive food and water. Move forward. You will be processed inside. You will receive . . ." How on earth, Peter thought, did they expect everyone to fit?

"Get moving," somebody said from behind Peter and jabbed his back.

Peter didn't have a choice; the people around him carried him and the girls forward. But for every step he took forward, he also tried to push sideways. If only he could get to the periphery. If only he could—

"Petel!"

He turned. Masha was pushing through the crowd toward them—God alone knew how she had located them in this mass.

Her coat was open over her chef's whites, and there was a spatter on them that looked like Burgundy wine, or blood.

"Mashi? Is it really you?"

She hurled herself at them. "Petel, Petel," she cried, "girls," and they stood in a huddle, all of them crying and shaking together until Peter was unable to tell whose limbs, hair, or tears was whose.

"We need to get out of here," said Masha, "quick."

"How? And go where? You should not have come, Mashi."

"And abandon you? And the girls? Are you crazy?"

"You were right, Mashi. They didn't care that you're Aryan and I'm *Geltungsjuden*. I should have listened. I should have listened . . ."

"None of that matters now," she said.

"Foolish, brave Mashi. You must go before they spot you . . ."

"Don't be silly, Petel. We'll all go. Come. I know a special way."

She took Peter's coat and started leading him through the crowd, Peter straining to keep his grip on his girls' bony bottoms. He had thought they would have to push, push, push, but the crowd parted magically for them as if Peter and his family were a hot knife slicing through butter. Over the loudspeakers came not the recorded voice telling them to stay where they were, they would all be processed, stay where they were, they would all be processed, but a recording of Prokofiev's *Peter and the Wolf*. "And now, imagine the triumphant procession! Of course, Peter was at the head," said the speakers. The girls missed it, their favorite story, because they were asleep, one head on each shoulder, their thumbs in their mouths. They reached the perimeter, and Peter saw the sun shining between two buildings, highlighting the golden alley through which they would make their escape. "And if you listened very carefully, you could hear the duck quacking inside the wolf. Because the wolf, in his hurry, had swallowed her alive," said the loudspeaker.

Masha turned and smiled brilliantly at Peter.

"See?" she said. "I told you I knew the way."

The relief in Peter was so great that his legs went weak, his arms. Masha saw and lifted the girls from him before he could drop them.

"Mashi," he said. "How can this be? You made it? The girls? You're no longer dead . . . ?"

*

When Peter first woke in the hold of the *Bubkes*, he flailed, sure he was back in the police truck—it was dark, and he was moving—or maybe the boxcar to Theresienstadt? Then he pitched off the bench onto the floor, heard the slosh of water and a *zzzzzzz!* overhead and remembered where he was: in a boat, on the Long Island Sound, in America. In 1966. He tried to sit up, but lifting his head produced such nausea that he quickly changed his mind. He lay very still, trying to think of something, anything but the dream.

The dream. The dream. The terrible roundup dream. Peter had thought he'd outgrown it. He hadn't had it in years. It had plagued him constantly when he first arrived at Sol and Ruth's; every night in Ruth and Sol's guestroom his dreaming mind had tried and tried and tried to rewrite history, to change what had happened, a different ending each time but with one important similarity: *No, you're wrong! They're still alive!* Each morning Peter had awakened, seen the glitter of the Sound beyond the window, turned his head to the wall, where the slanted-eyed red toile deer, eternally pursued by hunters, had looked inscrutably back at him, and wished he were dead too. To this day Peter could not see the shape of a stag in a photograph, tapestry, or painting without being transported back to the dread of those mornings. The fathomless black despair. He could not go back there. He could not. If the dream was starting again, he would . . . he didn't know what he would do.

Think of something else, he told himself. Focus.

The smell of cigar smoke drifted with diesel and fish guts into the hold. The two men talked overhead.

"What've you been bringing in this week?" Sol was asking Dutch.

"I got mostly eight-, ten-pounders—stuff you're supposed to throw back," said Dutch. "Baby blues and fluke. Though I heard a guy off Montauk caught a thresher."

Sol wheezed laughter. "You're kidding."

"Nope. Guy thought he'd hooked a buoy at first. Goddamned if it wasn't a shark. . . . Hand me those binocs."

"We got bubkes here today," said Sol. "We should change the name of the boat."

"Choppers said there were big blues running here over the weekend. Another half hour and we'll move. So how's your fishing been this month?"

"Pretty good," said Sol. "Not great but decent."

"How much you net?"

Sol said, "Three hundred K."

Dutch whistled. "That's some serious gelt."

"Young Zionists helped us out a lot," Sol said. "And the Friends of Israel. They coughed up a bundle. And I got Ruth to work her Hadassah girls."

"I'm impressed," said Dutch.

"It's good," said Sol, "but it could be better. Moshe needs more fast. Ever since the French pulled out . . ."

"Buncha gonnifs," said Dutch. "But whaddya expect from the French? The way they rolled over for Hitler—*puh puh.*"

"Not all of 'em," said Sol. "My cousin Avi had good connections outside Vichy. Impressive resistance."

"True," said Dutch. "Even still, I never felt a hundred percent about them. You should only really trust your own people, nu?"

"Yeah."

"So what's this month's catch gonna go for?" Dutch asked.

"Moshe says he's looking at Skyhawks mostly," said Sol. "Some M48s. Johnson promised to make up the difference when the French pulled out, but we know his promises are worth bubkes. He's no better than that momser Roosevelt. And it won't be enough."

"It's never enough," said Dutch.

"True. They need more AK-47s too. And Garands. And ammo. But mostly planes and tanks. Moshe says there's movement at all the borders."

"Egypt again?"

"And Jordan. And Syria. You know that Nasser, he wants to blow us off the face of the earth."

"Fucking momsers," said Dutch and made the spitting noise again. "You think Moshe'll get the appointment?"

"Hope so. Yeah. If we can get him the money fast so he can get the goods, that'll get him in extra tight with Defense."

"Good," said Dutch.

"Yeah," said Sol.

Footsteps overhead, then another *zzzzzzz!* as one of the men recast his line.

"Euh," Dutch said, "we got drek here. You wanna try another location?"

"Nah," said Sol, "I gotta get back. Ruth's having people. Lions of Judah."

"Oh yeah? That's a good group. Okay, let's go. Business is business." More walking overhead. "I don't know what happened to the blues," said Dutch, "but we got some nice mackerel for Sleeping Beauty down there. That should make him happy."

"He'll be thrilled," said Sol. "He'll wrap it in pastry or some meshuggaas."

"He know anything about . . ."

"What?" said Sol. "Defense? Nah. Far as he knows it's all hospitals and schools, the feel-good stuff."

"He doesn't know from anything?"

"No. That pretty face of his helps raise money, but otherwise I don't want him involved."

"I guess that's smart," said Dutch doubtfully, "not to bring in immediate family . . ."

"It's not that," said Sol. "It's that he's soft."

"Yeah, I got the impression he was kind of a peacenik," said Dutch. "No offense."

"None taken. He's got his head permanently up his tuches. Didn't even get his family outta Europe on time. That kinda help we don't need."

"I remember Ruth told me something about that," said Dutch, "when you first brought him over. Shiksa wife and . . . was it a daughter?"

"Two," said Sol. "Twins. Prettiest little girls you ever saw . . ."

There was a pause and the honk of Sol's nose.

"Aw, that's too bad," said Dutch. "Sorry, Solly. Poor kids. But life goes on, nu?"

"Yeah. Yeah, I guess so. . . . You should see what he's shtupping now."

"Oh yeah?"

"Yeah. Supershiksa," said Sol. "Ruth says she's some big model. Legs up to here."

"That right?"

"I'm telling you. If it weren't for Ruth, I'd like to . . ."

Whatever Sol wanted to do was lost in Dutch starting the engines, and from then on Peter heard only their noise and the slap of water against the *Bubkes*'s sides as it bounced over the waves. Peter was sitting up now, thinking. Skyhawks were fighter planes, that he knew. M48s—tanks. And any schmuck, as Sol would say, knew what Garands and AK-47s were. And Moshe was . . . Peter tried to remember the complex moving parts of Israel's political machine, but he had never paid much attention. He apparently hadn't paid much attention to many things. He thought of the meetings Sol and Choppers and their friends had taken at Masha's, tramping in through the kitchen, saying "Hey kid, send in some bagels and schmear when you get a chance, wouldja?" before shutting the door, locking Peter out of his own office. He thought of all Sol's fund-raisers—how the money had rolled in. Peter sat with his back braced against the bench, trying to keep his head from knocking against it, grimly putting pieces together.

*

"I feel like a dog," said Sol. "You wanna dog?"

"Do I want a . . . ," said Peter. It took him a minute to translate what Sol was asking. They were swerving along the Post Road from the marina in Sol's Volvo, Sol's characteristically carefree driving made worse by the whiskey he must have consumed on the *Bubkes*. It did nothing to help Peter's aching head or roiling stomach, the aftermath of seasickness, the stench of diesel in the boatyard, and fury.

"No, I don't want a hot dog," said Peter. "Watch it!" and he grabbed the steering wheel to bring them back into their own lane. Sol made a sweeping right turn onto Delaney Street.

"Keep your pants on," he said, "I know what I'm doing."

"What I want," said Peter, "is to know how long you've been using my restaurant to launder money."

Sol ignored this. He made a left onto Palmer Avenue without looking—luckily nobody was coming—and parked on a slant outside Walter's, a hot dog stand housed in a Chinese pagoda, complete with dragons bearing lanterns on its green copper-tiled roof. This was one of Sol's favorite places, and normally Peter was fond of it too, though more for the amusing architecture than the hot dogs, which he considered a bastardization of wursts.

Sol opened his door and got out. "I'm getting a foot-long," he said. "You want one?" Peter shook his head. Sol slammed the door and stumped across the sidewalk to the order window, where there was a line, even on a Monday afternoon. Construction workers, schoolchildren just released from class, a young mother cooing into a baby carriage, and a couple of what Sol would call other *alte kockers* like him: aging Jewish men in chinos, zipper sweaters, light jackets, glasses, their hands covered with liver spots, their hair graying and missing in patches and tamed with pomade, their backs slightly stooped. Sol looked just like the others as he took his place at the end of the line—maybe a little more florid. The only other difference was his mustache and his fishing hat with its brim of lures. Nobody would ever suspect him of running anything more illegal than a weekly poker game.

Peter got out of the car. He needed air. He walked to the bench a couple of feet from the hot dog pagoda, under some trees, and sat down. Eventually Sol came toward him with a white cardboard boat in each hand.

"I got you a Puppy Dog," he said, and he sat and leaned forward to take an enormous bite of his double foot-long. A splat of mustard and ketchup fell to the sidewalk.

"Whassamatter?" he said. "Quit looking at me like that, you're giving me shpilkes."

"I'm waiting for an answer to my question."

"What?" Sol said irritably.

"How long have you been laundering your money through my restaurant!"

Sol wheezed. It took Peter a moment to realize he was laughing. He coughed and thumped himself on the chest, then looked at Peter with watering eyes, a strand of sauerkraut clinging to his mustache.

"Listen to you! So it's your restaurant now. Aren't you some big macher." Sol shoved in another inch of hot dog. "That place would be a dry cleaner without my money, sonny boy, and don't you forget it."

"How long?" said Peter. "From the beginning?"

"Kid, you got it all wrong."

"Don't give me that. I heard you, Sol. I heard you talking to Dutch. About the Skyhawks and tanks and weapons. You're sending money to Israel, aren't you? For their war machine."

"What are you, a hippie?" said Sol. "It's not a war machine. It's defense. Defense of our people."

"Whatever you want to call it," said Peter, "you're laundering money through Masha's to do it. I don't want any part of it, Sol. I don't want you using my name, my reputation, my business, for your illegal activities."

"Illegal shmelegal," said Sol. "Hitler had plenty of laws too, you may remember, and that didn't make 'em right. What matters is the greater good. Taking care of your own."

"The end justifies the means," said Peter.

"Now you got the idea."

"Even if it means screwing your own family. We're just cogs in your machine."

Sol had been gazing philosophically out over Palmer Avenue as he chewed the last of his lunch, but now he looked at Peter with surprise.

"Whaddya talking about?" he said. "You got it backward. It's all about family. It's always about family. Haven't I helped you? Didn't I get you out of Europe, that miserable DP camp, take you into our home like a son? Didn't I give you money for your place—even though it's meshugga, a man wanting to be a cook, but that's your business. What you wanted you got. Because you're mishpocha—family. Family is everything."

"But it's not just my business," said Peter. "It's your business. You made it your business. Masha's is just one of your means to an end. A respectable front for your dirty money. Like all the suppliers you insist I use—the laundry and the linens and the printer." Peter thought of the nonagenarian owner of the company responsible for printing Masha's menus, flyers, matchbooks, his Bronx factory with the broken windows and cobwebbed machines, either the tufts of hair growing out of his ears or his age making him almost totally deaf. Charging three times what another printer would. "They're all your guys," Peter said. "Mob. Connected."

Sol wheezed some more. He took another swig from his flask. "Oy gevalt, the mob," he said. He drank and held up the flask. "Wanna toot?"

"No," said Peter.

"Too bad," said Sol. "Scotch goes good with Walter's. Eat your Puppy Dog."

"I don't want my fucking Puppy Dog," said Peter. "I want the truth."

"I'm giving it to you," said Sol. "You've got it all wrong, kid. Seen too many movies. Mob—that's rich! Wait'll I tell the guys."

"So you deny it? You deny that you and your friends—Choppers, Dutch, that doctor, the suppliers—you deny you're connected?"

"Sure we're connected," said Sol. "But not the way you think. Not Kosher Nostra—like Meyer Lansky and Bugsy Siegel and those guys. We're just a buncha guys who came up together, like I told you. We're not mobsters. We don't get involved with drugs and gambling and whores—we leave that meshuggaas to the Italians. We're numbers guys. The worst we do is maybe massage the numbers a little."

"To buy arms. And make a nice profit from it, too."

Sol reared back and glared at Peter, his eyes watering behind his glasses.

"We don't see profit," he said. "Whaddaya take me for? We're not criminals. We give back. I give back to the guys by giving them business, they help me raise money, every cent goes to defense. To protect our people over there."

"It's for war," said Peter. "And let me ask you something. These people you raise the money *from*, the people I *helped* you get money from, do they know what it's going for? Guns and tanks and planes?"

Sol shrugged. "A couple do. Most don't. But that's all right. We give some money to the up-front causes too. Hospitals. Orphanages. The Joint. Red Cross. We just stretch the contributions a little, creatively, to cover defense too."

Peter sat back. All the catering he had done for Sol's luncheons and dinners and brunches, in the law firm, in homes all over Manhattan and Westchester and New Jersey. All the years Peter had been the poster boy for Sol's good causes. How many darkened rooms had Peter sat in, while Sol clicked off slide after slide of emaciated Jewish children, of the melee in the DP camps, of trawlers full of survivors, bound for Palestine but sunk by the British before they could get there? Of men and women gazing out from bunks, skeletal, in rags, toothless, each bearing a tattoo like Peter's own? "We gotta help 'em," said Sol as people wept softly in the dark—by no means all women. "We gotta help our own. They survived Hitler's filthy camps—for what? To return to homes burned to the ground. To go back to shtetls that no longer exist. They want to come to this country—but there are quotas, waiting lines; our government says there's no room, sorry, we can't take 'em. Well, I'll take 'em," said Sol, "and with your help I'll make sure they'll all get here safe. Like this guy here," and he would gesture to Peter with his slideshow clicker, Peter who had been standing next to the podium in the dark, now stepping into the bright beam of the projector, rolling up his shirtsleeve to show his tattoo.

"I'm done," Peter said. "I'm through being your shill."

"Fine with me, Mr. Conscientious Objector," said Sol, relighting his cigar. "Guys like you, you sit around thinking about right and wrong, hold hands, sing 'Kumbaya,' and then when somebody's burning your house down, you say, 'Help! Help!' Before the war, when we were sounding the alarm, trying to get people out, you guys said, 'Nah, you're exaggerating, sit tight, it'll blow over.' Until they started herding you into the camps, and then who'd you turn to? The dirty-money guys. You think the world should be all flowers and sunshine, and maybe it should, that's nice. But the world doesn't work that way."

"You sound like my father," said Peter.

"Good," said Sol. "Now there was a smart man. A fighter.

Willing to put his mouth and his money on the line. If it weren't for him, there'd be a lot more dead Jews. If you'd been more like him—"

"—I'd be dead too," said Peter. "The Nazis would have dragged me off to Buchenwald too, and there'd be no one left."

"They hauled you off anyway," said Sol. "And you barely made it. Haven't you wised up by now? You of all people, I'd have thought you'd learned a lesson over there."

"My lesson?" Peter spat. He was so angry his lips were numb. "Don't you talk about my *lesson*. It is *not* the same—Israel and Germany. You have no idea what it was like. No idea at all. Don't you understand, we'd lived in Berlin for a *century*. It was our city—the way New York is yours. Germany our country. And then some strutting idiot, this little fool, this bigoted madman screaming idiocies with spit flying from his mouth—he comes in telling lies. Oh my God, the lies! The lies, the lies, the ridiculous lies. We never heard such stupid things. Every day a new one—our mouths were hanging open. We Jews had collapsed the economy—it wasn't the Versailles Treaty, oh no. We were bankrupting Germany. We had a Jewish master plan. Also—my favorite—he said we had declared war on Germany. War! We had! While our rights were being taken away from us one by one, first the movies and then parks and our pets and jobs and even riding on streetcars. *We* were undermining Germany. *We* were winning. Who could believe it? Who could believe such black-is-white horseshit? We laughed; we thought sooner or later people *must* wake up and say, 'All right, enough is enough, the emperor has no clothes,' and send him on his way. We never thought he'd stay. That things would get *worse*. We never thought that our friends—my parents' friends, the people we worked with, educated, civilized, cultured people, good people, people who *knew* right from wrong—we never believed they'd believe him. Or pretend they did, which was the same thing. Don't you see? There was no *precedent.* It was unbelievable that anyone could believe such lies lies lies lies lies!"

Peter stopped for breath, aware that at some point he'd jumped to his feet, that he had been shouting, that the people on line at Walter's were looking at him. Sol was considering the end of his cigar.

"Of course there was precedent," he said calmly.

"What the hell are you talking about?"

"People've always wanted to kill us," said Sol. "Cossacks. Pogroms. Nazis. Arabs. The uniforms change, that's all." He pitched the cigar stub toward the gutter. "Precedent or not, who cares? That's the trouble with you guys. Always thinking about ideas, when what matters is what's actually happening. Use your eyes. Use your ears. If you'd done that back in Germany—"

"Don't say it!" Peter shouted.

"—your family might be alive today," said Sol.

Peter's whole body clenched—and then all the fight went out of him. He felt very tired. He looked over at Walter's, at the people waiting on line for hot dogs; at the tiny leaves, just born, fluttering in the breeze above him; at the new daffodils and tulips springing from the mud; at the big American cars whooshing past on Palmer Avenue. Sol could talk all he wanted about how the world worked, but he was an American, and he would never know what it was like, how dumbfounding, how confusing, how paralyzing it was when it all went wrong, when the place you'd lived in your whole life, your city, your beloved country, abruptly and for no reason except the rants of a rabid fool, turned against you; when the place where you got your morning coffee and roll and had your hair cut and smiled good-morning to the neighbors as they walked their dogs—when that place started ejecting you. Suddenly you were invisible, and the next day worse: you were despised, you were filthy, you were vermin, and you stared in astonishment at the erosion of your life,

no more films, no more work, no freedom of movement, no citi-
zenry, no home, and by the time your mind caught up with events,
it was too late, and your government, friends, and neighbors were
joyously hunting you down like dogs.

"I want out," Peter said. "I won't bankroll war. Any war."

Sol shrugged. "Suit yourself. You want out, you're out. But if
you're too good to help me, you're too good for my money. You're
on your own. Don't come to me with your hand out."

"I won't," said Peter. "I'm done with that."

"You sure?" said Sol. "I'd think about it if I were you. Without
my money, you'll be outta business by the end of the year. Nothing
personal. Just numbers."

"I'll take the chance," said Peter. "I'd rather live on food stamps."

Sol planted his hands on his knees and pushed himself up.

"Okay, big talker," he said. "I'll give you a week to think about
it. Because you're family." He hitched up his pants. "You might
be fine eating government cheese," he said, "but that fancy piece
you've been shtupping, something tells me she won't be so happy
with it. How long you think she's gonna stick around when you're
living under some bridge like a schvantz?" And off he stomped to
his car.

*

Once Peter was on the New Haven line back to Grand Central,
having walked to Mamaroneck Station, he realized he'd forgotten the fish. He swore. Mackerel wasn't a popular entrée, too oily
for most people's palates, but he could have made a nice pâté out
of it. Aside from planting the garden, the whole day had been a
waste.

He took a seat by the window. At least the train wasn't too
crowded, since it was midafternoon. Peter scanned his fellow passengers' faces, wan in the spring sunlight. Two teenage girls in
dungarees, their hair plaited, a guitar case on the floor between

them. An older woman in a suit, with white gloves. A young matron with her eyes closed, head balanced and bobbing against the window glass—what had kept her up late? crying baby, angry husband? Suddenly Peter realized what he was doing: looking only at the women. Not that there were any men commuting at this hour, but still—he was searching for Masha. For the girls. Playing the looking game.

Disturbed, he got up and walked the length of the car, one of the young girls smiling at him as he passed. There was a daisy painted on one of her cheeks. Her hair and eyes were dark, and she couldn't have been more than sixteen: too young. Peter used the restroom, poured himself a Dixie cup of lukewarm water, and stepped into the compartment between the cars.

He stood with one foot on one part of the moving floor and the other on another, feeling the coupling swivel beneath him as the train took the track's curves. Outside the narrow window, the backyards of Westchester flashed past. Soon they would become highways, then the high-rises and swamps of the Bronx. Peter sipped his water. In the early days, in the 1940s when he first arrived here, the looking game had had a point. It had made sense for him to walk the streets and avenues of New York, staring at every woman he passed, seeking Masha's energetic stride and pale face, his girls' candy-floss hair. The war's end had been such a mess: people unaccounted for, too sick to remember their names, assuming or being assigned others' identities by mistake. It happened all the time. Peter had heard stories. There had been a rabbi on the Upper West Side who remarried, then opened his apartment door one day to find his dead wife standing on his welcome mat. Why shouldn't the same miracle happen for Peter? Why shouldn't the bell chime in Sol and Ruth's foyer one day, the door swing back to reveal Masha, or one of the twins clinging to a Red Cross worker's hand? Peter visited and revisited the relief office, asking them to check the rolls of the dead, to check again; on buses, in the subway, in stores, everywhere he went, he looked for a woman in her twenties, little girls who had grown from toddlerhood.

But it was useless, of course. Time had kept moving, as time did, and Peter kept having to push up his wife and children's ages, and one day in 1954 he had chased a woman up East Eighty-Sixth Street because of her quick step and white twist of hair, and she turned and hit him with her purse. After that, he had sworn: no more. Masha was gone, the girls with her, and the best Peter could hope for was that if there were some sort of afterlife, they had been reunited there. Someday maybe he would be with them. Now the roundup dream had come back; now the looking game. What did it mean? If they persisted, if they increased, Peter would not be able to stand it. This erosion of his sanity.

He put his hand on the exit door. It vibrated. Peter had read that when the train reached a certain speed, these doors locked to prevent jumpers. He had never tested the theory. Once he'd tried to step in front of an incoming train at Grand Central, but his legs had locked. The only other time he'd tried had been during that first miserable year, at Sol and Ruth's. They had gone on a cruise to Bermuda, and Peter had taken a packet of razor blades into their guest bathroom and sat on the side of the tub. Cut down, not across, he'd heard from a girl in the Bremerhaven DP camp, a Bergen-Belsen survivor who had taken her own advice and succeeded the next week. Peter had cut despite the incredible, nauseating pain. He had cut deeper. And then he had heard the voice. Peter had never believed in God, but he thought that if God had chosen to speak to him, He would sound like Charlton Heston in *The Ten Commandments*: "Peter, do my bidding!" Instead, what Peter heard was the voice in his own head, the one he thought of as his, except it was saying something very different from what it usually said. And what it said, firmly and calmly, was:

you are not allowed.

So he had put down the razor blade and wrapped his wrist in the cleaning rags Maria kept under the sink, and he had gone into the kitchen and taken an extra bottle of Sol's Cutty Sark down from the cupboard over the refrigerator and poured the whiskey over the wounds.

Peter crumpled the Dixie cup, turned, and went back to his seat. He put his hand in his pocket and found the ring, poked the prongs of its setting into his thumb, over and over. June. What was he going to do about June? Peter had thought she was his fresh American start—an idea as optimistic as something Roosevelt would say. Perhaps, if June were here, sitting in the next seat with her head on his shoulder, none of this would be happening: the memory shrapnel not working its way to the surface, the dead not reanimating. Peter would not be backsliding. But what if, instead of the cure, June was the cause? Peter thought of a PBS program he had seen about the *Titanic*, how it had not been a head-on collision with the iceberg that had sunk the great ship but the underwater slicing of its several watertight compartments. What if June, rather than being his lifesaver, was his iceberg? What if her presence in his life had punctured the sealed chamber into which Peter had put Masha and the girls? There was no way to know for sure.

Peter took the ring out of his pocket. The diamond made tiny sparklers of light against his palm. Peter had meant what he had said to Sol: he wanted out. It would mean finding another investor for Masha's, a process that could take months. Years. Peter might even have to close temporarily. He would be fine working in another kitchen, eating bachelor rations in his apartment. He had done it before. But what about June? Was it fair to her to saddle her with a pauper? And even if Peter cut ties with Sol, what if Sol was investigated, by the Internal Revenue Service, for instance? Would Peter himself fall under suspicion? Peter had done plenty of work bringing in money for Sol over the years—unwittingly, but who would believe him? Peter was family. Even if Sol was no Bugsy Siegel or Meyer Lansky—and Peter still had his doubts about whether Sol had told him everything—what he was doing was bad enough. Was it right to bring June into this situation? June, so young, so beautiful; she could have whoever she wanted. Was it not kinder to her to let her go? Peter looked out the window at the approaching city, turning the ring over and over in his hand.

6

PETER AND THE WOLF

One morning in mid-May, June talked Peter into having break-fast in Washington Square Park. It was on Peter's way uptown, she'd wheedled. "Let's stroll," she said, hooking her arm through Peter's, "get some fresh air, dine alfresco." Peter wasn't sure what they were doing now could be described as any of these things: they were sweltering on a bench near the Arch, June taking tiny sips of tea and feeding her breakfast sandwich to the pigeons, and the air in the park, far from crisp, smelled of pretzels, horseshit, and marijuana. Peter took out his handkerchief and daubed his forehead, the back of his neck. At least he wasn't on an uptown train, dangling from a strap, entangled with his fellow New York-ers like sauerkraut. It wasn't technically that hot yet, but lately Peter felt he was perspiring all the time. He would take a taxi.

"Want some?" said June, offering Peter a bit of bun containing a yellow disc of egg like a dog's rubber toy. He demurred and she tossed it to the birds, who immediately started pecking at each other for the privilege.

"There you go, Mortimer," said June. She elbowed Peter. "See that big one, with the silver neck? That's Mortimer."

"Ah," said Peter. He tucked his handkerchief away and subdued a sigh. He was not in the mood for the park today. Washington Square and June's West Village neighborhood were reliable barometers of his temper; on better days he found them raffish, even charming: the folk singers, the old men playing chess at stone tables, the bag ladies talking to the birds or trees or nobody at all. The peaceniks with their guitars and flowy pajama-like clothes; the mixed-race couples, Negro men holding hands with white women and vice versa—even the trash and drugs, the fellows whispering to Peter and June from the shade as they'd passed, "Smoke? Reefer? Maryjane?"—were all signs of, if not civil disobedience exactly, then a kind of tolerance that comforted Peter, that indicated that what had happened in his homeland would never happen here. After the young President Kennedy had been shot, Peter had feared it might; that had been a bad week, Peter afraid to leave his apartment, but not because he had been watching television like everyone else. He had been waiting for the crackdown, for Johnson, the new president, to implement martial law, for the tanks to start rolling down Lexington Avenue, for armed patrols on every corner. It had taken his own chefs coming to check on him to persuade him that it wouldn't happen, that the government had not toppled, that although the assassination was a tragedy, democracy was status quo. Blessed America! But on days like today, when Peter felt irritable and uncomfortable in his own skin, he wished for less quirkiness and laxity and a little more peace and quiet.

"What's up?" said June. "You're so restless."

"I don't mean to be. It's just that I have to get to—"

"The restaurant!" June sang, with an operatic flourish. The group of folk singers clustered near the fountain looked over, then applauded.

"You got pipes, girl," said one of them, a peacenik with a headband and smoked sunglasses. He grinned, his teeth crooked in his long, dark beard. "You wanna join us?"

June curtsied. She was wearing a pink-and-orange minidress today, patterned with jellybean shapes, and with the advent of warmer weather she had exchanged her boots for platform sandals whose cork heels made her taller than Peter.

"No thanks," she called, "but rock on."

She sat back down as the peacenik flashed her what Peter still thought of as the V for Victory sign, then fanned herself with her purse.

"Whew," she said, "I feel a little dizzy. Does it feel hot to you?"

"It does, actually."

"Some of the girls and photographers are going to DC next week," she said. "There's supposed to be a big antiwar rally at the White House."

"Are you thinking of joining them?"

"Me? No. I'm tempted, but I've got bookings. Gotta pay the rent. I'm not a kept woman yet." June put her hand on Peter's knee and squeezed. "Why, would you?"

"What," said Peter, "go? I don't think so. It's not for me."

June turned her big black movie-star glasses on him. "But you do support the protesters, don't you?"

"I do," Peter said truthfully, although his feelings about it were abstract: he appreciated that American citizens could dissent without being hauled off to prisons and camps; he thought the war in Vietnam was a travesty. Communism—what was so terrible about that, compared to fascism? Other than that, he remained detached; it wasn't his war. He wiggled his eyebrows at June and tried to sound hip: "It's not my bag, baby."

June laughed. "You'd better stick to the restaurant."

"Speaking of which," said Peter and looked at his watch. "There's a delivery of tomatoes from a new vendor coming in, and I should really be there."

June pursed her lips and looked away at the peaceniks. Poor June—this really was not fair to her. Perhaps this was Peter's

chance to ask her whether she really didn't want to be among people her own age—the Youthquake!—instead of an older guy like
him, set in his ways, wedded to his job. They had seen a revival of
My Fair Lady in March, and Peter had been dismayed how much he
felt like Rex Harrison's Professor Higgins. *A confirmed old bachelor and
likely to remain so.* Before June came along, Peter had been quite content with his life the way it was, avoiding romantic obligations, serene in his work. He still had the ring in his pocket; he had not yet
dissolved his partnership with Sol. Every time he thought about
taking action on either front, he felt the old inertia, the loathed
paralysis. It made him so very tired.

But surely there was some compromise, at least where June was
concerned. Peter could propose—he could *suggest*—that they take
a little time away from each other this summer. It was the age
of adventure; why shouldn't June have some, while Peter tended
to Masha's? The restaurant needed some reorganization, and he
wouldn't want to pin her in place, like a beautiful butterfly in a
glass box. Not a lot of time apart, just perhaps . . . seeing each other
once a week instead of every night; that sounded reasonable, didn't
it? He squared his elbows on his knees and leaned forward.

"June," he began.

She gave a small belch, a new habit she seemed to have recently
picked up that Peter found unbecoming.

"Are you all right?" he asked, irritated.

June held up her palm like a traffic policeman.

"Hold the phone," she said, then jumped up and ran to the
wastebasket next to the bench. She threw up into it most violently,
gripping its brim and heaving, and then did it again. Peter went
to her and held her hair back from her face—it was longer now,
swinging over her shoulders. He rubbed her back.

"June, June," he said. "I told you not to eat off a cart."

"Ugh, don't talk about it," she said. Peter handed her his handkerchief and she took it gratefully, using it on her mouth, then

turning it inside out and patting under her eyes, where her makeup had smeared from her exertions.

"Come, rest, sit down," said Peter, though he felt more impatient than ever. Now he would have to take her home, put her to bed, bring her some crackers and ginger ale from the corner deli; the whole morning, if not the entire day, would be lost. "Would you like something to settle your stomach—a seltzer?"

He returned to the bench and patted it, but June remained standing, refolding his handkerchief.

"Pete," she said, "I'm pregnant."

Peter looked up at her. She seemed very tall, a mannequin standing there in the sunlight with her hair adding another few inches to her height, her sunglasses back on, her face a mask. She was quite still, quite calm, but she was folding and unfolding his handkerchief. A breeze brought a gust of chestnuts and marijuana to Peter from across the square.

"Well?" she said.

Peter opened his mouth to respond, then shut it again. He wanted to answer, he really did, but something was wrong with him, something was wrong with his mind. His thoughts flashed past at rocket-ship speed while his body locked, a familiar and hated phenomenon. *I thought you were on the pill* was one option—but it was obvious the little tablets had failed. *Is it mine?* was another; however, June was faithful, and Peter knew the baby was his. He looked at his hands, curled on the knees of his lightweight gabardine trousers, in the left pocket of which was the ring. *Marry me*, he could say. *June Bouquet, will you be my wife?* What was to stop Peter from slipping to one knee right here on the asphalt, stained with pigeon droppings and spit and gum and God knew what? They could laugh about it later, make a funny story out of their beatnik engagement.

"Say something," June demanded. Her voice wobbled.

Peter cleared his throat. He found himself gazing off across the square, through dappled sunlight and shadow at the cars and people passing on Waverly Place. An old lady in a jeweled turban, pushing a shopping cart. A queenly Indian woman in saffron robes, holding a little girl in a matching gown by the hand. A mother and a daughter.

"Jesus," said June. "Pete? Hello? Are you there? Do you have *anything* to say?"

The mother and little girl vanished around the corner. Peter forced himself to squint up at June.

"I'm sorry," he said.

June stood knotting the handkerchief around her fingers for a moment, and then said, very low but clearly, "You bastard."

She threw the pocket square at him. It fell limply to the pavement.

"You goddamned bastard," she said. "I knew you would do this. I knew it!"

She backed away, and now she was crying, tears trickling from beneath the big sunglasses.

"Forget it, okay? Don't bother yourself. I'll take care of it. Have a nice life—in your *restaurant.*"

She turned, stumbling on her high cork heels but catching herself just in time, then walked rapidly with her head down out of the park, scattering litter and pigeons in her wake.

※

In every time of trouble in his life, large or small, Peter had gravitated to the kitchen. During his childhood, in flight from his father's bullying or his mother's disdain, Peter had sought the large square room in the back of the house where Hilde let him stir soup, roll dough, and—most excitingly, and provided he held the knife just as she showed him—chop vegetables. During his teens, Peter's sole act of rebellion had been to apply for a job as Adlon *commis* instead of clerking in the family law firm. He had kept his apprenticeship nights and weekends while attending university, and when the Nazis declared Jews could no longer participate in higher education, Peter had gratefully decamped from the study of law to full-time at the Adlon. In front of his parents and their friends—at least until they disowned him for marrying a gentile—Peter had been careful to pull a long face about his humble employment. How awful, the only son of one of Berlin's oldest and finest families, forced to work as a kitchen boy! Disgraceful! Hitler would be the ruin of them all. But at the time, promoted to prep chef and newly married, Peter had secretly, stupidly thought that the Nazis coming to power was the best thing that had ever happened to him.

At Auschwitz, his reassignment to the kitchens had saved his life; in America his first years, tortured by dreams and thick-tongued in his new language, Peter wandered nearly mute through a landscape of misery until the afternoon he walked into the Oyster Bar for a sandwich and came out with a job. After he lost that, his year of traveling: working his way from short-order cook to deli counter boy to prep chef in Chicago, Minneapolis, Atlanta. By the time Peter returned to New York and landed at Giuseppe's, he had discovered something: no place on this earth was home without Masha and the girls, but at least here there were more Jews—and restaurants. And if cuisine varied from country to country—in America no Spargel or *Johannisbeeren* but plenty of barbecue sauce, hot dogs, pizza, and the abomination Americans considered mayonnaise— then food itself was essentially the same. Julienning carrots or chiffonading basil was the same in Skokie and Berlin. A rutabaga was a rutabaga. Vegetables, meat, and technique had no language. The kitchen, any kitchen, was Peter's home.

In the week after June's revelation, he went to ground at Masha's. He opened every morning and closed each night, sleeping on the cot in his office and returning to his apartment only to shower. Although Peter had managed to be at the restaurant and cook most of his shifts even while dating June, he had not eaten, drank, and slept at Masha's since his opening days. He knew his behavior raised some eyebrows; he could practically feel the staff drawing straws to see who would ask him about the change, making up theories and bets behind his back. But it was a full week before anyone said anything, and then it was Lena—Peter should have known—who came in one morning at six to find Peter already there, surrounded by a glistening mound of sliced cucumbers and shallots, and said, "What is going on?"

"What does it look like?" Peter said, wiping his eyes on his sleeve—the shallots were pungent. "I'm making pickles."

"I see this," said Lena. "Where is little *zhopa* Steve? Is his job."

"I gave him the week off," said Peter of their prep chef.

Lena folded her arms over her chest. "Why you do this?"

"Because I'm here, and his wife just had another baby."

"She should keep legs together," said Lena. "*Tupa blyad.*"

She stood glowering at Peter like an aging traffic policeman—he could feel her gaze on the side of his neck—then huffed and left. Peter packed the vegetables into jars with dill flowers and a pickling mix he had invented himself: cloves, yellow and black mustard seed, anise, fennel, turmeric, red pepper. He funneled salted vinegar into the jars and dropped them into the ferociously boiling twenty-quart vat, then swapped out his cutting boards and began chopping day-old challah and baguettes to toast for croutons. Some of the cooks liked the radio on while they worked; some swore they solved problems in their heads. Peter preferred quiet but for the *pockpockpock* of his knife and, in this case, the chattering lid of the canning vat. It was only during these times that he was able to stop thinking; when his hands were occupied, his head was at rest.

Lena returned in whites and clogs, a bandanna hiding her short gray hair. "What is special today?"

Peter nodded at the chalkboard.

"Endive salad," Lena read under her breath. "Chicory, butter lettuce—produce delivery already came?"

"Five this morning."

"And cheesemonger?"

"I went yesterday," said Peter. "He had some excellent Roquefort."

"Probably stole it off truck," said Lena, "cocksucker," but she went to the walk-in for her *mise en place* and began setting up her station a foot away from Peter's. The two worked in silence broken only by Lena's heavy breathing. She was fileting bluefish and Peter was lifting the pickles out of the vat with the rubber-tipped claw when Lena said, "What happen to skinny whore?"

"Don't call her that," Peter said. He set the final jar on a baking sheet and turned off the heat under the pot.

"Okay," said Lena agreeably. "Where is stupid whore?"

Peter took a fresh rag off his stack and wiped his face and neck. "Lena, I'm warning you."

Lena shrugged. "Warn if you want. You think I am scared? I snap you over my knee like twig."

"I mean it, Lena. I'm in no mood."

Peter began tossing the challah and baguettes he had cubed in a mixture of olive oil and rosemary. Lena lowered the bluefish filets into a mustard marinade.

"I am not in mood either," she said. "Today on subway man piss on my foot. This fucking city. And Linda out all night again whoring. Next time I see her I break fucking neck."

"Ah," said Peter. Linda was Lena's girlfriend, who worked as a hostess and sometime dancer in one of the boardwalk clubs on Coney Island.

"You know what else I am not in mood for?" said Lena. "This," and she nudged Peter. She put her knife down and used her fingers to pull her eyelids down into a horrible grimace.

"All this moping," she said. "Boss who mope around like sick dog. Like dog that get run over. Like dog that get run over after finding out his bitch fucking some other dog."

"Yes, I take your point," Peter said.

"So?" said Lena. She returned to painting marinade on the filets. "What happen with *yebanutaya suka*?"

"Lena," said Peter—he knew she had just called June a fucked whore. But he also knew it was useless to tell her again to stop. "That woman despises me," said June, when Peter had asked her to spend more time at the restaurant. "She has a thing for you, Pete, she's carrying a torch like the Statue of Liberty." Peter had told June about Lena's girlfriend by way of assuring June it wasn't true, but June had not been convinced, and although it wouldn't have helped the situation to admit it, Peter knew what she meant. Lena had no romantic designs on Peter; she no more wanted to sleep with him than with any other male cocksucker. Lena's attachment to Peter ran deeper: that of an employee whose boss had given her a chance when nobody else would; that of an almost-partner in a business she cared about more than anything else; that of—if not a friend exactly, then a companion who had worked alongside another in the same pattern for a decade and a half.

Lena began deboning rabbits. "I have right to know," she insisted. "First you are all over town like this," and she lolled out her tongue and crossed her eyes, "running around with skinny whore like lovesick boy. Lena, take charge, you say. Then *toshchaya blyad* is gone and you are like pathetic dog who—"

"Yes, all right," Peter interrupted. "No more about the dog. June is—"

He stopped speaking, even as he continued shaking sea salt over the croutons, because he wasn't quite sure how to finish the sentence. June is angry with me? June is gone? June is in the capital, protesting the Vietnam War? June is devastated? So many times that week Peter had intended to call her, had found himself with the office phone receiver in his hand, his finger in the dial, or standing in a phone booth, putting a dime in the slot. But then he—couldn't. Something came over him, an apathy, an exhaustion like a suit of lead, and he hung up the phone and walked away.

"She is *beremennaya*," said Lena and cupped a hand in the air over her stomach. "Knocked up."

Peter was astonished. "How did you know?"

Lena shrugged. "She is whore, like all models. Open her legs enough, get knocked up. Is math."

"Lena!" Peter roared.

Lena began dicing the rabbits for stew—poor hairless creatures, Peter could not watch. "Is little bastard yours?"

Peter sighed. He slid the trays of croutons into the oven and stood suddenly at a loss. "Yes," he said.

"At least she tells you this."

"And I believe her. June's no liar."

Lena shrugged philosophically. "She will have abortion?"

"I don't know."

"What, you don't know?"

"I haven't talked to her."

Lena nodded. "This is smart. You avoid her. She wants marriage?"

"I don't know," said Peter.

"She wants husband," said Lena. "All skinny whores want husband. But this way you don't get tied down."

"That's not it at all," said Peter. "I've been meaning to propose to her for months."

Lena slid him a sly look. "But you don't."

Peter shook his head, not in negation but confusion. "I need to start the pea soup."

"Why don't you ask?"

"I don't know."

"I don't know, I don't know," Lena said. "This is little-boy answer."

"Go fuck yourself, Lena," Peter said in her language. Lena laughed.

"I think you are little boy," she said. "I think you want to marry skinny whore. Is this good idea? No. Will she bring nothing but trouble? Yes. But you make baby, you take care of baby. One way or another. Coat hanger or wedding. Enough bastards in world already."

Peter balled his hands before he could seize the nearest object—a meat pounder, a frying pan—and strike Lena with it. He had never hit a woman before, but this seemed like the perfect opportunity. He stood wrestling with his temper while Lena serenely tournéed potatoes and carrots for the stew. He had known her for fifteen years, since her twenties; she had been with him when he first opened the restaurant as Masha's. She had been a prep chef then; there had been no question of putting Lena anywhere near the front of the house, as a waitress or even a busser, where she would terrorize the customers. Lena didn't want that anyway; according to her, waitresses, hostesses, and coat girls were also whores. She had requested to cook from the start, and Peter had hired her even though it was extremely rare for a woman to work in a professional kitchen as anything other than a pastry chef. For one thing, his other staff had not immediately realized that Lena, who threw anyone who offended her up against a wall to dry-hump him, was a woman in the first place. For another, her knife skills were unparalleled—in this way, if no other, she had reminded Peter of Masha. And there was the moment, during her audition, when Peter had requested Lena make beef Bourguignon, that she rolled up her sleeves and he saw the row of crooked green numbers on her skin. "What?" she had said, when she'd caught him looking. "I was political prisoner in Nazi camp," and she had spit in the sink. "You have problem with this?" No, not at all, Peter had said. It was the only moment in all his time in America that he almost unbuttoned his cuff of his own volition to expose his own tattoo. Almost.

Lena had been his right arm for all these years, and she could say things to him that nobody else could—not Sol, Ruth, or June. In fact, Peter had told Lena about Sol, and Lena had said, *"Da,* Jewish mafia, big deal. If were Russian mob, then you worry." Peter had still not cut ties with Sol. He suddenly found his own inertia, Lena, and even his beloved kitchen intolerable. He threw down his rag on the cutting board.

"Watch the croutons," he said. "I'm going for a walk."

*

One of the best things about Masha's Upper East Side location— which Peter would not have chosen had he not inherited the restaurant; he would have preferred the West Fifties, near the theaters and Carnegie Hall—was its proximity to Carl Schurz Park. It was three blocks south and three east, at Eighty-Sixth and East End Avenue, and many were the restless hours Peter had spent there, pacing along the East River, admiring the Triborough Bridge and absently petting the heads of amorous dogs. In his English classes, one of his more demanding instructors had assigned *Moby-Dick,* and in Carl Schurz Park he always thought of the passage about the calming effects of being near water. He also often thought of the novel's final epigraph: *And I only am escaped alone to tell thee.*

Today he quickly found a bench and sat, mopping his face and neck with the sleeve of his chef's whites—his handkerchiefs, like his street clothes, were back at Masha's. The morning was not hot, but it was damp, the sun a distant silver coin trying to break through the fog, gulls wheeling and crying over the river, the air smelling of diesel and fish, pedestrians passing with coffee, white paper bags, and dogs, each encapsulated in his own early morning thoughts. Peter watched the barges pushed by stalwart tugs, the water lapping at Roosevelt Island and its salt-shaker lighthouse. In the early days, Peter had sometimes wondered how hard it would be to scale the fence, with its sharp iron points, but then he had realized the drop here was not very steep, and probably the worst thing that could happen to a person who jumped into the East River from Carl Schurz Park would be some foul skin disease from the polluted water. Now he knotted his hands and leaned forward, as if in doing so he could see past the river, island, and the bridge all the way to the Atlantic and the continent he had left behind.

Lena was quite right: he was being a coward. But Peter had always been a coward; he had always known that about himself. It was his worst, most damning trait, the one that defined him, the secret at his core he tried and tried to keep hidden but that inevitably surfaced, time and time again. It was his inability to act, his paralysis in crucial situations. His inability to jump. To cut. To call. To decide. To keep his family safe. To leave Germany while there was still time. For of course, Peter had had ample warning of what could happen. His own father had told him. His father had worked with Sol to get Jews out by any means possible, first legal—before the Night of the Broken Glass—and then illegal. That was why the Nazis had sent Avram to Buchenwald in 1941. That was why Peter's mother had been detained and had caught her fatal flu in the detention center. That was why Peter had the constant argument with Masha that reminded him of the physics conundrum about the unstoppable force meeting the immovable object: they had to get out, she said. It was too dangerous, he said. They had to leave. They had to stay. Over and over and around and around, Masha suggesting ridiculous things like alternate identities, hiding in attics, in church basements, hiking over the Alps at night. You sound like a spy novel! Peter retorted. This insanity will end; the outside world will realize what's going on and put a stop to it. Besides, the girls, Peter said, pointing to the newborns sleeping in their laundry basket, the infants in the cradle he had fashioned from a crate and discarded rocking chair, the toddlers in their parents' bed. The girls, the girls, what about the girls?

In the end, what happened was very like the roundup dream, except without the alternate conclusions Peter's mind kept trying to write for it. Peter and the twins were rounded up in what was now known as the Fabrikaktion of 1943. They had been taken in a truck to one of many processing camps, theirs at the Clou Concert Hall—several thousand people crammed into a space meant to hold a few hundred. Masha had come running from the Adlon's kitchen, still in her whites, a sympathetic supplier having alerted her to what had happened. By some miracle, she had managed to find them in the melee—that was one thing the dream got right, the miracle of Masha locating them amid all those people. Peter had scolded her as they stood together huddled and crying, their arms interlaced around their children, a tiny buoy in a heaving, wailing human sea. "You should not have come," he said over and over, kissing Masha's cold wet face. "Foolish Mashi, brave Mashi! You can't stay. You must go. Go now. Go."

"And leave you?" she said. "Never."

"At least all these other people keep us warm," said Peter, trying to smile. "Mashi, please. Go. Get the papers from Dietrich—"

"It's too late for that," said Masha, "don't you see? Can't you see that, Petel? There are thousands and thousands of people here."

She stood on tiptoe, then jumped, trying to get a view over the hats and kerchiefs and shoulders and bare heads. "Sorry," she said to an old woman whose foot she trod on; the lady just looked at her with the befuddlement Peter had seen on air raid survivors. Masha put her hands over her face.

"It's hopeless," she said, "it's all over," and she cried very hard for a minute. Peter comforted her as best he could by pressing his body against hers—his hands holding both girls against him by their bony little bottoms.

"Shhh, Mashi," he said, "we're together, we'll be all right. . . . Shhh."

As abruptly as she had started, Masha stopped crying.

"Stay with them," she said, "I'll be right back," and before Peter could stop her, she began eeling her way through the crowd.

"Mamaaaaaaa!" wailed Vivian, "where's Mama going? Mama!" Her outrage woke Gigi, who was too weak to match her sister's sobs but keened in Peter's other ear.

"Shhh, girls," said Peter. "Mama will be right back."

A woman next to him—about Masha's age, nursing an infant—gave him a half pitying, half scornful look, and for the first time Peter thought: But maybe she won't. Despite the crush of people, he felt as though he were falling.

"Shall we sing, girls?" he asked. "What shall we sing?"

Vivian patted Peter's cheek and said, "Sing you, Papa. Sing you."

She meant *Peter and the Wolf*, Prokofiev's children's composition, which both girls thought had been written about Peter—they loved the musical story of the hero boy vanquishing the wolf. Peter whistled the opening bars of their favorite part, when the menace had been captured: "And off they started to the zoo!" he began.

Vivi recited with him: "Now just imagine the triumphant procession! Of course, Peter was at the head . . ." They had sung their way to Grandfather and the cat, Peter and Vivi saying in the deep Grandfather voice, "And what if Peter hadn't caught the wolf? What then, eh?" when Masha did come back, pushing her way through, an all-white apparition with her pale skin and hair and chef's jacket, except for her red and streaming nose.

"Good news," she said, "they're processing Aryans and *Geltungs-juden* at another center, at Rosen Street. All we have to do is get to a guard and show our papers to prove we're married. They'll take us over there straight away."

"Is that true?" said someone nearby, and "If you're Aryan? If you're married to an Aryan?"

"That's what I heard," said Masha.

The breastfeeding woman, whose armband over her shearling

coat bore the Star, smirked. "A fat lot of good that does most of us," she said.

Masha gave the woman a look of great sympathy. "Courage," she said. Then she took Vivi from Peter and said, "Come, girls."

"Papaaaaaa," cried Vivian, "I want Papa," and she lunged toward Peter. "I want Papa! I want more Peter! I want to go home!"

"I know, sweet love," said Masha. She took Peter's arm and kissed Ginger's forehead, then recoiled in alarm. Gigi was lying with her head on Peter's shoulder, her eyes glazed with fever, her thumb sliding listlessly out of her mouth.

"Pete, she's burning up," said Masha. "We have to do something."

"Hold the girls," he offered, "I'll take off my shirt and put it over her."

"Don't be silly," said Masha, "you'll catch your death." She was right; it was February, ice and frozen mud treacherous beneath their feet, their terrified breath puffing with thousands of others' into the air. Masha stood on tiptoe and looked around.

"See there," she said, "that older lady? She looks like she might not put up much of a fight. See if you can get that fur hat off her."

"Mashi! I can't do that."

"We have to do something."

"But not that. Here. I'll put Gigi beneath my coat—"

Masha made an impatient noise. "That won't be enough. I know how you feel, but it could mean Gigi's life against some stranger's, somebody who might not last very long anyway, I'm sorry to say . . . I'll be right back."

"No," said Peter, "Mashi, stay! I'll do it."

But Masha had already let go of his sleeve and was sliding through the crowd toward her target, a drooping woman who did indeed look as though she might expire at any moment. Masha crept up behind her and tweaked the woman's hat off her head, and she was turning triumphantly to Peter when there was an outcry on the far side of the square. It was a jumper: a woman who plunged from a top window straight as an arrow, feet pointed earthward and arms at her sides, her skirt flying up around her.

"Masha!" Peter yelled. "Stay put."

He began battering his way toward her, clamping Ginger's hot damp head to his shoulder. "Don't look, baby," he panted, although Ginger was unconscious. "Don't look." He felt a spreading warm wetness on his side as Ginger's bladder let go.

"Masha!"

More screams and shouts, and Peter knew there must be another suicide. He focused with all his might on the flash of Masha's white coat, on shoving toward her through the crowd. But panic seized the detainees, and it was as though Peter's feet were thrown off the ground by an earthquake. With everyone around him pushing and screaming—mouths wide open, spit stretching from teeth, sour breath, a crush of wool, outstretched hands—Peter lost sight of his wife. More frightening still, somebody shoved Peter so hard he and Gigi almost went flying; he clung to his little girl, trying desperately to keep his footing and not get trampled.

"Come, baby," he panted; her head lolled, her eyes were rolled up; had she had a seizure? "Let's find Mama."

There were gunshots. More screaming. "Halt," said the loudspeaker. "Stay where you are."

Peter saw Masha about a dozen people away. She caught sight of him at the same time. She waved the fur hat.

"Masha!" he shouted.

"I'll see you . . . Rosen Street!" she called.

"Papa," called Vivi, and Peter saw a wink of her hand in the weak winter sun, and then the throng surged over them.

"No," Peter screamed. "Masha!" He began thrashing through the wall of backs, shoulders, bodies. But that was when the guards started separating the crowd, wading in and using their rifle butts and whip handles, and Peter went flying. He overbalanced, hit the ground on his back, and lost his grip on Ginger—one minute he had her gripped to his side for dear life, and the next she was gone.

Peter got to his knees, peering through a forest of shoes and pant legs and skirts. This couldn't be happening. She had been with him! He had been holding her! How could she be gone so quickly! She had to be here. She couldn't be more than a meter away. Two at most.

"Gigi!"

He crawled. Which direction had she gone? She was wearing a pink nightgown. Only a pink nightgown. He saw boots and cuffs. Somebody stepped on his right hand, a woman's sharp heel, piercing deep into the skin between the veins. The shoe's owner was shoved and she fell and Peter's hand was freed. He scrambled forward on the icy cobbles.

"Gigi!" he screamed. "Gigi!"

He pulled himself up using the nearest man. "My little girl, have you seen her?"

The man stared past him, walleyed with fear. The guards were getting closer. "Gigi!" Peter yelled. "Gigi! Has anyone seen a little girl?"

He flailed in every direction. Everywhere a wall of strangers. Peter was crying. "Gigi! Gigi!"

He staggered up against a guard, an impassive young man in uniform and helmet. "I lost my daughter—Gigi—she's Aryan—please help me, I lost my little girl!"

The guard looked at Peter's hand on his sleeve and shook it off with a grimace. "Everyone's Aryan today," he said, and hit Peter across the face with his baton.

By the time Peter came to, he was indeed at Rosen Street—how he got there, he did not remember. He did not remember the people who had picked him up and found his papers and shown somebody in charge that he was *Geltungsjuden*—married to an Aryan. Peter was duly processed and sent to the work camp for such privileged Jews:

Theresienstadt. But there were so many people at the Clou Concert Hall that day, and at Oranienburg and Grosse Hamburger Strasse and the Putlitz train station; regrettably, given the scope of the Fabrikaktion, the processing wasn't as efficient as it might have been and mistakes were made, so that while Peter was transferred to Rosen Street, Masha and Vivian were sent with another transport of full-blooded Jews to Oranienburg, then to Putlitz, where their train took them to Auschwitz. No record of Ginger Rashkin, age three, was ever found.

*

When Peter left Carl Schurz Park, he didn't have a plan in mind, but as his feet carried him automatically back toward Masha's, one started to grow. Instead of returning to the restaurant, he hailed a cab; he was halfway downtown before he realized he was still in his chef's whites. But that didn't matter. This would either work on first sight or not at all. Peter asked the cabbie to stop near the Washington Square Arch, where a blind man was selling carnations from a plastic bucket; when they reached Minetta Lane, Peter asked the driver if he minded waiting.

"Whatever, man, it's your dime," the cabbie said.

Peter stood in the quiet winding street outside the little beige three-story building with its neat black shutters that reminded him of a doll's house. He checked his watch: it was 8:30 a.m. No wonder there were no signs of life at 16 Minetta Lane; its inhabitants were its owners, two Broadway performers known for their tap-dancing abilities and very loud arguments; three stewardesses on the second floor; and, in the top-floor apartment, an aspiring opera singer and June. Not an early riser among them. Peter felt bad disturbing them, but it couldn't be helped: he had no key. He rang the doorbell marked DAHL/BOUQUET. Nothing happened.

He waited a polite interval and tried again, then, wincing,

pressed all the bells. Finally the door buzzed and he pushed it open. "Is that you, Sven?" said a man waspishly from the front hall. "You'd better have some Alka-Seltzer and a damned good explanation."

"I'm sorry, Michael, it's only me," said Peter. He held up his carnations in a salute and Michael, in a kimono and green face mask, looked him over and sniffed.

"Bring roses next time, lover," he said and slammed his door.

Peter climbed the spiral staircase to the top floor and knocked. "Hold on," a woman's voice said—not June's. Peter gazed out the rear window at the garden as he waited: a little pocket hideaway with brick walls, soda-fountain table and chairs, slender willow weeping into a pond presided over by a stone Lorelei and presumably containing koi—or doomed sailors lured by her voice. Over the Village rooftops the sun was still fighting the mist.

The door opened and June's roommate Dawn squinted at him with some irritation. She was a tiny woman with shoulder-length chestnut hair, now bound up in curlers, her eyes the same bright blue as her robe. She was from Minneapolis, June had told him— the Minnesota connection—and was studying at Juilliard; she's very good, June had said, although Peter had doubts about a big voice emerging from such a diminutive body; he had always thought sopranos were meant to look more Wagnerian.

"She's not here," Dawn said. "But nice flowers. Tea?"

"Please," said Peter.

He followed Dawn in and stood in the center of the room as Dawn, yawning, lifted the carnations from him to put them in the sink, then lit the kettle and opened cupboards to assemble mugs, sugar, honey. Peter had been here only twice before, both times at night; because June shared the apartment, it had always made more sense for them to stay at Peter's. During his last visit Sven and Michael had been having people, which translated into a night-long carnival that spilled into the street. Now Peter admired the peaceful light pouring through the skylights, the purple-painted brick fireplace and the slanted honey-colored floors. The bathtub was beneath the skylights, towels slung over the saddle of a carousel horse standing next to it. On the walls were framed playbills of Dawn's plays, covers of June's magazines.

"Do you take milk?" Dawn asked. "Lemon, sugar?"

"Just sugar, please," said Peter.

She gestured to the purple velvet couch, salvaged, June had said, from an off-Broadway production of *A Streetcar Named Desire*. Peter sat. Dawn curled against the arm, tucking her bare feet beneath her like a cat.

"Forgive my speaking quietly," she said, "I have to conserve my voice."

"Understood," said Peter and accepted his tea. But he couldn't drink.

"Is she on a shoot?" he asked. "Please tell me she's on a shoot."

Dawn surveyed him over the lip of her mug as she blew and sipped.

"Do you know," Peter began.

"I know about the baby."

"Do you know if she . . ."

"She hasn't decided yet," said Dawn.

"Thank God," said Peter. He set his mug on the floor.

"She'll have to do it soon, though," said Dawn. "Otherwise it'll be too late. She said she'd take this trip to think about it, and if she decided not to have it, she'd go straight to Mexico."

Peter stood up. "Where is she now?"

"I don't know if I should tell you," Dawn said. "You hurt her pretty badly."

"Please," said Peter.

Dawn examined him, her blue eyes frank and suspicious. "Hawaii. Honolulu. The shoot's for *Cosmo*. They'll be there two more days."

"Thank you," said Peter. "Thank you very much." He started for the door. Dawn remained on the couch, watching him like a cat, amused and disdainful.

"Good luck," she called.

Peter was relieved to see the cab was still at the curb. "Thought you fell asleep up there, man," said the driver. He was a long-haired college-age kid, maybe a dropout, wearing little glasses and a newsboy's cap; he looked like he might have been having a nap himself.

Peter got in. "Idlewild Airport, please," he said.

"JFK, you mean."

"Yes, right, JFK," Peter said. He had forgotten about the new name.

"Welcome to the future," the driver said and pulled away from the curb.

Peter watched as they made their way through the warren of streets that comprised the Village, passing Washington Square again, then turning onto West Fourth, Bowery, Broadway. He had expected the driver to take the Midtown Tunnel, but they were heading east instead of north. Peter tapped the plastic divider. "Excuse me, why are we going this way?"

"It's faster, man," said the driver. "There's an accident in the tunnel. But I'll go whatever way you want."

"No," said Peter, "the faster the better," and he sat back. The driver turned on the radio, 1010 WINS. It was the top of the hour, nine o'clock: *You give us twenty-two minutes; we'll give you the world.* Peter ran through what lay ahead of him: at the airport he would purchase a ticket for the first flight to Honolulu. Thank goodness June's shoot was in Hawaii rather than Europe; that would have tested Peter's resolve, but he thought he would have gone nonetheless. He must also call Lena and inform her of the trip, ask her to cover for him; he would buy travel clothes and toiletries. Peter patted his pockets and swore: he didn't have the ring. Of course—he was in his checks, and the ring was in his suit trousers back at Masha's. Well, then, he would get another one. Surely they had jewelry stores in Honolulu. The cab circled up the ramp onto the Williamsburg Bridge, passing garbage, graffiti, dark water, the colossal cement columns and rusty girders that held up all the bridges in Peter's adopted city, and as the tires thumped onto the bridge, the sun finally broke through the clouds. Peter watched Manhattan slide away on his left, the other cars and buses and taxis and trucks schooling about them, going about their errands, as he was on his. He might have no business trying to be a husband again, and he certainly had been a failure as a father. The past had proven that. But here Peter was, and whether it was the name of an airport, the trends in cuisine, a decade on a calendar or one's nationality, things kept on changing. Peter knew only that once upon a time, he had let go. He would not let go again.

II

JUNE, 1975

*The thoughtful wife has a simple beverage
(cold in summer, hot in winter) ready for her weary husband when
he comes home at night. The simplest are fruit and vegetable juices
served in small fruit juice glasses.*

—BETTY CROCKER'S NEW PICTURE COOK BOOK

TENNIS LESSONS

The Glenwood Bath and Tennis Club was atop the first and low-est mountain in the Watchung Range in New Jersey, overlook-ing the Eagle Ridge reservation, the town of Glenwood, and, in the distance, New York. It wasn't as ritzy as Glenwood's most exclusive club, the Briars, which didn't allow Jews, but Glenwood Bath and Tennis was fancy enough. To reach it, June Rashkin turned into an unmarked wooded road—if a person didn't know where the en-trance was, she might drive right past it, as June had done when the Rashkins were first accepted. The road wound through stands of birch, pine, and oak growing diagonally from the rock that com-prised the mountain and eventually reached the top, as announced by a brass sign reading, beneath a crossed-tennis-racquet insig-nia: GLENWOOD BATH & TENNIS CLUB, EST. 1924. The parking lot, cleared from the forest, opened to the sky and was bordered on one side by wooden courts caged by chicken wire for paddleball, where June and Peter's five-year-old daughter, Elsbeth, who had tough soles, could be let loose to run even on the hottest days.

The clubhouse was unremarkable, a one-story stucco structure whose timbers and mullioned windows gave it, at least from a distance, the air of an English cottage. Just inside the door, where members and visitors signed in, the check-in desk boasted the club's wares: polo shirts, tennis visors, sweatbands, and wristbands with the club's logo; books of the perforated cardboard tickets used instead of currency. The floors were tile, to handle the water the children tracked in from the pools—the whole place reeked of chlorine. The main eating area beyond the snack bar was a screened-in rotunda with picnic tables. At the very top of the mountain peak, at the end of a gravel path marked with another brass sign that read OVER 18 ONLY! was the adult pool with its terrace and, on clear nights, a spectacular view of the skyline of Manhattan, where the male members worked during the day. By night the adult pool was a place where there were many parties, which invariably ended in shrieking nudity, drunken cannonballs, and regret.

This morning June wasn't anywhere near the adult pool inferno; she was on the other side of the club, standing with two other women in front of Glenwood's clay courts, awaiting the tennis pro. June's husband, Peter, had given her the lessons for her birthday this past week, on June 10—June's thirty-fifth. June had blinked at the certificate, lying next to her cake—angel food, which Peter always made for her because it was low-fat. "Mrs. Peter Rashkin," it read on Glenwood Bath and Tennis stationery; "6 group lessons. Good until August 30th." The handwriting was big and careless, not Peter's spiky bird-track script. "Surprise," Peter had said, smiling at June over the melting wax of her many candles. "Surprise!" Elsbeth had echoed, clambering around the booth; they were in their traditional corner banquette at Peter's restaurant, the Claremont. Peter frowned over his bifocals. "Oh dear, you're not happy," he said. "I thought you might like a change from jewelry."

"No, this is really very original," said June. "Thank you."

"You said you wanted to do something about your feedbags."

June couldn't help laughing. "My saddlebags."

"Yes, those—although I think you are imagining them," said Peter, and then he was summoned to the kitchen because the New Jersey state health inspector had paid a surprise visit. June had waited, feeding her cake to Elsbeth, and waited and waited, and eventually she had slipped the certificate into her purse and taken Elsbeth home alone.

It wasn't that June objected to the lessons, although she'd never had the slightest interest in tennis beyond whacking a couple of balls around on the cracked courts of her hometown in New Heidelberg, long ago in high school, and usually after a couple of boilermakers. It wasn't even that, unlike in Minnesota, here on the East Coast tennis was serious business. June had had to purchase a whole new wardrobe at one of the two establishments Glenwood Bath and Tennis approved: its own pro shop or It's a Racquet!, the sporting goods store downtown in Glenwood Plaza. It was a racket, all right, June thought; $47 later, she owned two dresses, three pairs of bloomers, Tretorns, and seven pairs of socks with colored balls on the ankles—each a different pastel, June supposed for the days of the week. Glenwood Bath and Tennis did not permit women to wear shorts on the court; tennis, like much else in Glenwood, New Jersey, was geared toward the pleasure of the male animal—chauvinistic and ball-heavy. But June didn't mind even that, beyond the principle. It was that the lessons, and Peter's attempt to do something different, reminded June of how much in her life was indeed stagnant. So much left undone, so much more she had wanted to do. Thirty-five: June was officially middle-aged.

The morning was hot and damp, the dew evaporating into mist that steamed around the women's bare legs and beaded in the velvety grass, the hawthorn hedges separating the courts from the pool area, and June's regulation tennis bra—no nipple display permitted on the Glenwood courts, either. Sweat trickled from beneath the fringed edges of June's new shag cut. She'd grown her hair long when she stopped working, but she'd had it all chopped off last week, and she was getting reacquainted with the feeling of sun and wind on her neck. She wiped it with a wristband, then took her pack of Marlboros from her bloomers, where the balls were supposed to go, and lit one.

"Oooooh, smoking near the courts? You're so bad," said Helen Lawatsch, next to June. "Give me a drag."

June passed her the cigarette. She and Helen weren't close friends, exactly, if by friends one meant spending the majority of one's time together and exchanging deep, dark secrets; June hadn't had such a friend since she left New York. But she liked Helen, whom she'd met at Mr. Hatrack's HappyTime Preschool, which both their daughters attended. June and Helen had passed many pleasant hours trading cigarettes and mild complaints while their children urinated in the sandbox and twanged the banjo. The third woman with them, little Liesel Lambert, June barely knew at all, beyond being introduced to her at the club's opening Memorial Day party, where Liesel's husband, Steve Lambert, a bigwig at Ogilvy & Mather, had shamed her by sticking his face into the bosom of one of the waitresses and making an outboard motor sound.

June took her cigarette back from Helen and dragged, although the Marlboro was now ringed with Helen's bright pink lipstick. "Where's the pro?" she asked. "I'm broiling like a pork chop out here."

Helen was staring at the pro shack, from which a man was emerging.

"There he is," she said.

"That can't be the new pro," squeaked Liesel.

All three women stared. Glenwood Bath and Tennis had recently had to hire a new pro to replace their old one, Kevin, when he failed to report for work one day; the official story in the club newsletter was that Kevin had relocated to Florida to help his ailing mother, although his reputation and activity at the club pointed to his caring for much older women in an entirely different way.

"Maybe this guy's ground crew," said June.

"He's huge!" squealed Liesel.

"He's gigantic," said Helen. "Maybe he's Russian?"

June thought of Lena, Peter's former sous-chef—she had been a brute. "I am Igor, tennis giant," said June in a deep Frankenstein voice.

"Shhh, he's coming!" said Liesel.

Igor the tennis giant lumbered up the hill from the shack toward them, twirling a racquet in one hand. He really was freakishly tall, six-six or six-seven, reminding June of the supersize farm boys she'd grown up with. And indeed he was still a boy—from his long hair, held off his forehead by a Björn Borg–type sweatband and the peace sign stickers on his racquet cover, June guessed he was in his early twenties. He also had five-o'clock shadow at eight in the morning, big teardrop-shaped glasses, and a dent above his brow, as if somebody had at one time thrown a soup can at his head.

He stopped in front of the women, legs bulging out of white shorts.

"I could climb that," muttered Helen to June. June swatted Helen's behind with her racquet.

"Morning, ladies," said the giant and smiled. He had very white teeth. "I'm Gregg with two G's, Gregg Santorelli. I'm the new pro."

Liesel adjusted her visor to peer up at him. "I thought tennis players were supposed to be . . ."

They all waited for her to finish her sentence. On a lower court, somebody called, "Forty-love!"

"Supposed to be what?" Gregg the giant said finally.

"Um, smaller," said Liesel, and all the women snickered. "I didn't mean that the way it sounded; I'm sure you're perfectly proportioned," Liesel squeaked and covered her face with her hands. "Oh Lord. Just shoot me."

"No, I dig what you're saying," said Gregg. "A lot of the pros are smaller, more wiry. So as to get around the court more quickly, is that what you meant?"

"Uh-huh, yes," said Liesel, recovering.

Gregg shrugged. "You're right. I'm built more for football than for tennis, but I have one advantage those guys don't. Do you want to guess what it is?"

"I do!" said Helen.

"Control yourself," June told her.

"I have longer arms," said Gregg, and he startled them all by dropping his racquet and pounding on his chest like a gorilla, making *Ooo ooo ooo ahh ahh ahh!* noises.

"I," he said to his stunned audience, "have stupendous reach." He retrieved his racquet from the grass. "My arms are almost twice as long as a regular guy's. You ladies won't be able to put a single ball past me, I guarantee it. Who wants to try me?"

"I do!" said Helen.

"You're hopeless," said June.

"Okay," said Gregg, pointing his racquet at Helen. "You, Mrs. Eager Beaver, get the ball hopper from the pro shack. You two other ladies, please join me on the court."

Helen, pouting, slunk off down the hill. Liesel and June obediently filed past the pro; June thought she saw him smirking, just the slightest purse of the lips, but when she looked back it was gone.

For the next hour, as the sun climbed higher, the giant evaluated their grips—"Shake hands with the racquet!"; demonstrated swing—"Low to high! No, Mrs. Lambert, not a loop. Just straight back—niiiiice and easy," and circled them, analyzing their form. "When you swing," he called, "put your weight on your leading foot. Let me see it! Good, Mrs. Rashkin—you got it," he said to June, who said, "I'm a Ms."

"Sorry, *Ms.* Rashkin." He reached around her and joggled June's right arm—she wanted to yank it away, conscious of how the skin on its underside must be wobbling. "Relax, Ms. R," he said in her ear, and June felt startled by a weird déjà vu. As he tapped her hip to position her leg, then demonstrated the stance himself, June realized what it was: tennis was like modeling. The physical guidance; how the pro was assessing June's body as a tool, a means to an end; how he called out what he wanted her to do and she did it, easily. *A little to the left! Give me more, lift your body. That's it, beautiful, terrific, good girl.* Physical movement was a language June's body had learned very young, forgotten, and was only now, for the first time since she'd had Elsbeth and stopped working, remembering. It was blissful.

She stretched, pivoted, aimed, and ran. They stood at half-court as Gregg lobbed easy shots to them—June hitting them back, the other women into the net. *That's it, Ms. R! Everyone watch her—she's got a natural swing!* When the wire baskets Gregg referred to as the hoppers were empty, they circled the court with them, picking up the balls. June squashed the fuzzy fat orbs up through the mesh without much thought beyond how hot the sun was, like a hot studio lamp, Gregg's deep voice joking with the other girls like a photographer's.

He came up beside her, pinching a ball up between foot and racquet and slipping it into June's hopper. "You're doing really well, Ms. R," he said. "This is your first lesson?" and when June nodded and smiled up at him—it was a rare man she had to tip her head back to see—Gregg said, "Let me guess, you were an athlete in college."

"No college," said June, "but I was a model."

She wondered if he'd recognize her, if he might have seen some of her covers; even today, people sometimes stopped June in the playground, at the supermarket: *Hey, aren't you somebody? Patti Hansen— Cheryl Tiegs?* But of course this guy would have been in diapers when June's career was at its zenith.

He was nodding, though. He said, "I should have known; your form's fantastic. A model, huh?"

"For a while," June said modestly.

"Sure thing, I can see it," he said, peering at her through his big glasses. "An older model now, but still a good one."

And just like that, all the pleasure went out of the day. The sun seemed to dim as though a cloud were passing over it. June wanted to hit the pro with her racquet, to swing it at him and feel it connect. Instead she released the hopper, so her balls went all over the Har-Tru. "Excuse me," she said, "I think I have sunstroke," and she turned and walked off the court.

*

That evening June decided to rearrange the furniture. She had promised Peter she would try to stop; he hated it when he came home late from the Claremont and barked his shins or fell over a chair that hadn't been there that morning. But it was what June did when she felt restless; it soothed her to consider how the perspective could be changed just by moving a couch from one side of a room to another. It made everything look different, if only for a little while.

Tonight she was working on the master bedroom. It was hot— they hadn't gotten around to putting air conditioners in all the rooms in the old house, which had been built in 1910 as a summer retreat for wealthy New Yorkers fleeing the steam and stink of the city. Only the kitchen, so far, had a window unit—Peter had said he needed it for when he was testing recipes, although that made no sense because, aside from cooking lessons with Elsbeth, he did most of his trial runs at the restaurant. June was more of a TV-dinner chef herself, and there was no reason why the kitchen should be comfortable while they sweltered and suffered every night in the bedroom; if June had been able to lift the huge air conditioner, she would have moved it up here and installed it herself. The whole upstairs was about a thousand degrees and equally humid and smelled like hot carpet and old wood, like an attic.

June had taken all the drawers out of the highboy Ruth had

given her when the younger Rashkins moved to New Jersey, when Elsbeth was two. The dresser was solid mahogany, with bow-front drawers and scrolled handles, something that belonged in a house where George Washington might once have slept. It wasn't June's style at all, but she had transformed it with three coats of high-gloss white paint, replacing the handles with Lucite knobs. "My mamele's dresser," Ruth had cried when she saw it; "I barely recognize it!" That's the point, thought June. "I'm sorry, Ruth," she'd said. Now the highboy was extracting revenge on Ruth's behalf; it might have been made of iron for how much it weighed.

June lit a fortifying cigarette, then began pushing the highboy, which lurched grudgingly over the tired maroon carpet. June had thought they'd replace it, but it had turned out that starting a new restaurant, even in the suburbs, was much more expensive than she had known. Most people were house-poor; the Rashkins were Claremont-poor. June strained and shoved and braced her feet, grunting, her goal to position the highboy across from the fireplace, and all the while she was replaying a conversation she'd had that morning with Helen, when Helen found June by the pool after the tennis lesson. "How's the heatstroke?" Helen asked, and June said, "I'm okay, I just needed to get off that court," and Helen said, "Cramps? Do you need a Kotex?" and June said, "No, I don't have my period. I think I have the thirty-five blues." "Oh," said Helen. "Hang on." She left and returned with two Tabs from the snack bar, then sat on the chaise next to June and kicked off her Tretorns and little-balled socks. They drank deeply from the sweating cans. The sun was a blister in a white sky; the kids shouted in the pool, and the sprinklers whirred.

"Helen," June said presently. "Do you ever feel like you're in the wrong life?" Helen had squinted at her beneath her sun visor. "What d'you mean?" she said. June looked out across the blue chlorinated water. "I don't know exactly how to put it, but this isn't what I signed up for. When I left Minnesota, it wasn't to be a wife and mother. I could've stayed there and done that. I was supposed to do something different." "Like what?" said Helen. June shrugged. "I'm not sure," she said. "I always knew modeling wouldn't last forever, so that's not it. Nor travel the world—I'd already done that, for work. Just—something bigger. Something *more*." Helen had wrinkled her nose at June. "You sound like one of those women's libbers," she said. "Well, maybe I am," said June, "though I certainly don't want to burn my bras. I'm thirty-five. I need them." Both women laughed, then sighed. "But don't you just think it's so *boring*?" June burst out. "I love Pete and Elsbeth, don't get me wrong. But every day's the same: you get up, make the bed, cook breakfast, play Candyland, put away the toys, do laundry, go grocery shopping, plan dinner—and none of it matters because you just have to do it all over again the next day. And nobody ever notices. What's the point?" "Unless you don't do it," said Helen. "Then things fall apart pretty fast." "True," said June. Helen sipped the last of her Tab, which rattled in her straw. "I get it," she said. "It's not exactly what I expected, being married to Marvin the Carpet King, having sex once a month—and did you know he never takes his socks off in bed?" "No," said June. She thought: Once a month? Helen nodded. "He has cold feet. Poor circulation. And I sure didn't mean to have three kids in four years. But I'm not like you," she said shyly. "I don't look like you, June. Nobody around here does. If I did, I might have expected my life to be different too. But I'm doing pretty much what I thought I'd do." She'd reached over for the cigarette June had lit, and June handed it to her. They watched smoke float off across the pool.

June had maneuvered the highboy into place and was straining to push the bed into the vacated space when Peter said, "Knock knock," from the doorway. June looked up, strands of damp hair falling out of her bandanna and into her eyes. "What's going on in here?" Peter said, looking at the drawers on the floor, his undershirts and June's scarves spilling out. "It looks like a bomb went off."

"Ha ha," said June, "very funny. Here, help me with this, would you?"

Peter took off his suit jacket and hung it on the doorknob, since his route to the closet was blocked; then he joined June and they pushed in tandem. June could smell the Claremont on her husband's shirt and skin: Thousand Island dressing, pastry, stale cool air—of course the restaurant was fully air-conditioned.

Everything was much easier with two, and soon the bed was in place against the wall. June put her hands on her hips and surveyed the room; now she only needed something to go beneath the windows, and she was done. The wicker chaise from the sun porch, maybe? No—the rocking chair!

"June," said Peter, stepping over the clothes on the floor. "I thought we weren't moving the furniture anymore."

"Sorry," said June. "I just thought with the bed catty-corner from the window, we'd get more of a breeze."

"You may be right," Peter admitted. He removed his trousers and tucked them in the hamper. "It is rather stuffy in here."

"Can we get another air conditioner?" said June. "During Fourth of July sales?"

"We'll see," said Peter. "It depends on this month's figures."

He took off his top shirt as well, then stood in his briefs and undershirt. June knew what he was waiting for: for her to leave the room so he could finish undressing in peace. As if she hadn't seen his scars so many times over the past decade, while Peter was sleeping, glimpses in the shower: the horrible raised white ropes that could still, after so many years, make tears of outrage come to June's eyes.

"Pete," she said, taking her cigarettes from her overalls pocket and lighting one.

"June," he said, coughing and waving at the smoke. "Please, not in the bedroom."

"Sorry," she said and dropped the Marlboro in her Tab can,

where it sizzled as it died. "But I've been meaning to talk to you about something: I want to go back to work."

Peter sat on the side of the bed to remove his socks. He was still very handsome—at fifty-five, Peter was among the older husbands in their circle of friends, but on him age was distinguished rather than diminishing. His hairline was higher than when June had met him, the waves more silver than gold—except at his temples, where there were wings of pure white. He was slender still, and whenever he wasn't in a chef's jacket and checks, he wore suits, charcoal in winter and fall, light gray in summer. If not for his hands, with their encyclopedia of burns and scars—missing fourth fingertip, the deep whorl on the back of the left whose origin June had never learned—he could be mistaken for a diplomat or captain of industry.

"May we have this discussion in the morning?" he said. "It has been a long day."

"Sure," said June, but then, because she knew he'd be gone by five, and she was excited, she continued: "I'm too old for modeling, except maybe catalogs. But I thought maybe a design firm?"

"Design?"

"Home decorating. You know I'm good at it. You've said it yourself—many times."

Peter sighed and rubbed his eyes. "You do have a knack. You've done a beautiful job with this place, on a shoestring, and you transformed the Claremont. But June, we cannot afford it."

June laughed. "That doesn't make sense. If I'm working, I'll bring in money."

"And who will take care of Elsbeth?"

"I'll hire a sitter for her."

Peter raised his eyebrows.

"Oh, for God's sake, Pete, it doesn't have to be Mary Poppins. There're plenty of teenage girls around here who need pocket money."

"And this is whom you would have raise our daughter, some teenybopper?"

"Not raise her," said June. "Just watch her. A couple of days a week." She was losing ground. "I meant only part-time," she said. "To start."

"June," said Peter, "I don't mean to sound dictatorial. Actually, I think it is rather a good idea. But wait until Elsbeth is in school full-time. Then we can reconsider it."

"But that won't be until next year," said June.

"Is that so long?" Peter asked. "Why this rush, this impatience now?"

"Because——," said June, then bit down on the words just in time. She'd been about to say, *Because I'm dying here, Pete*. It was a common enough turn of phrase; June heard it every day: *I'm dying of heat, I'm dying of hunger*. But it was one she could never say to her husband. Not after what he'd been through. Nor could she use the word so many women's magazines did, *unfulfilled*, since to complain about being a wife and mother to a man who'd lost a wife and daughters—it was unthinkable.

"I just want to do something more," she said. "I told you this before we were married."

"I thought you'd grow out of it," Peter said.

June flinched. "And I thought you believed in women working," she snapped. "Masha did, didn't she?"

Peter looked down at his feet—knobby, with yellowing nails.

"Yes," he said evenly. "She did." The subtext being: until she was murdered.

"I'm sorry," said June. "That was below the belt."

Silence thickened in the room. Peter removed his watch, looking around for the little change dish June had given him for their seventh anniversary, the one symbolized by copper and dissatisfaction. Since it was across the room on the bedside table June had not yet moved, he settled for laying the watch on the carpet beside the bed.

"I am very tired," he said.

"Pete—"

"I need to sleep."

He straightened the sheets June's furniture-rearranging had rumpled, then slid in on his side—even with the bed in the new place, Peter stayed on the right. He closed his eyes. After a minute, June left the room, switching off the overhead light.

✳

She went downstairs first to get a cold Tab and secure the house for the night: turning off lamps, making sure windows were closed and doors locked. Ever since the oil crisis and the recession, crime had been spreading up from Newark; muggings and burglaries were rampant, even in Glenwood. Just last week Linda Apple had come home to find a thief running down the sidewalk with one of her best pillowcases filled with silver, jewelry, and a frozen chicken. June checked on Elsbeth next, easing open the door Elsbeth had plastered with rainbow stickers. Her daughter slept on her back as always, hands on her chest like a sarcophagus, the solid little mound of her stomach peeking out from between the top and bottom of her Holly Hobbie pajamas. June made sure Elsbeth was breathing, then set her stuffed animals— Pooh, Piglet, Snoopy, Woodstock, Henry, and EekAMouse!— back in the mysterious order only Elsbeth understood, so Elsbeth would not scream if she woke and found them disarrayed. She was so like Peter in this way, in her neatness and order—and in every way, so much so that if it had been medically possible, June would have thought her child had sprung from her husband's brow without June's aid, like Athena from Zeus. Elsbeth had June's stubborn chin, but otherwise everything about her, from her springy curls to her temper and prodigious appetite—surely these had all come, if not from Peter, then from ancestors on his side of the family, long-dead, nameless, and perhaps murdered but nonetheless responsible for all the traits in her daughter June could not understand.

June kissed Elsbeth, who frowned—even in sleep she preferred her father to her mother, an inclination she'd shown from the first moment she was placed in June's arms in the maternity ward, when Elsbeth had arced her back and screamed so violently June had feared she was having a seizure and thrust her at Peter, in whose embrace she instantly quieted. If June had not miscarried the first child she and Peter had conceived, would that one have been more like her? June backed out, making sure Elsbeth's rainbow night-light was on and the door open a precise half-inch.

She went down the hall to the bathroom and showered, after-ward assessing her face and body for wear as if they were items of clothing. June was lucky, she knew; although she no longer met cover-girl standards, she had no jowls or eyelid sag, only the start of crow's-feet. Her stomach was flat, and her breasts, despite her joke to Helen, needed no support—they'd always been pretty much nonexistent anyway. But there was June's cesarean scar, which looked like a shark bite, and motherhood's graffiti of stretch marks and varicose veins; her thighs, elbows, and upper arms were crepey. June put on a baby-doll nightgown, the coolest she owned, that came just to her crotch, and made a face as she went to the bedroom. Crotch, such a crude word, like something that giant Gregg would say. Why had June used it?

She got into bed next to Peter, who was either asleep or play-ing possum. Like his daughter, Peter was a quiet sleeper—except for occasional and galvanic nightmares. Tonight his chest barely rose and fell. June turned from him, then back. The room was so hot. The silvery light from the window fell across the bed in a way she wasn't used to; normally this would have pleased her, but now it seemed too bright. Her leg brushed Peter's, and June snuggled closer to him despite the heat. Peter didn't move. June rested her lips on his shoulder—he still smelled like restaurant—

and reached down to cup him through his briefs, a soft mass in a cotton hammock.

June slipped her hand under Peter's elastic waistband and squeezed once, twice. Peter murmured and tried to shift away, but his cock responded to her, pulsing happily. June kept squeezing, rhythmically, and when he hardened she slid her hand up and down as well. Peter's body still liked her—it was his head that was the problem. So many times June had wished she could just un-screw it from his shoulders and set it aside. He was leaping in her hand now, his breathing changing—he could no longer pretend he was asleep. Suddenly he rose, flipped June onto her back, pushed up the baby-doll hem, and entered her. He hadn't checked to see if she was ready—but she was. Readiness had also never been June's problem.

She kept her eyes closed to let the sensations mount—but it was as though she'd had novocaine; she knew she wasn't going to get there tonight. She also knew from *Cosmo* and *Mademoiselle* that she was within her rights to demand her satisfaction from Peter, but that wasn't what June wanted, at least not now. What *did* she want? She felt so sad, detached from Peter even while he was in-side her—there was no lonelier feeling in the world. "Open your eyes," she whispered, "look at me," but Peter didn't hear—he was reaching his own climax. One, two, three more thrusts and he was there; he exclaimed something June couldn't make out, relaxed on top of her for a moment, then kissed her cheek and rolled off. Another minute and he was, if June believed his breathing, asleep again. June didn't, but it didn't matter; what did was that she couldn't remember the last time Peter had looked at her when they made love. The early days of their courtship? The first year of their marriage? Maybe June was being overly suspicious; maybe Peter wasn't really thinking of his former wife while making love to his current one. Maybe he was wandering through some inte-rior landscape of his own. But if June knew one thing for sure, it was that she would never access it. There was a door closed in Peter that June could never open, as much as she'd tried; it was in all the things she couldn't say and he couldn't talk about; in memories of atrocity and tenderness June could never comprehend. And somewhere behind that door, they were still trapped too: his poor little girls. And their mother, Masha.

*

On Friday, June went to her first suburban encounter group. She'd known a lot of women who'd attended back in the city, having their consciousness raised on a regular basis; June had tried one with her friend Dominique, in an apartment near the Brooklyn Bridge. June had strongly supported the ideas in theory, but she found the experience to be kind of bullshit: a lot of unshaven people—men and women—sitting around chanting, raising their fists, and talking about sticking it to the Man, then doing mushrooms and LSD and starting a group grope. The apartment had been full of incense and roaches, and when a few of the more sentient women pulled out pocket mirrors to examine their vaginas, June had gotten up and, on the pretext of seeking the bathroom, sneaked out.

She hoped tonight's gathering would be different; the setting certainly was. June had parked her Dodge on a tree-lined street near Glenwood Middle School—not the very best neighborhood, which was Upper Glenwood on Watchung Mountain, but quite respectable. June had gotten the address from a tab she'd torn off the flyer in the A&P—WOMEN: WHAT HAPPENS TO A DREAM DE-FERRED? TIRED OF BEING OPPRESSED? WANT EQUAL RIGHTS? JOIN US FRIDAYS AT 7!—and the house was a white brick colonial, a Negro jockey holding a lantern at the end of the driveway; apparently women's rights didn't necessarily equal black rights. The street was lined with Buicks, Fords, and wood-paneled station wagons.

June traversed the brick walk, skirting a tricycle and skateboard. Taped to the screen door was a handwritten note: "Want your consciousness raised? Join us in the den!" Inside, the house was identical to several others June had visited in Glenwood: dining room to the left, living room on the right, hallway straight ahead to the kitchen. The difference here was that everything was decorated as if the owners had recently returned from safari. The rugs were zebra and leopard; bronze urns bristled with peacock feathers and spears, and there was a snarling rhinoceros head over the living room mantel. June couldn't help frowning—not because she didn't approve of the homeowners' taste, although she didn't; it was that the African vibe was all wrong for a turn-of-the-century colonial. Houses had personalities, June believed, and their decor ought to fit them; otherwise it was like sending a child into the world dressed in the wrong clothes.

She knew the den would be off the living room, and indeed she could hear voices from that direction, a babble of talk and a shout of laughter. Feeling suddenly shy, June tapped on the French door. "Hello?" she said, and a dozen faces turned in her direction. A woman in a denim jumper, rainbow knee socks, and clogs jumped up from a hassock and came over.

"Welcome to the Glenwood consciousness group!" she said, holding out her hands to June, her broad face creased in a smile. Then she stopped and squinted.

"June?" she said. "June Bouquet?"

"Yes," said June, "although it's Rashkin now," and she peered back at the woman, trying to figure out who she was. Then she cried, "Frederica? Frederica Haupt? I don't believe it!" and the two women embraced. When they separated, Frederica held June's arms out from her sides so she could look June up and down.

"You look just the same," she said, "I'd recognize you anywhere. Although the clothes are a little different."

June had worn her paint-spattered decorating overalls as a preventative measure in case of a vaginal exam. "No more micro-minis for this girl," she agreed. "And you! What . . ."

She stopped short of saying "What happened?" and instead said, "What a coincidence!" But Frederica laughed.

"Ten years," she said, "three boys—all with big heads; that's what happens to a girl," and she ran her hands down the front of her dress. June smiled; the Frederica she remembered was a painter, nearly as tall as June herself, with Modigliani eyes, black hair she could sit on, and cheekbones like crescent moons. Now she was zaftig, her hair a frizzy gray halo.

Frederica took June's arm and turned her toward the group. "Friends," she announced, "we have with us tonight a genuine celebrity: June Bouquet—sorry, June Rashkin. She was Bouquet when I knew her, and you might recognize her: she was one of the most famous models in New York when we met, even hotter than Twiggy!"

"Ha, I wish," said June. She gave a little wave. "Hi, everyone."

There was a chorus of *hi*s and *welcome*s; the group was seated around an ottoman, most on the floor, some on folding chairs. Frederica patted the hassock she'd been sitting on, which was tufted with white fur like a woolly mammoth. "Sit, sit," she said. "Wine? Are you hungry? There's some cheese and crackers, and guacamole . . ."

"Wine would be great, thanks," said June.

"So you still don't eat," said Frederica, perching on a couch arm next to June's head. "Which explains why you still look like that and I look like this."

"You look great," said June, twisting her head to smile at Frederica. "Besides, it's what's inside that counts, right?"

"Hear, hear," said a lady on June's right, passing her a glass of white wine. She was older, about June's mother's age, with a severe gray bob and a clipboard. She clicked the top of her ballpoint pen. "Welcome," she said. "Would you like to tell us what brought you here?"

"That's our moderator, Patricia," said Frederica. "She's getting her sociology master's at Glenwood State."

"Oh, terrific," said June. She sipped her wine. "Sorry, I'm a little nervous."

"Take your time," said Patricia.

"Thanks," said June. "I guess I'm here because—well, lots of reasons. But to put it simply, I want to go back to work and my husband has some objections . . ."

She had been looking at her paint-blotched lap while she said this, but now she raised her head and saw, on the far side of the circle in the shadowy corner of the room, the giant Gregg. He was sitting on the floor, between a girl in a *MS!* T-shirt and a lady in a peacock chair who was as tiny as Gregg was huge. He smiled sweetly at June.

"How's the sunstroke?" he said.

June turned to Frederica. "What's he doing here? I thought this was a women's lib group!"

"It is," said Frederica, "but we welcome anyone who supports equal rights, regardless of sex. Why? Is there a problem?"

"*I* don't have a problem," said Gregg. Was it June's imagination, or was he smirking at her? His wiry black hair was loose tonight, his tennis shirt replaced by a dashiki. He tipped his head, smiling a little pursed-lipped smile.

June started to get up. "I'm sorry," she said, "I don't think this is for me." But she felt Frederica's hand on her back again.

"Please," said Frederica, "just give it a chance. I know a man's presence can be threatening, but—"

"He's not threatening," said June furiously, "he's just a big lunker!"

Everyone laughed, and Gregg grinned. He said something to the tiny woman in the peacock chair—she wore big dark square glasses—and she nodded.

"I just told my mom that sounds like something my nonna would say," Gregg said. "She doesn't speak English."

Patricia touched June's hand. "If it's not too uncomfortable for you," she said, "I'd love for you to stay so we can explore this. It's exactly the kind of dynamic we've been talking about: how sexism works both ways. Both gender groups are trying to get stronger by excluding each other, whereas in reality women need all the help they can get."

"Right on," said the girl in the *MS!* T-shirt.

Frederica swung down so she was in June's line of vision. "Will you stay?" she asked, "and help us?" and the group said, "Stay, stay, stay!"

"All right," said June, "but I need more wine."

Everybody cheered, and a mother with a baby attached to her breast in a sling refilled June's glass to the brim.

"So, June, you've told us why you're here," said Patricia. "Your husband doesn't want you to work—which is certainly something we've heard before."

"Boo," said the group, and the *MS!* girl said, "Down with the Man!"

"Yet it occurs to me," said Patricia, turning to Gregg, "that I don't think we've ever asked you. You've been coming to this group regularly for months now, and we welcome you, but we don't know what brings you here."

"That's an easy one," said Gregg, grinning. "None of you libbers wear bras."

He ducked, laughing, as the women threw pillows and balled-up napkins at him, shouting "Pig!" and "Chauvinist!" and "Off with his head!"

"Okay, okay! You win. Boy, you libbers are vicious," Gregg said and rescued a stalk of grapes somebody had thrown before they could get squashed in the rug. "Seriously, I'm here because of her," and he tipped his head toward his tiny mother.

"As her translator?" asked Patricia.

"No, she couldn't care less about any of this stuff. She thinks it's a bunch of baloney—no offense." He said something to his mother, and she raised her hands and replied rapidly in what June thought was probably Italian. Gregg grinned. "Yeah, you don't want to know what she just said. But I brought her because I keep hoping she'll get something out of it—that something will stick. And I started coming because my pop beats the crap out of her. And my gramps did the same thing to my nonna. And I'm tired of it," he said. "I'm so fucking sick and tired of all the macho shit, the dick-swinging—'scuse my French. I saw enough of it in 'Nam. I see it at home. And I'm sick of what it leads to." He stopped for breath, and the room was so quiet June could hear the hiss of the Duraflame in the fireplace. "That's why I'm here," he said. "Fuck the patriarchy. Equal rights for everyone."

The group erupted in cheering and applause, and several of the women leaned over to hug Gregg. The girl in the *MS!* shirt was wiping her eyes; Frederica handed her a napkin off a stack of them that proclaimed, "A Woman's Place Is in the House—and the Senate!" Gregg was smiling, accepting the petting and praise, but when he looked over at June, his face turned serious. He pushed his big glasses back up on his nose with his pointer finger and nodded. June nodded back, then gulped her wine. Through it all Mrs. Santorelli sat upright and unmoving as a queen.

*

The next tennis lesson was the following Monday, and it wasn't until that morning that June decided to go. She had spent the weekend repapering the guest bedroom, using fabric instead of wallpaper—a design innovation she'd read about in *House & Garden*—and it had been a total disaster. The red-and-blue flower-sprigged linen June had chosen at Fabricville did what she'd hoped it would do, refreshed the room without being fussy, but the article hadn't specified that the process would require two people, one to apply the paste and the other to smooth the cloth. June had done it all herself, or rather with Elsbeth's assistance; her daughter had appropriated a length of linen for herself, demanding June sew it into an apron, and then stomped around the room wearing it, chanting, "I'm a princess, look at me! I'm a princess, look at me!" and tracking paste all over the carpet. June clambered up and down a ladder, arms trembling with strain, vacillating between embarrassment at having misread Gregg and anger over what he'd said on the court. So he went to an encounter group—that didn't negate his sexist comment! He was no more feminist than—than Archie Bunker! Probably Gregg was using the encounter group to pick up chicks—like the *MS!* girl, whom June could imagine Gregg balling in the back of some carpeted van. Finally June sat on the gluey carpet and lit a cigarette, staring at her lumpy walls. She was putting way too much thought into this; all this time without adult company, with Peter always at the Claremont, was making her neurotic. Of course she'd go to her lesson, and the hell with what some dumb young tennis pro thought.

Yet by the time June drove up the mountain in her dress and bloomers and socks with the little balls on; by the time she'd signed in and walked Elsbeth to the kiddie pool; by the time she had applied zinc to Elsbeth's nose and wrestled her into her bathing cap—"It hurrrrrrrrrts! It's squeezing my head!"—and given up on persuading her out of her apron—"No, Mommy, I'm a princess!"—by the time June had left her child happily dog-paddling in a foot of water, the apron clinging to her legs, all she wanted to do was go back to bed. The morning was gray and oppressive, and she felt headachy and bloated, as though she were about to get her period. But she'd just finished a week ago. Was it maybe—the onset of the dreaded Change?

June slogged toward the courts with her racquet dragging. She was late; she could hear the balls *thowcking* and the women laughing. A moonball arced high above the hawthorn hedge; "Oh, shoot!" she heard Helen say, and Gregg called like an umpire, "Ooooooout!" June stood watching them scrambling around from the top of the rise, Helen and Liesel the size of Elsbeth's Fisher-Price figures from this distance, and Gregg too—except he of course was a Fisher-Price giant. June turned and moved quickly away, crouching like a grunt in the Vietnam jungle, before they could see her.

She wasn't quite sure what to do with herself after that; there were two moms she somewhat knew on the chairs by the main pool, watching their kids bounce off the diving board, but June wasn't in the mood to make small talk. She waved and went into the snack bar, where a teenager served her a Tab.

June wandered out the back door and onto the path to the adult pool, clutching her greasy waxed paper cup. The sun was trying to break through now, and cicadas whirred in the trees. Past the rhododendrons and big boulders, up up up June went, until she emerged onto the terrace surrounding the adult pool and over-looking the city. She toed off her Tretorns and socks with relief, then carried her Tab to the railing. She looked down: the treetops on the side of the mountain were like broccoli at this height. It was a sheer drop. June wondered, as she sometimes did, what it would be like to step over the railing, hold on to it from the other side, let go—in the same way she sometimes thought when driving that she could, at any time, spin her wheel into oncoming traffic. It was less anything she really wanted to do than the reminder of how close they were to death, inches away, all the time. Her marriage to Peter had taught her that—what had happened to him, his wife, those poor little girls! June could hardly imagine it, although she tried to, often: Peter and Masha and his girls had been going along in their daily lives, business as usual, and suddenly history had tipped them off into the abyss. June ought to be thankful; she should be on her knees each day thanking God for what she had, which was all most women ever wanted: a handsome husband, a house, a healthy child. Safety. And she was grateful. She never forgot.

But.

June lit a cigarette and stared at the skyline. The tallest skyscrapers—the Twin Towers, the needle of the Empire State—

were still hidden by smog, but June could make out the Chrysler and the offices of Midtown. Into that most impressive collection of buildings young June Bouquet had emerged in 1961, alighting from a Greyhound at Port Authority with one suitcase and a hatbox. She had been thrilled not only by the number of people but the way they all knew where they were going—and June was one of them, her arrival a point toward which her life, a conveyor belt, had carried her all along. Gerber Baby in 1942 to Little Miss Dairy Princess, '53, '54, '55; Butter Queen, 1958; modeling auditions in Minneapolis in '61. Now a porter hailed June a cab that she took to the Ford Agency, where a scout had set up her appointment; the booker took one look at June, put her suitcase and hatbox in a locker, and sent her straight to makeup. June's first shoot, for *Vogue*, had been that afternoon. Finally she was on her way.

June drank her lukewarm Tab. Somewhere over there, in Central Park and photographers' studios and Washington Square, all of that was still going on: women were hailing taxis, rushing to bookings with portfolios under their arms, wearing four-inch heels and three-inch hemlines, having their hair sprayed and eyelashes applied and bending forward to drink from straws inserted into cups that assistants held for them, all the better not to muss their lipstick. Over there, too, in the Village, was Parsons School of Design, where women alongside men learned tricks of the trade that June, with her floral wallpaper cloth, could only emulate. She was an amateur, and unless she could convince Peter otherwise or did something drastic, she would remain one. But once upon a time she had been a professional, before her body had tricked her by becoming pregnant, then betrayed her by miscarrying that baby after June and Peter were already wed.

She crushed out her cigarette and turned from the railing. Somebody was coming up the gravel path toward the pool: she could hear footsteps, *crunch crunch crunch*. She cupped her hands around her face and bolted for the nearest shelter, the pool equipment shed:

whether it was a maintenance man or a sunbathing mommy, she didn't want anyone to see her when she'd been crying this way.

The shed was sheet metal, the size of a walk-in closet. June stood in the dark amid the sacks of crushed rock, grass seed, and mulch, trying to calm her breathing. The air was chokingly hot and smelled of fertilizer. Whoever had come up the path was going for a dip; there was a *sploosh!* as a body hit the water, then splashing as whoever-it-was churned back and forth. June waited, wiping her face on her tennis skirt, sweat running like oil down her body.

Suddenly the shed door opened, letting in a glare of light, and Gregg the giant was standing there. He was wearing his ubiquitous tennis headband with goggles and a Speedo; his mountainous body was more padded than June would have thought from looking at him in his clothes, with a belly and a layer of postadolescent flesh his tennis shirts had concealed. He looked as if he were still wearing one; his arms and neck were deeply tanned, but the skin of his stomach and chest was so white and sleekly plump beneath its smattering of black hair that it seemed as if it might, if stroked, squeak.

"I heard a noise," he said, "I thought it was a raccoon."

"They're nocturnal," said June.

Gregg pulled down his goggles. "You're not supposed to be in here."

June was about to make some witty comeback, like, Oh yeah? when Gregg asked, "Are you *crying?*"

"No," said June, "allergies."

"Then the last place you should be is in a shed full of grass seed," Gregg said reasonably. He squinted. "Your face is all swollen. I can get you some ice . . ."

Later June would tell herself she didn't know who started it, or rather that Gregg did, that he came a couple of steps closer and the next thing she knew, she was in his arms. But the truth was that it was June, that without thinking about it, she launched herself at him the same way she had reached the high bar in high school gymnastics: *step step step bounce!* Gregg had to act fast to catch her, to hold her steady as he staggered backward, June's legs locked around his big wet slippery belly and his hands cupping her ass in the ridiculous bloomers. He was clutching her like a bag of groceries or a child, and he walked forward until he could set her on the nearest stack of sacks, which crunched beneath her like rice.

"What the hell, lady," said Gregg, staring at her. He was breathing hard, and his eyes without any lenses turned out to be brandy-colored. Steam rose from his skin.

Then he must have kicked the door shut behind him, because all June remembered after that was how dark it was again in the shed, only sparks of light coming in between the cracks in the walls, and how hot it was and how strongly it smelled like lime and chlorine, and how Gregg had held his hand over her mouth to keep her from making any noise, how hard it was to not be heard by anyone who might have come up the path to the pool, and how unlike anything June had ever known, it was so wet and simple and easy and free.

8

LARCHMONT, 1975

The last Saturday of every month the younger Rashkins visited the senior ones, piling into the Volvo that Sol had given
them when they moved to the suburbs and taking the Garden State
Parkway to the George Washington Bridge to the Cross-Bronx
to the Hutch and, eventually, to Larchmont. Peter drove; he was
always fretful on these Saturdays, though only someone who knew
him as well as June did would be able to tell. Peter in a bad mood
looked much like Peter in a good mood or even at peace: polite,
elegant, contained. Impenetrable. The only signs that he disliked
being away from the Claremont for even a day were his blotting
his forehead with his handkerchief more often than usual and his
shifting in his seat, as though he were sitting on his keys.

June herself usually dreaded going to Larchmont—despite her
best efforts, she knew she was not Sol and Ruth's favorite person,
and vice versa—but today she felt reprieved. She was grateful to
be away from the club—and from Gregg, with whom she had
had three more encounters. One in the men's locker room. One
in Gregg's car, which had proven awkward, since he drove a Pinto.
And one in the wooded no-man's-land near the Club's property

line, up against a chain-link fence that had rattled alarmingly and imprinted June's back with diamonds for the rest of the afternoon. Each episode, irresistible at the time, now had the quality of dream.

June looked at her husband. What had she been thinking? She and Peter had their troubles, but what couple didn't? Was that any reason to risk everything? Peter frowned as he guided the Volvo down the steep, curly off-ramp from the George Washington Bridge; he sweated in the fetid air coming off the Hudson, which flowed so slowly through the bridge's great cement legs that it didn't seem to be moving at all. Beyond Peter's window, a homeless man slept in the dirt; glass glittered on the expressway, testimony to an earlier accident. It was a tough old world—as Peter knew better than anyone. What he had seen and endured! What he had survived! He moved in his seat again to get at his handkerchief, but June used a tissue from her purse to catch the sweat that trickled toward his spade-shaped sideburn, his sole concession to fashion. Peter glanced at her and smiled his thanks, and June vowed that there would be no more calls to the pro shack, no more meetings. If only her dear, square husband was spared knowledge of June's activities, she would find another way to broach the subject of work; she would be an ideal wife from now on.

She lit a cigarette with the Volvo's lighter, and for a change Peter didn't say anything; maybe he was regretting their recent discord, too. "What's up?" she said, for he was still frowning.

Immediately she wished she hadn't asked—because what if Peter knew? Or suspected? Had June said something in her sleep; did she have a bruise in a strange place, smell different; had she somehow given herself away?

But Peter said, to her relief, "Just the usual," then admitted: "I wish we didn't have to go today."

June didn't voice agreement even to show solidarity; she'd learned long ago that while Peter could gripe about his relatives, it was like blond, Jewish, Polish, or Negro jokes: you had to be one of those things to be able to make fun of it.

"It's a bad time to be away from the Claremont," Peter added.

"More than usual?"

"I think Maurice is stealing," Peter said.

"No way," said June, although it didn't surprise her in the least. Maurice, the manager Peter had brought with him to New Jersey, had once been a waiter and then maître d' at Masha's and at the Claremont continued to exude an unctuous Mediterranean charm June had never trusted. Though she did find Maurice much less sinister than Peter's former sous-chef, Lena, who had not made the transition and was now overseeing something called a brigade kitchen on a cruise ship. And good riddance.

"If it's not Maurice, it is somebody on staff," said Peter, "but he is the only one besides me with access to the safe. And the books are badly out of balance."

"That's a drag," said June. "What are you going to do?"

Peter sighed. "Make sure. Set a trap. Leave cash in the office, and if it's gone . . . I'll have to look for somebody else."

June *tsk*ed. Peter slowed to toss a quarter in the Cloisters toll-booth basket and smiled over at her. "It's kind of you to be concerned," he said.

"Sure thing."

The driver behind them honked and shouted, "Move it, buddy!" As Peter pulled forward and cleared the tolls, the guy shot around them—a man with a crazed Afro and huge smoked sunglasses. He gave Peter the finger.

Peter sighed. "Sometimes it seems like the whole world is angry," he said, and then, "I like your outfit today."

"Thank you," said June. It was a silk jumpsuit with bold horizontal stripes of white, orange, and navy blue, the material gossamer and see-through. Originally June had tried it on at Gimbel's with the idea of somebody else appreciating her in it, but she was glad she'd worn it today.

"And your hair," said Peter. "I am happy you cut it. I am not fond of short hair on women as a rule, but it suits you. It reminds me of when we met." He touched June's neck beneath the wispy ends. "Maybe later . . ."

"Daddy!"

Peter rolled his eyes. "Our little contraceptive device is awake," he said, and June laughed. He looked into the rearview mirror at Elsbeth with a mock scowl that was designed to send her into paroxysms of laughter. "Yesssssssssss, Ellie?"

Elsbeth giggled madly. "Daddy, did we pass the Wash Georgington Bridge?"

"The George Washington, Ellie. We did indeed."

"Nooooooo," cried Elsbeth. She drummed her Mary Janes against June's seat. "I wanted to see it!"

"You'll see it tonight, darling, when it's all lit up," said June. Elsbeth gave her a scowl so fierce it was comic, then whipped her face away to stare lovingly at the back of Peter's head.

"Daaaaaaddyyyyyy," she said.

"Yes, Ellie?"

"What time is it?"

"Time to get a watch."

Elsbeth fell over herself, laughing. "Can I have some Nilla wafers?"

"May I," said Peter, "and ask your mother."

"After lunch at Nana and Papa Sol's," said June, "all right?"

"No," said Elsbeth.

She aimed such a kick at the back of June's seat that June was thrown forward.

"Hey," said June, turning. "Do not do that. Do not be wild in the car."

"You shut up," said Elsbeth.

"Hey," said both parents, and Elsbeth started to buck and thrash beneath her seat belt. "I want Nilla wafers," she howled, "I want them now!" and she would not stop wailing even when June told her Peter was going to pull over, and what did Elsbeth think would happen then? Did she want to find out? Did she want a spanking? Did she? June was going to give Elsbeth three seconds to stop behaving like an animal, and then Elsbeth was really going to get it. One . . . two . . . two and a half . . . two and three-quarters . . . Finally June handed her daughter the sleeve of cookies in her purse. It was after lunch somewhere.

✻

When they pulled into the motor court at Larchmont, Ruth was waiting for them on the terrace; she clasped her hands triumphantly over her head in a boxer's salute, then laboriously descended the stone steps. "Hi, you people!" she called. "Hello, dolly," she said to June when she reached her, standing on tiptoe to take June's face in both palms, and June knew she'd have Louis Armstrong in her head for the rest of the day. *You're looking swell, Dolly / it's so nice to have you back where you belong!*

"Hi, Ruth," she said, "don't you look elegant."

"Sha," said Ruth, who was wearing a caftan printed with peacock feathers and a head wrap to match, secured by a turquoise brooch. "I just didn't have time to get to the beauty parlor. And you, what's this you're wearing?" she asked, fingering the silk of June's jumpsuit.

"It's just something I picked up. I thought it'd be nice and cool."

"Glamour puss," said Ruth. She turned to Peter next. "How are you, movie star?"

"Fine, Raquel Welch," he said, bending so she could kiss him. Ruth licked her thumb and swiped at the orange mark her lipstick had left on Peter's cheek; he held up a Claremont shopping bag.

"Some treats," he said, "and the special dessert."

"Ooooh, let me see," said Ruth, and they all peered in at a cake June knew would be yellow with vanilla frosting and strawberry filling, a little quotidian for Peter's taste but Sol's favorite. "Happy 67th, Sol!" was written in cursive across the top—Sol's birthday was really the middle of next week, but they were celebrating today.

"I even brought candles," said Peter, shaking a small box. "How many are we?"

"Not so many," said Ruth, "just us and the Websters from across the lane."

"Great," said Peter, and then the garage door rumbled up in its tracks and Sol boomed from the interior, "Wait'll you see Lionel Webster's new Leica—that thing's got a zoom lens that could shoot Mars. And take a look at this," he added to Peter, rattling the ice in his highball glass—for Sol, the time was always after lunch. "New rod. Top of the line. And lures."

Peter, who didn't care a fig for cameras or fishing, smiled politely and went into the garage nonetheless, and Ruth bent to the back seat of the car. "Sweetheart," she cried, holding her arms out. "Bubbeleh, *shayne madele*, come give Nana a kiss!"

Elsbeth was flattened like a badger against the far door, one of her ponytails undone and her face streaked with drying tears. She shook her head.

"What's going on with her?" Ruth asked June.

"She had a tantrum on the way here," said June. "She's pouting."

Ruth leaned in again. "Bubbie, how would you like a nice glass of fruit punch?"

"No," said Elsbeth. "I'm staying here. I'm baking—I'm a cake in the oven!"

"Oh, for God's sake," said June. "She's doing it for the attention. Just leave her."

"Leave her," said Ruth in horror, "as if she were a dog in a hot

car? Bubbie," she crooned, "I wonder if you know any little girls
who like Pepperidge Farm cookies?"

Elsbeth sat up. "I do," she said.

"Mint Milano? Are they still your favorite?"

"Yes!" said Elsbeth, and just like that she bounced out of the car
past Ruth and her mother and bounded up the stone steps, the taffeta ruffle of her dress, a gift from Ruth, bouncing over her rump
like a duck's tail. "Maaaaarrriaaaaaaa," they heard Elsbeth scream
to the maid, and the screen door banged behind her.

"There you are," said Ruth, "you just have to know how to talk
to her," and she took June's arm. "Come, let me show you what I've
done with the gardens."

Insects chattered in the tall trees as they crossed the grass, the
pool gleaming in the natural bowl of the grounds. The sun beat
down on June's head; her heels sank into the lawn, and she paused,
sitting on the stone lip of a pool into which a waterfall chattered,
to slip her sandals off. June was more interested in the insides of
houses than their outsides; to her, a garden was for vegetables—
like the VE plot her mother Ida still had pictures of from the war.
But June had to admit Ruth and her gardener Yoshi had done
a gorgeous job here, creating a fairyland of Japanese maples and
rhododendrons, mini pagodas and exotic blooms. June had never
met anybody who lived like Sol and Ruth before she came to New
York: people who took several trips a year just for pleasure and
brought back trinkets and treasures; who had season tickets to
the Met, the symphony, and the ballet; who spent their weekends
at museums and art exhibits, when not at their club. "Oh my,"
Ida had whispered, the only time she'd visited Larchmont, for a
hastily arranged get-together after Peter and June's elopement,
so the small families could meet. "It must be true what they say
about Jews: they must have so much money." June had said "Shhh,
Mom!"; since dating Peter, she'd taken much more notice of anti-
Semitic slurs—*Everybody knows Hebes stick with their own kind; I Jewed him*

down good. But she had to agree Sol and Ruth had done beautifully for themselves, all the more impressive since Sol's own father had been, on the Lower East Side, a plumber.

"Tell me, doll," said Ruth, gripping June's elbow for balance as the two drifted toward the pool, the garden tour over. "How are things? How's my Peter?"

"Fine," said June, "busy. You know how he is—always at the restaurant."

Ruth clucked her tongue. "He works too hard. And you? Everything all right? You look a little . . ." She swirled a hand in front of her own face to indicate how June looked. "Something. Are you maybe pregnant?"

"Oh, no," said June, and she must have had a tone because Ruth stopped walking and lowered her big tortoiseshell sunglasses.

"Would that be the worst thing in the world?" she asked.

"Of course not," June said, although it would. She had never told Ruth and Sol, and she had made Peter swear not to disclose it either, that she had almost died having Elsbeth. Elsbeth had been breech, so June had a cesarean, and then she hemorrhaged and they had to pack her uterus, and June's obstetrician told them he didn't recommend having any more children. Fine with me, June had thought; she was still so weak that she was unable to hold infant Elsbeth for more than a minute. Clearly her body was not designed for pregnancy: she had miscarried her first and nearly died with her second. She had been on the pill ever since to make sure.

She was spared further inquisition by Elsbeth charging down the terrace steps and across the lawn, now in her Jantzen one-piece and water wings, her bedraggled fabric apron knotted around her waist. "Not so fast, Bubbie," called Ruth, "you'll give yourself cramps." Elsbeth ignored her and shot toward the pool.

"Mommy," she called, "no bathing cap!" She held her nose and jumped in.

"Oy gevalt," said Ruth, feeling behind her for one of the lawn chairs and lowering herself into it. She patted her chest, smiling and waving as Elsbeth climbed out, raced around to the deep end of the pool, and hurled herself in again. "What's that schmatta she's wearing?"

"That's her princess apron."

"Princesses wear aprons?"

"Tell me about it," said June. "I can't pry it off her. She even wears it to bed."

She readjusted the back of her own lawn chair to a comfortable angle. Ruth called up to the house to ask Maria to bring drinks; the phone, a source of fascination to Elsbeth and, June had to confess, to herself, had been installed in a Plexiglas box strapped to a big oak so Sol could take calls down here by the pool as if he were a Hollywood mogul. "Iced coffee for me and Peter," said Ruth, "mint tea for June, Scotch for Mr. Sol, and extra ice. And maybe some of those purple grapes. Thank you, Maria." She set the phone down. "Hoo," she said, fanning herself from the exertion. Sol and Peter came strolling across the lawn, Peter now in his swim trunks as well.

"Daddy," called Elsbeth, "Papa Sol, watch, watch!" She threw herself in backward and emerged sputtering. "I'm a mermaid princess!"

"You are, snickelfritz," said Sol, "you surely are." He set his highball glass on the cement walk surrounding the pool to adjust the camera around his neck. He was wearing a Guatemalan shirt today, his skin dark as mahogany. The first time Ida met Sol, with his golf tan and crinkly gray hair, she'd whispered to June, "He's colored? I thought you said he was Jewish!"

Peter entered the pool using the steps, his white button-down shirt belling up around his waist. "Come to me," he said to Elsbeth, "let's see your crawl," and Elsbeth swam over, kicking wildly. "Good girl," said Peter. He sank down under the water so Elsbeth could climb on his shoulders, then sounded, spouting water like

a whale. "Are you ready?" Peter asked. Elsbeth shrieked. "One . . .
two . . . ," and he leaned forward and tipped Elsbeth into the water.

"Again!" she said when she bobbed up.

"Beautiful," said Sol, clicking away with his camera. "Beautiful.
Just look at that beautiful, beautiful girl."

He took off his glasses to wipe his eyes, and June saw he was
crying, as he sometimes did when he'd started with the highballs
at breakfast. He had wept during their wedding brunch, too, and
June had known what Ida was thinking without her having to
whisper it: *Goodness, Jews are a sentimental race.* June thought in Sol's
case it was less sentiment than Scotch, but he did have a soft spot
for Elsbeth. "Beautiful," he said again, honking his nose in a big
handkerchief, and aimed his camera.

The maid came with drinks, and she must have misunderstood
Ruth's instructions, for June's mint tea had bourbon in it; it was
more of a julep. June wasn't much of a daytime drinker—it made
her sleepy—but the afternoon was hot, and she drank gratefully.
Sol took more photos and Ruth fanned herself and Peter spun Elsbeth in the pool; the alcohol started working on June, turning her
languid, and the smell of chlorine made her think of Gregg. That
first day by the adult pool when they'd emerged from the shed:
"Where'd you get that?" June had asked, reaching toward but not
quite daring to touch the curious dent above Gregg's brow, "from
Vietnam?" "Nope," he'd said briefly, "my pop." They had both
been soaking wet, the sun amplifying the smell of their sweat from
their exertions in the shed, a sweet musk. Quit it, June told herself
now. Forget him. She lit a cigarette and looked at her husband,
who was balancing Elsbeth with one hand under her belly while
she practiced her butterfly; Peter's shirt, soaked, was transparent,
his hair dark as honey from the water. Peter must have felt June
studying him, because he glanced up and smiled over Elsbeth's
head; he'd had exactly this same expression, June remembered, in
the maternity ward when Elsbeth was born. It was the only time

June had ever seen him look truly content. She toasted him with her julep, then tipped her head back to watch the sun filter white through the trees.

*

The Websters arrived shortly after two, whereupon lunch was served in the solarium. This was a room June coveted, not because of Ruth's indoor garden, which June found a little creepy—all those cacti with their needles and fur—but because of its contemporary design. Ruth had recently had it redecorated, her gift from Sol for her sixty-fifth birthday, and although June was hurt Ruth hadn't consulted her, instead hiring a designer recommended by one of the other wives from Sol's law firm, she admired the result. The black ceramic floor tiles! The wet bar and hi-fi covered in grass cloth to make them blend in; the couch and matching chaise upholstered in orange leather. June took her seat alongside Peter and Elsbeth, across from the Websters, Sol at one end of the table and Ruth at the other, and brushed at a cattail tickling her bare neck. If not for the plants, the room, in June's opinion, would have been perfect.

The Websters made amiable small talk as Maria, creaking around the table in her putty-colored orthopedic shoes, set out the food: deli meats; baskets of challah bread Peter had baked; a tomato and cucumber salad; cold brisket; and the pièce de résistance, a bluefish from the Sound with accompanying dill sauce and its head still on. Elsbeth wailed at the sight of it and buried her face in Peter's side. I'm with you, kid, June thought. In the ten years she'd been coming here, she still hadn't quite gotten used to the food. She'd been raised on peanut butter, canned peas, and Wonder Bread, and her palate hadn't adjusted to dishes like borscht, lox, or the cow tongue the Rashkins favored, with bumps on it. Luckily, she barely ate anything anyway.

"How are you, my dear?" said Lionel Webster. "You look ravishing, as always."

"Thank you, Lionel," said June. She liked the Websters; unlike Sol's art crowd or his buddies with the strange nicknames and mahjongg-obsessed wives, the Websters were small, civilized people, neat as garden gnomes, with matching gray hair and sandals made from recycled tires.

"How are you?" June asked, touching her own throat to indicate the bandage wrapped around Mary Webster's. "Did you have surgery?"

Mary nodded. "Polyps," she rasped.

Lionel smiled at Elsbeth, the expression stretching his pointy white wizard beard. "My, haven't you grown since we last saw you. How old are you now, forty-seven?"

Elsbeth giggled, then scowled. "No," she said. She held up her hand.

"Four fingers and a thumb old?" said Lionel.

"No," Elsbeth said, "I'm five!"

"Ellie, sweet pea," said June, "use your lady voice inside, please."

"Of course she'll use her lady voice," croaked Mary, "she's a real grown-up lady now, aren't you, honey?"

"No," shouted Elsbeth. "I'm a princess!"

"For God's sake," said Sol irritably. "Pipe down over there."

"Sorry," said Peter to the Websters. He whispered to Elsbeth and she kicked her chair legs, but then she started eating a heel of challah Peter had buttered. Peter stroked her curls. "She's had quite a day already," he said. "I think somebody needs a N-A-P."

"I do not," said Elsbeth. She reached for the sugar bowl and poured a pyramid on her tomatoes.

Ruth gasped. "Bubbie, no, what are you doing?"

"It's okay, Ruth, it's a Minnesota custom," said June. "That's how I ate all my tomatoes growing up."

"Isn't that unusual?" said Lionel. "I might try it myself!" He dabbed his tomato in some sugar and proclaimed, "Delicious."

Sol made a gagging noise and picked something out of his mouth. He held it up to the light. "Maria," he bellowed, and the maid came in from the hall. "Fish bone," said Sol, handing it to her. She palmed it without a change of expression and tucked it into her apron pocket.

"So sorry, Mr. Sol," she said. "I can bring you something else?"

"More ice," said Sol, indicating the bucket in the wet bar over his shoulder. Maria picked it up and departed.

"Goddamned woman," said Sol, "in ten years she hasn't learned to debone a fish."

"I have offered over and over to show her how," Peter said.

"In my house men don't do women's work," Sol said.

He bent over his plate again, scooping bluefish flesh onto his fork. June wished she were brave enough to say something—*What exactly is women's work, Sol?*—but she knew it would only cause trouble and upset Peter, so she remained quiet.

"It's so hard to find good help these days," Mary whispered.

"Maria's a good girl," said Ruth. "She's just getting a little forgetful."

Lionel ate some fish, chewing rapidly. "Delicious fish. One of your victims, Sol?"

Sol grunted. "Caught off the Point yesterday. Twelve-pound blue."

"Excellent. And the brisket . . ." He kissed his fingertips. "I believe I recognize one of your signature dishes, sir," he said to Peter, "from your former establishment?"

"Indeed. We served it at Masha's, and we serve it at the Claremont, too."

"Yes, yes. The Claremont. How is life in suburbia treating you?"

"Very well, thank you."

"And business? Still brisk?"

"More or less," said Peter. Napkin tucked into his collar, he was cutting a slice of brisket for Elsbeth. "Summers are typically slow. But we have been doing fine, and we are looking forward to things picking up in the fall."

"Bullshit," said Sol.

They all turned to look at him. "Excuse me?" said Peter.

"I said, bullshit." Sol leveled his knife at Peter. "The books have been off for months now. Somebody's stealing you blind, buddy boy."

Peter took a swallow of iced coffee. "Let's discuss business later."

"Let's discuss it now. It's that schwartze manager of yours, isn't it?"

Peter sighed. "Maurice is Greek, not colored," he said. "And I am not sure that—"

"You'd better get sure," said Sol. "You'd better get sure in a hurry. Because I'm not sinking any more money into a failing business just so some schwartze can line his pockets, understand?"

He glared at Peter, who cut his fish into smaller and smaller triangles. Elsbeth was squirming in her chair, rubbing her eyes and grizzling. Ruth stood.

"I think it's time the princess had her nap," she said.

"I'll take her," said June, starting to get up, but Peter lifted Elsbeth out of her chair. "Go with Nana. Thank you," he said to Ruth.

"My pleasure. Come, Bubbie," and Ruth coaxed Elsbeth from the room.

June had a terrible fish taste in her mouth, although she hadn't eaten any. She was so angry with Sol she couldn't look at him. What right did he have to treat Peter that way? Sol would say he had every right; that because he was Peter's patron, Peter's business was his business. Peter had tried to get out from under Sol's thumb; he attempted to run Masha's on his own when he and June were newly married, but the restaurant had suffered without Sol's cash infusion, and it had never recovered. June knew that without Sol they would be living in Newark, and Elsbeth would be playing amid needles and condoms. Still, just once June wish Peter would tell Sol to shove it.

"What are you up to these days, dear?" Mary rasped. "Besides staying beautiful?"

June forced herself to smile. "A little of this, a little of that."

"Playing tennis at that schmancy club I pay for," said Sol.

"Actually," said June, "I was thinking about going back to work."

She felt Peter's foot press hers beneath the table. She drew hers away.

"How nice," said Mary. "Doing what? Something volunteer?"

"No," said June, "real work. Something that makes money. Like interior design."

"You already have real work," said Sol, "staying home and taking care of my grandchild."

"Right, you mean *my* daughter. And I want to set a better example for her than a mom who's just some Suzy Homemaker."

"Euh," said Sol, "typical women's-lib bullshit." He turned his red-eyed glare on Peter. "What wrong with you? First you can't control your business, and now you can't control your wife?"

"Hey," said June, and Mary said, "Oh dear, I didn't mean to start a ruckus." Peter himself said nothing; he kept eating, as if he hadn't heard. Maybe June should be grateful for her husband's restraint; "I just ignore him," Peter had told June when they were first married, "Sol's bark is far worse than his bite." Peter's greatest strength was his endurance, and God knew he had outlasted worse bullies than Sol. Still, June silently implored him to say something. Get up and walk out, she thought; I will if you will.

But it was Lionel who stood, folding his napkin. "I for one am stuffed," he announced. "Anyone care to join me for a walk?"

*

June did not want to go for a stroll; she wanted to leave. But since this was out of the question for the time being, she went in search of her daughter. While Sol showed the Websters his new darkroom and Peter helped Maria in the kitchen, June checked the guest room, where Elsbeth usually napped when they were here. It was empty but for its single bed and, a recent addition, the big loom on which Ruth was learning to weave her own cloth; June foresaw many beautiful but unwearably itchy sweaters in her future. Next she glanced into Sol's study and then the maid's quarters; finally she came to the end of the hall and the master suite.

If Peter had certain rooms in the house he avoided—he was not a fan of the loom room, for some reason, although June liked its view of the Sound and hunting-scene toile wallpaper—June was not fond of Sol and Ruth's bedroom, with its adjoining bath, which was where June had first learned about the existence of Peter's little girls. Of course, the way this day was going, that was exactly where Ruth and Elsbeth were now; Ruth must have given Elsbeth a bath, to get the chlorine out of her hair. June walked through the bedroom, with its peony-covered walls and twin beds, and was about to tap on the door when she heard her daughter say, "Tell me, Nana, tell me about the little girls."

"What little girls?" said Ruth, but her voice had a singsong that hinted at a ritual, and sure enough Elsbeth chanted, "My sisters, my half sisters, the ones who got deaded."

"Well," said Ruth, and then—"Hold still, Bubbie, Nana can't get your snarls out when you're fidgeting like that."

"Nannnnnnnaaaa," said Elsbeth. "Tell, tell, tell."

"All right, darling," said Ruth. "Once upon a time—"

"—my daddy lived in a faraway place called Germany and was married to a lady named Masha. Right?"

"Right, Bubbie, but who's telling this story?"

"Me," said Elsbeth and giggled. "No, you, Nana, you."

"Very well. Your daddy lived in Germany with a lady named Masha, and they had two beautiful daughters—"

"—who looked like princesses," said Elsbeth. "Let me see, Nana, I want to see."

There was the sound of a drawer sliding open, and Elsbeth breathed, "Ooohhhh."

"Yes, weren't they pretty?"

"Yessssss," said Elsbeth. "Go on, Nana."

"Well, for a while, they all lived together in peace and harmony, but then a very bad man came to power. And his name was—"

"Hitler. *Puh puh puh.*"

"That's right, Bubbie, we always spit when we say his name. *Puh puh puh.*" More energetic spitting. "So this Hitler, who wasn't really a man at all but a kind of *dybbuk*, a demon, took over the land, and he said very bad things about your daddy and his family, about the Jews. He said that they had horns and tails and that they ate little gentile children—can you imagine your daddy doing such a thing?"

"No," said Elsbeth. She sounded awed.

"Of course not," said Ruth. "For a while, your daddy and his wife and your sisters went into hiding like little mice and they survived that way. But one day Hitler's men, the Nazis, found them, and they—"

"—I know, I know," cried Elsbeth. "They took them away. They said 'Come with us, little girls, and you'll go to a special camp with nice showers.' But when they got there, the showers didn't have water in them but gas, and the Nazis put them in there and they got deaded. All except my daddy, because he got away. Right, Nana?"

There was a pause, and then Ruth said, her voice watery, "Yes, Bubbie."

"And then the bad men putted them in special ovens and baked them and eated them all up!"

June flinched. She hadn't realized she had sunk onto the chair next to the bathroom door, nor that she'd been holding her breath—but enough was enough. She rapped firmly on the door.

"Ruth," she said, "it's time for Elsbeth's nap now."

She opened the door. Since June was last in this room, it had been redecorated as well; the walls were all mirrored, so dozens of Junes and Elsbeths and guilty-looking Ruths dwindled into infinity. Elsbeth was sitting on the counter, in the little pink satin robe Ruth kept for her here. She was clutching a silver-framed photo.

"Mommy," she said, "Nana was telling me a story."

"I heard, sweetie pie, but it's time for your nap now."

"Noooo," Elsbeth cried, but she let Ruth help her climb down off the counter, with the aid of her step stool in the shape of a duck.

"I thought she should have a bath," Ruth said, "after being in the pool earlier. Come, Bubbie, Nana will give you a cookie."

She started to lead Elsbeth from the room, but June said, "Ruth. I heard what you were telling her. I don't want you to talk about that anymore with her, you understand?"

Ruth had been avoiding looking at June since she'd come in, but now she said, "She has a right to know about her family."

"We are her family," said June, "Peter and I."

"And Sol and myself."

"Well, of course," said June. "And she knows that. But I don't want you talking about them, or I won't B-R-I-N-G her here anymore. It'll give her nightmares, and you know how Peter feels about it. He refuses to discuss it at all. If he knew what you'd said, he'd be so upset."

Ruth evaded June's eyes and mumbled something.

"Pardon?"

"I said fine."

"Fine, then," said June. "Thank you."

She looked into the bedroom, where Elsbeth was sitting on the carpet, playing with a bowlful of Ruth's beaded necklaces. "Nana," she said, "can I have these?"

"Maybe when you're older," said Ruth. "Let's go get a cookie, shall we?"

When they were gone, June ran cold water on one of Ruth's washcloths and pressed it to her neck, her chest and cheeks. The bathroom was such a luxurious little nest, with its rosy carpet, its mirrored walls, and Ruth's vanity tray of perfume bottles. One would never imagine it to be a place of terrifying revelation. June was about to turn out the light when she noticed, half hidden beneath a hand towel where Elsbeth must have set it, the photo. The only surviving picture of Masha and the girls.

June picked it up, cool and heavy in its ornate frame. She hadn't seen it in years, since Ruth first showed it to her, but she remembered it all too well—sometimes, when she was half-asleep, she saw it still. Peter had had the portrait made and sent to Sol and Ruth in 1941, right before he and Masha and the twins went into hiding; the photographer's name was C. Alsop, and the shoot must have been in a studio, for there were no furnishings, only the velvet chair on which Masha sat. She had a toddler on each knee; in their dirndls, with their spun-sugar hair in looped braids, their light eyes, they might as well have been dolls. Masha was in profile, though whether by her own inclination or the photographer's, June couldn't say; she was gazing up at Peter, her pale hair in a chignon, her equine face alight. And Peter—he stood behind her with a hand possessively on her shoulder, wearing a suit and pencil-line mustache; he stared straight at the camera, handsome and proud and so achingly young.

June traced the photographer's stenciled signature with her fingernail, not daring to touch Peter or Masha or the girls. What courage this young woman—barely out of her teens—had had! To die trying to save her daughters. To have married a Jewish man in the first place, when she knew, she must have known, what the penalty could be. The danger to herself and her girls. Had Masha been horrified to learn she was pregnant? Or had she been ecstatic despite the abysmal timing, the terrible times? Had she been thrilled to bear Peter's children, to produce life at any cost? June stared at Masha's face, permanently turned up to Peter's, telling June nothing—until she heard footsteps coming along the corridor and Maria calling, "Mrs. June, you in there? Mr. Sol wants everyone outside." June slid the photo into a drawer.

*

The Rashkins reassembled on the terrace, where Lionel Webster was fussing with a long-lensed camera on a tripod. June had forgotten about this part of Sol's birthday: the taking of the annual family portrait, which was then used for holiday cards. Sol sat with Ruth on an iron love seat, and Peter stood behind them holding Elsbeth, who was wearing a dress June hadn't seen before: another Ruth special, a white frock frothing with lace. Elsbeth looked like Little Bo Peep, except for her bedraggled fabric apron trailing from her waist.

"Almost there, almost there," said Lionel, teeth clenched around his pipe. He advanced the film in his camera, and as she moved to her place next to Peter in the humid afternoon, June thought how different this was from the shoots of her youth.

Peter was stroking Elsbeth's hair; she was beyond tired now, her head on his shoulder and her thumb in her mouth, a habit she had long outgrown. He put his free arm around June, who stood perfectly straight. How dearly she wished she could share with him what had just happened—but of course she couldn't; telling Peter that Ruth had not only kept the photo but filled Elsbeth's head with what had happened to his lost daughters would be like rubbing salt in his eyes.

"All right?" he murmured.

"Fine," she said.

"I'm sorry about earlier."

"Thank you."

"I owe you."

"Yes," said June, "you do."

She slid a glance sideways at him and saw he was doing the same to her. He smiled wryly. Sol said, "Jesus Christ, what's taking so long?" and Lionel said, "It's this new lens, it's temperamental. But I think we're in focus now. . . . Everybody say Cheese!"

"Cheese," they chorused, and there was a pop and a whine.

"Darn it," said Lionel, "I forgot a new flash cube. One more second, folks."

The Rashkins grumbled and sagged, and as they daubed their perspiration and blew hair out of their faces, June suddenly thought for no reason at all of when Peter came for her in Hawaii, when June had returned to her hotel in Honolulu after their last shoot, laughing with some of the other models, and Peter was waiting in the hotel lobby on a couch. He had risen when he'd seen her, and June was so surprised she'd stopped right inside the revolving door, causing the person behind her to crash into her. Peter had been wearing a rather ill-fitting white linen suit and yellow lei; he was holding a spray of identically colored orchids, and June would never forget the look on his face, equal parts hopeful and wary. He dropped to one knee right there in the Honolulu Continental: "June Bouquet," he said, "will you marry me?" and she put her hand over her mouth and said "Yes, of course!" and everyone, from the other tourists to the reception staff, clapped. They had been married the next day, by a judge at Waikiki City Hall, Peter in the linen suit and June in a lavender minidress and white go-go boots. They both wore leis, and their witnesses were two tourists they'd grabbed off the street; June couldn't remember their names now, but they had been married themselves thirty-seven years, they said, and she and Peter had taken that as a good sign. They all had mai tais afterward at the Pink Palace, and their wedding dinner was a luau pig roasted with pineapple.

June looked at her husband now as he shifted their daughter and murmured to her, his hairline higher, his face tired. How different he was from the man she'd thought he was, the man he'd turned out to be. Was it the same for everyone? Was the magnitude of discrepancy between the person you thought you were marrying and the person you got similar for most couples? Was the barrier in Peter, the territory he kept to himself, the disappointment, the conflict, greater or less for the Rashkins than for, say, Helen and the Carpet King? Or Sol and Ruth, or Lionel and Mary? Peter gave June a sheepish smile. "Almost done, God willing," he murmured, and Sol said, "Stand up straight, everybody, goddamn it," and Lionel Webster said, "Say cake, folks!" and Mary pointed and whispered, "Look!" and they turned to see Maria staggering toward them with Sol's cake on a platter, ablaze with candles. *"Happy birthday to you,"* Ruth started, in her quivering soprano, and they all joined in: *"Happy birthday to you, happy birthday, dear Soooooooool, happy birthday to you! and many moooorrrre,"* and Lionel Webster said, "Three . . . two . . . ," and took the picture.

9

BRIGADOON

By the end of the month, June had started meeting Gregg in motels. They were on Route 23 or 46 or 10, surrounded by diners and car dealers and knockoff furniture outlets, motor lodges where the carpets smelled like mildew and payment was accepted by the hour. June was afraid to take her shoes off in the rooms or guess what might be in the bedspreads. But they were places where nobody she knew would go and safer than their other assignation sites: parking lots, the Watchung Reservation woods, and, once, beneath the paddleball courts at the club, where Gregg spread a sleeping bag and a ball-chasing child almost found them. Also, the no-tell motels, which June despised, were a form of punishment.

Today's was called the Pilgrim, although the only sign of those intrepid travelers was a peeling sign in the shape of a buckled hat out front. It was nearly three, which meant that June had to get home in an hour and pay the sitter, little Barbie Ryan from down the street. June had told Barbie that Elsbeth was getting over an ear infection, which was why June was keeping her home from the club today, away from the pool. Had Barbie believed her? Had June explained too much? She wasn't used to subterfuge, and she wasn't very good at it. It wasn't a skill she wanted to perfect.

She lit a cigarette and sat cross-legged on the sheets, watching Gregg nap. After sex he fell asleep instantly, like a child—which of course he was, although not as young as June had feared. She had sneaked a peek at his driver's license while he was showering one afternoon, and he was twenty-seven. Eight years younger than June, which made Gregg almost a more suitable match for June, chronologically, than Peter with his nineteen years' seniority. Almost.

It didn't matter. It wouldn't last. Every time June did this, she swore it was the final time—until the next. It was like eating chocolate, which June never, ever did, because she knew if she took one bite, allowed even one dark square into her mouth to melt, she would not be able to stop. And if Peter was marzipan, an interesting taste June enjoyed, Gregg was a jumbo Hershey bar. Time would take care of it, June told herself; if she was too weak to break it off, the club's courts would be closed in fall, and Gregg would do—whatever pros did in winter, probably go south to teach in warmer climes, and June could do . . . what? Make amends to Peter for the damage he didn't know she'd wreaked; figure out what to do with her life. But no. She couldn't wait that long. She'd have to tell Gregg today. This afternoon. No more. It was over. June screwed her cigarette out decisively in the Pilgrim ashtray.

"Stop looking at me," Gregg said without opening his eyes.

"I'm not looking at you."

"Yes, you are. I can feel it."

He bolted up without warning, seizing June's ankles and pulling her onto her back.

"It's rude to stare at people when they're sleeping," he said, licking her neck. "Don't you know that?"

"I wasn't," she said breathlessly. "Conceited."

Gregg kissed her—June had forgotten how delicious kissing

could be—and then just as suddenly as he'd sat up, he flopped onto his back, tugging June on top of him. He took her hips and slid her against his hard-on.

"You're sopping," he said and smiled. "I love that. Do your worst."

This was the thing: it was wrong, of course; it was morally reprehensible; it was no answer to a marriage's problems—but Gregg talked. "Oh, June," he said. "That's it. You're almost there. Oh, God, yes." Yes, he was young, and his skin had that lovely satiny rubbery bounce-back quality—somehow he had managed to survive his tours of duty without a single shrapnel mark. He was giant, his legs like tree trunks and his cock a huge purple club—with a little freckle June had discovered at the base, like a secret friend. Gregg was the only man next to whom June had ever felt dainty. Most importantly, he didn't shut her out. He told June what she felt like to him, and what he wanted to do to her, and he kept his eyes open until the very end. Sometimes even then. He was there. "I love watching you," he'd say. "Do you know your face flushes when you're about to come? Like right now. Oh yes. I can tell. Do it, June. Come for me."

When they were done—when June had ridden him until she was soaked and shaking and Gregg had made sure she was satisfied, then flipped her over and held her ankles up like wheelbarrow handles and thrust into her until he roared—after this, he collapsed on his back with June's feet still locked around his neck, which was sweet but a little awkward. She withdrew them, and they both lay getting their wind back. June reached for her cigarettes and checked her watch: 3:30. She had a half hour left.

"That's so bad for you," said Gregg of June's Marlboro. "It'll kill your wind."

"That's okay," June said, "I don't think I'll be Chris Evert anytime soon—hey, you hypocrite!" and she laughed, because Gregg had taken a baggie from the pocket of his tennis shorts and was rolling a joint. He did it quickly, methodically, and expertly, producing a reefer the size of a lollipop stick.

"Ladies first," he said, offering it to June, but she shook her head. Gregg lit it with a Zippo, punched the thin pillows into shape, and lay back.

"You don't turn on?" he asked.

"I used to, sometimes," said June. "Not anymore."

"How come? Your old man doesn't like it?"

"Not really," said June. That was true; the one time Peter had smoked hashish, with June and some of her friends at Electric Circus, he had had a bad reaction to it; he'd gotten severe leg cramps, and of course because June and the other models were high, it was the funniest thing they'd ever seen. Peter hopping first on one leg, then the other, swearing in German! Or maybe it had been Russian. Whatever language it was, it had been energetic. Poor Peter. He never smoked again, and June abstained partly to keep him company but mostly to keep her figure. Pot in any form gave her terrible munchies; the last time she indulged, in the laundry room of their East Ninety-Sixth Street building while Elsbeth was napping, June had eaten a whole jar of peanut butter, scooping it into her mouth with Elsbeth's zwieback biscuits. She just couldn't afford that kind of thing.

"Your old man strikes me as kind of square," said Gregg ruminatively. He was following the path of the smoke straight up toward the ceiling, where it then got tangled in the fan.

"Oh, really?" said June tartly. "You've met him?"

"No," said Gregg, unoffended, "but I think I've seen him at the club. Tall blond guy, a little older—always wears a suit and tie, right?"

June nodded. Gregg squinted one eye, then the other. "Never takes off his shirt, even on the hottest days. Real formal. Establishment type."

June reached for the joint after all and took a small toke. What the hell—there was no food in this awful place, and her appetite would wear off by the time she got home.

"That's not why he keeps his shirt on," she said, her voice squeaky from holding in the smoke.

Gregg turned on his side to look at her. His hair, unleashed from its rawhide and tennis headband, was a wild black electrical tangle. "Why is it, then?"

June released her breath. "It's because of his scars."

"What scars?"

"From the war."

Gregg sat up. "He was in 'Nam?" he said. "No way. He must be at least fifty—what was he, an admiral or something?"

"Not your war," June said. "World War II."

She got up and went to the mirror over the sink. "I look like *A Clockwork Orange*," she said, running water.

"Atlantic or Pacific?" Gregg persisted.

June looked at him over her shoulder. "What?"

"Where did he fight?" Gregg clarified.

June drew a washcloth under her eyes to get rid of the pooled mascara there, then reapplied it. "He didn't. He was in the camps."

"He's Jewish?" Gregg said.

"Yes."

"I never would have known."

June glanced at him again as she rubbed in some blusher. "And how would you know a thing like that?"

"I don't know," said Gregg. "My pop always said Jews had a look."

"That's what I heard growing up too," said June, "but it isn't true. If you go by stereotypes, Peter's the least Jewish-looking guy I've ever seen. And his wife and little girls looked like Alice in Wonderland, but they still all went to the camps."

"What? Oh no. Really?"

"Yes, there was some mixup, and . . . I really don't know much more," she said. "He never talks about it. Everything I know, I know from his cousin's wife."

"Wow," said Gregg. "I can see why. I wouldn't talk about it, either."

June suddenly felt unbearably lonely, the shabby room depressing. She also realized she was naked. It was surreal, to be talking about this. Maybe the pot was stronger than she'd thought.

She retrieved her halter top and shorts from the floor and sat on the side of the bed to put them on. Gregg tied the strings of the top for her, then touched the nape of her neck. June shivered. "He's still in love with her," she said.

"Who?"

"My husband. With his first wife."

"June," said Gregg, "do you really think so? Maybe he's just really sad."

June was struggling to buckle a sandal—it was hard to see the little holes on the strap in the dim room, let alone guide the tiny prong in. She gave up and said, "She wasn't very pretty—Masha. I think at best she was kind of elegant, in a certain light. But she was so brave. And the little girls . . ."

"How old?"

"Three. Twins."

Gregg made a sound in his throat.

"She died trying to save them," said June. "Try to compete with that."

"I wouldn't," said Gregg. "You can't compete with ghosts."

All the breath went out of June. It was true. She would never win.

Gregg reached for his glasses and got off the bed, kneeling in front of June to fasten her sandal straps.

"I'm sorry for both of you," he said. "And now I understand why you're so lonely . . ." He looked up. "Hey. I didn't mean to make you sad."

June shook her head. "You didn't. It's just this whole situation . . ." She waved around the dismal little room.

"Well, let's cheer it up, then," said Gregg. "You know what I do when I'm sad?"

"What, Julie Andrews, jump on the bed?"

"No," said Gregg. "Dance."

He stood and pulled June into his arms before she could think. She staggered a little, her heel catching in the shag carpet. Gregg caught her and whirled her, humming:

Here's to you, Mrs. Robinson
Jesus loves you more than you will know . . .

"Very funny," said June, but she was laughing. Gregg was still naked except for his glasses. He dipped her expertly. "Where'd you learn how to dance?" she asked breathlessly, upside-down.

"Arthur Murray," said Gregg. "My ma made all us boys take lessons."

He planted a kiss on June's throat and pulled her upright. "Thank you, Mrs. Robinson."

"You're welcome," said June. She looked around for her purse. "I really have to go."

"Wait up, I'll walk out with you," said Gregg. He pulled on his tennis shorts—today he was wearing them with leather sandals and a red-and-blue-striped polo shirt. June couldn't help rolling her eyes. What a fashion sense! But she smiled as Gregg tied his hair back with its rawhide, and for the first time, as they checked the room to make sure they hadn't left their wallets or keys, she felt a little sad. Usually she couldn't get away fast enough, guilt driving her—but today she wanted an ice cream. She wished they could go to Applegate Farm, just her and her boy lover, and split a mint chocolate chip cone, or maybe watermelon sherbet.

"So your name wasn't on the sheet for the July Fourth tourney," said Gregg, opening the door. "You out of town?"

"Yes, I'm taking Elsbeth to see my mom. We fly out every summer."

"To where?"

"Minnesota."

"Minne-soda? You're a farm girl?"

"Not exactly," said June. "My mom owned a dress shop."

"Still," said Gregg. "I can see you in gingham, baking pies. That kinda turns me on."

He slid a hand into the back of June's shorts as they stepped into the parking lot, and she jumped away—they were out in public now. She went to her tan Dodge, Gregg his orange Pinto. The air smelled like melting tar.

"I'll see you when you get back?" he said, squinting at her—the lot was dazzling after the darkness of the room.

"Sure," said June, sliding on her sunglasses. "I'll call you."

Would she? She didn't have to get in touch with him when she returned. Maybe over the long holiday weekend, this whatever-it-was would die a natural death.

Gregg smiled at her over the Pinto's roof as if he knew exactly what she was thinking.

"You'd better call me," he said, "or I'll call you." He blew her a kiss. "Hurry back, Mrs. Robinson. I already have withdrawal."

*

When June and Elsbeth landed in Minneapolis in the afternoon on July 2, June's mother, Ida, was there to pick them up. June was relieved and a little surprised that Ida was still driving; Ida was only sixty-five, but ever since she sold Bouquet's LadiesWear and retired, June had watched her mother anxiously for signs of old age. Today Ida was wearing a natty olive-green pantsuit that matched her Buick, and she managed the airport traffic with aplomb. Her hair was still a neat acorn cap of brown. But June could see the white of her roots bleeding through, and Ida had to lift her chin to squint over the wheel in a way that let June know her mother's glasses prescription needed to be strengthened, and her chin wobbled periodically for no reason. It was disconcerting.

They drove south over the Mendota Bridge onto Highway 52. Elsbeth slept in the back seat, exhausted from the excitement of the TWA wings pinned to her OshKosh overalls, the glimpse into the cockpit, and breakfast on the plane—"Mommy! Eggies in the sky!" Ida asked how Peter was, how was the restaurant, what were the fashions like in New York these days? She filled June in on all the New Heidelberg gossip: who had died, who had married, who'd had more babies or gotten sick or become a hopeless drunk, who was stepping out on whom.

They reached New Heidelberg at twilight, which lasted a long time in July, the sun not setting until after nine. June twisted in her seat to look for all the familiar landmarks in the evening's orange haze. "Plus ça change, plus c'est la même chose," June's friend Dominique, a French model, used to sigh about her suitors; in New Heidelberg, as with faithless men, the more things changed, the more they were the same. There was one stoplight, downtown at the intersection of Elm and Main. The pharmacy was closed, but Ida could fill her prescriptions at the Ben Franklin instead of going all the way into La Crosse. There was a second water tower, two big blue pushpins holding the town in place, and on the west side, just before the sign saying WELCOME TO NEW HEIDELBERG! WILD TURKEY CAPITAL OF MINNESOTA, a new housing development was going up, named, without any irony that June could see, Green Acres. "I don't know who they think's going to live there," commented Ida as they passed. "It's all so fancy."

Ida still lived in the house where June had grown up, in the older postwar subdivision called Brigadoon. Ida pulled into the driveway, and they sat looking at the house, Ida with satisfaction:

when she sold her shop, she'd been able to pay off the mortgage, concluding a thirty-year financial journey she'd begun with her husband Oscar's death benefits in 1945—government compensation for Iwo Jima. "Uncle Sam and I bought this house," Ida liked to say. It was small and neat as a Monopoly piece, the grass in front cut on the diagonal, tubs of marigolds bracketing the front door. The trees that had been saplings when June played hopscotch and roller-skated on these sidewalks were now mature elms, shading the street.

Ida looked fondly at her granddaughter in the rearview mirror. "Should we wake her? I hate to when she's sleeping so nicely . . ."

"I know," said June, "but she'll be up in the night if we don't give her some dinner."

"Does she still have such a good appetite?"

"She does. Like a trucker."

"Oh, now," said Ida, "I wish you were little more like that. You were always picky. . . . Let's see, I could make sandwiches—I have some olive loaf. Or would you girls like to go out?"

"Out, I think," said June diplomatically. She would never forget Peter's horror during his visit here, his barely suppressed shudder over the sliced bologna studded with pimentos. "It looks like typhus," he'd whispered.

Going out in New Heidelberg after 7:00 p.m. meant one of two places: Wilmar's Supper Club, where there were polka bands on weekends and Duke Ellington was rumored to have once played, or the A&W. Since the supper club was no place for a little girl, Ida drove them to the root beer stand with its orange roof and drive-in bays, casting beckoning fluorescence into the fields.

June hadn't been to the A&W for years, so Ida ordered for them: roast beef sandwiches, onion rings, two frosted mugs of root beer, and a child's float. Elsbeth stirred, awakened by the voice on the squawk box. "Mommy," she said in wonder, "are we in a spaceship?"

"No, sweetie pie, we're in Minnesota with Grandma," said June, and Ida waggled her fingers over the seat.

"Look who's awake," she said. "Did you have a good nap, honey? Would you like to sit up here with us?" Elsbeth nodded shyly: yes, please.

June got out to help Elsbeth slide out of the back seat and into the front, aware that in the other cars diners were staring at her, her macramé dress and cork heels, trying to figure out who she was. June waved, and they returned the gesture or lifted fingers off steering wheels, then turned to each other to talk.

The waitress roller-skated to the Buick with their food, attaching the tray to Ida's window, and Ida unwrapped their sandwiches. The car filled with the smell of grease. June's mouth watered. She'd forgotten how much she'd loved the beef, the horseradish, and— her favorite—the onion rings; she nibbled the breading off one, eating around its circumference while helping Elsbeth with her napkin and ketchup.

"Use both hands," she said as Elsbeth lifted her float; "you don't want to spill in Grandma's car."

"Oh, she won't," said Ida, "she's a big girl now, aren't you, honey?"

Elsbeth nodded and smashed a whole onion ring into her mouth. Ida smiled. "Just look at those curls," she said, threading her finger through one and pulling, then letting it spring back. Elsbeth grinned up at her, chewing.

"A gift from her dad," said June.

"Oh, I know," said Ida. "Everyone around here still talks about his movie-star hair." She wiped her fingers on a paper napkin and began winding Elsbeth's ringlets around them. "Do you know my mother tied my hair in rags to give me curls when I was little?"

Elsbeth laughed. "Grandma," she said, "that's silly."

She leaned back against Ida, letting Ida twist her hair into long, shining tubes. Elsbeth's face was blissful in a way June rarely saw it at home, unless Peter was reading her a story or helping her stir something on the stove. June sighed. She was thrilled Elsbeth got along so well with her mother, but she was jealous, too. Ida had whatever June didn't have—as did most women. What it was, what June lacked, was natural maternal instinct. She'd never had it; she'd been born with it left out of her. She'd hated dolls, their clicky eyes scaring her, and unlike all her friends, June had never wanted to babysit, didn't understand how they could sound so dreamy when they talked about having babies of their own. *Oh, I want at least four or five, all girls so we can play dress-up!* June liked to play dress-up by herself. She was perfectly content in her mother's shop, clomping around in scarves and faux fox stoles and clip-on earrings and heels far too big for her.

June had confessed this flaw to Elsbeth's pediatrician, when Elsbeth was four months old and had colic and June was going out of her mind. Nothing, nothing she did could help her baby stop crying, she'd said; it had started the first moment she'd held Elsbeth, and it was all June's fault, because Elsbeth knew June had never wanted to be a mother. There was something wrong with her. "You're right," the doctor had said, "there is: your neurotic fantasies. You're letting them run away with you. All women are meant to be mothers," he'd said, ripping a prescription for Valium off his pad; "it's simple biology, it's what you're designed for, and you're no exception. You're not special, Mrs. Rashkin. Put her in a bouncy chair or drive her around when she's fretful, and stop feeling sorry for yourself."

June had, for the most part. Her maternal deficit was somewhat easier to bear in New York, where a woman could, even should, question her options; where she could wear T-shirts that read "A Woman Without a Man Is Like a Fish Without a Bicycle." But June felt alien here, where women were wives and mothers and did not work—unless thrown into some difficult and pitiable circumstance, as young Ida Bouquet had been by her husband's death. What had made June so different? Why did she want other things?

Was it restlessness inherited from some pioneer ancestor lying over the hill in the New Heidelberg Lutheran cemetery? Some gift, like Elsbeth's curls, from the heroic soldier father June didn't remember? June lit a cigarette, cranking her window down so the smoke would float off into the night. The sun was finally going down behind the horizon in stripes of watermelon and gold; the air smelled sweet, of hay and clover and a hint of manure. The loudspeakers played cheerful ditty-bop music from June's own childhood—*Chantilly Lace and a purty face / and a ponytail hangin' down!*—and beyond the highway cows were lowing. Finally June relaxed against her vinyl seat; whatever her troubles, it was good to be home.

*

The Fourth of July was a highly anticipated event in New Heidelberg, the morning parade with the Sons of Norway and their wives dancing the polka, and of course fireworks—but for Ida, nothing was as important as the luncheon she had arranged for June the next day. Two of the guests were usual suspects, Ida's best friends Minnie and Lois: her bridge partners, former employees, honorary aunts to June. The third woman, Pat, June didn't know at all, even though Ida said, "Oh, you must—Pat Peeper; she was in your grade at school!" Sure, of course, June said finally, to make Ida happy, though the truth was she had no recollection of this Pat. June suspected Ida had invited her because all of June's close friends from growing up had married and moved away, to Des Moines or the Twin Cities or even Texas, but Ida still wanted June to have a girl her own age to play with.

The luncheon was set for noon, and the moment the siren went off at the fire station there was a corresponding knock on the door: in they trooped, Ida's friends and the mysterious Pat, bearing in Tupperware yesterday's transformed leftovers. They hugged June, exclaimed over her Halston dress and how thin she was, made much of Ida's new pantsuit—light blue today—and filed into the parlor off the sun porch, all the better to fold back Ida's accordion door and peep through it at Elsbeth, who was lying on her stomach next to the hi-fi, enraptured by Ida's album of *My Fair Lady*.

"Can you please say hi to the ladies, sweetie?" said June, and Elsbeth said, "Hi, ladies!" then resumed listening, chin propped on her fists and heels swinging idly in the air. She was wearing the new lavender dress Ida had taken her to get at Doerflinger's in La Crosse and let Ida coil her hair into fat sausage ponytails, though she had insisted on also wearing her princess apron.

"Oh my, that hair!" said Minnie, as they arranged themselves at the card table June had helped Ida set up that morning and cover with her best tablecloth. "It's to die for."

"She's a regular Shirley Temple," boomed Lois, who was built like a silo and had a voice like Foghorn Leghorn.

"How's your hubby?" asked Minnie, taking out her cigarettes and setting them next to her plate for after they ate. She was a doll-like woman with a brown perm—they all had brown perms—and eyes the color of cornflowers. Before June came along, Minnie had been the prettiest girl New Heidelberg had ever seen, except for that German war bride who lived out on the Swenson farm and didn't count because she was an import.

"I bet he's handsome as ever," Minnie continued, bumping elbows with June. "I always thought he looked just like Errol Flynn."

"God, you're old," bellowed Lois, "I was going to say Leslie Howard myself," and they all laughed, even Pat, although she had yet to speak, and when June smiled at her she flushed the color of her red jumper.

"Please, everybody, help yourselves," said Ida, and the ladies started dishing the food. There were many exclamations over the cleverness of the recipes: Minnie's July 4 fried chicken was now salad, with the addition of mayonnaise, bacon bits, and cheddar cheese; Lois's deviled eggs had been chopped and mixed with celery and Miracle Whip. The most ingenious transformation, however, belonged to Pat, who shyly confessed that yes, her salad was ham—only she'd put it in Jell-O and poured it in a mold, so it was now octopus-shaped and studded with pineapple, olives, and— were those stars?

"They are," said Pat, the flush creeping up her neck again. "They're cranberry sauce? From the can? I slid it out and made the stars using a cookie cutter?"

This drew exclamations of high praise from everyone, including June, who was taking mental notes with which to torment Peter— and the olives, she would say, were *canned*. Pat looked shyly at June and smiled, and suddenly June knew exactly who Pat was, and felt her own face grow hot. Pat Peeper had once been Pat Mueller, but all the kids had called her Fat Pat—she had weighed close to three hundred pounds. June knew this because some of the football team had carried Pat, screaming and struggling, to the livestock scale at the county fair and held her down until they got her weight. That had been in sophomore year, and the reason June didn't remember Pat was that she'd gone to stay with an aunt in Cedar Rapids af- ter that, although some said she'd had a nervous breakdown and had to go to Black Wing Asylum. The world was not kind to fat women.

But here Pat was, reinvented—almost as thin as June herself. She took a slim segment of the ham salad mold and cut the pine- apple ring into slivers with the side of her fork, a maneuver June recognized. "You look terrific," June told her.

"Thanks," said Pat, "so do you. But you always did," and her face grew so red June feared she would have an embolism. "Are you still modeling?"

"Not as much anymore," said June, "since I had Elsbeth."

"Every time I drive to La Crosse I look for you at the stationery store," Pat burst out, "in *Vogue* and *Glamour* and *Mademoiselle!*"

"That's sweet of you. But honestly, I'm too old now. It's a very competitive industry."

"Oh, I don't know, June Ann," boomed Lois, "you could always do catalogs. Don't they need older models?"

"Sure, to play the moms," said Pat. "You could model for Dayton's."

"Or Macy's," said Lois.

"Or Sears!" said Pat, "I bet you'd look so cute on a rider mower!" and then she glared at her plate again.

Minnie patted June's hand. "June Ann doesn't need to work now, with her husband to provide for her."

"Well," June said, "actually—"

"How's his business, June? Your mom says he's got a whole chain of restaurants."

June raised her eyebrows at Ida, who suddenly found the beaded necklace her glasses were attached to very interesting. "He has *one*. In New Jersey, where we live. He used to have one in New York, but it closed."

"Oh, that's too bad," said Minnie. "Though I wouldn't want to go into New York City to eat, myself. The dirt! and the crime! They say there's a mugging there every minute."

"Well—," June started again.

"Your mom says you're doing real good, though," Lois bellowed. "She showed us the pictures you sent of your house. It's beautiful."

"Thank you," said June.

Minnie nodded enthusiastically. "I love those turn-of-the-century homes. Big, though—hard to keep up. I suppose you have a girl."

June was momentarily bewildered. Of course she had a girl; hadn't Minnie just seen her? Then she realized Minnie didn't mean Elsbeth; she meant a maid.

"Not anymore," she said. "We did have a cleaning lady a long time ago, but when the recession hit we had to let her go."

Minnie looked confused. "I thought your husband was Jewish."

June felt equally confused by the non sequitur. "He is."

"But I thought all Jews were—" Minnie rubbed her thumb and forefinger together. "Ow! Who kicked me?"

"I did," said Lois. "You are plain ignorant, Minnie. Sure, plenty of Jews have money. But lots of them are just as poor as we are! Like those immigrants who came over after the war, from the camps. Like June Ann's husband did—right, June Ann?"

"Well, I know that," Minnie said. "June Ann knows I didn't mean anything by it. Goodness, Lois, you're so sensitive."

"That's true," Lois agreed, "I am."

"But he did have some wealthy relatives who helped him get started here, didn't he?" said Minnie. She looked anxiously at June.

June reassured Minnie it was true and decided she'd waited long enough for a cigarette. Minnie didn't mean any harm; all she wanted to hear was that June was well taken care of. But how Peter would hate to hear himself described this way, after putting as much time and effort between himself and the past as humanly possible. It had been hard for him, coming here where most people had never seen a Jew before—except maybe in the service. In New Heidelberg, Peter had become the instant poster boy for Judaism. Peter wore a suit and tie every day? All Jews wore suits and ties! He never rolled up his sleeves? No Jews showed their wrists! Peter talked with a slight accent? It was Hebrew! He ordered his grilled cheese with tomato? All Jews ate tomato in their grilled cheese. On Peter's last night they had taken him to Wilmar's, where he had been filling a plate at the salad bar when a little towheaded boy ran over to him. "Are you the Jew?" he'd asked, and when Peter said, "Why, yes, I am," the boy had run back to his parents in the booth, yelling, "He don't look like he killed Jesus!"

"Speaking of husbands," said Lois, "guess who I ran into the other day."

"Who?" said Minnie, Ida, and Pat.

Lois slid a sly glance at June. "Dwayne Knutsen."

"No," said Minnie.

"Yup."

"I thought he'd moved to Iowa," said Minnie.

"Well, he did," said Lois, "but I guess he was back visiting his mom and dad." She looked expectantly at June; they all did. June smiled and sipped her coffee.

"Well, June Ann," said Minnie, "don't you want to know how he looked?"

"Not particularly," said June, but when all the ladies said "Awwww," she laughed and said, "All right, since you're obviously dying to tell me. How'd he look?"

"Bald!" said Lois triumphantly. "Bald as a Ping-Pong ball. And fat—whew. He must have three chins!"

"All those Knutsen men get heavy," said Ida. "Would anyone like more coffee?"

"I would, thank you," said June and handed Ida her cup. She was trying to manufacture some satisfying response for Lois, who looked a little disappointed, but the truth was, June didn't have any feelings about Dwayne Knutsen at all. They had gone together senior year, which had been preordained since June was head cheerleader and Dwayne the quarterback, and they had been briefly engaged, and Dwayne had even taken June's virginity, if one could call that brief stab of pain in his pickup truck a sexual encounter. But a month later June had gone up to Minneapolis with some girlfriends to the modeling auditions at Dayton's, and that had been that. "I knew it'd never stick," Dwayne had said sadly, coming to get his ring back the morning June left for New York. "But it was fun while it lasted." June hadn't thought of him in years.

"Guess you had a narrow escape, June Ann," said Minnie. "Ow, *now* why are you kicking me?"

"Just for fun," said Lois.

"Is he married?" said June, because some response was expected of her, and when Lois said "Of course," she asked, "Kids?"

"Five," said Lois, "and one on the way."

"Wow," said June. "Six kids. Imagine that," and she smiled into her cup. A farmer with six kids. She'd have to remember to tell Peter.

*

As if she had summoned him up, the phone rang. Ida went into the kitchen to answer it and came back saying, "June, honey, it's for you, long distance." Awwwww, all the ladies chorused again, and Minnie said, "Somebody's husband misses her. That's sweet! Tell him hello from us."

June promised she would and went into the kitchen, where Ida had left the receiver on the stool she sat on while she took calls. "Hello? Pete? How are you?"

"Hi," said Gregg. "Do you miss me?"

June was so startled she nearly dropped the phone. She glanced toward the living room; the ladies were entangled in some new conversational topic, and from the sun porch Julie Andrews was singing, *"All I want is a room somewhere!"*

"Hello?" said Gregg. "Are you there?"

June walked across Ida's kitchen as far as the phone's curly cord would stretch, which was to the refrigerator. "How did you get this number?"

"I just asked the operator for Bouquet, in New Heidelberg. No sweat. Anyway," said Gregg, "I'm here."

"What?" said June. "Where?" She looked wildly out the window over the kitchen sink, as if Gregg might be lurking in Ida's lilac bushes.

"In Minnesota, silly. Minneapolis."

"Why?"

"Why d'you think? Because I want to see you."

"Oh," said June.

"I wanted to see you in gingham," Gregg said. "And if you'd baked me a pie."

"Not exactly," said June.

"Well, that's disappointing." He laughed. "It's nice here," he added.

"I'm glad you like it," said June. She walked back to the threshold; her mother was doling out coffee cake now, but Lois looked up and winked. June winked back.

"So when can I see you?" said Gregg.

"I really don't think that's possible."

"Anything's possible. Can you get away for a night?"

"I'm with my mom," said June, "and my daughter."

"Sure, I know. I figured your mom could watch Elsbeth for a night or two. So we could have a sleepover."

"You're nuts," said June.

"Nuts about you," said Gregg. "So are you coming up? Or should I come down there?"

"You don't know where I am," said June, but then she realized if he'd found her number, he could have Ida's address. Sure enough, Gregg was saying, "That's what maps are for." Would he really do it? Would he show up here? June could invent some cover story, but the town would talk about nothing else for years.

"Listen," Gregg said, "I dig if you really can't, but it's an awfully long flight out here just for room service, and I do miss you. One night? Please?"

June had knotted the phone cord around her hand; her fingers were turning purple. She loosened it and said, "I'll try."

"Really?"

"Maybe tomorrow. Just for one night."

"Far out!" said Gregg. He sounded surprised, as if he hadn't expected this plan to succeed. "I'm excited to see you, Mrs. Robinson."

"You too," said June.

"I'm at the Radisson," he said. "Don't stand me up, baby," and the line went dead.

June hung up and went to stand by the sink, watching the clothes turn on Ida's spinning clothesline until her heart rate had gone back to normal. Thank God Ida no longer had a party line! She went back into the living room.

"Mom," she said, "I have to run up to Minneapolis for a night. Can you watch Elsbeth?"

"Sure, honey," said Ida. "But why? Who was that on the phone?"

"An old friend," said June. "A photographer I worked with in New York. He shoots for Dayton's now, and he offered me a day's work."

"Well, what do you know," said Lois. "Weren't we just talking about that?"

"We're psychic," said Minnie. "We should open a palm-reading business."

"How did he know you were here?" said Ida.

"I ran into him at the airport," June said, "didn't I mention that?"

"I don't think so, no."

"That's funny. I was sure I had. Well, anyway, it'd be fun to see him again, and it'd be nice pocket money, but if it's too much bother . . ."

"Oh, heavens," said Ida, "it's never a bother to spend time with my granddaughter. You run along, honey. Have fun." She cut a slice of cake and set it in front of June with a fork, but behind her glasses her eyes were troubled.

*

The Radisson was in downtown Minneapolis, near the Foshay Tower, which was the tallest structure June had seen before going to New York, and the new IDS Center, which when completed would be taller. June consigned Ida's Buick to the valet and stepped through the revolving door with her overnight bag. She was perspiring, her stomach churning, full of anticipation and dread. On the drive up here, she had half convinced herself the whole thing was a practical joke. Now she almost hoped it was.

She scanned the lobby, seeing several businessmen, in chairs and on couches and by the elevator bank; she saw them seeing her too, but she didn't spot Gregg. She walked to the reception desk. If he really wasn't here, June would have one martini in the bar, do a little shopping at Dayton's to make the trip worthwhile, and drive straight back to Elsbeth and Ida.

"Santorelli," she said to the girl at reception, who had a toothsome smile and a name tag that read MIMS. "Is there anyone here by that name?"

The girl leafed through the reservation book. "No, ma'am, I'm sorry."

"It's Ms., please. How about Bouquet, or Rashkin?"

"Let me just check. No, I don't. . . ."

"Actually, it's Robinson," said Gregg at June's elbow. "Mr. and Mrs. Robinson."

June turned and stared in astonishment: Gregg had been totally transformed. He was in a suit, sober pinstriped black; he had a striped red tie and shining new shoes. Most surprising of all, his shoulder-length hair had been cut short. Only his size and his large glasses were the same.

June started to laugh. "You look like a banker."

Gregg grinned. "You dig?" he said and revolved in a slow circle.

"I do," said June. "No wonder I didn't recognize you!" She was shaking a little, from the surprise and the strangeness. "Are you really here?"

"I really am." He bent to hug her. "You look gorgeous," he said in her ear, "as usual. I missed you, Mrs. Robinson." He smelled of new cologne, too, spice and lime.

"Your room has been cleaned, Mr. Robinson," said Mims, "and I have an extra key right here. May I get a signature?"

"Of course," said Gregg. He signed the register for both of

them: "Mr. and Mrs. Gregg Robinson!" He nodded to the clerk, took June's overnight bag, and guided her across the lobby with a hand on the small of her back, the very model of decorum until they were by the elevator, whereupon the hand slipped down to her buttock and remained there. They watched the bronze arrow descend.

"I've never stayed here," said June. "It's swanky."

"Isn't it?" he said, and then the elevator went *ding!* and the doors slid open. They stepped inside, and Gregg pressed 14.

As soon as the doors slid closed, he dropped June's bag and picked her up off her feet; she wrapped her legs around him to keep from falling over. They kissed deeply, violently, Gregg's hands kneading June's buttocks, hers running over his new short hair. He fumbled up the hem of her dress, trembling; he used his thumb to push her underwear aside and hooked it inside her. June gasped and he made a noise deep in his throat.

The elevator dinged, and June slid back down to the floor just in time for two more guests to get on, a middle-aged couple in matching aqua leisure suits. "Going down?" the man said.

"Up," said Gregg and leaned forward to press the Close button. The woman and man glanced at them suspiciously; June fought the urge to fix her hair. They rose.

"I like your outfits," said Gregg. "Nice day for a jog."

The man coughed; the woman cleared her throat disapprovingly. "I like your dress too, miss," Gregg said to June.

"Thank you," said June, "it's Pucci."

"It's short," said Gregg. "I like that in a dress." He was standing behind her, and on June's right side, the one the couple couldn't see, he slid his hand under her shift and pinched her thigh. June bit the inside of her lip. The bell pinged, and the doors slid open.

"Have a nice day," said Gregg; "Enjoy your visit," and they tumbled out into the hall, laughing.

"You're incorrigible," said June. "Couldn't you wait?"

"Obviously not. It's your fault. Temptress."

"Sex maniac."

"Hussy."

"Child."

"Child molester."

He laughed as June hit him on the shoulder. "Mr. Robinson," she said. "Really. So clever. Like they've never heard that one before," and she shimmied away from him down the hall, backward, doing a little can-can and flipping up the hem of her dress. Gregg put on a burst of speed and caught up with her, grabbing her elbow and spinning her around to frog-march her to their room.

"Here we are, Mrs. Robinson," he said and opened the door.

"Wow," said June, surprised. The room was more contemporary than June would have guessed from the lobby's traditional marble floors and chandeliers; up here the furniture was modular, the hanging lamps white globes, one wall mirrored in smoked glass. There was a wet bar and, framed by open Levolor blinds, a view of the Mississippi.

"This is nice——," June started to say, but that was all she had time to get out before Gregg propelled her to the window. He pulled her dress over her head and tossed it aside, and June felt his breath on her neck and the clink of a belt buckle and then he was inside her, pressing June against the glass with each thrust so every nude inch of her was splayed like a starfish, the whole of the city spread at her feet.

*

When June woke, it was to a darkness so complete, it felt as though she were floating. She was frightened for a moment, not knowing where she was—Ida's? the guest room?—and then Gregg's arm tightened around her, and she remembered. His grip must have been what awakened her; his muscles contracted around June's rib cage, seizing so hard she cried out. It was like being crushed by a python. Gregg was making a noise too, whining in his throat; he kicked out with one foot, and June realized he was dreaming.

"Gregg," she said, "Gregg, wake up."

He didn't, but his breathing changed; his big body went slack, and his arm fell away. Then one hand slid up the backs of June's thighs and inserted itself between her legs. It eased forward, slowly, slowly, inch by excruciating inch, until he found what he was seeking and pushed first his fingers and then himself inside.

"June," he said. "Ah, Jesus."

Afterward he catapulted from the bed full of energy; he went naked to the window and opened it. "Helloooo, Minneapolis!" he called into the evening—June was surprised the digital clock read 7:30; she'd thought it was the middle of the night. Gregg laughed at something on the street. "Come check this out," he said.

"In a minute," said June. She was flattened, pulverized by the same dread she'd felt walking into the lobby, the fear she'd felt in the dark. Only it wasn't for herself—or rather it was because of her, what she was doing here, that something bad was going to happen to her loved ones. She was suddenly sure of it. They might not know; Ida might not suspect that June wasn't on a shoot nor Peter have any idea June had a lover, but fate would even the score. Nothing like this could go unpunished, and whatever it was wouldn't happen to June; her sentence would be to remain fine while her family suffered. Even now Elsbeth might be slipping in the tub; Peter would have a terrible migraine that would turn out to be a stroke, or a car would run over him, or a boiling vat fall off his stove.

"You've got to see this," said Gregg, beckoning to June. She made herself get off the bed and go look out the window: far below, in the fountain on the Nicollet Mall, a band of naked hippies was frolicking nude in the water; they had put dish soap in it, for it foamed with bubbles. They cavorted happily, splashing and shouting, until there was a whistle and the clop of hooves and one of them yelled, "Scram, man! Fuzz!" And they scattered, nude behinds bouncing off into the night as a mounted policeman galloped along the pedestrian zone toward them.

"I like Minneapolis," said Gregg. "It's a happening place."

He reached over to draw June to him, but she said, "I need a shower—and do you mind if I make a couple of calls?"

Gregg yawned and scratched his chest. "Not at all. Want company?"

"For the calls?"

"In the shower."

"Oh," said June. "Well—give me a minute, okay?"

She carried the room's phone into the bathroom and called New Heidelberg first, her stomach sinking with every ring that went unanswered—but when Ida picked up, she assured June that Elsbeth was fine; they had made cookies and listened to *My Fair Lady*, and Elsbeth had gone down like a dream, and was June having a good time?

June said she was; she thanked her mother again and hung up. She sat on the side of the tub with her finger on the disconnect button for a moment, then released it and dialed the Claremont. There was no way Peter would be at the house; he wouldn't be there even if June and Elsbeth were home.

The hostess put June right through to Peter's office, but June waited another two minutes before her husband said, "Good evening from the Claremont, this is Peter, how may I help you?"

"Hi, Pete. It's June."

"Yes, I recognize the voice," said Peter. "What is the matter?"

"Nothing—why would you think anything's wrong?"

"Because I am in the middle of dinner service," said Peter.

"Right!" June said heartily. She was messing this up already. She went to the door and peeked out at Gregg; he was sitting on the side of the bed, rolling a joint. She shut the door as far as it would go.

"Well, I'll say good-bye then," she said, and added idiotically,

"I'm in Minneapolis." What the hell was wrong with her? But maybe it was better this way; what if Peter had called New Heidelberg tomorrow asking for June and found she wasn't there?

"Why are you in Minneapolis?" Peter asked.

"Because I got a job. I met a former coworker on the plane, a photographer who lives here now, and he offered me a catalog shoot. For Dayton's," she added, not that Peter would know what Dayton's was.

There was a pause. "You're working in Minneapolis now?" Peter asked.

June laughed. "Oh, no no no no. Just for a day."

"I see," he said. Another silence, longer this time; the line ticked and hissed. June desperately wanted to know what it meant: Had she said something wrong? Did Peter suspect? Was he furious? Or was he looking over the night's tickets, checking to see which specials had run out?

"Is Elsbeth with you?" Peter asked finally.

"No, she's at my mom's," said June.

"You left her with your mother?"

"Jeez, Pete, it's not like she's in a gutter or something. My mom is probably spoiling her rotten."

"That is true," Peter admitted. He sighed. "All right. Have a good time, and I will see you—remind me, what day are you coming home?"

"Thursday. Three days from now."

"Very well. I will call the airline and meet you at Teterboro."

"Thanks," said June. "Pete?"

"Yes?"

June clung to the phone. She wasn't sure what she wanted to say—I'm sorry. I miss you. I love you. Won't you love me back? Can't you even try? She couldn't speak, but she couldn't hang up.

"Are you still on the line?" said Peter.

"Yes. Sorry. I just . . . how are you doing?"

Peter laughed, or maybe it was a huff of exasperation. "I am fine, thank you, June. Now I really must go—we have a full house tonight—"

"Sure. Go ahead."

"Give Ellie and your mother a kiss from me," and then he was gone.

June hung up. The restaurant, always the goddamned restaurant! Although of course the Claremont was just Peter's excuse for staying away, for his perennial absence. June opened the door.

"I'm starved," she announced. "What time's dinner?"

Gregg was slumped in an armchair, watching *All in the Family.* The room was resinous with the skunk smell of pot. On-screen Archie called his son-in-law a Polack meathead, and the audience laughed.

"Want to join me in the shower?"

Gregg stared stonily ahead, then used the remote to turn off the TV. The picture dwindled to a small white cube and blinked out. "Sure. If you're done with your *calls.*"

His voice had a nasty edge June hadn't heard before. "What's the matter with you?" she said.

"Nothing. Why would you think anything's the matter?"

"Because you're acting like a jerk."

"That's a matter of opinion."

"Well, that's my opinion."

Gregg took a toke from the joint. June waited. "I'm going to get ready," she said finally. "Can you please pass me my cigarettes?"

Gregg reached for the pack on the bedside table and pegged it in June's direction. June ducked, and the Marlboro box bounced off the bathroom door.

"What is your *problem?*" she said.

Gregg pinched out the joint and turned the TV back on. Now it was the Jeffersons, movin' on up.

"Fine," said June. "Up yours. I'll go to dinner by myself."

"Oh no, you won't."

"Oh yes, I will."

"You don't even know where our reservation is."

June laughed. "Like I care. I'll go somewhere else."

"Not without me, you won't," said Gregg and got up.

"Fine."

"Fine."

*

It turned out Gregg had booked a table at the Radisson, in the famous Golden Flame Room on the top floor. They awaited the elevator in silence; when it came, they boarded and stood a foot apart, June in her green halter gown, Gregg in his suit. There was Muzak: raindrops kept falling on their heads. Gregg stood at parade rest, hands clasped in front of him, gaze straight; the dent on his forehead was more prominent now with his short hair, in the overhead light. Their afternoon interlude in this very elevator seemed to have happened to other people. Who *was* he, this big silent boy? They ascended, watching the lighted numbers.

June had heard about the Golden Flame Room, but she had never been there; it was much like the Rainbow Room in New York, a rooftop restaurant surrounded by windows. All the men in June's life seemed insistent on taking her to dine in the sky. June remembered Peter pretending he couldn't waltz and felt a pinch of pain. The hostess led them to their table: a ringside seat to the dance floor, with a fine view of the Minneapolis horizon, the Mississippi and beyond it the Gold Medal Flour sign glowing red, and the Golden Strings Orchestra. On either side of the musicians' platform were the Golden Flames: two plumes of fire shooting regularly to the ceiling from two torches and, to the *ooooh*s and *aaaah*s of the diners, turning rainbow colors. The orchestra, seven tuxedoed young men and seven damsels in gowns, plucking away at cellos, violins, guitars, and harps, was playing "Tea for Two." They looked like refugees from *The Poseidon Adventure*.

They segued into "Candle on the Water" as Gregg shouted something at their waitress that ended with ". . . martinis!" June took a cigarette from her clutch and waited. When Gregg didn't lean over to light it, she picked up a Golden Flame Room matchbook and did it herself. They stared at the Golden Flames; the fire shot up, and the lenses of Gregg's glasses flared orange, red, green, and blue. "Oooohhhhhhhhhh," the diners said. "Aaaaahhhh." Over the music came the soft roar of propane.

The waitress returned with their martinis, and June picked hers up. "Hold on," said Gregg. "We haven't toasted." He smiled sweetly and lifted his glass. "To your husband. *A salut.*"

"Very mature," said June.

"How do you think that felt?" Gregg said. His lips pulled back from his teeth, and behind his glasses June could see the whites of his eyes around the pupils; she realized he was truly furious, and for the first time she felt a little afraid. "Sitting there like a chump while you sweet-talked him like that?"

"Sweet talk?" said June, "that wasn't sweet talk! That was a wife trying to sound normal so her husband wouldn't suspect anything. Which I think he might, by the way."

"Good," said Gregg. "It's about time."

"What are you talking about! How can you say that?"

Gregg drained his drink. "If he doesn't know by now, I'll tell him myself."

"Don't . . . you . . . dare." June stood up, fists clenched, nails digging into her palms. "I'll kill you if you do."

"Go ahead," Gregg nearly shouted. "This is killing me already. What do you think this is for me, June?" and June was astonished to see his eyes reddening with tears. He took his glasses off and pinched his nose. "Some little joke? A summer fling? You think I ball every horny wife at the club, that I came halfway across the country for fun and games? I love you, June."

June stood very still, holding the back of her chair. "What?"

"I said I love you."

The waitress returned. "Two chicken Kiev specials," she sang, "with rice pilaf . . ."

Gregg took the plates from her. "Okay, thanks," he said. He looked back at June, who hadn't moved. "You have no reaction to my telling you I love you?"

June had many, the most prevalent being confusion, like the roaring of a big shell on her ears. "You don't even know me," she said.

"Sure I do."

"No, you don't. You just think you do. You think you know me because we've spent a couple of months screwing—"

"I know you think you're old even though you're the most stunning woman I've ever seen. I know you have a raspberry birthmark. I know you're double-jointed. I know you're funny. I know you're lonely. I know you've tried, but your marriage isn't working. I know you want more. I know you want more from your life, June."

That did sound convincing, June had to admit. But—

"You don't know what you're talking about," she said, and fled.

She was halfway to the door when Gregg caught up with her. He grabbed her arm.

"Wait," he said.

"Let go," she said.

"I will if you listen. Will you listen?"

"Go ahead," she said.

Gregg took both of June's hands in his. They were standing half on, half off the dance floor, on carpet and parquet, sequins of light from the disco ball scattering in their eyes. Waitresses eddied around them, carrying folding stands and big trays.

"I came here," Gregg said, "to ask you to go away with me."

"We're already away," said June.

"I mean away-away. For real. I'm going to California, June. After Labor Day. As soon as my contract at the club is up."

"How long have you known this?"

"All along."

"And you're just telling me now?" June tried to wrench free. She had predicted Gregg would leave, hoped for it, even—why was she feeling tearful now? It was this whole upsetting scene. "Give me the room key."

"I will, I promise. Just one more minute."

June wrestled with him. She was strong from tennis and house-work, but Gregg of course was stronger. She stopped.

"Thank you," he said.

June glared. "What else, macho man," she snapped—which was in fact the song the Golden Strings Orchestra was now playing.

"I always knew the club was a temporary gig," Gregg said. "I was just saving up money. I can't live in my parents' basement forever. I've been there since I was discharged. It's been a long two years."

"I get it, but—"

"*Listen.*" Gregg put his hand on June's cheek. "So I got in touch with a buddy of mine I served with—he's in Long Beach. He says I can crash with him until I find my own place. That housing's cheap. I can go to USC or UCLA on the GI Bill—finally finish college. Sun. Sand. New beginnings. Sounds pretty good, June, doesn't it?"

It did. June asked, stalling, "What are you going to study?"

"Oceanography."

"Oceanography!" She started to laugh.

"What?" said Gregg, looking hurt. "I like whales."

June laughed. She laughed and laughed, until tears ran down her face. She bent at the waist, but she couldn't stop. She saw ladies' pumps and skirt hems, men's loafers and trouser cuffs, whisk past on the dance floor; Gregg's giant shoes remained in place. When June straightened up, he was standing with his arms crossed, just watching.

"Better?" he asked.

June wiped her eyes. "Yes, thanks."

Gregg used the tail of his tie to dry June's face. She thought of Peter then, how he was never, in any circumstance, without his handkerchief, and stepped back.

"I'm flattered," she said. "It's very sweet, what you're asking me to do. But—"

"Don't," said Gregg. "Don't do that, June. Don't say no before you've really thought it over, given it a chance."

"But—"

"What'd I just say?"

"It's impossible. I have a husband. And a daughter you've never even met!"

"A husband who, with all due respect, doesn't love you the way you deserve. This is 1975—people get divorced every day. As for your daughter, I'd love to meet her. I'm really good with kids."

"B—," June started to say, and Gregg put a hand on her mouth.

"Just for now," he said, "just for tonight, don't say no. Think about it. I know you want a fresh start as badly as I do, June. Just think about it for one night, okay?"

June sighed. Lassitude overcame her, from laughing and crying and from having gotten very little sleep the night before. She looked over at the Golden Flame Orchestra. They were all so young, these girls in their gowns and boys with beards; who knew where their lives would take them, what wretched decisions they would face?

Gregg lifted her hand and kissed it. "Dance with me," he said.

He drew her onto the floor. The orchestra was playing "Honey Bun" from *South Pacific*. "That's you," Gregg said, as he pulled June in; "my doll, dainty as a sparrow. Compared to me, anyway." He sang along:

Where she's narrow, she's as narrow as an arrow,
And she's broad . . . where a broad . . . should be broad!

He squeezed June's corresponding body part and she whacked him on the shoulder. "Hey!" she said.

Gregg grinned. "I didn't write the lyrics, Mrs. R."

"Excuse me," said a man next to them—a portly gentleman in a tuxedo, dancing with a lady who had an impressive gray beehive. "Pardon me, young fellow. Care to settle a bet for my wife and me?"

"Sure, if I can," Gregg said.

The man winked at June. "Are you two honeymooners?"

"We are, as a matter of fact," Gregg said, just as June opened her mouth to say no.

The man turned to his wife, who was rolling her eyes. "You owe me a dollar, Jeanette," he said. "I told you—it's easy to spot the ones in love. You can always tell."

*

The next morning they got up early, not wanting to squander their rapidly dwindling time. Gregg suggested room service, but June said, "C'mon, I want to take you to one of my favorite places," and after they dressed, she led him out onto the Nicollet Mall. The sun was bright, the bricks shining, the shopkeepers just rolling the grates up the windows. At Burt's Shoes, Gregg chose a hideous pair of green platform clogs for June, the toes curled as if elves had made them; at Brown's Contemporary Clothing, June selected circus-striped pants for Gregg. "I think I'd rather wear a mini," he said. In fact he was still in his banker's suit, which was starting to look a little rumpled. It was the only thing he'd packed, he admitted sheepishly. He stood behind June and put his arms around her, turning her to face their reflection in the glass. "What d'you think, Mrs. R?" he said. "Pretty cute couple, huh?"

"You sure are, Mr. Rockefeller," said a voice from a nearby bench, and up rose one of the hippies they'd seen last night—in a stovepipe hat and bell-bottoms, though sans shirt. "You take care of her," he said, "take care of that angel."

"I intend to," said Gregg, "if she'll let me."

"That's why we're all on this earth, to take care of each other," said the hippie, and he whipped off his hat. "You wouldn't happen to have a quarter, would you?"

"For you," said Gregg, "I've got a dollar," and he dropped a bill in the hippie's hat and bowed back to him, and they strolled on.

"That was generous of you," said June as they reached where she'd wanted to go—Bridgeman's lunch counter. "By the way, if you don't mind my asking—how are you affording all this?" The Radisson wasn't cheap.

Gregg drew back in mock offense. "You think I'm just some po'-ass tennis pro? I'm a vet, baby. Uncle Sam be payin' for this trip. You got yo'self a real liiiive sugar daddy."

"I've got myself a real jive turkey, is more like it," said June. She stepped daintily over the threshold in her platform sandals as Gregg held the door.

"Groovy place," he said, looking at the long lunch counter, the checkered green and gray floors, the row of red vinyl booths.

"I used to come here when I was a kid," said June, "on buying trips with my mom." The waitress nodded for them to take a seat, so Gregg chose the window booth.

"Welcome to Bridgeman's, home of the LaLaPaLooza," the waitress chanted, dropping menus on the speckled Formica.

"Thanks," said Gregg. "What the heck is a LaLaPaLooza?"

"That," said June, pointing to the photo on the sun-faded menu, and the waitress recited, "Our famous sundae, eight scoops of ice cream—pineapple rings—pineapple caramel and strawberry topping—mixed nuts—bananas slices—whipped cream and maraschino cherries—eat the whole thing and it's free."

"Well, obviously that's for me," said Gregg.

"For breakfast?" said June.

"Santorelli's rule," said Gregg. "If there's an in-house sundae, you have to eat it."

"Same for you?" said the waitress.

"Oh, God, no," said June. "I'll have half a grapefruit and coffee. Black."

She lit a cigarette as Gregg pulled over the glass of crayons near the jukebox and the waitress poured coffee. June just wanted to savor this moment: the sun slanting across the table; her muscles sore in a way that spoke only of pleasurable activities; Gregg's hair still damp from the shower and combed in furrows. June still wasn't used to how he looked with short hair. Nor was he; "I don't have a forehead," he'd said that morning in the bathroom, squinting at himself in the steamy mirror; "I have a fivehead." His hair, at twenty-seven, was already thin at the crown; would he be completely bald in five years? June wondered. Ten?

"So," said Gregg, without looking up from the place-mat puzzles he was working on: circle the hidden words, find what's wrong with this picture. "Have you given it more thought?"

"What?" said June.

He glanced up at her. "What we talked about last night," he said, and then he sat back as the waitress served his sundae. "Good grief," he said.

"Don't forget," June said with a sadistic smile, "you've got to eat the whoooolllle thing."

"No sweat," said Gregg and applied himself to his ridiculous mounds of ice cream. June sipped her coffee and watched, both repulsed and amused. Naturally Gregg would order ice cream for breakfast—he was practically still a child, after all. But June had to admit there was something refreshing about his appetite, how he ate and enjoyed whatever he wanted without considering its pedigree. June admired Peter's dedication to his profession, of course she did, along with his proficiency at it—but he could be so . . . fussy. Did anyone but chefs really care whether tomatoes came from a local farm or the A&P? Or go into raptures over white asparagus, or fly into rages about a broken-yolked egg? June had once seen Peter fire a man for oversalting a sauce, scream at another for not wiping down a plate's rim before he ran it to the dining room. They were among the few times she'd seen him truly angry. She didn't understand it—his passion *consumed* him. What did it really matter whether the Brie was served at the ideal temperature or the beef for brisket Wellington came from flank steak or top round? Food was food.

Gregg held out a spoonful of ice cream to June. "That's cheating," she said.

"I won't tell if you don't," he said, and June accepted the bite. Butter pecan—a flavor she hadn't tasted since childhood. She'd forgotten how much she loved it.

"Well?" Gregg said again.

"Well what?"

"You know well what," he said.

"It's only been twelve hours," she said. "Give me a few more minutes."

"Fine," said Gregg.

He set the empty sundae boat aside and returned to his puzzles, pushing his glasses up onto his nose with his pointer finger. June watched him circle a beach ball on a stove, a duck with a bow tie, an upside-down lamp. Was she even going to consider this? Was she really? California: home of the silver screen, of Hollywood hopefuls, of—as Archie Bunker said—fruits and nuts. June didn't want to be in pictures, but finally she could work! There had to be plenty of movie stars' wives with pots of money and no taste who would welcome June redecorating their mansions.

But Peter. This would hurt. Badly. He would be shocked, his pride injured, and he would miss June—in the academic, abstract way a husband misses the wife who has shared his bed and set out his suits and shoes. Sol and Ruth would be thrilled, their opinion of June and all slippery shiksas confirmed, a brand-new opportunity to fix Peter up with a nice Jewish girl. Maybe somebody Peter's own age; maybe a widow, so they'd have that essential grief in common. Although June imagined Peter would scorn such attempts. Without June, he'd probably return to the bachelor ways he'd been set in when she met him, working twenty hours a day, seven days a week—testing recipes, stalking the best meat and produce, sleeping at the restaurant. The kitchen was Peter's real love, after all—and the memories it contained.

"Oh no," said June.

"What?" said Gregg.

"Elsbeth," June said. What about Elsbeth? Elsbeth, who couldn't stand to have her stuffed animals out of alignment, who couldn't bear when her night-light went out or her bedroom door was left open an inch too wide. She was not a child who would take kindly to transplantation. And Elsbeth and Peter . . . if there was a vault in Peter that was shut to everyone but himself, his heart was open, to the degree it was, to his daughter.

"If you think I'm not old enough to help take care of her," said Gregg, "don't worry about that. I've wanted to be a dad since I can remember."

"Then you're a much better parent than I am," said June, "because I never wanted to be a mom," and she started to cry. She couldn't believe she had said this; she hadn't told anyone since Elsbeth's doctor scolded her. June waited for Gregg to comfort her, but he didn't, and when she was done, she opened her eyes to find a pile of napkins on the table in front of her and the waitress giving them the fisheye.

"I bet you're a wonderful mom," said Gregg.

"I'm not," said June. "My daughter hates me. She's always hated me."

"That's ridiculous," said Gregg. "Kids don't hate their parents. They might say they do, and maybe they even mean it, but it's temporary, like after a punishment or something."

"You don't understand," said June. "Elsbeth's a daddy's girl through and through. How can I even think of taking her from him?"

"Listen," said Gregg, "there's such a thing as joint custody, right? She could spend holidays with him, and summers—all summer, every summer. That's more time than I've ever spent with my old man in my life." He handed June a napkin and she blew her nose. "Besides," Gregg added, "nobody who cries over her kid like that could be a bad mom. Look how much you care! My ma barely says two words to me. She never once stepped in when my old man was beating on us. But I still love her."

"Do you?"

"Always," said Gregg firmly. "Anyway, we don't have to decide all of this right now. Let me meet her first, and then we'll see what happens. Okay?"

"There's one more thing," June said. "I want to go back to work."

"Doing what?"

"Home decor," said June. "Interior design."

"Neat," said Gregg. "Then you can be my sugar mama while I go back to school."

"I'm serious," said June.

"So am I," said Gregg. "I dig it. You think I was really at that encounter group to get laid? I'm all about women having jobs."

"Oh," said June, "would you cut it out? Stop saying all those perfect things. You're making everything so much harder."

"Good," said Gregg. His grin broke out, white and radiant. "I look forward to complicating your life for a long time."

He got up and crouched next to June's side of the booth, patting his crumpled shirtfront. June slid over and put her face against his chest; beneath it, she could hear the lollop of his big heart. She didn't have to marry him; she didn't have to go through with any of this if she didn't want to. They could, as Gregg had suggested, just take it a step at a time. Gregg cradled her head as gently as if June herself were a child. He kissed the top of it.

"It's going to be okay, June," he said. "Everything's going to be all right. You'll see."

✻

"June Ann, are you all right?"

"What's that, Mom?" June said. It was Wednesday, the day before she and Elsbeth were to fly back to New Jersey, and June and Ida were having another cup of coffee in the breakfast nook while Elsbeth played outside with June's old paper dolls. June had been watching her through the window but thinking about Peter, and packing, and the logistics of the return trip—and Gregg. She was helpless, it seemed, to stop thinking about their last hours together, which replayed in her mind like a broken record. How when they had left Bridgeman's, they had gone back to the hotel, where they had made love quickly, quietly, missionary, no fancy tricks or acrobatics, as if to seal with their bodies an agreement their mouths had made. How they then took a shower together, for once not playing with the soap, and got out and somberly packed their separate bags. How Gregg had called the front desk and said they were running a little behind, could they possibly have an extra half hour to check out, please? And how he had taken June's hand and led her to the bed, making her sit on the side while he undressed again, and pushed her back, and made her watch as he entered her, said, Look, June, look at us. I want you to remember, and she said, I will, and he said, Promise, and she said, I promise, and he said, Ah, God, June, I love you, and she said, Gregg . . . and he said, Say it, and she said, I love you too, and then they were saying it together, I love you, I love you, like a canticle, and then it was over.

June had tried her best to stop thinking about this, because it would do her no good while she was here at her mother's and it certainly wouldn't help in New Jersey, where she would have to try to clear her head and make some difficult decisions. But something of it must have shown on her face, because Ida repeated, "I asked if you were all right. This whole visit you haven't been yourself."

"Sorry, Mom," said June. "I guess I'm a little preoccupied."

She was playing with a pin under the tablecloth, a button Gregg had pressed into her palm in front of the Radisson before June got into Ida's Buick and Gregg caught a cab to the airport. It was a small navy circle embossed with a cheerful cartoon character proclaiming "I Ate a Whole LaLaPaLooza!" June had gotten used to fiddling with it, idly poking her thumb on the pin; now she stuck it into her pocket and smiled at her mother.

Ida got up to refill their coffee. "Are you having troubles at home?"

Both women glanced toward the window, but Elsbeth was making one of the paper dolls sing, her voice just audible through the glass: *"Pickering, why can't a woman be more like a man?"*

"Everything's fine, Mom," said June, but then she said, "Yes, a little trouble."

"Oh no," said Ida. Her chin wobbled, and her hand rose to fiddle with her glasses chain. "Is Peter stepping out?"

"No, Mom."

"Is it drinking? Gambling? Oh, I just can't believe that of Peter."

"It's not those either," June said. "It's hard to explain."

"You don't have to," said Ida and put her hand on June's. "But if you want to, try."

June looked at their hands, small and long-fingered, Ida's knuckles knobby. Her wedding ring, unlike June's thick gold band, hung loosely, silver and thin as a dime from a quarter-century's ceaseless wear.

"He doesn't want me to work, for one thing," June said.

"Well, why should you have to?"

"I want to."

"That's just silly," said Ida. "Why would you want to do that when you could stay home and take care of Elsbeth?"

Because it's boring, June wanted to say; because I want to do other things with my life. But that would have been an incendiary and worthless argument. If everyone had at least one alternate life she wanted to be living, Ida's was that Oscar had never been killed; that he had come home from the war, maybe missing a limb or prone to odd tempers or drinking too much, like some of the other veteran husbands, but returned nonetheless, to eat breakfast with his family every morning, toast and eggs and bacon, juice in the Fiestaware glasses they had received as wedding gifts, then put on his hat and coat and go downtown to his job as an accountant. Ida would have stayed home with baby June; she would have washed and dried and put away the dishes, then vacuumed; on Tuesday she would have laundered the sheets, on Wednesday ironed, Thursday baked. In the afternoons she might put June in her carriage and fasten her own hat and walk downtown, or she might have met some of the other mothers to play bridge. In the evening her husband would come home. On weekends they would go for a Sunday drive, and Oscar would wash and wax the car, and maybe June would have had brothers and sisters. Instead, Ida had gone to work and June had stayed home alone, and they had had suppers from cans or aluminum TV trays, and Ida had never again dated, not gone to so much as a church supper or ice cream social, and June would never forget growing up in the deep underwater silence of a house where the population was a female two.

"Peter . . . ," said June. She sipped her coffee, which was cold. "He's a lovely man. But he's difficult. He keeps things to himself."

Ida's chin trembled. "Like what?"

June debated whether to try and explain about Peter's lost family, about which Ida knew nothing but the simplified version June had given her after the elopement: *Peter's first wife and daughters died in the war.* But June feared Ida would not understand; Ida, too, was in love with a ghost. June also could have told her mother about when Peter hadn't confided in June about Masha's going out of business, so June had had to read that for herself in the *New York Times* entertainment section. Or when she'd found out from Ruth, not Peter, that Sol had helped Peter buy the Claremont, that Sol was Peter's partner again. Or when Peter had said the move to New Jersey was for Elsbeth's good—a toddler needed green space to run about in—when really, June suspected, it was to start afresh after losing Masha's. But she didn't tell Ida those things because Ida would worry about June's financial position, and that wasn't really the problem. Peter's secrecy was, his closed door, and June being permanently on the other side.

"I'm not just sure it was a good match," June said finally.

Ida squeezed June's hand, then let go. "Oh, June Ann," she said sadly.

"What?"

"What do you think a marriage is?"

"Two people joining their lives together."

"A marriage is a vow," said Ida. "A vow you took, in case you've forgotten."

"I haven't forgotten," June said. The denial came out more sulkily than she would have liked. She stopped herself from saying, *What would you know about it?* Ida had lived with her husband only a few weeks before he shipped out; the next time she had seen Oscar, he had been in a coffin. Instead June said, "Things have changed since you got married, Mom. Women don't have to be beaten or be married to drunks or gamblers to get divorced. We have other options now—it's the equal rights movement, women's lib. We can find other ways to be fulfilled."

Ida folded her arms and looked at June. Oh Lord, thought June, not the Look. This stern, level gaze of Ida's was the one thing in the world guaranteed to make June rise out of her chair, like a zombie, and do whatever Ida wanted.

"June Ann," she said, "do you know what your first word was?"

"Mom?" June guessed.

"More," Ida said.

June laughed. Ida nodded.

"It's true," she said. "Ever since you were born, this is how you've been. More juice. More cookie. More than anyone else had, more than this place could give you. I always loved you for it, honey. Even when it took you away from me, all the way to New York, I never tried to stop you. Maybe I even spoiled you a little."

"Probably you did," said June, "for which I thank you."

She was smiling, but Ida looked grave.

"It was fine when it was just you," she said, "or even when it was you and Peter. But you've got Elsbeth to think about now, June Ann. It's time you settled down. Life doesn't always work out the way you want. You made your bed."

She reached out and cupped June's face with a hand that shook only a little.

"It's time to grow up, honey," she said.

✳

After this disturbing conversation, June took Elsbeth for one last swim. Elsbeth was ecstatic; she loved the New Heidelberg town pool, where, as in Larchmont, she didn't have to wear a bathing cap. She scampered alongside June, chattering as they walked, her apron dragging over the cracked sidewalks. The sun was like a hammer.

At the pool, June paid the fifty-cent entrance fee and walked Elsbeth behind the chain-link fence, where Elsbeth first ran up to the life-size ceramic lion spitting water from its mouth and stuck her head in, then charged toward the pool. "No running," called the lifeguard, in exactly the same tone of bored authority June had used when she'd sat on that throne, wearing a faded red suit and squeezing lemon juice in her hair. Elsbeth leaped in among her shrieking New Heidelberg counterparts, and June watched until she was involved in a game of Marco Polo. Then June left the pool area, got a Tab from the pop machine, and took it to the parking-lot pay phone. The pool was on a slight rise, all the better from which to survey the playing fields, the baseball diamond, and the tennis courts, whose nets sagged on this windless day.

June inserted a dime and dialed. "Good afternoon, Claremont," said the hostess, Shawna. "Oh, hi, June, he's in the kitchen. I'll put you through." But nobody answered, and after listening to the line ring fourteen, fifteen times, June hung up. She fished her dime out of the slot and dialed again.

"Glenwood Bath and Tennis Club," said a girl's voice.

"Pro shack, please," said June.

"This is pro shack," said the girl, who sounded about fifteen and also as though she were chewing gum.

"May I speak with Gregg Santorelli?"

"Who's calling?"

"Mrs. Robinson," said June.

"Sure thing, Mrs. Robinson," said the girl. "Hold on, I'll see if he's available."

She must have set the phone on the desk, because from Minnesota June heard the ambient noises of the country club in New Jersey: the *pock! pong!* of tennis balls being hit; a woman talking about restringing her racquet; a man's deep voice and laughter—Gregg?

"Hello?" June said. "Hello?"

But the girl must never have found Gregg or forgotten June was on the line, for after a while there was a scuffling noise and then somebody hung up, leaving June with the *wah wah wah* of a broken connection.

10

THE FUN HOUSE

One morning in early August somebody rang June's doorbell. She wasn't expecting anyone, so she thought it must be an ambitious Girl Scout or Jehovah's Witness. She was annoyed; she had been watering her plants, which didn't make much sense if she were only going to leave them after Labor Day anyway—she hadn't yet made up her mind about that matter. But it would have been cruel to let them die of thirst in the meantime, so she had been moving among them with her bronze can, pinching off unhealthy babies and dead leaves.

The doorbell ringer turned out to be Gregg, in tennis whites and carrying a shopping bag. "Hi," he said. "Can I interest you in a set of encyclopedias?"

"What are you doing here?" June hissed. She craned around his bulk, and sure enough, his orange Pinto was parked at the curb. "Get in here," she said, pulling him in by the shirt. She wasn't sure what to do about the car; on the one hand, everyone in Glenwood could see it, but on the other, maybe it was better Gregg hadn't driven it around to the back door, which would have been an admission of guilt impossible to explain.

"Wow," he said, walking into June's living room. "This is your house? It's so nice." He turned, taking in the window seat piled with mirrored Indian pillows, the ferns and flokati rugs and hardwood floors. "I can see why you want to be a decorator. You've got great taste. I especially dig this," and he sat in the bishop's chair June had rescued from the curb in front of a burned church and painted bright red.

"Thanks," said June. "What are you doing here?"

Gregg nudged the shopping bag with a sneaker. "I came to see Elsbeth."

"She's not here. She had a birthday party. They went to Turtleback Zoo."

"Oh," said Gregg. He sounded genuinely disappointed. He had met Elsbeth a couple of times: first at the club, where he'd lobbed balls to her on the paddle court that she'd swung at with her short-handled racquet; then, last week, at Applegate Farm. Gregg had arrived before them; he was sitting on a bench in front of the red barn, but when he saw June and Elsbeth he jumped up, grinned, and waved.

Elsbeth hung back. "What?" she said, meaning, What is he doing here?

"You know Gregg, sweet pea," said June, "from the club. He's going to have ice cream with us; isn't that nice?"

"No," said Elsbeth.

But she allowed herself to be led over, and Gregg had crouched down to her eye level. "Hi, kiddo," he said. "Gimme some skin." He held up his palm and Elsbeth slapped at it. "Now go low," he said, and she did it again. "There you go. You wanna see what I've got for you?"

Elsbeth nodded. Gregg produced a set of alphabet letter magnets. "Somebody went to Toys 'R' Us on Route 46," murmured June.

"You bet," said Gregg. He opened the plastic packaging and set the magnets on the curb. "What's the matter, kiddo?"

Elsbeth had backed away from the letters. "Those are wrong," she said.

"Elsbeth," said June, "that's not polite. What do we say when someone gives us a gift?"

"The A is green," Elsbeth cried. "That's not right. A is blue. And the T is not 'opposed to be yellow!"

"Wow," said Gregg. "You know your own mind, huh, kiddo? That's cool. Hey, I'm awfully hungry for ice cream. You wouldn't know anyone else who wants some, would you?"

He stood and rubbed his big belly. Elsbeth looked up—and up and up. She glanced back at June, then let Gregg take her to the counter for a watermelon cone.

Now Gregg said, "That's too bad. I was looking forward to seeing her. I brought her this," and he pulled a carton out of the shopping bag. It was a toy called a Lite-Brite, an electric box with a perforated pegboard and black sheets of paper to be taped over it, along with hundreds of different-colored pegs to make designs.

"See," said Gregg, "when you turn it on, the pegs glow! I thought because she digs colors so much . . . Don't worry," he added, "I checked the box. It's for over age five."

"Thank you," said June, although all she could think of was how hard those little pegs would be to vacuum out of the deep-pile rug in Elsbeth's room, not to mention how they would feel when June inevitably stepped on them barefoot. "I'll give it to her when she gets home. But you can't be here. Why aren't you at the club?"

"I was, but I told them I had a medical emergency," he said. He stood. "Which was true. I'm having June withdrawal."

"Gregg, honestly."

He kissed her. "And I've got good news. I officially gave notice this morning. One more week. Plus my buddy Steve found us a place. It's just a studio, but it'll do until we can get settled."

"Gregg—"

"I wired the deposit last night," he added. He stepped back. "So are you going to give me the house tour?"

"I'd love to," said June, "but I don't think it's a good idea."

"Fine," he said, "I'll sightsee on my own." June stayed where she was and listened to Gregg prowling through the foyer, looking into the kitchen. "Your pad's great," he called, "but it doesn't look like you've packed much."

"Of course not," said June. "I don't want to give the game away."

Gregg returned. His head bumped the living room chandelier, and it swung back and forth, white globes trembling.

"You aren't going to tell him?"

"I'm still trying to decide that. It might be easier if—"

"You mean you're still trying to decide if you're coming."

"That's not what I said."

"It's what you mean, though, isn't it? Otherwise you would have told him already."

"That's not true," said June. "It's more complicated than that. You don't know Peter, you don't know—"

"I know that I'm hearing a lot of hesitation, June. I don't like that. It makes me nervous."

"Oh," June cried, "why don't you just back off! You have no idea what this is like for me. I'm not some twenty-seven-year-old vet who's footloose and fancy-free. I've got a family, a whole household to pull apart. There's nothing harder."

Gregg looked contrite. He came back to June and took her in his arms. "You're right. I'm sorry. How can I help? Tell me."

He soothed her, stroking her hair; he kissed her sweetly, then more deeply. He slid his hand under the panel of June's overalls, found her nipple beneath her shirt, thumbed it.

"I like these," he murmured, unhooking the straps. "Your grubs."

June wouldn't take him upstairs, but to avoid carpet burn she did lead Gregg to the den, which was where people were supposed to sit to listen to the piano nobody played. Instead the Rashkins used the room mostly to watch television. June and Gregg put the couch, a midcentury green leather castoff from Sol's office, to good use, and afterward, when Gregg fell asleep, June lay awkwardly wedged in next to him—half beneath him, really, with his heavy arm curled around her waist. She felt his breath on her neck and watched, through the window over his shoulder, the flickering leaves of the oak that sheltered Elsbeth's sandbox. The big old trees were one of the reasons June had agreed to this property, although she had been reluctant to leave the city. If she stayed now, she would wither and turn brittle like the plants she had been tending earlier. But how could she go? What was she going to do?

Gregg twitched in his sleep, a whole-body jerk that almost bumped June off the couch. She glanced at him with annoyance. A minute later it happened again, then again. June tried to extricate herself, but he was too heavy. "Gregg," she said, nudging him with her elbow. "Gregg, you're dreaming. Wake up."

"Huh!" he said, but he was still asleep, the whites of his eyes showing between the lids. He started clicking his jaw, biting rapidly, making a sound like castanets. His mouth fell open and omitted a high whine that made the fine hair on June's neck and arms stand up.

"Gregg," she said again, but then she paused: she'd heard if you woke a person during a nightmare, he could go crazy. And Gregg was surely having a nightmare; he was crying now, tears streaming down his cheeks from his half-open eyes, the thin scream still emerging from his throat. He shuddered and jumped, muscles writhing all over his body. June couldn't stand it. It was as though he were on a planet where only bad things happened and he was being tortured there.

She pushed with all her might against his chest and broke free, sliding to the floor beside the couch. Gregg's eyes popped open.

"It's me," said June. "You were having a bad dream. Are you okay?"

He stared at her with absolutely no recognition. Then his arm shot out and he punched her in the face.

June howled—at least, she thought she did. She couldn't tell. The pain was instant and world-swallowing, a supernova blotting out everything but itself. The only thing she had to compare it to was when she'd been in labor with Elsbeth, before the cesarean: "You're doing great, sugar," a nurse had kept saying, "real good, sugar, keep it up," until finally June had screamed, "Don't call me fucking sugar just give me something to make it stop!" She had not known until then that pain could turn her into an animal, that she would do anything—kick, bite, scream, kill—if only it would go away.

"Oh my God," she heard Gregg saying. "June! June, can you breathe?"

She must have thrown her hands over her face, for she felt Gregg trying to pry them away. This was an improvement, the consciousness that she had limbs, a face, and body, instead of just being obliterated by pain.

"Oh my God," Gregg said again. "Oh, June. Your face. Your beautiful face. I'm so, so sorry."

June tried to force her eyes open to look at him. The whole right side of her head throbbed.

"Can you breathe?" he asked. "Are you hearing me?"

"Yes," said June. She snuffled and tasted blood. She would have spat, but she was coming back to herself enough to know it would ruin the rug. She swallowed instead and instantly felt nauseous.

"Can you hang on?" said Gregg. "While I get a cloth and some ice? I'll be right back."

June heard him run toward the kitchen, his heavy footsteps shaking her furniture. She leaned against the couch, snuffling and swallowing, trying not to throw up. She could open her right eye now, just a slit, although the vision in it was red. Her cheek pulsed in and out like a cartoon character who'd been pounded with a mallet.

Gregg returned with a dishtowel and an ice tray. June heard him cracking its metal spine and the cubes hitting something—a bowl? Then she felt the wet towel on her face. She hissed.

"I'm sorry," said Gregg. "I know it hurts. But I need to see if anything's broken. Can you count to ten for me? In your head?"

June did, focusing on the numbers in the red sea of pain. The dishtowel brushed lightly over her face.

"Okay . . ." Gregg muttered. "I don't think anything's broken. That's the good news. Your cheekbone's intact, and your nose and teeth and jaw. The bad news is, I must have really clobbered you one in the eye."

"No kidding," said June. She hadn't considered her teeth. She used her tongue to check them, but Gregg had been right; nothing wobbled.

"I should take you to the hospital," said Gregg, "just to be sure."

"No way," said June.

"Yes way."

"No," she said and swallowed—the blood taste was diminishing, but it was still sickening. "What would I tell them, that I walked into a door?"

"You could tell them they should see the other guy," said Gregg. He tried to smile.

"It's not funny."

"No," he agreed. "It's not. Sorry. Oh God, June, I'm so sorry. I would do anything to take this back. I'd rather set myself on fire than hurt you—you know that, right?"

"Yes," June said, and she did. But she couldn't help adding, "When you're awake, anyway."

Gregg said nothing, and June opened her right eye farther and peered at him: he was blurry but no longer red, which was a good thing. As she blinked, the blur began to clear as well. Gregg was making an ice bag of the dishcloth and cubes; he started to apply it to June's cheek, but she stopped him.

"Let me," she said. "It hurts less that way."

Gregg sat on the floor with her, a hand resting on June's bare knee—she realized she was still in the pink T-shirt she'd been wearing under her overalls and nothing else. Her face throbbed. For the first time she was grateful she was too old to model, because she would have been hysterical with panic. Her most valuable property, ruined! Now she just felt scared and very tired.

"Can you bring me a mirror, please?" she asked. "I want to check the damage."

"I don't know if you should . . ."

"My handbag's hanging on the knob of the kitchen door."

Gregg left and returned with June's purse. He sat on the floor with her, knee to knee, as if they were playing Connect Four. June took out her compact.

"Oh my God," she said. The left side of her face looked relatively normal, just wet and pink. The right side was swollen beyond recognition.

"I look like Boom Boom Mancini," she said. "What am I going to tell Elsbeth? Or . . ." She stopped, but she knew both she and Gregg were thinking: Peter.

"You could say you got mugged," Gregg suggested.

"That might work," June agreed. She started assembling the story—she'd been leaving Willowbrook Mall with her wallet open, putting change into it; stupid, she knew, but it had been partly her fault . . .

Gregg said, "The swelling's going down some already. It's not as bad as it could be, thank God—although we should put a steak on it. That's what my ma and Nonna always do." Suddenly his face changed, draining of expression as if somebody had pulled a plug.

"Jesus Christ," he said. "I'm just like Pop."

"What?"

"I hit a woman. The one thing I swore on my life I'd never ever do."

"You were sleeping. You were having a nightmare—"

"That's no excuse," Gregg said, and he started to cry. He turned to hide it, but his shoulders heaved.

"Gregg," she said. "It's not the same."

"It doesn't matter. It's 'Nam. It's fucking destroyed me."

"What are you talking about? This doesn't have anything to do with—"

"It does, though," he said grimly. "That's what I was dreaming about." He wiped his face on his forearm—at some point he had pulled on his briefs. "They told me when I was discharged that this might happen. That I might have shell shock. Bad dreams." Gregg scoffed and ground the heels of his palms into his eyes. "Bad dreams. Jesus!"

June sat holding her dishtowel ice bag, water trickling down her arm, as Gregg got himself under control. She felt resentful, tricked: not by Gregg but by war. It was such a wily opponent. It had punched such big holes in June's life—a father-sized one, smaller ones belonging to a woman and two children June had never met. It had left June's mother widowed, June half orphaned and with half a husband. She had thought, with Gregg, that he had miraculously escaped damage. Now she knew his scars were all on the inside.

She watched him now, his big head in his hands, and asked the one thing she'd never dared to ask Peter, the question that could never be answered by Walter Cronkite, by newspapers or *Time* and *Life*. She asked, "What was it like?"

Gregg didn't lift his head. He said, "What was what like?"

"The war," said June.

Gregg didn't respond, and June thought maybe he hadn't heard her. She was about to ask again—if anyone could tell her, he could; he was young, he was a different, open generation—when he said "What do you want to know?"

"I don't know," said June, "that's why I'm asking. Did you . . . kill anyone?"

Now Gregg did look up; he glared at June in disbelief from wet red eyes.

"Did I kill anyone?" he repeated. "Did I kill anyone? Fuck, June, what do you think my job over there was, to play Monopoly with Charlie?"

"Sorry," June said.

"Yeah, I'm sorry too. Sorry I wasted four years of my life in some stinking shithole fighting a war it turns out nobody believed in anyway. Sorry it messed me up so bad I can't sleep without turning on. Sorry it turned me into such an animal I did this to you," and Gregg reached toward June's face. She flinched back.

"Look what I've done," he said, "you won't even let me touch you," and his eyes filled again with tears. "I wasn't like this before. I was pretty normal, I think. But 'Nam did things to me. It got into my head. You want to know what it was like, June? You really want to know?"

"I'm not sure," said June.

"It was like the fun house," Gregg said. "The one my pop took us to when I was a little kid, down at Asbury. You know those places? The kind where the floors move up and down and the walls are mirrored and people jump out at you, dressed like mummies and ghosts. And it was a maze, so you couldn't find your way out. It scared me so badly I just gave up and sat in a corner. Until the park attendants came to find me. I'd wet myself, and my pop belted me good for that. Yeah."

He flexed his big hands, frowning at them as if he weren't sure they belonged to him. Those big hands that had cupped June's head, her breasts, her buttocks; had held her child's hand, had been inside her. What else had they done?

"That's what 'Nam was like," said Gregg. "Except with a thousand more bodies and shit and fire and bugs and rot and death. And you never get out."

He looked up at June, his eyes drooping at the corners.

"I'd understand if you kick me out right now," he said. "If you tell me you never want to see me again. I'm sure you don't want to come to California with me now."

"Don't be silly," said June.

She said it reflexively, as if she were reassuring Elsbeth after a fall: You'll be all right. Gregg looked stunned.

"Really?" he said. "Really, June?"

"I think you should see a doctor," she said quickly, "and get some help. . . ."

"Oh, I will," he said. He got up on his knees. "I will. I definitely will. I'll do anything you say—as long as you're still coming. I can do anything if you're with me."

He touched her face with one finger, as gently as if he were removing an eyelash.

"I love you, June," he said, and June thought: Oh God, help him. Help us both. How was she going to get out of this? She let Gregg apply her ice pack and closed her eyes.

*

It took a week for June's face to heal enough for her to go out in public, except to visit the family physician, who told her she was lucky she hadn't detached a retina. Peter had been horrified, demanding they call the police, but June said, "For what? I didn't see the guy who mugged me, and I'm sure he's long gone by now." After an evening and morning of solicitude and aspirin, Peter had returned to the Claremont—and June had seen nobody but Elsbeth and Helen Lawatsch, who mercifully came to take Elsbeth to the club for afternoon swim. "I won't tell anyone the real story," Helen had said; "was it just eyes?" and June realized Helen thought June had had work done. She had smiled enigmatically behind her big sunglasses; better that Helen believed this and spread this rumor than guess what had really happened.

By the time her mandatory convalescence was over, June was jumpy from isolation—and she had formulated a plan. She waited until late afternoon, then dressed Elsbeth in her lavender Ida frock—Elsbeth had relinquished her princess apron, but now she refused to wear anything that wasn't purple—put her in the back of the car, and drove up the mountain. At the turnoff to the club June glanced over, but she kept going. She hadn't seen Gregg since the incident; he had agreed with her on the phone that it was better if they cooled it while June's face healed. She wondered what he was doing at that very moment: giving a private lesson, coaching men's doubles, belly-flopping into the adult pool after finishing for the day? He might even be at his parents' house, continuing to pack. June missed him so terribly it felt like vertigo.

At the bottom of the mountain she turned left and drove along Route 23 past the Woodcrest Golf Club, with its neoclassical club-house and sweeping greens; the next turnoff was the Claremont. The restaurant's proximity to the Woodcrest was both a boon for business, since people often came to the restaurant for fine dining after playing eighteen holes, and a hazard because rogue balls flew over the fence to dent the cars of Peter's patrons. He had been negotiating with the Woodcrest about installing a net. June parked and let Elsbeth run into the restaurant ahead of her, crying, "Daddy, Daddy, Daddy!"—it was only five, so the lot was empty. June followed at a more sedate pace, pausing to light a cigarette.

The Claremont's air conditioning was a welcome shock after the August humidity and glare; sometimes it seemed this month would never end, with its orange sun and smell of fires. June took off her sunglasses to let her eyes adjust. The hostess, Shawna, came from the back in a long burgundy gown, her black hair winging away from her face in feathers. They exchanged air kisses, careful not to touch each other's skin.

"Nice to see you, hon," said Shawna. "How's the shiner?"

"Much better."

Shawna came closer for inspection. "Looks good," she said finally; "you can hardly tell." Shawna was engaged to a police officer who was enthusiastic with his fists; she knew about black eyes. "Did you put a steak on it?"

"No, ice," said June. "And frozen peas."

"Peas! I'll have to remember that. I told Bobby about the jigs who jumped you. He said they'll put an extra detail on at the mall."

"Thanks," said June, "but I don't think he was black. And there was only one."

"Of course he was black," said Shawna. "They're all coming up from Newark these days, haven't you heard? And the riots? You've got to be more careful."

"I will," said June, following Shawna to the Rashkins' habitual corner banquette.

"Mr. R will be out in a sec," said Shawna. "You want a drink?"

"Martini?"

"You got it," said Shawna. She tipped a long red nail at June and sashayed off.

June lit another cigarette and looked around. The dining room was nearly empty; only one early-bird pair sat by the window, or maybe they were lingering after a very late lunch. From the banquet room came the sound of vacuuming. A waitress brought June's drink, and she sipped it meditatively. The Claremont had changed so much since the first time Peter had brought June here, in 1972; it had previously been a Greek diner, its owner mysteriously disappeared, and Peter had gotten it at auction. "A fire-sale price," he had told June, who'd said, "I can see why." She had paced the dining room, with its tired vinyl flooring, pink plastic tablecloths, the smudged display case that was meant to showcase cakes and pies but now rotated empty; she had shaken her head at the mirrored walls and sun-faded mural of Mount Olympus and said, "This is why you moved us to the suburbs?" Peter had smiled. "This is why I need your help," he said.

The Claremont was the first space June had decorated beyond the apartment on East Ninety-Sixth Street and their Glenwood home; Peter had given her a strict budget but carte blanche with style. It had been June who had chosen the gold carpet and starburst chandeliers; June who had come up with the idea to spongepaint the mirrored walls in gold leaf to antique them and hang red velvet curtains to make them look like windows. "Better than paying to remove them," she'd told Peter, "and think of all the years of bad luck you've avoided." She remembered the excitement of hurrying across the parking lot on opening day, clutching a takeout coffee, and assuming her position behind the hostess stand—this was before Peter had hired a regular girl. *Welcome to the Claremont, how are you this evening?* She and Peter had made the Claremont together; after Elsbeth, it was their best collaborative effort.

Peter came through the kitchen door now, holding Elsbeth's hand; he was in a light gray summer-weight suit. He smiled at June as he helped Elsbeth into the banquette, and she smiled back; no matter whatever else had happened between them, June never tired of seeing Peter in his element, cutting across a restaurant floor.

"May I join you?" he asked.

"Of course." June slid over, and Elsbeth did too, so Peter could sit on her other side.

"A vodka tonic, please," he said to the waitress who materialized, and—"June, another? Yes? Beefeater martini, very dry; Shirley Temple, three cherries; and one hamburger, plain, no bun. Otherwise known as . . . what, Ellie?"

"Hamburger Walter," Elsbeth said, scribbling on the back of a place mat with the crayons June had passed her.

"Very good. And how is that cooked, for grown-ups?"

"With pepper and brandy," she said. "Au poivre."

"Excellent. That deserves a strawberry ice cream—after dinner."

The waitress lit the candle on their table and departed. Peter scanned the dining room, making sure it was ready for dinner service. "How is your eye?" he asked.

"Better, thank you."

"Let me see," he said, and June turned obligingly toward him. "Ah, yes. You can barely tell."

"Thank God for Cover Girl," June said.

"Thank God that bastard didn't hurt you any worse than he did," said Peter grimly.

"Daaadddddy," said Elsbeth. She was drawing herself, in a purple princess dress with an apron and jeweled crown. "You said a bad word."

"So I did." Peter shifted to get at his pocket and pushed a nickel across the table. "One for the swear bank," he said, and Elsbeth tucked the coin in her purple purse.

"And who is that you are drawing?" said Peter, tipping his head to look at Elsbeth's paper. "That big person?"

"That's Gregg," said Elsbeth.

She was coloring in a monolithic rectangle with legs and glasses. June shook her head and shrugged in response to Peter's questioning glance: *I don't have any idea.* "Maybe somebody from the club," she said.

The waitress returned with their drinks and Elsbeth's burger, along with a silver dish of her favorite pickles. "Cheers," said Peter, and the three Rashkins clinked glasses. Elsbeth ate a cherry and returned to scribbling; June and Peter sipped and sat watching the dining room fill. Shawna swanned among the tables in her wine-colored gown, leading patrons to their seats, waiters and waitresses then appearing to take drink and appetizer orders in well-rehearsed choreography.

"To what do I owe the pleasure—" Peter said, as June started, "This is a nice—" They looked at each other and smiled.

"Go ahead," said June.

Peter inclined his head. "After you."

"I was just going to say this is a nice change of pace," said June, "after being in the house all week. It was too hot to cook."

"Indeed," said Peter. "It is beastly. Even with the air conditioning, the air is like soup in the kitchen." He consulted his watch. "I should go back in."

June lit a cigarette. "Actually, I was hoping to get a word with you—"

"Can it wait until after I get home?"

June's hand shook as she lifted her drink; she set it down before it could spill.

"Honestly, Peter," she said, "I don't think it can."

Peter had been signaling something to a waiter across the room, restaurateur's semaphore, but something in June's tone or her use of his full name stopped him.

"What is it?" he asked.

June stared at her martini and took a deep breath through her nose.

"June? Is something wrong?"

"I've been meaning to tell you," she said, and then her voice caught and she looked away, across the dining room.

Peter said nothing, but in June's peripheral vision she saw his handkerchief appear. She nodded her thanks and picked it up, touching it beneath her left eye and then, very carefully, her right.

Peter knocked his knuckles against the table. Presently he said, "Is this about what we've been discussing, you going back to work?"

"In a manner of speaking," said June.

"Or is it Sol's comments? I have been regretting letting him get away with that," said Peter. "Sol can be a bully, but you know his opinion has no bearing on our personal life."

June made herself look over at him. Peter was smiling at her with his head lowered and his brows raised, an expression she knew meant, Forgive me?

"Peter," she said, "I have to tell you something."

She watched as his face changed. When Elsbeth was little, Peter had played a game with her that consisted of making a comical smile, then drawing his hand over it and frowning, then repeating the gesture and grinning again. Now it looked as though somebody had swiped his face with comprehension. He sat back.

"I see," he said. "Very well. But I suggest we talk tonight at home. I will try to leave at a decent hour. I don't think we should discuss it in front of——"

And he tipped his head toward Elsbeth. But Elsbeth wasn't there. There was only her drawing, her napkin, and her empty plate.

"Where did she go?" Peter stood up.

June did too. "I don't know."

"She must have wriggled out under the table. But where is she?"

"I can't see her anywhere," June said.

Both parents surveyed the room. It was busy now, most tables filled; waiters and waitresses swerved among them, balancing heavy trays of drink and hot food. June thought of the kitchen, where Elsbeth was expressly forbidden to go without a grown-up; of knives, stovetops, boiling pots. The parking lot with its incoming traffic. Route 23, where the speed limit was fifty-five miles an hour. Peter had summoned Shawna and was speaking quickly to her; Shawna hurried into the kitchen.

"Pete," said June, "you don't think——"

Then she glanced at Elsbeth's drawing, which was all done in purple, and Elsbeth's purple satin purse, and she knew where Elsbeth was; when she looked back at Peter, she could see he did too. They bolted from the table. "Excuse me," said June as she moved through the dining room, "pardon me." She headed toward the ladies' lounge, which, like everything else at the Claremont, June had decorated herself. She had used the most au courant color in 1972, which, like everything Elsbeth wore, drew, and surrounded herself with these days, was purple. Everything in the ladies' room was some shade of that color, from the tiles to the stalls to the African violet prints. Even the toilets were lavender, and it was there that June, banging open the first stall with Peter behind her, found Elsbeth: hugging the porcelain bowl. "Mommy," announced Elsbeth, "look, my purple princess throne! I love it." And as both parents said, "No no no no no no!" she lowered her face to kiss the seat.

*

That night June was in the guest room when Peter came home. She had moved from the master bedroom after the incident with her face, claiming it was easier for her to sleep sitting up—which, as far as it went, was true. But June had been doing precious little sleeping the past week, and it hadn't been due to the residual ache in her cheek.

She looked at the clock on the bedside table: ten past midnight. This was what Peter called a decent hour? But it was, really, for him; most nights he didn't leave the restaurant until two or three. June lit a cigarette and sat alert with it, listening. She heard Peter's footsteps cross the kitchen floor. The refrigerator opened and closed—no doubt he had brought home leftovers from the Claremont's nightly special, as he always did. The creak of the cupboard in which the glasses were kept; the faucet running. The clank of a glass being set in the sink. Then he was coming upstairs. June watched the door.

There was a knock. "June? Are you still awake?"

June set aside the paperback she had been holding and extinguished her cigarette. "Come in."

Peter walked into the little room, then stood looking around. "I'd forgotten what a pleasant space this is," he said. "I don't think I've been in here more than once or twice since it was Ellie's nursery."

"I redid the wallpaper."

"Ah, is that it? I thought there was something different. It looks nice," he said, either not seeing or pretending not to notice the way the flowered cloth sagged and bowed away from the walls.

June waved at the rocker in the corner. "Have a seat."

"Thank you," Peter said. He crossed to the chair and sat, set his palms on his knees, and smiled at her. He had gray bags under his eyes, and the breeze from the fan as it moved its wire face from side to side loosened his hair from its gelled waves. Time had carved lines across Peter's forehead and from his nose to his chin; June thought, as she sometimes had before, that if youth was being unmarked, age was a sullying, and she wished there were some special sponge she could use to wipe her husband's years away.

"Well, June," Peter said. He had taken off his suit jacket, maybe downstairs, and was in his shirtsleeves. The shirt looked rumpled. "Here we are."

"Yes," she agreed. Outside a car passed on Park Street; a dog barked down the block.

"So," said Peter, "there is somebody else?"

June looked at her lap, her legs crossed beneath her nylon nightgown.

"Yes," she said.

"That is what you wanted to tell me. At the restaurant."

"Yes."

"I see," he said. "How long?"

"Not very. A couple of months."

"A couple of—! Who is it?"

"That's not important."

"Like hell it isn't," said Peter. "Like hell!"

He got up from the chair so abruptly that it hit the wall, then rebounded. He strode back and forth. "Goddamn it, June!" he shouted. "Who is it? This photographer you were supposedly working with in Minneapolis? Someone from the club? Tell me!"

She shook her head. "It doesn't matter. I think it's over—"

"You think! You think. Ah, that's terrific. You think it's over."

"What do you want me to say?" she shouted back. "That it's not over? That I'm leaving you? Is that what you want?"

Peter stopped pacing. "Are you?"

June looked back down at her lap. She shook her head and pinched her eyes shut. A couple of tears fell on her thighs.

"And now you're sad about it," said Peter. "Ah, that's wonderful. I'm so sorry you're not running off with your lover."

"Don't tempt me!"

Peter threw himself back into the chair, which cracked but continued to hold him. A lock of hair, loosened from his pacing, waved wildly in the breeze from the fan.

"Why?" he said. "If you won't tell me who, at least tell me that. I've been a good husband to you. I've provided for you, I've been faithful—"

"—you've been a good father to Elsbeth," June finished for him. "Yes."

"Then why, goddamn it?"

"You really have to ask me that?" said June softly.

He stared at her. "What are you talking about?"

"You know what I mean," she said.

"Enlighten me."

"You really want me to? You really want me to tell you what it's like for me while you're working twenty hours a day, seven days a week—"

"To keep the business going. I've always been dedicated to what I do, you've always known that—"

"We both know you don't have to work as hard as you do."

"Lots of men work hard."

"Come on, Pete. Why are you making me say it? You know what the problem is. You know why you work so hard. It's the only place you feel good, in your kitchen. Right? It's where you shut everything out, pretend nothing bad ever happened. The war never happened. You never lost her. You never lost them."

"That . . . is . . . enough!"

"No, I'm not finished. I think about them too, did you know that? I do. Those poor babies. And Masha. I wish I'd been able to meet her. I admire her. She must have been so brave. . . . But the fact is, she's gone. And you are too. There's a part of you that's not there at all. It's shut down, or maybe it doesn't even exist anymore. All I know is, you're only half there." June's throat hurt. She put her hand on it. "And it's really lonely."

Peter looked at her as though he'd never seen her before.

"June," he said, "you knew all this when you married me. You knew what had happened."

"Yes, of course. But I didn't know it would last. I guess I was naive, but I thought, well, you're always strangers to each other at the beginning, right? People grow together. I thought you would thaw." She shook her head. "You didn't."

Peter looked down at his feet, his scuffed black chef's shoes on the carpet.

"Sometimes I think you never should have gotten married again," said June. "You might have been happier if I hadn't come along."

"That's not true. You made me happy."

"Let me ask you something. If I hadn't been pregnant, would you have proposed?"

Peter paused long enough to let June know he was considering his answer. "I wanted to marry you."

"That doesn't answer my question."

Peter ran his hands over his hair. "June," he said finally, "this is all ancient history. What do you want me to do?"

"Remember before we were married, when I asked you to see an analyst?"

"Yes."

"Did you?"

"Ah, June, who knows? It was so long ago—"

"You didn't," she said. "Don't bother fibbing. I know."

"And how would you know that?"

"I followed you," she said. "When you left your apartment. You said you were going to the appointment, but you went to Masha's as usual."

"You followed me," Peter repeated. He closed his eyes. "Of course you did."

"I want you to go now," June said. "With me. I don't know if it'll fix anything, but something has to change. Something. And maybe it'll give us a chance. Will you?"

Peter seemed to be considering the carpet. At long last, he sighed.

"June," he said. "I am sorry, but I cannot. I am too old a dog for that trick. I told you a long time ago that there were some things I wouldn't talk about. And I still can't."

"Won't, you mean."

"Won't or can't, it is just not something I am going to do." He looked at her without lifting his head. "Perhaps I should not have married you. I thought at the time it might not be fair to you. You are, you have always been, so vital, so open to life's possibilities. And I have been missing something all along. I thought it might come back. Or that we could do without it. But in the end, this is who I am, and this is the best I can do."

He lifted his hands and let them fall. "I am sorry, June. I'm sorry I am not who you want me to be."

June waited. "Is that it?" she asked finally.

"For now," said Peter. "Except I do love you, June, as best I can. And that is as true as anything we have said here tonight."

He stood, then winced and pressed his side.

"What is it?" said June.

"Nothing. A stitch. I must have lifted something the wrong way at the stove." Peter forced himself upright. "I know this isn't the end of the discussion," he said. "We will talk more. But please excuse me for now. I have gone as far as I can tonight." He opened the door and nodded politely at June. "Good night," he said, and went out.

✳

The next morning, June awoke very early, and she knew what she must do.

She got up, made the guest bed, washed her face, brushed her teeth, and combed her hair. She dressed in the clothes on the back of the bathroom door, bell-bottom jeans and a T-shirt. She went quietly downstairs. The door to the master bedroom was closed; either Peter had also arisen early and gone to the restaurant, or he was still asleep. The house was filling with the gray light of dawn.

Elsbeth was already up; she was sitting in front of the television in the den, frog-legged in her Holly Hobbie pajamas, watching *The Pink Panther*. This was her routine before June and Peter woke: she was allowed to watch TV if she kept the sound low, and she could have a couple of sugar wafers June left for her in Elsbeth's special kitchen drawer, but she was not to disturb her parents.

She whipped her head around when June said, very quietly, "Good morning, darling."

"Look!" said Elsbeth. She rose on her knees and bounced, pointing at the screen. The Pink Panther lit Inspector Clouseau's cigarette. It promptly exploded, leaving Clouseau smoldering. Elsbeth jiggled, giggling. "Isn't he silly, Mommy?"

"Very silly. Come on, let's get dressed, hurry hurry. Mommy's got a surprise for you."

"What?"

"It wouldn't be a surprise if I told you, would it?"

"No," Elsbeth agreed. She jumped up.

June got her dressed, plucking clothes from the basket in the laundry room off the kitchen, a ruffled yellow blouse and a clean pair of OshKoshes. She stuffed a few more outfits into a shopping bag. In Elsbeth's lunchbox June packed carrot sticks and Laughing Cow cheese and Oreos, averting her eyes from the food Peter had brought home the night before: "rst chix / crmd pots / spch souff / 30 aug," it said on the Styrofoam container, in Peter's pointy script. The chef's habit of always listing contents and date.

"Can I have some apple juice, Mommy?"

"May I."

"May I have some apple juice, please?"

"Yes, you may," said June. She filled Elsbeth's Beatrix Potter mug. "Stay right here and drink that. I'll be back in a sec."

She darted upstairs, careful to avoid the step that creaked under the carpet. In Elsbeth's room, June grabbed *Charlotte's Web* and *Stuart Little* from the side table, stuffed Pooh, Piglet, Snoopy, Woodstock, Henry, and EekAMouse! into a sling she made out of her shirt. The master bedroom door was still closed. June crept quickly downstairs. She put on her sunglasses and picked up her purse.

"Ready, sweet pea?"

"Where are we going, Mommy?"

"On a special trip."

"Yayyyyyy!" Elsbeth shouted. June put a finger to her lips.

"But quietly," she said. "Like baby mice. Can you be quiet?"

"Yes," Elsbeth stage-whispered.

She tiptoed exaggeratedly toward the back steps, lifting her feet in huge arcs. June took a last look at the kitchen and shut the door behind them.

Outside the big trees were wreathed in mist, the grass glittering with dew. The light was mysterious, the birdsong lively and sweet. June would miss her plants, the yard with the brook. She buckled Elsbeth into the back seat.

On the way to the interstate, June stopped in Glenwood Plaza to get gas, a cup of coffee, and a new map. "Hiya, sunshine," the station attendant said to her, "you're up early for a Saturday." June smiled behind her sunglasses and added a handful of pretzel sticks for Elsbeth. The pavement steamed; the shopkeepers were just unlocking their doors, putting out sandwich boards. In yards along the way, people shuffled out in robes to get papers, set sprinklers fanning back and forth, walked dogs, unfurled their flags. Then Glenwood fell away behind them as June drove up over the mountain. The road wound through the Watchung Reservation, where June had once made love in a stand of birches with Gregg; she drove past the Eagle Ridge Diner and Pal's Cabin, and took the exit for 280. It felt strange to be traveling west instead of east to Larchmont or New York, the city at her back. The interstate was nearly empty.

June felt a rising excitement she hadn't felt since boarding the Greyhound bus for Manhattan when she was twenty-one. It had something to do with getting up so early, going on a trip, but it was more than that. It was the thrill of embarking upon an adventure she had chosen, with a purpose in mind but no guarantee of what would happen next. June would start by going to Ida's; Ida might not be too pleased to see June and Elsbeth initially, not under these circumstances, but she would soften, June was sure—and wasn't home the place you went where they had to take you in? June and Elsbeth would finish the summer there, then go to Minneapolis, where some of June's high-school friends might help her get oriented. There was no Parsons in the Twin Cities, but there was the Minneapolis College of Art and Design; there were decorating firms; there were correspondence courses. June could be the mother in a few catalogs to bring in some money, smiling in housedresses and pedal pushers at children not her own. And then, degree in hand, maybe California was next—who knew? June didn't. That was the point. She was free. She laughed aloud.

"What's so funny, Mommy?"

"Nothing, darling. I'm just happy."

Elsbeth thought about this. "Where are we going?"

"Well, sweet pea," said June, smiling at Elsbeth in the rearview. Elsbeth had put her sunglasses on too, her Minnie Mouse ones. She looked back at June impassively. "I thought we'd visit Grandma Ida. What do you think?"

"But we just saw her," said Elsbeth.

"That's true. But I thought it'd be nice to go see her again. So you can swim in the pool without your bathing cap and go to the A&W. And then maybe go to Minneapolis!"

"Is Daddy coming?"

"Not this trip, darling. He has to work. But we'll call him later. Okay?"

Elsbeth looked out her window, swinging her sandaled feet. "Can we see the big lion?" she asked eventually.

She meant the fountain at the pool. "Absolutely," said June. "Okay?"

"Okay," Elsbeth said.

"Good," said June. "Should we sing some road trip songs?"

They sang all the way through New Jersey. "Free to Be . . . You and Me," "She'll Be Coming 'Round the Mountain," "I've Been Working on the Railroad"—that was sort of a travel song—Jim Croce. *"Movin' me down the highway . . . movin' ahead so life won't pass me by,"* June and Elsbeth sang lustily. There were more cars on the road now; June kept an eye on the lane ahead of her as she spread the map over the steering wheel. It confirmed what she already knew: they would take Interstate 80 through Pennsylvania and Ohio.

She didn't start to flag until around noon, when they were approaching the Delaware Water Gap. Elsbeth was feeling it too; she had dozed for a while after the sing-along, her head hanging to her chest, but now she was awake and cranky. "Mommy," she said, "I have to go to the bathroom."

"All right, sweetie pie. Can you hold it until I find a gas station?"

"No," said Elsbeth. "I need to go *now.*"

"I know." June handed a baggie of Oreos over the seat. "Just give me a minute."

June drove and drove, but all around them were other people's cars, trucks, mountains, nothing but trees. She knew the Catskills were a popular vacation destination, but she had always found them hostile. Wasn't this the area with Rip Van Winkle, the Headless Horseman? Why would anybody come here for a holiday? June had a headache, a dull pressure squeezing her temples, from eyestrain or from getting up too early. Her right socket ached beneath her sunglasses. A sign flashed by: DEL WATER GAP 12 MI LAST EXIT IN NEW JERSEY TOLLS AHEAD.

"Mommy," said Elsbeth, "I want Daddy. I want to go home."

She started to cry. Of course she did—Elsbeth was tired too despite her nap, her regular routine disrupted. Sometimes, on Saturday mornings, if the Claremont had had a good night the evening before, Peter didn't go in right away. He got up with Elsbeth, and they made breakfast: fresh-squeezed orange juice— naturally, Peter would not hear of juice from a carton or can. Bread toasted in the oven so it would crisp all the way through, Elsbeth turning it carefully with tongs. And Peter's special scrambled eggs: first he caramelized onions in a pan, cooking them very slowly in butter until they were translucent; then he added eggs whipped to a froth, heavy cream, ham, fresh dill, and the secret ingredient: a dollop of Neufchâtel cheese. Elsbeth was always allowed to drop this last onto the dish from a wooden spoon. She had her own jacket with her name stenciled on the lapel, a mini chef's hat, rubber clogs, and a special stool to stand on while she helped Peter stir and mince and measure. The Fabulous Rashkins, they called themselves, and when the food was ready to be served, they presented it to June at the table with a bow, Peter sweeping his hand to the right and Elsbeth to the left. "Ta da! The Fabulous Rashkins! Lo and behold!"

At the exit before the Water Gap, June got off and found a gas station. While the attendant filled their tank and squeegeed the windshield, June got a key and took Elsbeth to the ladies' room. Then she pulled the Dodge off to the side near the pay phone and placed a collect call, her free hand on her ear to block the highway noises, keeping watch on Elsbeth. Elsbeth kicked moodily at the seat, her face sullen; her chest hitched with hiccups from her crying fit earlier.

"Your party does not answer," said the operator. "Would you like to make another call?"

"Yes, please," said June and gave the number. She plugged her ear again and rehearsed what she might say. *I'm so sorry, I didn't mean to scare you, I just had to do it this way before I lost my nerve. We're fine, we're going to my mother's. I'll call you from Ohio tonight. We'll talk . . .*

"Claremont," said an unfamiliar male voice.

June frowned. "Who's this?"

"This is Tony in the kitchen. Who's this?"

"June Rashkin. Is my husband there, please?"

"Oh. Oh, Jesus, June." Tony was one of Peter's prep chefs; what was he doing answering the phone? "Where are you, sweetheart?" he asked.

"I'm out with Elsbeth. Is something wrong?"

"Thank God you called. We've been trying your house all day. Shawna's driving all over looking for you—"

"Tony, just tell me what's wrong!"

"I'm sorry to have to tell you this, hon," he said, "but Peter had a heart attack this morning. He's at Glenwood Memorial."

11

THE AMERICAN DREAM

Peter remained at Glenwood Memorial only until the next morning, when, as soon as it was safe for him to travel, Sol had him transported by ambulance to Mount Sinai in New York. What was the point of making contributions if they weren't even going to use the goddamned place? Sol demanded of June. Sol knew the best heart man in the world, and did June know he was in the city? Didn't June want Peter to have top of the line care? June assumed all the questions were rhetorical.

She followed the ambulance in, Elsbeth having been relinquished to the care of Helen Lawatsch. "Don't you worry about a thing," Helen had said, her eyes huge with sympathy, when she came to pick Elsbeth up at the hospital. "I'll take care of her as long as you need me to." June had burst into tears. She had been numb during her return drive from the Catskills, during which she had gone a good thirty miles an hour over the speed limit the whole way, and her emotional anesthesia had persisted into intensive care, even upon seeing Peter attached to all those machines. It didn't seem quite real. But Helen's kindness undid her.

Now, after a night in an orange plastic chair, June drove very carefully, the heat and her exhaustion making her feel as though everything were melting. Once again it was early; the highway, Route 3 this time, was deserted. In the city, June sat at the first stoplight outside the Lincoln Tunnel and let the windshield washer guys scrub her window without bothering to turn her wipers on or wave them off. She didn't pay them, either, and they yelled resentfully after her. The only pedestrians unfortunate enough to be out scurried from one air-conditioned place to the next; the tops of the buildings disappeared into gray-yellow smog. When June parked her Dodge and got out, her sneakers made imprints in the tar.

Peter was no longer in intensive care, and Sol must indeed have made some healthy donations to Mount Sinai over the years, for Peter's room in the cardiac ward was a single, overlooking the East River. June waited outside until a nurse told her she could go in. She moved quietly, pulling a chair over to the bed; its legs tangled in some tubing attached to Peter's hand, tugging at the tape there, and June swore. Why didn't she just clobber Peter over the head and be done with it? She sat next to him and cradled his free hand, which was dry and cold; she squeezed it and got no response. She turned to the view, the skyscrapers and the water beyond, tugboats and barges moving on it, miniature cars zipping back and forth along FDR Drive and the bridge. It was hard to believe each one contained its own tiny universe, a person or people living out private joys, sorrows, trouble, and dreams. The clouds drifted, curdled like cottage cheese in a white sky.

"June."

Faint pressure on June's hand; when she turned, Peter's eyes were open. She bent to the bed, smiling.

"Hi, Pete. How are you feeling?"

"I've been better," he said. His voice was faint, raspy—from having had the breathing tube in his throat, June thought. But his gaze was lucid. "How long have I been here?"

"Just since this morning. Before that, you were at Glenwood. Sol moved you."

He nodded and winced. "Elsbeth?"

"She's at Helen Lawatsch's. She doesn't know anything—just that you weren't feeling well, so you went into the city to see a special doctor."

"Good," said Peter. "Thank you."

"You're welcome. Is there anything I can get for you?"

"Some water, please," he said, and June fetched it from the plastic pitcher on the bedside table, adjusting the bending straw in the cup.

"June," he said. "What we were talking about before—"

"Forget it, Pete. Just concentrate on getting well."

"I don't want to forget about it. I was thinking about it when . . . this business happened. I don't want you to . . . to be unhappy . . ."

"I'm here," June said firmly. "I'm not going anywhere—understand?"

Peter examined her face over the rim of the cup, his eyes scanning back and forth. Was it possible, June thought, that his hair had thinned overnight? It stood up on his scalp, wispy. She smoothed it, then leaned forward and kissed his forehead. It felt cool and slightly oily under her lips, and he smelled of rubbing alcohol.

"Thank you, June."

"You're welcome, Pete."

The door opened, and a doctor strode in. He was very tall and blond, gloriously mustachioed and sideburned, like an actor playing a doctor on a soap opera. He beamed at Peter, picking up Peter's chart.

"Mr. Rashkin? Dr. Alberts, your cardiologist. How are we feeling today? Anything hurt?"

"Mostly my pride, Doctor."

"A comedian," said the doctor. "That's good. Laughter's the best medicine, et cetera." He took Peter's pulse, still flipping through the paperwork. "Mmm hmm, ta dum, hmmm, very good. Any pressure in the chest?"

"No," said Peter.

"Faintness? Shortness of breath?"

"No."

"Very good, very good. .... Mr. Rashkin, you've suffered a fairly serious cardiac incident—in other words, a heart attack. We'll be keeping you here for a few days, and then, if you don't give us any more trouble, we'll send you home with this lovely young lady." His smile beaconed over at June. "Your daughter, is it?"

"My wife," said Peter.

"Well! Lucky man." The doctor opened Peter's hospital gown to apply his stethoscope to Peter's chest, which June now saw had been shaved in spots to accommodate electrodes. The bare patches among Peter's silvery tufts of hair seemed to June a terrible indignity—perhaps because in their married life she had seen her husband's penis far more frequently than his exposed chest. Her eyes smarted with tears, and she looked away.

"All sounds good," said the doctor. "Your heart's definitely still in there. Do you mind if I borrow your wife for a moment?"

"As long as you return her," Peter said.

"Good man. Keep up the jokes." The doctor closed Peter's gown, made a notation on the chart, and clasped Peter's shoulder. "Get some rest. I'll see you soon."

"Wonderful," said Peter. His eyes had closed again already, the lids purple and waxy.

"Mrs. Rashkin, may I speak to you?" said the doctor.

June kissed Peter's cheek. Outside in the hallway, the doctor was lighting a cigarette, and when he saw June he offered her one.

"Thank you," she said. It was a Pall Mall, stronger than what she usually smoked, and she felt instantly lightheaded.

"You're welcome," said the doctor. His eyes flickered over June in an assessment that didn't feel quite medical; they were very blue, strikingly so, and June suddenly realized who he must be: the man Sol and his friends referred to as Dr. Gorgeous.

"Mrs. Rashkin, I won't lie to you. Your husband's a very sick man."

"Will he be all right?"

"He should be. With proper rest and care. And some dietary and lifestyle changes. But he's had a major coronary. He's lucky he was in the presence of fast-acting people when it happened and got treatment right away."

"Yes," said June faintly. "Very lucky."

"His medical chart says he was in the Nazi death camps?"

"Yes, Auschwitz and . . . I'm sorry, I can't remember the other one. It must be the stress."

"His heart suffered serious damage from that early experience— the starvation and abuse his body took. Given his age, it's a miracle it didn't happen sooner."

"Lucky," June said again. "When can he come home?"

"Oh, four-five days, maybe a week, pending no further incidents. We'll give him an EKG, get him on nitro. He'll have to be kept very quiet. No exertion. No stress."

"I understand."

"Your father-in-law says your husband's a restaurant owner?"

"Yes. He used to own Masha's on the Upper East Side."

"That's it," said Dr. Gorgeous. "I knew I'd met him before. Far out! I loved that place." He mashed out his cigarette in the hallway ashtray. "He might consider doing something else for a while. Even retiring early. That's a high-stress environment for a cardiac patient."

"I see," said June. "We'll figure it out."

Dr. Gorgeous held out his Pall Malls again, but she shook her head. "Is there anything else you want to ask me?" he said.

"No, thank you, Doctor, you've been very helpful. Oh—you mentioned diet?"

"High fiber, low fat, no cholesterol. I'll have the nurse send you home with a care sheet." Dr. Gorgeous smiled. "No more cream puffs."

"No, I guess not."

"God, I loved those," he said. "With that chocolate fondue on the side!" He shook his head. "Of course, Ms. Rashkin, the most important factor in your husband's recovery is the love of his family. But I can't imagine that'll be any trouble. Not with a peach like you at home."

He winked, lit another cigarette, and ambled off down the hall.

*

June stayed with Peter until that evening, when a nurse told her it would be better for them both if June went home to get some rest. Peter had slept most of the afternoon anyway, except when the staff came in to check his vitals. When June kissed him and whispered she would be back tomorrow, his eyelids barely flickered.

In Glenwood, the house was dark, with the waiting air that precedes a thunderstorm. It was too quiet without Elsbeth, the hum of the refrigerator and AC and the tick of the stove clock the only noises. June switched on the kitchen overhead and beheld Elsbeth's rabbit-encircled mug, the mismatched Tupperware lids, and Peter's coffee cup in the sink from their last morning here. They seemed like archaeological relics. June flicked the light back off and went upstairs.

In the master bedroom, she kicked off her sneakers. The bed, the pillow, was redolent of Peter: his skin, his hair gel, spicy and sweet. June intended only to nap, then to get up and call Helen, check on Elsbeth—Elsbeth did not as a rule like sleepovers, claiming other people's houses smelled funny. June also needed to update Sol. She closed her eyes, and the next thing she knew it was morning.

And somebody was pressing the doorbell, alternating the chimes with the front-door knocker. June jolted up and sat stupidly on the side of the bed. Was it Helen? Had Helen been trying to bring Elsbeth back all morning? Now June remembered, or seemed to remember, the phone ringing earlier, and ringing and ringing. Had something happened to Pete? She ran downstairs.

"I'm coming, I'm coming," she called.

But once again it was Gregg at the door.

"Hi," he said.

"Hi," said June. She was suddenly aware of her physical being for the first time in days: her morning breath, her crazy hair. She was still wearing—what was she wearing? The T-shirt and bell-bottoms she'd grabbed the dawn she'd put Elsbeth in the car. How many days ago was that—two, three?

Gregg handed her a white paper bag, in which was a Danish and a takeout coffee.

"May I come in?" he said.

June stepped back, and he came into the foyer. He was wearing jeans too, the first time, besides his suit trousers, that June had ever seen Gregg in anything but shorts. She realized the air was cooler, damp—it must have stormed in the night.

Gregg stood formally in the middle of the rug. "How is he?" he asked.

"Stable," said June. "How did you know?"

"I called the restaurant," said Gregg, and June must have made some noise or expression of alarm because he said, "Don't worry, I didn't tell them who I was. I was just worried because I couldn't reach you, I'd been calling and calling and nobody at the club had seen you, so finally I tried the Claremont. And the hostess told me you were in New York with your husband because he'd had a heart attack."

"Oh," said June.

Her legs suddenly felt jellified, and she sat on the window seat. Gregg sat next to her and helped her take the lid off the coffee. It was sweet, light, and strong.

"I didn't think you took sugar," he said, "but the guy just put it in."

"It's good. Thank you." June sipped, then pinched off a bit of Danish. Cherry, with frosting. Gregg put his elbows on his big knees and looked down.

"So I came," he said, "to say good-bye."

June's stomach lurched. She set the coffee on the rug. "You're going already?"

"June. It's September."

June looked across the foyer at the windows going up the staircase. Beyond them it was raining, drops wending down the glass. "I guess it is."

"Tell me the truth," said Gregg. "You were never going to leave him, were you?"

"No, that's not true," said June. "I was. You gave me the courage to do it. You woke me up."

Gregg grunted. He reached out an arm and hugged June as if they were two pals sitting on a park bench, and then suddenly her head was on his shoulder and they were both crying.

"June, June," he said. "I don't think I can stand this."

"I know," she said. "But you can."

"Can you?"

"I'll have to."

Gregg wiped June's cheeks with his big thumbs. "Your face is all better," he said, "your beautiful beautiful face," and he kissed her. They clung and kissed and cried and hugged until June's nose was so stuffed she could barely breathe.

"Will you write to me?"

Gregg swiped his wrist over his eyes. "I don't think I should."

"Will you send me a postcard with absolutely nothing on it? Every once in a while, so I know you're okay?"

"That," he said, "I can do."

Gregg stood and pulled June to her feet. She stepped toward him one last time and laid her head on his heart.

"Nice purple shirt," she said, muffled.

His voice was a rumble against her cheek. "I thought Elsbeth would like it. Say good-bye to her for me, would you? Tell her keep swinging the racquet low to high."

June trailed him disconsolately to the door, then onto the porch. They were still holding hands. The orange Pinto was at the curb, packed to the roof with bags and cartons. Slumped in the passenger's seat like a person was a duffel: PVT SANT, 3RD INF, she saw stenciled on its side.

Gregg bent his head to kiss her once more, very gently. June felt the flick of his tongue, and then his mouth was gone. "You're the only girl I never had to stoop to kiss," he said. "You know how much I loved that?"

He stepped back and pushed his glasses up on his nose.

"Please go quickly," she said.

"I will."

"Good luck out there, Gregg Santorelli," June said.

"You too, June Bouquet Rashkin."

He jogged down the steps and along the brick walk to his car. June watched with her hand on her throat. She turned and went into the house before she could see him get in and drive away, so her last sight of Gregg Santorelli was of him standing next to his Pinto in his purple shirt, one big arm raised in farewell.

*

Dr. Gorgeous was as good as his word, and Peter was discharged from Mount Sinai a week after he'd gone in, once an angioplasty and another EKG showed that no further procedures—at that time—were necessary. June went to pick Peter up in his Volvo; it was roomier than her Dodge, and she thought he might be more comfortable. A nurse wheeled Peter down to the curb in a chair despite his protests that he was quite able to walk, thank you. He had lost weight, the shirt and slacks June had brought for him sagging on his shoulders and waist, and had also grown a beard. It was more white than blond and made him look, June thought, like an ambassador or visiting dignitary, somebody worthy of being treated with the utmost respect.

She settled Peter in the master bedroom, which she had stocked with the plants, cards, bestsellers, food baskets, and magazines people had dropped off for him, including a *Penthouse* the Claremont kitchen staff had sent as a joke—ha ha, June had thought, tucking it into the bedside stack of *Gourmet, Time,* and *Bon Appetit!,* very funny. The house was full of flowers. June spread the mohair blanket Ruth had loomed on the foot of Peter's bed; she switched on the bedside lamp. The season had turned, the weather continuing cool and rainy, and although June knew they would see another episode of Indian summer, hazy days when the temperatures soared back into the eighties, she had turned the air conditioner off.

"Is there anything else I can get you?" she asked Peter, who was propped against three pillows in new blue pajamas and making a rueful face.

"Not a thing," he said. "You have thoroughly spoiled me." He looked around the room. "It is rather like being at one's own funeral, except not dead."

"Thank God for that," said June. "I'll just go check on Elsbeth."

"June?"

"Yes?"

"Stay a minute." Peter tapped the bed by his knee.

June crossed the room and sat next to him. She reached into her dungarees pocket for her cigarettes, then remembered she wasn't supposed to smoke anywhere in the house anymore—per Dr. Gorgeous's orders.

"Are we all right?" Peter said.

"Sure, Pete. We're fine."

Peter was smiling at June over his bifocals, head lowered, in that wry, self-deprecating way that he thought looked bullish—which it did, but it also meant, June knew, he was seeking forgiveness.

"That business we spoke of earlier, in the hospital and before I went in—"

"I told you, forget it. I have."

"Have you?"

"Yes."

Peter watched her, the smile fading now. Rain trickled down the window next to the bed, making shadows on his face. He was no longer the ghastly no-color he had been in the hospital, as translucent as if he were his own ghost, but his skin was still tinged the bluish white of the skimmed milk he disdained, claiming it tasted like water. June knew she had to be careful with Peter. He could not be upset. And yet she did not look away. She met her husband's inquiring gaze and held it, and she felt as if she were traveling an emotional umbilicus into him, arcing into what it must be like to be Peter, lying in this bed, helpless in this room; to be Peter in his kitchen, measuring, tasting, content; to be young Peter arriving in this country, an unwilling immigrant, pushed this way and that by shoving, muscular crowds who had been born here, finding his way and place among them nonetheless. And to be even younger Peter than that: working in a kitchen in a Berlin hotel, spotting across it a girl more junior than he. But one who was unafraid; maybe she had put out her tongue at him; maybe he had tried that night to take her hand. Closing after hours, volunteering to stay late and sweep up the scraps, do the dirty work of scrubbing up the greasy fat and blood and lug out the rubbish so he could have the chance to be alone with her, to kiss her, to walk her home. Maybe that first hasty coupling had been in the supply cellar or on Chef's butcher-block table. And then the miracle of it, discovering she felt the same about him as he did about her; the joy like a shout in the heart, the invincibility, so that defying the parents was a wisp to be pushed aside. The whole world with its ugly politics and stupid brutality was something to be ignored, in that exuberance of love found and returned and doubled, so that by the time Peter and Masha had married and formed their own family, created two more bodies out of their two, it was too late. Too late. June knew about the echocardiogram and the angioplasty, the clogged arteries, the muscle weakened by malnutrition and age—but she also understood that Dr. Gorgeous, for all his scientific knowledge, was wrong. Peter's heart had been broken long ago.

"June?" he said. "What is it? Your face . . ."

"Nothing," June said. She would be damned if she'd cry in front of Peter. She would not. She stood and patted his leg.

"I'm just glad to have you home," she said. "I'll bring you some toast."

And after a brief listen at Elsbeth's door to ensure she was content with her snacks and albums, downstairs June went. But she did not stop in the kitchen, didn't put bread in the toaster or straighten up the breakfast dishes or even pause to fit another piece into the puzzle Ida had sent Peter for his convalescence, a thousand-part jigsaw called "The American Dream" that June had been working on night after sleepless night here at this table, cigarettes piling in the ashtray. It was multi-image, barns and horses and flags and sunsets, but what June had been thinking of while she searched for the right pieces, tried this one here and that one there, was how it was like a marriage, the accretion of details, of small joys and sorrows and catchphrases and hurts and rituals all adding up to a bigger picture eventually, even if it was impossible to see, while doing it, how it all fit.

June walked out through the backyard, beneath the great dripping trees, wishing she had brought a sweater. Behind the garage was a willow with roots forming a natural seat at its base, its fronds weeping into the brook. It was a private space; nobody used it except Elsbeth, in summer, to dam the water with rocks and catch minnows. June had sometimes fantasized about making love with Gregg back here. Now she never would. She sat in the willow seat and fished her cigarette pack out of her pocket, and something pricked her finger.

She drew it out. The pin, the little navy-blue disc with the cartoon man proudly proclaiming "I Ate a Whole LaLaPaLooza!" June lit a cigarette and sat with the pin, flipping it over and over in her palm. Suddenly she threw it into the water.

Instantly she regretted it; dropping her cigarette, she scrambled down the bank and jumped in. She clambered around in the shallow water, soaking her sneakers and dungarees, twisting her ankles, slipping on the mossy rocks. The pin was nowhere to be found; the current might have already carried it downstream, or more likely the silt June had stirred up had obscured it. June bent and dug, turning over rocks, sinking her fingers into the muck, once falling on her ass with a great splash. But the pin was gone. She hauled herself, using the roots of the tree, up the slippery bank.

Back in the willow seat, she put her face in her slimy, algae-smelling hands and cried. These fits of grief had been coming over her since Gregg's departure a week ago, ugly and raw, more like vomiting than weeping. June's only consolation was that she had been able to conceal them from Elsbeth and, now, Peter. But back here June could sob as noisily as she wanted, and she did, gasping and moaning. "What am I going to do?" she asked. "What am I going to do?"

Finally June was cried out. She found a cigarette that was only half wet and broke it in two to smoke it, exhaling over the brook. The water ran on, dark and shining, pockmarked by rain. The willow rustled overhead. What could June do? Only what she had been doing—except more. This afternoon, for instance, she would go back inside. Wash her face. Tidy up the kitchen. Cook something low-fat and cholesterol-free for dinner—skinless chicken breasts

and broccoli. Sit with Peter, watch TV with him and Elsbeth—
June had moved the television into Peter's room. Bathe Elsbeth.
Read her a chapter of *Charlotte's Web*. Tuck her into bed. Do dishes.
Fold laundry. Work on the puzzle until she grew sleepy or did
not. Do it all again tomorrow. This week Elsbeth would start
kindergarten; there were labels to be sewn into clothes, pencils
to be put into a case, crusts to cut off sandwiches. Her daughter's
hand to hold on the way to school.

And beyond this, once Elsbeth was settled, once a sitter could
be hired for afternoons when Peter needed rest, there were the
want ads. This was not what June had hoped for, not the way
she would have wished it to happen in a hundred years—but it
had happened nonetheless: Peter could not work. June didn't know
what she qualified for, catalog shoots or a secretary in a decorating
firm or even, eventually, interior design school, but she would find
out. She would make it happen. She had to. She would keep on
truckin', keep on keeping on, and if there was one thing she knew
for sure, it was this: no matter what happened next, with Peter or
with Elsbeth or to June herself, June would be in charge of her own
life. She would never depend on another man, ever again.

III

ELSBETH, 1985

What's your definition of dirty, baby?
What do you consider pornography?
—GEORGE MICHAEL

12

SYNESTHESIA

It was the last Saturday of the month, which meant the Rashkins had to visit Elsbeth's Papa Sol and Nana Ruth in Larchmont, which in turn meant they were all in a foul mood. Elsbeth's mother, June, a real estate agent who specialized in "home facelifts," redecorating houses to sell them for more money, was cranky because she had to take a valuable weekend day away from her clients. Elsbeth's dad, Peter, who once upon a time had been tense about the Saturday visits for a similar reason—they had removed him from his restaurant, the Claremont—now disliked them because they disrupted his schedule of sleeping all day and testing recipes for his cookbook by night. Elsbeth herself dreaded going to Larchmont because of (a) her parents; (b) her grandparents—although Sol and Ruth weren't her grandparents, really, they were her dad's cousins or something, but they doted upon Elsbeth as if she were a toddler still in diapers instead of almost sixteen—and (c) the battle between June and Elsbeth over what Elsbeth was going to wear. When Elsbeth was little, the issue had been moot: Elsbeth had to dress for Larchmont in frocks Ruth sent, of taffeta or scratchy lace, quite unlike her usual and preferred OshKosh overalls or shorts.

But now, as with every time Elsbeth left the house, she had to try to sneak her sartorial choices past her mother.

This morning, for instance: "Oh no no no no no," said June, when she caught Elsbeth darting across the kitchen in a hot pink T-shirt, lace capri leggings, and a white rhinestone belt. "That outfit is all wrong for you; that waistband hits you just at the wrong place, and the belt emphasizes your double stomach." "That's your opinion, *Mother*," said Elsbeth, whereupon June said, "That's right, and I'm the expert. Go upstairs and put something else on." "No," said Elsbeth. "Yes," said June. "I categorically refuse," said Elsbeth, and June said, "Fine, have it your way, but no phone for a month," and Elsbeth said, "You are hateful," and June said, "I'm just trying to help you, darling." As Elsbeth stomped out, making the dishes rattle in the cupboards, June had called, "And don't *trample*, like an elephant. Wear my new dress—it's on the back of my closet door."

Elsbeth hadn't been sure whether this command was a concession or a way to make sure all her embarrassing rolls and bulges were covered; June's latest purchase was a white calf-length thing with tiered ruffles. Elsbeth had yanked it off its hanger and on over her head, then gone to her own room, where she sat eating Doritos and Bacos from her stash in the roof of her old dollhouse. Both foods would have horrified Peter and June had they known about them, for different reasons. Elsbeth had crunched all the Bacos straight from their jar.

Now in the back seat of the family Volvo, Elsbeth regretted it: her stomach beneath June's dress pooched out like the bellies of the Ethiopian orphans in the Save the Children commercials; she felt fatter and more uncomfortable than ever. It was about 800 degrees and 900 percent humidity, so hazy that Elsbeth could barely see the steel web of the George Washington Bridge, and the air conditioner of the old Volvo, a hand-me-down from Sol, was broken. Elsbeth tugged the elastic neckline of June's dress down around her shoulders. On June, who was tall and angular and looked, despite her new perm, like Christie Brinkley, the dress was a Grecian column. On Elsbeth, it made her look like a sturdy peasant about to stomp a tub of grapes. Elsbeth pulled the neckline down more, beneath her clavicle, and fanned herself with her hand.

They were almost to the tollbooths now, inching forward in a metal sea of vehicles all doing the same thing. Waves of heat shimmered from hoods and roofs; radios babbled from everywhere, Spanish music, Casey Kasem's Top 40, 1010 WINS. They were in an official heat wave, with dangers of a brownout in the greater metropolitan area; tempers were short all over. Elsbeth's parents were no exception. "I hate these command performances," June was complaining. "Especially with Sol's artsy-fartsy crowd."

Peter tried to cut into the left lane—his trick was to look for the line with trucks in it, since the length of one eighteen-wheeler equaled four cars, and technically, this meant they would reach the toll faster. "Don't even think abouddit, cocksucker!" yelled the driver in the Honda next to them, and shot Peter the finger.

"Same to you," said June and returned the gesture.

"June," said Peter. "Is that really the brightest thing to do when we are completely boxed in?"

June lit a cigarette. "I didn't want to just let him get away with it," she muttered, "unlike some people."

They rolled forward three inches and stopped. TEANECK, Elsbeth read off a nearby sign: green, light blue, navy, yellow, light blue, mustard yellow, orange. Those were the colors of the letters—it was a little habit she had, a trick she used to distract herself when the situation she was stuck in seemed unbearable.

"I don't see why you and Elsbeth couldn't go without me," said June. "You know they don't really want to see me."

"I know nothing of the sort," said Peter. "They want to see you very much. They want to see us as a family and know we are happy."

"Ah," said June, "right," and she ashed out the window and pulled the pink silk shell beneath her power suit—which she had worn today out of habit, Elsbeth guessed, since she wouldn't be showing any houses—away from her breastbone. "You mean they want to see a good return on their investment." she said.

"June," said Peter. "You know that is not fair."

"I know nothing of the sort," June said, mimicking Peter's slightly clipped accent—what Elsbeth's friend Liza called his Oh Captain, My Captain voice. "Your dad's so Von Trapp," Liza had observed one night when Liza and Veronica—Very—and Elsbeth were sitting around the kitchen table, watching Peter make them grilled Gruyère and chutney sandwiches. "Except blond, and the geriatric version. Still, I'd do him," which had made all the girls squeal and Elsbeth shove Liza so hard she fell off her chair.

Peter sighed and shifted to take his handkerchief out of his trousers pocket; he was sweating, which Elsbeth knew he hated. It didn't help that he never, ever wore short-sleeved shirts because of his tattoo.

"June," he said, "even if what you are saying were true—which it is not; I know Sol and Ruth can be difficult, but they do care for you, in their fashion, very much. But even if it were true, what would you have me do? We do owe them, you know."

"Yes," said June. "I am all too aware, Pete, that what I make doesn't cover us. I am painfully conscious of Sol's *contributions* to our household for taxes and braces and such. But that's the irony, don't you see? If I didn't have to deal with these interruptions, I could pull in enough that we might not need him."

"I fail to see that one day makes such a difference," said Peter.

"Wake up, pal," yelled a driver behind them and lay on his horn. Peter lifted a hand and moved the Volvo forward another half-foot.

"It can make all the difference," said June. "One property, if it's the right one, could keep us for a year. And that five-bedroom on Upper Watchung, with the tennis court—its open house is today, and I'm missing it. It makes me sick, Pete. Sick!"

"Will your boss not stand in for you? What's his name, Hamilton?"

"Harrison. He is, but . . ." June let out a stream of smoke and threw herself back against the seat. "First of all, I don't want to split the commission."

"He must be a slave driver if he makes you do all the work and then takes half the commission for one day. Frankly, I think he works you too hard in general."

June sat up a little straighter. "What is that supposed to mean?"

"I mean you work nights, weekends, at his beck and call seven days a week. He crooks a finger, and you come running. It seems excessive."

"Look who's talking," said June, and then there was a silence in the Volvo, if being surrounded by a thousand other people's engines and voices and music could be called that. Peter's dependence on Sol as well as his wife, since Peter could no longer work, was something he despised even more than perspiring.

"Sorry," said June. "That was uncalled for. I'm just so damned hot. It's a furnace in here." She leaned over to turn up the dashboard fan all the way. Heat blasted into the car, flipping Elsbeth's carefully feathered bangs back from her face.

"*Mom*," she said.

"*Elsbeth*," said June. She sighed. "Besides, Pete," she said, "it's hard to make a name for yourself as a woman in this industry. In any industry. To get half as far as a man, you have to work twice as hard."

From what Elsbeth could see of her dad's face in the rearview, he seemed as if he might concede the point—he looked tired, which worried Elsbeth, as the day's festivities hadn't even really begun—but then they crept, thank God, into the shadow of the tollbooths, and Peter became preoccupied with digging out correct change. George Washington Bridge, Elsbeth said to herself. GWB. Green, brown, orange. Peter tossed coins into the basket and maneuvered into the traffic on the bridge; June lit another cigarette. Elsbeth blinked up at the mighty girders, then turned to look for the tiny city on her right. NYC, where she had been born: orange, yellow, yellow-orange. She was relieved to be on the bridge at last; it meant the drive was halfway over, even if things generally got worse on the other side.

*

Because of the traffic, which didn't really lighten until they got out of the Bronx, they reached Larchmont a little past two, which meant—by Elsbeth's estimate—that most of Sol and Ruth's guests would be well into the cheese, dips, and cocktails part of the program, and the maid, Bertha, would be setting up for lunch. Indeed, the motor court was full, and Peter had to park back by the road, next to one of the shining, canted sheets of rock that protruded through the ground. They got out of the Volvo—*ker-chunk, ker-chunk*, went the doors, a sound that hit Elsbeth's stomach with dread; now there was no way out. The next few hours would be a hell of discomfort: Peter blotting his forehead and responding politely to Papa Sol, who would be halfway into a bottle of Cutty Sark and show-off mode; June smiling brightly and escaping as often as she could to check messages on her brand-new mobile phone; Elsbeth trying to avoid her grandparents' friends, who meant well but, when they couldn't avoid talking to her, asked questions that were all but unanswerable like "So, how's school?" or "What do you kids do for fun these days?"

The Rashkins slogged up the driveway, the tar soft underfoot, water running down the rock faces, the air smelling of minerals and humidity. Elsbeth loved the property, which had been an enchanted playground to her when she was little: the shining boulders she could climb on, the waterfall chattering into its secret pool, the flowering shrubs Ruth and the ancient gardener, Yoshi, tended so Sol could photograph them with his special telephoto lens. And the pool. Elsbeth looked longingly at it as she and Peter and June wended through the car maze in the motor court; it gleamed aqua in its grassy setting, beneath the tall oaks. *Come in*, it whispered, *get cool!* Elsbeth loved the water; beneath it she was not fat but weightless, agile as a mermaid.

But— "There you are," called Ruth from the terrace, and "Solly? Sol! They're here." There would be no swimming until after lunch. Elsbeth's parents were already ascending the rock steps, Peter in the lead and June next, her order floating back to Elsbeth: "Pull that collar up, young lady; did you think I wouldn't notice? And suck in your stomach!" Elsbeth yanked the dress's neckline even lower, to just above her bra, and, although she knew it was childish, stuck her tongue out at her mother's bony back.

Then, "Hello! Hello!" the Rashkins cried, younger and older generations, embracing and kissing each other on the cheeks. Sol had abandoned his guests temporarily to greet them; he stood by Ruth's side, highball glass clinking with ice. Every time Elsbeth saw her grandparents, they seemed to have shrunk a little: Sol melting ever more downward, as though he were made of wax, and Ruth drying out, like a tiny mummy. Sol was oxblood-colored to Elsbeth, although maybe that was just because that was his skin tone in summer, when he fished and golfed as well as drank. Nana Ruth was a soft, dusty beige. "Bubbeleh," she cried, crushing Elsbeth's head to her little birdy chest, her arms shaking with effort. She smelled of mothballs, Shalimar, and Pepsodent. "My *shayne madele*. Let me look at you," she said, as if it had been years since Elsbeth had last seen her instead of only a few weeks. She smoothed Elsbeth's bangs off her forehead, the better to see Elsbeth's whole face.

"Nannnaaaaa," said Elsbeth, ducking away, "don't, please," but then she had to deal with Sol, who pinched her chin in one hand and covered her cheeks with kisses that smelled of whitefish dip and Scotch.

"What a girl," he boomed, as if the terrace were packed with an invisible audience of dozens; "what a beautiful girl, isn't she beautiful?" and to Elsbeth's embarrassment he started to cry. Every time Papa Sol saw her, this happened, and Elsbeth was never sure what she had done to cause it or if there were anything she could do to prevent it.

"She looks more like Rivka every day," Sol said to Peter, who nodded. Sol always said this too; he meant Elsbeth's real grandmother, Peter's mother, who had died of pneumonia before the Nazis could kill her. Elsbeth had seen a photo of her only once, a lady who looked both dumpy and regal, with her stocky build and crown of braids. Of course Elsbeth *would* look like her, instead of like her own mother, or even her beautiful little half sisters—the twins, Vivian and Ginger, named after movie stars.

"Don't just stand there, you people, you're letting all the air out," said Sol, switching abruptly from sentimental mode. He turned and stumped into the kitchen, Peter following. Elsbeth and Ruth and June stayed on the terrace, June lighting a cigarette.

"Around the child?" said Ruth to June, waving at the smoke. She smiled at Elsbeth. "Look at you, so big—every time I see you, you grow another foot. What are you eating?"

It was a rhetorical question, but June said, "I'm trying to get her to stick to fruit and vegetables, but I know she sneaks junk," and Elsbeth said, "I do *not*," and Ruth said, "Sha, she's a growing girl, it's good to have a little extra padding, you never know what could happen," and June said, "Maybe in wartime Europe that was true, but we know better now, Ruth; it's not healthy to carry too much weight," and Ruth said, "She's just big-boned, aren't you, darling. How much do you weigh now?" she asked, and Elsbeth said, "Nanaaaaa," and June said, "About ten pounds more than she should," and Elsbeth muttered, "Screw you," and June said, "What was that?" and her mobile phone rang. She took it out of her purse and pulled up the antenna; it was big and black, the size of a brick. "I've got to grab this, excuse me," she said and clicked away down the steps on her high heels. "June Rashkin," she said.

"What is that contraption?" said Ruth.

"That's her mobile phone," Elsbeth explained. "Her boss gave it to her." And indeed Elsbeth was pretty sure that was who June was talking to, Harrison, a man Elsbeth did not trust in the slightest. Harrison used her name all the time when he spoke to her, the way a soap opera actor or car salesman would: "How are you today, Elsbeth? You look wonderful today, Elsbeth! Elsbeth, isn't your mom the greatest?" When he smiled, he seemed to have at least three rows of teeth, like a shark.

"Oy," said Ruth, as she and Elsbeth watched June pace among the cars in the motor court, phone pressed to her ear, looking like Realtor Barbie from this height. Ruth *tsk*ed and turned to Elsbeth. "You must be starving after that long trip," she said, as if Elsbeth and her parents had dragged themselves across the Russian steppes instead of driving from New Jersey. "Would you like a snack before lunch? I got the caviar spread you like, from Zabar's. And how about a nice cold drink? Iced tea?"

"I'm fine, Nana," said Elsbeth. "You go ahead, I'll be in in a minute. I forgot something in the car."

"It can't wait?" Elsbeth vehemently shook her head. "All right, darling, don't be long," Ruth said, and went into the house. Elsbeth heaved a sigh of relief. There was nothing in the Volvo she needed; she had just wanted another minute to herself, or as many as possible, before she had to go in. For this moment, it was just as she liked it: she was alone on the terrace except for her mother far below and the cicadas like maracas in the trees.

*

But—there was somebody else outside after all, Elsbeth discovered to her dismay, somebody who might have witnessed the whole humiliating arrival scene. There was a crashing in the bushes on the far side of the terrace, near the bonsai grove, and from them a man emerged, zipping his pants. Unaware of Elsbeth's presence, he yanked up the fly of his white jeans and, from the breast pocket of the Cuban shirt he wore, which was misbuttoned so one half of the bottom hung lower than the other, he slid a pack of cigarettes. Elsbeth felt instant sympathy for him. She too often left the house with her blouse fastened the wrong way, or socks that were different colors, or once, most embarrassingly, her skirt tucked into the back of her underpants. The man gazed around as he shook out the match he'd lit his cigarette with, and he looked startled when he saw her.

Then: "Heeeeeey," he said, as if he and Elsbeth were old friends, "how's it going?" and he held out his cigarette pack toward her. He smiled and shook it a little as if enticing a squirrel with nuts: *Come on, come and get it.* He had a friendly, very tan face, brown eyes, and wavy dark hair, his open collar showing a patch of fur on his chest. Like Peter Brady, Elsbeth imagined telling her friends later, if Peter Brady were older, maybe twenty-five. And although Elsbeth had always thought Greg was the cutest Brady brother, she revised this opinion instantly.

"No, thanks, I don't smoke," said Elsbeth. She sucked in her stomach and flipped her hair back behind her shoulders. "Not because I'm too young, of course. Because it's bad for you."

The man shrugged and tossed his cigarette pack to the coffee table. "You're right, you're right," he said. "But you've got to have some bad habits, right? Don't drink, don't smoke, what do you do," and he smiled at Elsbeth. His teeth were very white and straight.

"I guess," she said. "Were you—um, urinating in the bushes?"

He said somberly, "I might have been watering the plantings, yes." He winked at her. "Don't tell anybody, okay, Charlie?"

"Of course not," she said, and then, "Why did you call me Charlie?"

"Isn't that the perfume you're wearing?"

Elsbeth's cheeks felt suddenly much hotter than was warranted even by the temperature of the day. "How did you know?"

"I'm a connoisseur," he said, and then, pointing his cigarette at her, "Plus, you look like a Charlie."

"I do?" Elsbeth said. She was thrilled; she had always hated her name, which Peter and June had chosen out of a phone book in the maternity ward because, they said, they wanted her to be completely her own person. They had closed their eyes and opened the book and put their finger on the Es, and here Elsbeth was, stuck with the name of an old lady, somebody who wore orthopedic shoes; a name that dragged itself along: Elssss–BETH. Elssss–BETH. What her dad called her, Ellie, was not much better, and his childhood pet name for her, Ellie-Belly, was, as it drew attention to the part of her body she loathed most, worst of all.

"My actual name's Elsbeth," she said. "But I like Charlie."

"Elsbeth," the man repeated, and Elsbeth was impressed: he neither mispronounced it, the way most people did upon first hearing it—Elizabeth? Liz Beth?—nor said how unusual, how interesting. "I think Charlie suits you better," said the man, "and not because you look like a boy." He blew out smoke. "Do you mind if I call you Charlie?"

"No," said Elsbeth, "that's fine, if you want." Holding in her breath, she strolled to the railing and gazed out at the view: the lawn and pool and trees and marsh and Long Island Sound, a stripe of glitter in the distance.

"What's your name?" she asked, as the man came to stand beside her. Which was when Elsbeth realized he was drunk, or at least had been drinking: he smelled of alcohol, although rising from his skin it smelled warm and rich, instead of pickled and rotting, the way Sol smelled when he'd had too much.

"I'm Julian," said the man. "How do you do?" He held out his hand. Elsbeth shook it. Julian's palm was dry and smooth despite the heat.

"Are you one of Sol's artsy-fartsy . . . I mean, one of Sol's friends?" Elsbeth asked.

Julian laughed, a deep, happy, vital sound that came all the way up from his stomach. "Friend I don't know about," he said, "but definitely artsy-fartsy. I'm the taste of the hour, the flavor of the day."

"Excuse me?" said Elsbeth.

Julian leaned next to Elsbeth on the railing, propping his elbows on it. He was like a toothpaste model; Elsbeth had never been this close to anyone so handsome and yet so normal-looking.

"Sol bought out my first show," he said. "And he's still my biggest patron."

"Oh," said Elsbeth, "I see." So this Julian was one of the artists Sol sponsored, a painter or a photographer. She was about to ask which when Julian said, "Excuse me, I've got to shake the lily again," and he walked off the terrace.

"Why don't you just go inside?" Elsbeth called.

"I don't want to have to deal with everybody," said Julian, and then he put his finger to his lips and glided out of sight beyond the bonsais.

Elsbeth certainly understood that. She sat on one of the iron deck chairs to wait for him, its metal hot through the material of June's dress, and toyed with Julian's cigarette pack. "Marlboro," she murmured, "maroon, navy, red, light blue, orange, purple, red, purple—"

"What're you doing?" Julian said behind her, and Elsbeth jumped and put the pack back.

"Nothing," she said. "Sorry. It's just this dumb habit I have—"

"You think letters have colors?" said Julian. Elsbeth nodded, embarrassed. "You're synesthetic!" he said in great delight.

"I'm what?"

"You're a synesthete," he said and sat beside her. "So am I. We have synesthesia. We think letters and numbers have colors."

"You do too?" Elsbeth said. She had never met anyone else who did this.

"I do," Julian said. "We're two of a kind. There aren't many of us synesthetes, but there are a few. It's our synapses. Something up here"—and he tapped his temple—"is scrambled, but in what I consider a marvelous way. Our senses are cross-connected, so that tastes have colors, and music and numbers, and abstract concepts—like months and days—have shapes. Tell me, for instance, how do you think of the calendar?"

"It's round," Elsbeth said, "like a clock. January's at the top and June's at the bottom."

"Exactly," Julian said. "And numbers?"

"They march into infinity! In a horizontal line that's light at the beginning, but the higher up you go, the more it shades into darkness. And the numbers have colors too: five is red, and seven is green."

"It isn't, though," Julian said. "Seven is blue."

"Seven is not blue," Elsbeth said indignantly. "Three is blue."

"Three is so not blue," said Julian. "It's beige."

"It is not!" Elsbeth cried. "Next you'll be telling me your name doesn't start with yellow."

"It doesn't," Julian said. "J is red."

"No way," said Elsbeth. "Your name is orange-yellow, yellow, navy blue, black, blue-black, mustard yellow."

"And your name is yellow, forest green, navy, red, neon pink, charcoal."

"E is not yellow!" said Elsbeth. "It's blue."

"Ah, but I didn't spell Elsbeth. I spelled Charlie. That's who you are. Charlie the synesthete."

"Right," said Elsbeth. She was laughing. "Excellent."

Julian picked up his sweating glass from the table, sipped from it, and handed it to her. Elsbeth drank gratefully: gin and tonic with lime, hot and flat from the sun.

"Would you like to pose for me, Charlie?" Julian asked.

"What?" Elsbeth said.

"I'd like to shoot you. You've got a unique quality, a look. And I've never shot a synesthete before."

"Shoot me?"

Julian let out that deep vital laugh again. "I'm a photographer."

"Oh, duh," said Elsbeth. She had forgotten to ask his medium in her excitement at discovering somebody else who did what she could do. "You want to shoot—me?"

"I do," said Julian. He stood up, took a brown leather wallet out of his back pocket, and handed her a business card.

"Think about it and let me know. You can call me anytime, okay, Charlie?"

"Okay," said Elsbeth, and Julian smiled at her. Then he turned and went without another word through the sliding door into the solarium.

Elsbeth looked down at the card. It was warm from being in Julian's pocket, next to his body: *julian wilton photography*, all in lower-case letters on a white background, and there was a number and an address in New York. That was it. Elsbeth glanced at the house, then held the card to her nose. It smelled of damp paper. She tucked it carefully into her bra.

*

Lunch was served in the solarium on the side of the house, Elsbeth's favorite room because within its glass walls she could pretend she was eating outside. The shelves ringing its circumference now displayed Ruth's gardening obsession: cacti. There were plants with broad leaves and pink flowers; teardrop-sized pods; sharp four-inch spines or white fuzz that looked deceptively soft until Elsbeth stroked it and came away with tiny splinters embedded in her fingertips. She had learned not to touch anything in here, that whatever a plant's beauty, it might be painful or dangerous. Some were and some weren't, and there was no way to know for sure.

Usually Elsbeth tried to be invisible, positioning herself near the coffee table on the orange couch and eating as many hors d'oeuvres as she could before June caught her—Ruth went into the city to specialty-shop for these occasions, and Elsbeth loved the pâté and Brie, the stone-ground crackers, the scallion cream cheese and the caviar dip whose tiny eggs popped in her mouth with delicious flavor. Today, however, she was more interested in Julian; she hovered near the living room doorway, trying to track him among the other guests and wondering where he would sit. This was indeed Sol's artsy-fartsy crowd, not his regular childhood buddies with their fleshy noses and funny nicknames, pretending to pull quarters from behind Elsbeth's ears, their soufflé-haired wives whose kisses left thick lipstick on Elsbeth's cheeks. These people were art critics and collectors, their inquisitive faces vaguely familiar to Elsbeth from the times she met them here and at galleries Sol took them to, from museum openings and newspaper columns. They began filtering in when Ruth clapped her hands and announced lunch was ready, Bach and argumentative conversation accompanying them. Julian was in the rear, talking to a younger man in electric-blue-framed glasses and a Don Johnson white suit; Elsbeth waited, then pounced into the chair opposite from the one Julian chose, elbowing a man out of her way whom she then realized might be the art critic for *Newsweek*.

"Sorry," she said to him.

"That's all right," he said and gallantly held Elsbeth's chair out for her.

Julian smiled at Elsbeth as the maid poured a glass of wine over his shoulder. "We meet again, Charlie," he said and raised his drink to her.

"You've met before?" said the *Newsweek* man, and the woman on the other side said, "Are you surprised?" and there was some laughter that didn't sound to Elsbeth quite convivial. She smiled at Julian, then noticed that the woman taking a seat next to him and fluffing out her napkin was June. Elsbeth scowled.

"What?" June said, feeling Elsbeth's glare. She bared her teeth: *Lipstick?* Elsbeth shrugged. June winked at Elsbeth in a just-us-girls kind of way, but Elsbeth wasn't buying it. That was the trouble with June: she did have her moments, but she was like the sun coming out from the clouds on an overcast day; just when you were enjoying the warmth, she disappeared again, leaving you longing for what you didn't know you'd been missing and even colder than you'd been before.

Ruth tinged her fork on her water glass and said, "L'chaim," and up and down the table everyone lifted their glasses and toasted. Conversation hummed again as the guests passed platters, handed along baskets of challah and trays of cold cuts, pinched up lettuce in silver tongs. Elsbeth grabbed whatever came her way, watching Julian from the corners of her eyes. He piled his plate with cucumber salad, salmon, bluefish, and remoulade.

"Oh, Elsbeth," June said. "So much roast beef? And two rolls?" She herself had taken nothing but a cup of gazpacho, sans the sour cream that went with it. She pushed it toward Elsbeth. "Here, I don't need all of this."

"I'm fine," said Elsbeth.

"Come on," said June, "we girls have to watch our figures, right?"

"June, doll," said Ruth, "you want she should starve?" and Elsbeth, desperate to stop this conversation before Julian noticed—he was talking to the man on his other side—said, more loudly than she'd intended, "I *know* how to feed myself, *Mother.*"

"Hey," said Sol, irritated, "pipe down. We're trying to have a discussion here."

"Sorry," sang June. She picked up her wine. "I give up. Eat whatever you want," and she turned, to Elsbeth's horror, to Julian, who had now started in on his lunch.

"Teenagers," she said, "such an impossible age, am I right?"

The *Newsweek* critic scoffed, and the lady beside him murmured, "Ask the expert."

Julian glanced up and raised his dark eyebrows, then ate a fork-ful of salad.

"You have children too, Mr. Wilton?" June asked, and now Elsbeth heard, very definitely, a snort. It came from the man between her dad and Sol; he was laughing.

"Pardon," he said, "I couldn't help overhearing. Really, it's just too delicious."

Julian buttered a piece of challah. "I don't have children, Mrs. Rashkin," he said.

"But he *is* the Pied Piper of the art world," said the *Newsweek* critic.

"More like Humbert Humbert," said the lady next to him, and there was more of that sharp laughter.

"Oh!" said June. "Now I know why your name sounds familiar; I read about you in the *New Yorker*. You're that photographer . . ."

"Yes," said Julian, "I'm the one who shoots children. I do love them. That's why they're my subject. Their unself-consciousness, their purity and joie de vivre—"

Suddenly the Humbert Humbert woman crashed her fork down on her plate. "I don't know how you can live with yourself," she said.

"I don't know what you mean," Julian said mildly.

The woman stood, her chair legs producing a violent scrape on the tiles. She was about June's age, with painfully short hair and what looked like a miniature cuckoo clock pinned at the throat of her black shirt. Her mouth shook.

"Art should never be used to justify immorality," she said. "There's a line that shouldn't be crossed, and you have crossed it."

"That's enough," boomed Sol. "Mr. Wilton is our guest of honor."

"Mr. Wilton is a pornographer," the woman said.

"Oh, I think that's a bit reductive," said the waxed-mustache man, and the *Newsweek* critic muttered, "Plebian morality."

Julian looked calmly at the woman, though Elsbeth noticed his fingers pinching and pinching the seam of his jeans under the glass-topped table. "I create images," he said. "I'm interested in the play of light and shade on the human form, as artists have been for millennia. Would you level the same accusations at Michelangelo? At Renoir? Impurity's in the eye of the beholder, and I think it says more about your mind-set than—"

"They're children," shouted the woman.

Now the whole table quivered with quiet, even Sol. Then Peter cleared his throat.

"Perhaps Ellie should go for a swim," he said, and to Elsbeth's tremendous mortification every head in the room swiveled toward her.

"That's a wonderful idea," said Ruth. "Go on, Bubbie."

"But I'm fine here," Elsbeth said.

"Elsbeth," said Peter, "*go*," and at her dad's rare use of her full name, Elsbeth laid her napkin on her plate. She got up and, feeling as though she were in the dream in which she'd come to school naked, walked stiffly from the room. She didn't dare look at Julian. She was followed by the lady in the black shirt, who brushed past Elsbeth in the living room and stormed through the swinging door into the kitchen. A minute later, over the limp of restarted conversation in the solarium, Elsbeth heard the growling engine of Julian's accuser's car as she started it and drove away.

*

Elsbeth waited to see if anyone else would come out of the solarium—her dad, maybe, to make sure she was all right, or Julian!—but when nobody did, she wandered into the living room. When she'd been younger, she would have seized this chance to search for the photo: the forbidden, the fascinating, the secret picture of her dad's first family that Ruth used to keep in her powder room. Elsbeth knew rationally that the photo had disappeared the day her mom had caught Ruth showing it to her and telling her again the terrible story of Masha and the twins, but for years she had kept searching for it anyway, hoping she would turn over Ruth's silver-backed hairbrushes or panty hose and there they would be, her unfamiliar young dad and his first wife and Elsbeth's half sisters. They had the same glamour as the scrapbook Ruth kept of Peter and June's courtship: menus from Peter's famous restaurant, Masha's; magazine covers, *Harper's* and *Vogue*, with June's face on them; gossip columns showing June and Peter dancing at the Rainbow Room or a place called ElMo. They were all memories Elsbeth coveted; they belonged to her, even if they had happened before she was born, and she'd spent so much time trying to occupy them that she felt as if she had actually lived them. How many hours had she spent poring over the photos of Masha's, the restaurant almost like another person: its red walls, the laughing patrons with hats and furs and cocktails, the giant chandelier? How many times had Elsbeth pictured herself in clogs and chef's jacket, whisking up recipes in its kitchen? Her imaginings of her dad's life before the war, the real Masha, her twin sisters—they had been like that too, except sadder.

But Elsbeth had long moved beyond the need to look for the photo; she was mature now and accepted that it was gone. She was easing back toward the solarium to eavesdrop when she saw the book, lying on the coffee table amid a crumple of napkins, glasses half full of liquid and the pulp of desiccated fruit. *luminous beings: images by julian wilton* was printed on the glossy cover, beneath a photo so intensely colored that it reminded Elsbeth of the time of day just before sunset, when the vibrant light made her feel melancholy for no reason. The image showed a girl about twelve or thirteen, with long, light hair, a chest flat as a boy's except for pushpin nipples that pointed at the viewer, and a challenging stare. She was straddling the fork of a tree—and she was naked.

Elsbeth appropriated the book, swiping it from the coffee table along with a half-eaten tray of cheese and crackers and carrying it all to a wing chair, which she turned to face the bay windows—from behind, if she pulled her legs up, nobody would know she was in it. She arranged herself so the book was on one knee and the food on the other and leafed and ate, leafed and ate, careful to hold the pages by their edges. They all featured the girl on the cover and another who was probably her sister: a second blonde with light eyes who stared almost angrily at the camera. They swam in ponds and lay on riverbanks; they ate tomatoes in fields, the juice running down their bare arms; they sunbathed on a city rooftop deck, the faces of office workers visible in tiny windows across the street. In all of the photos they were naked. It was all on display.

When Elsbeth got to the last image, the cover model sitting alone on a boulder, she closed the book. Who *were* these girls, who displayed their nudity with such unself-consciousness, such lack of shame? It was totally alien to Elsbeth, who in every locker room and at each slumber party hunched in corners to hide her cone-shaped breasts, the rolls of fat at her stomach. She had been different for as long as she could remember: a matryoshka doll among puppets. In first grade she'd been called Elsbeth the Elephant, in fifth the Doughnut after she'd been caught eating a box of them. In the lunchroom one day, while Elsbeth was blissfully unwrapping her Laughing Cow cheese cubes, Christy Albertson, thin and popular with two long braids, had wrinkled her nose and said, "Are those *butter*?" Snickers, and everyone moved away. At camp, Elsbeth's peers weighed 45 pounds, 48, 50; when Elsbeth stepped on the scale, clumsy with shame and dread, the nurse announced, "Ninety-six-point-three pounds!" Now, as a sophomore, Elsbeth was five foot three and 145 pounds; she had been surpassed in height by some girls and in cup size by others, and she could hide among the tall and the busty. But she still knew that every bite she took would congeal in lumps on her body; she would never be like the others, who ate candy bars, ice cream sandwiches, and Fritos because they were hungry, because they wanted them, without a second thought. And Elsbeth was even more bitterly envious of Julian's models, showing everything with careless confidence. Everything—in front of Julian!

Chairs scraped back in the solarium, and Elsbeth implemented a hasty strategy. She raced through the kitchen, grabbing a Pepperidge Farm cookie from the tray on the table—"Did you get enough to eat, miss?" the maid called, and Elsbeth said, "Yes, thanks!" as she escaped down the basement stairs. She had to shout it; Bertha, the new maid Ruth had found after Maria retired, was a little deaf, a kindly, grandmother-age woman with Brillo hair and missing teeth. "She's far too old for any real work," Ruth had whispered to Elsbeth one day, "but she went through the Shoah like your father, so I took her on as a mitzvah." Apparently the Nazis had damaged Bertha's hearing, though whether by bomb blast or torture with a hot poker or something, Elsbeth didn't know. She couldn't imagine anyone doing that to Bertha, let alone Bertha having the kind of secret anyone would want that badly.

The basement was dim and cool, the linoleum squares kind on Elsbeth's bare feet. She navigated the warren of rooms: Sol's wet bar, with the six-foot stuffed marlin over it; Sol's projector room, where he made them watch slideshows; Sol's framed prints of boats, flowers, peasants in Italy, the onion-dome churches of Leningrad. Sol had won a couple of minor prizes in amateur competitions before realizing that he would never be a professional photographer and sponsoring them instead. But he still used his darkroom, which was down here too, and Elsbeth gave it a curious glance as she passed. She would have liked to peek in, to educate herself a little more about Julian's world, but she had once opened the door while Sol was developing photos and ruined a batch of film, so she had avoided it ever since. Instead she went to the closet off the laundry room, called the changing room because here Ruth kept the family's swimsuits and rainbow-striped towels for swimming, and pulled off June's dress.

Elsbeth faced herself in the mirror with the usual loathing. Her soft breasts, her blubbery belly—as much as she hated the term, Elsbeth understood why June called it a double stomach. She pinched it viciously, her fingers digging into the flesh and leaving pink marks, then turned to the toilet in the corner. She had never tried this before—something her friend Liza had told her about. "It's only for when I've really pigged out," Liza had said, "like gone *absolument fou* at Carvel and scarfed a whole cookie cake. Which actually is not bad because ice cream is a cinch to throw up." Elsbeth bent. She slid two fingers down her throat and waited. Her stomach hitched, once, twice, but nothing else happened.

"Come on," she mumbled. She pushed her fingers down farther and forced herself to think of how many slices of cheese and sleeves of crackers had been on that tray, and the Mint Milano cookie she'd snatched from the kitchen just out of habit and apparently eaten without even thinking about it, and that morning's food: the breakfast Peter had made, an omelet with Boursin and sautéed mushrooms; croissants fresh from the oven and his homemade raspberry jam and about a stick of butter—Elsbeth loved butter. She crammed her whole hand in her mouth, gagging, and then she remembered something else Liza had said: "If you're having trouble, just tickle that little hangy-downy thing at the back of your throat. That'll make everything come up."

And it did. The cheese and cracker ball emerged in a satisfying gush, some half digested. Elsbeth did it again and again until she was retching only thick, clear fluid, and then she stood, flushed, and washed her hands and face. Her eyes were bloodshot and her ears were ringing, but she felt as if she were floating. She was serene, empty, and calm. She stripped off her underwear and reached for her Jantzen one-piece, hanging on the back of the door, and Julian's card—*julian wilton photography*—damp and curved, fell out of her right bra cup.

Elsbeth retrieved the card and hid it in her clothes, which she tucked onto a shelf, behind extra towels. Then she pulled on her suit—was it her imagination, or did it squeak up a little more easily over her bulges already?—and went out through the garage to the motor court. The afternoon was bright and humid, the sun white in a steamy sky. Elsbeth walked at a queenly pace across the melting tar, between the heat-shimmering cars. The air whirred with cicadas. The pool shone among the tall oaks. Elsbeth could see, from the very corner of her left eye, that Julian was on the terrace again, smoking while a man in a maroon suit talked animatedly to him. Elsbeth didn't look back, but she could hear Julian's voice in return, smell his cigarette. She proceeded toward the pool, holding her breath and swinging her hips just a bit from side to side. She knew he was watching.

13

THE SHOOT

A week later Elsbeth stood on the top floor of a brownstone on Riverside Drive, outside Julian's apartment door. She had knocked twice already, once quietly, then a little louder. Maybe she had still been too timid, because he hadn't answered. It was the right day, wasn't it? Swing by Saturday, Julian had said, when Elsbeth had called him from the pay phone at the Glenwood Deli; come around two. But what if Julian was in his darkroom, and Elsbeth was disturbing some new outpouring of genius? Or what if—as Liza had suggested—Julian was a pervert, and after shooting Elsbeth he would chop her up into little pieces? "If he's a porno," said Liza, her eyes alight, "God knows what else he'll do." Elsbeth had wanted to defend Julian, to say he was no pornographer, but the fact was, she wasn't sure. The only real, undisputed porn Elsbeth had ever seen had been their friend Very's brother's *Penthouses*, which his parents had discovered and thrown out in a screaming fit of rage and humiliation. Liza had snatched them from the recycling, and Elsbeth had stolen one from her and flipped through it in her room. There had been a blonde centerfold biting a strand of pearls; a layout of two women touching each other by a swimming pool, the photos growing more and more graphic until Elsbeth could see parts of the women she'd never seen even on herself, red and pink flesh glistening, tongues and fingers everywhere. That was pornography, Elsbeth was sure: it had to expose the most secret places. Julian's girls might have been nude, but they seemed tame in comparison.

Elsbeth looked around the landing: cage elevator; Egon Schiele print of a dancer hugging one knee; skylight with a fern hanging from it. Nothing to indicate that a murderous pervert lived here. She had to go to the bathroom, and her hair was inflating in the humidity; it puffed itself up more with every passing minute, like an angry animal. Sweat would ruin her carefully chosen outfit, her white blouse and red culottes with suspenders, and she had a very bad feeling that the dog shit she'd stepped in outside the Port Authority was caking the treads of her Capezios. Elsbeth had tried to scrape it off on one of those little iron fences surrounding a sad city gingko tree, but she feared she could still smell it wafting up.

She was dragging her foot across Julian's bristly mat when the door flew open and there he was, smiling his toothpaste-model smile as if there were nobody in the world he would rather see on his landing than Elsbeth.

"Hey, Charlie," he said, "you made it! Sorry to keep you waiting; I just jumped in the shower," and indeed his hair was in damp ringlets and his Hawaiian shirt plastered to his chest as if he'd thrown it on without drying off first.

"Did I come too early?" Elsbeth asked, although in the elevator her Swatch had said it was twenty past two.

"No, no, I'm moving slowly today," said Julian. He stepped back and opened the door a bit wider. "Here you are," he said, "how wonderful! Welcome. Come in."

*

Elsbeth stepped past Julian into a marvelous room. It was a loft space: shining wooden floors, bank of windows overlooking the

Hudson, more skylights. The rugs were zebra, the furniture white leather and chrome; there was a red beanbag chair that looked like an actual bean. Running along the length of the windows was a huge architect's table covered with sheets of contact paper, photos, grease pencils, lenses; a six-foot lamp, a silver globe on a stem, arced over it. Cameras lined the bookshelves on either side of the fireplace, and a forest of tripods bristled in one corner. Over the mantel Julian's cover girl glared at the room, naked from the waist up; her, Elsbeth could have done without, but otherwise she had never been in such a masculine, magical place in her life.

"I love your studio," she said.

"Do you?" said Julian; he was rushing around now, collecting newspapers, an ashtray, smudgy glasses. "Thank you. Actually my studio is downtown; this is my apartment. But I do a lot of editing here." He dumped his armload, ashtray and glasses and all, into the kitchen sink, which was in a line of cabinets against one wall. "Are you hungry? The fridge is pretty bare, but I can order from the deli—"

"No, thank you," said Elsbeth. "I couldn't eat a thing."

"How about something to drink?" asked Julian. "It looks pretty sultry out there." He opened the refrigerator. "Let's see, I've got orange juice, tonic, milk—whoops, expired. How about gin? Ha, ha."

"Sure," said Elsbeth, pleased; he must have been remembering last week, when they'd shared his gin and tonic on Ruth and Sol's terrace. It would be their theme drink.

Julian, backing out of the fridge, looked startled. "Really?" he said. He laughed. "You had me going a minute there, girl. How about coffee?"

"Sure," Elsbeth said again, disappointed. She watched Julian measure grounds into a French press; his curly hair, like hers, was fluffing as it dried, and his Hawaiian shirt was misbuttoned. Oh, Julian, she thought, helpless with longing.

"Can I use your ladies' room?" she asked.

"Last door on the left," said Julian and jutted his chin toward a narrow hallway off the kitchen. "I'll get things set up out here."

Elsbeth's stomach jumped; that meant she'd have to take off her clothes. She'd done well this past week, eating nothing but pita bread, cottage cheese, and grapes—except once, when she'd gotten so hungry she'd eaten an entire pint of Vanilla Häagen Dazs ice cream, but then she'd used her secret weapon and thrown it all up. She'd been practicing in the mirror in her room, holding her breath, standing at oblique angles to minimize her pudge. She'd lost four pounds, but here under Julian's skylights, it didn't seem like nearly enough. The phone rang then; Julian scooped it up, listened, laughed, and said, "Richard, you scurvy bastard." Elsbeth escaped into the hall.

*

It was long and dim, festooned with eight-by-ten photos clipped to clotheslines that Elsbeth looked at as she passed. The blond girl again, making a mustache out of the end of her long blond braid; a boy about ten playing in a lake; the same kid standing on a dock, his penis a button mushroom. On the right, a door was tantalizingly ajar; Elsbeth looked in—Julian's bedroom! Unmade bed, black sheets spilling onto the floor, one checkered Van sneaker. And on the far wall, a most curious thing: a clock whose face glowed every pastel imaginable, shifting colors every few seconds, lavender, rose, lime, lemon. Its hands were circles, each their own color, and as they swept past each other, they changed hues as well as shifting the colors beneath them.

Elsbeth was mesmerized by the wondrous clock until a bark of Julian's laughter freed her. She located the bathroom at the end of the hall. It reminded her of the one in her family's first apartment in New York, which everyone said she couldn't possibly remember because she'd been only two when they'd moved to Glenwood, but she did: here were the same black-and-white hexagonal tiles, frosted window in the shower, pedestal sink with rust flowers under the faucets. Elsbeth used the facilities, checked herself in the mirror, and scowled—her hair was a travesty. She wet it down with water from the tap, though she knew it was useless. Then, since Julian was still on the phone, she opened the medicine cabinet.

Waterpik; razor and blades; economy-size bottle of aspirin; a lot of prescriptions—was Julian sick? What was diazepam? Cologne that Elsbeth opened and inhaled rapturously, though she'd never smelled fragrance on Julian at all. Vaseline, Q-tips, a box of condoms—glow-in-the-dark, extra sensitive. Elsbeth smirked; why luminescent ones? Did Julian need help finding something? Most importantly, there was nothing in the cabinet at all to indicate that a woman had ever been there.

She was closing it, relieved, when she spotted something else behind the Waterpik: a large purple . . . penis? It was; girthy and rubbery, speckled with gold flakes. It was a dildo, it had to be—something else Elsbeth recognized from *Penthouse*. She knew what it was for, but—why would a man have one? She was trying to puzzle this out when Julian, finally released from his conversation, called, "Charlie? You okay in there, did you fall in?" and Elsbeth hastily shut the cabinet, glared at her hair once more in the mirror, sucked in her stomach, and opened the door.

*

As she emerged into the main room, she was temporarily blinded by a white flare, accompanied by a sound like *vssssh!* "Ooops, sorry, didn't mean to startle you," said Julian. "I forgot the flash was on."

"That's okay," she said, as Julian took her arm to guide her farther into the room. "I'm used to it from Sol. Except with him it's in reverse: he's always like, Okay, people, get ready, and then his flash never works."

Julian laughed. "He's using a much older model," he said, "a

Pentax, if I'm not mistaken. This is a new Polaroid Supercolor the company sent me to test," and Elsbeth, blinking, saw he was holding a black box with a rainbow on it. Julian aimed it at her and pressed a button—*vssh!*—and a white-bordered gray square slid from it.

"Now," said Julian, "watch," and he set the square on the architect's table among a vast array of others, like puzzle pieces. Elsbeth stood next to him as they looked at it together; she could smell him, warm cotton and cigarette and skin. In the gray center of the white-bordered square an outline was emerging: a body, a face.

"It's like magic!" Elsbeth said.

"It *is* magic, Charlie," said Julian. "It's photography. You know what photography means, right? Writing with light. *Photo* is light; *graph* is writing. That's what you're seeing here."

"Awesome," breathed Elsbeth, but as more of the image appeared, she cried, "Oh, no, I look like a moon."

Julian laughed. "I assure you, you don't; it's just that I shot you straight on. Nobody looks good from that angle."

June did, Elsbeth thought. Julian walked away to secure a different camera to a tripod set up next to the big arcing lamp; he bent and peered through it, adjusted a lever on the top and pressed a button. *Clickclickclick vssh!* Elsbeth hovered uncertainly by the table, turning sideways and sucking in her stomach. "Are we shooting?" she said. "What should I do?"

Clickclickclickclick. Clickclick vsssh click. "Nothing," said Julian, "you don't have to pose, just act natural," which made it worse because Elsbeth had no idea what she was supposed to be doing. What would June do? Elsbeth gazed with worldly disdain toward the windows, but because Julian had pulled down blackout shades, there was no view.

Julian glanced up from his camera and smiled at her. "Should we have some music?" he asked. "Sometimes that helps."

Elsbeth's eyes burned. She was blowing this. "Sure."

"Go ahead," said Julian, pointing to a stereo in the corner, "ladies' choice."

Elsbeth crossed the room, holding her breath. *Clickclickclick vssh clickclick.* The on light of the stereo glowed red, and there was a record on the turntable already, so she just set the arm on it. "Ssssssexxxxx," said a man's voice, and a blare of chords and throbbing beat blasted the room.

"Whoops!" said Julian, leaping out from behind the tripod and hurrying over, "not that one, hahaha," and he scraped the needle off the record. "How aboooout . . . some classical? Something more genteel."

"Sure," said Elsbeth, and then, wincing, "except maybe not this?"

Julian looked surprised. "You don't like Prokofiev?"

"Not especially," said Elsbeth, rubbing her arms, which were suddenly covered in goose bumps. Prokofiev terrified her: once in third grade, she'd had Bethany Chase over to play, and they'd been listening to albums in her room when the door slammed open and her dad ran in. "Who put this on?" he demanded, his face so red and furious that Elsbeth barely recognized him. "Who brought this music into my house?" She had jumped up, fearing he was having another heart attack. "Daddy," she said, "what's wrong?"

Peter yanked the album off the turntable. He tried to snap it, but when it proved too thick, he threw it into the hall like a Frisbee. "I don't want to hear this ever again," he said, "never, understand?" and he'd stormed out. Bethany, whose record it had been, had gone crying home—Elsbeth could hardly blame her. Ever since that day, Elsbeth had never been able to listen to *Peter and the Wolf*, or anything by its composer, ever again.

Julian put on a third album. "How's this?"

"Better," said Elsbeth with relief; he had chosen *Cats*. "*Oh, well, I never was there ever / a cat so clever / as magical Mr. Mistoffelees!*" Elsbeth had seen *Cats* on Broadway with her parents and Sol and Ruth, and she remembered Mistoffelees, a baritone in black, leaping off the stage right in front of her. Julian looked a lot like Mistoffelees, lithe and sinewy and brunet, and Elsbeth imagined him materializing in her bedroom in an *explosion* of smoke, in black unitard and tights——*poof!*

Clickclickclickclick vssssh clickclick. "There you go," Julian murmured, "very nice, very nice." *Clickclickclick.* "So, Charlie, how old are you?"

"Almost sixteen," said Elsbeth, padding her age by a few months.

"Have you done any modeling before?"

"*Moi?* Please."

Julian laughed. *Clickclickclickclickclick.* "I'm surprised, Charlie. Your mother was a very famous model in her day, no?" *Clickclickvsssssh.* "I remember one shot of her by Avedon——she had a birdcage on her head. She was magnificent."

"Well, that's kind of the problem," said Elsbeth.

"Oh, Charlie," said Julian. "Don't you remember what I told you at your grandparents' house? You've got a look. You might not see it yet, but I'm trained to notice composition, to see structure beneath the surface of things, and you've got it." *Clickclickclickclickclick.* "In a few years——bam! You'll be a bigger supermodel than your mom ever was, if you want to."

Elsbeth shook her head, and one of the big hoop earrings she'd borrowed from Liza popped out and rolled away. "Shit," she muttered.

"That's all right, we'll find it later." *Clickclick vssh clickclick.* "It's true you don't look like your mom, though," said Julian, "or your dad either, though he's a handsome guy. You've got your own thing going on. Who *do* you look like?"

"Probably my grandmother," said Elsbeth, "the potato."

Julian laughed. "Ruth? She's hardly even a spud."

"Ruth's not actually my grandmother——she's my dad's second cousin or something. They took him in after the war. I meant my real grandmother——his mom, the one who died during the Nazis."

Clickclickclick vssh. "Your dad was in Europe then, too."

"How did you know that?" said Elsbeth, forgetting herself and looking directly at the camera. *Clickclickclickclickclick.*

"I saw his tattoo," said Julian.

Elsbeth sighed. She couldn't believe he had noticed it—her dad was so careful to keep it hidden. Then again, as Julian had mentioned himself, he had unusual powers of vision.

"My dad was in the camps," she said, "Auschwitz and . . . Theresien-stadt." She pronounced the name carefully, not at all sure she was getting it right; she'd had to look them both up in the school library, and she hadn't wanted to ask the librarian.

Clickclickclickclick vsssh click. "I figured as much," said Julian. "For all his elegance, I sensed something very sad about him. I'm sorry, Charlie."

"For what?" Elsbeth said. She didn't know why she was suddenly bristling, but she couldn't help it. What did Julian know about anything? "What are *you* sorry about?"

Julian clicked away, undaunted. "It must be hard," he said, "to know somebody you love went through such an ordeal."

Elsbeth's chest hitched once, twice, as though she had hiccups. "I lost sisters, too. My half sisters. Twins, Vivian and Ginger— the Nazis killed them. They were only three." Elsbeth thought of sitting in Ruth's pink bathroom, the mirrors upon mirrors upon mirrors, Ruth brushing her hair with long, soothing strokes while telling Elsbeth about the little girls who'd burned in the ovens. "You know what else," she said to Julian, "it's pathetic, but I used to imagine they were still alive. In real life they'd be old now, like in their forties, so more aunts than sisters, but in my mind they're still little, and I get to take care of them. I used to pretend I was giving them dinner and baths, and I'd braid their hair and read them stories, and we'd all sleep in the same bed, and wear the same nightgowns, and I had this place in the attic where we could go if the Nazis came again, where I could keep them safe."

Julian didn't say anything; there was only the sound of his camera, clicking and whizzing, and Elsbeth realized she was crying.
The tears seemed detached from her, as if she were a cloud that was
raining, but they streamed down her cheeks nonetheless. Angrily
she wiped them away.

"Isn't that the dumbest thing you ever heard?" she asked, and
cried harder.

The clicking stopped, and Elsbeth felt more than heard the big
light go off; there was a sudden absence of warmth on her skin,
making her realize how hot the lamp had been. They were done,
she'd ruined it, crying like this; Julian would never use her as a
model now. He probably thought she was a lunatic.

But then he did a wonderful thing: he came to her with a dishtowel, gently prying her hands from her face. "Here," he said, "it's
all right, Charlie," and Elsbeth felt the material on her skin, stiff
and a little musty. He gently daubed her cheeks.

"Better?" he said finally, and Elsbeth nodded. She sensed him
moving away, and when she opened her eyes, he was perched on the
arm of the couch, lighting a cigarette.

"Smoke?" he said, holding out the Camels, and then, when Elsbeth shook her head, he said, "That's right, you don't," and tossed
the pack onto the coffee table.

"You did great today, Charlie," he said. "I knew you would. Do
you like the beach?"

"Excuse me?"

"I thought we might go to the Hamptons," said Julian. "I want
to do a series on you, mostly outside. We could meet here, say on
Saturday again, and if it's nice weather we'll shoot on location. Are
you available?"

"But—" Elsbeth stammered in her confusion. "But I didn't
even . . ." She pantomimed undressing, taking her suspender straps
down.

Julian looked a little startled. "Oh, no no no," he said. "Sorry

I wasn't clear. Today was just a test shoot." He smiled at her. "So what d'you think, are you free next week?"

She'd have time to lose five more pounds—at least. "Next week should be fine," Elsbeth said.

＊

When Elsbeth got home, she was unhappily surprised to find her dad awake, puttering around the kitchen. What was he doing up? Normally—abnormally—Peter slept all day and cooked at night, testing recipes for what June called "the famous cookbook," one that would feature dishes from Peter's first restaurant, Masha's, but updated for a new decade. Peter had been working on it for years, ever since the Claremont was sold; a publisher had given him a nice advance, and for a while even June was excited about it, but somehow the recipes were never quite ready, requiring more adjustments, and it had been so long that not only had the money been spent, the publishing house had gone out of business. Yet this was still all Peter did. Elsbeth stood in the doorway, watching her dad tend a stockpot on the stove. It was hard to reconcile this man—his baggy khakis, slight stoop, and neatly trimmed white beard—with the stern, polished fellow in a suit and hat Elsbeth had seen emerging from Masha's in photos, or even her impeccably elegant, commanding-yet-kind chef dad of later years. Women still looked at Peter; he was still handsome, but in a more faded, ghostly way.

Peter must have sensed Elsbeth measuring him or heard her come up the stairs, for he turned from the stove. "Ah," he said, "the world's greatest *commis* and taste tester! What luck." He came at Elsbeth with a ladle. "I need your unparalleled palate."

Maybe after one spoon, he would let her go. Elsbeth sipped what turned out to be Peter's mushroom soup, thick with cream and brandy, dolloped with crème fraiche. Her stomach, which had had nothing in it since last night's fat-free yogurt, gurgled; her mouth filled with saliva. Danger, she thought.

"It's good," she said, handing the ladle back.

Peter's brow, of which there was more than there used to be, furrowed beneath the waves of his hair, which crested higher on his forehead. "Not great?"

"It's the world's most excellent soup," said Elsbeth, edging closer to the hall.

"I may not be fluent in sarcasm, but I recognize it when I hear it. Come, what's wrong with it?"

"Nothing! Seriously, Dad. Put it in the book."

"Not enough thyme? Too much? Should I have browned the roux a bit more?"

"Dad. I really have to go."

"But you just came home."

"I have to call the girls."

"Did you not just see them?"

Elsbeth remembered the lie she had constructed to sneak into the city: "Gone to mall with Liza & Very, back later," scribbled on one of June's sticky notes—"Doe$ your hou$e need a face-lift? Call June Ra$hkin TODAY!"—and stuck to the refrigerator with a magnet featuring her mother's face and phone number.

"What could you possibly have to discuss in the fifteen minutes since you left them?" Peter was saying. "Come, have one bowl of soup with your old man."

"*Dad*," Elsbeth said. Fury rose in her: Why now? Why had Peter chosen to notice her now, when all she wanted to do was pore over her glorious afternoon with Julian in peace and privacy? Not only was Peter's attention inconvenient, it was years too late. Where have you been? Elsbeth wanted to shout at him—but as always, she tamped the anger down. It wasn't Peter's fault, she knew. It was the medicine, his beta blockers, his nitroglycerin, his angina pills. "He's sweet as ever," Elsbeth had heard June telling one of her tennis buddies on the phone, "but he's just so *vague*; it's like he doesn't know where he is half the time. And his schedule's completely upside-down." There was no alternative, though; if Peter stopped taking his medication, he could die at any moment, and was that what Elsbeth wanted? She had thought she'd stopped missing him long ago.

He was holding out a chair now, one of the bistro chairs June had salvaged from the Glenwood dump and recaned herself. Elsbeth sat, resigned.

Peter bustled to the stove and filled two bowls, bringing them to the table with a basket of baguettes.

"Lo and behold!" he said, bowing.

Elsbeth's eyes filled with tears. She cleared her throat.

"Lo and behold," she repeated and bent to the bowl. She dipped her spoon and touched it to her lips so Peter would think she was eating. Crème fraiche melted in a puddle on the surface; the smell, of rosemary and chanterelles, was driving her mad.

Peter joined her and took a thoughtful bite. He savored it, squinted, lowered his bifocals, and took his spiral-bound notebook from his back pocket, where he had carried it every day Elsbeth could remember.

"Something is still off," he said. "The onion? Should I have used Vidalias?"

"I think it's good," said Elsbeth, though she could taste what Peter meant—but she didn't want to eat more of the thousand-calorie soup, and besides, what did it matter? He'd never write the fucking cookbook. She began to tear a slice of baguette into pieces.

"Good is never good enough," said Peter. He put the notebook down and looked at Elsbeth. "How was your day?"

Again, Elsbeth wanted to laugh—or to hit something, or to say *Great, Dad, just great, I spent my afternoon with that photographer from Sol and Ruth's house, the one that lady called a pornographer, the one who shoots naked kids, and guess what? Next week he's going to photograph me. Nude.* Then a truly horrible thought occurred to her: Was this why Peter was awake? Had some dormant parental radar alerted him to the fact of Elsbeth's sneaking out to Julian's apartment? She stuffed bread into her mouth.

"Your note said you went to the mall with Very and Lisa," said Peter, as Elsbeth chewed and chewed. "Remind me, who are they?"

Elsbeth brought up her napkin and spat the bread into it. "It's *Liza.*"

"Is she the pretty Oriental?"

"Dad! That's so prejudiced. That's Very, and she's *Asian.*"

"My apologies. So who is this Eliza?"

"Liza."

"That's what I said. Is she the tall one, with the rather provocative manner?"

"Dad!"

"What?" said Peter. "I didn't mean anything by it. I just seem to remember she has a certain air about her."

"Well, she is kind of a—she's not shy," said Elsbeth, who had been going to say *slut.* "She can't help it, though. Her mom and dad are divorced, and her mom's out all the time with different guys."

"Ah," said Peter.

Elsbeth pushed herself back from the table. "Anyhoo, I've got to—"

"So what did you do?"

"Excuse me?"

"With your friends."

"We went to the mall. I said."

"And what did you do there?"

"Jeez, Dad, what's with the inquisition?" But Peter was looking at Elsbeth so sadly that she relented. "We hung out."

"You hung."

"Yes, we just chilled. You know."

"Ah," said Peter again. "I see."

He smiled at her. When had it gotten to be this way? After he'd gotten sick, around her eighth birthday, when the Claremont finally sold. Before that it had been just the two of them and nobody else, Elsbeth and her dad, the Fabulous Rashkins—that was to be the name of their restaurant, the one they would open together once Elsbeth was grown up and had gone to culinary school. At first it was a crêperie—Elsbeth, a big fan of the Magic Pan, was crazy for the thin sweet pancakes; later it was fine dining. Her earliest memories were of balancing on tiptoe on her special stool, her dad's hand over hers as she stirred batter on the counter; of his small spiky handwriting in his spiral-bound notebook. The drawings he made for her, the tap of his pen against the words. Bread. Butter. Lemons. You see, Ellie? Peter and his favorite *commis*, standing beside him rolling dough, chopping celery, sliding eggs into boiling water: the Fabulous Rashkins against the world.

Because the quiet was so awful, because her throat ached with everything she couldn't say, Elsbeth dumped some soup on it. The flavor was rich and complex, with crème fraiche and Courvoisier, thyme and chives, slivers of chanterelles and Portobello. You have the best palate of anyone I know, Ellie, her dad used to tell her; you'll be the top chef in the world, or food critic, if that is what you want. Suddenly Elsbeth couldn't eat the soup fast enough. She gobbled it down, her eyes watering; she would have picked up the bowl and drank from it if she hadn't known Peter would scold her.

"It is the onions," she said when she was done.

"What do you mean?"

Elsbeth pressed a belch against her wrist. Her shrunken stomach, now overloaded, groaned and gurgled; she could practically feel the fat invading her veins, her cells, plumping them up, making her bigger.

"What you said before," she said, "about Vidalias? I'd use shallots, the way you usually do, but I'd caramelize them first. To make them sweeter."

Her dad nodded slowly, stroking his beard. "Yes," he said, "you're exactly right, that's what it needs. And perhaps I should add a dash of balsamic?" He grabbed his notebook. "Ellie, you're a genius!"

"*De nada,*" Elsbeth said.

She got up and kissed Peter on the forehead while he scribbled away; his skin was warm, a little oily. She had to get upstairs. The sooner she got rid of the soup, the less chance the fat would have to pervade her system.

Yet something made Elsbeth pause at the door separating the kitchen from the foyer. She looked through it at her dad. Peter was sitting at the kitchen table alone; his scalp gleamed beneath his hair in the glare of the overhead light. He ate more soup, paused to make some notations, then gazed straight forward again—at nothing. What was he seeing when he looked into the middle distance like that? His kitchen at the Claremont? at Masha's? Masha herself? The little girls? Elsbeth took a last look at her father, then shut the door. She walked up the three flights to her attic suite, went into the bathroom, lifted the toilet lid, and knelt.

14

THE HAMPTONS

On the morning of the first naked shoot, Elsbeth met Julian on the sidewalk in front of his apartment, where he was loading camera and tripod bags into the back seat of a car that looked very much like the General Lee in *The Dukes of Hazzard*—minus the Confederate flag on top. Elsbeth rather hoped Julian would vault through the driver's window, but he instead came around to her side and opened the door. "Your chariot, Charlie," he said.

Elsbeth tried to drop gracefully into the low seat. "Thank you," she said. Julian was in shorts and a ruffled tuxedo shirt today, the checked Vans on his feet. The sun haloed his hair, which was curling in the mid-July haze. Elsbeth had given up on hers, pulling it over to one side in a banana clip. Her white jeans skirt had ridden up when she'd gotten in the car, but she left it as it was: her legs, sturdy and curved from years of swimming, were her best feature.

Julian drove them somewhat jerkily down Riverside Drive and across town, while Elsbeth tried to watch him without looking like she was. He was unshaven again, his eyes hidden behind Wayfarer sunglasses, and a tiny cross dangled from his right ear. Had he had the earring before? Elsbeth was sure not. She would have noticed.

She tried to think of something sophisticated to say as they entered Central Park at Ninety-Sixth Street—Julian didn't seem as inclined this morning toward sprightly conversation.

"I like your car," was the best she could come up with, having discarded an anecdote about her favorite childhood spot, the Whale Room at the Museum of Natural History a few blocks south.

Julian took a sip from a to-go cup of coffee, and his hand shook. Some of the hot liquid spilled on his bare leg, and he swore. "Thanks," he said. "It is bodacious, isn't it? I don't really drive stick, but a friend was putting it up for sale and I just couldn't resist."

Elsbeth wondered how many other girls had sat exactly where she was now, in the front seat of the non–General Lee en route to a shoot with Julian, their thighs adhering to the cracked vinyl. It didn't matter. She was here now. She would be unforgettable.

Julian slalomed the car along the curving road through Central Park, sunlight and shadow sliding over the windshield. Elsbeth tried to pick up what color mood he was in today. People's hues, like those of numbers and letters, weren't always immediately visible—thank goodness, because that would be distracting. But if Elsbeth concentrated, she could make the colors appear, and Julian, who was usually a supernova, a dark center surrounded by prismatic rays, was today preoccupied and refracted, so that his light spoked out at broken-umbrella angles.

Elsbeth considered whether to share this observation with her fellow synesthete but decided to keep it to herself. Instead, as they passed her old building on East Ninety-Sixth Street, she said, "There's my first apartment."

"Is that so?" said Julian, merging onto FDR Drive.

"For real," said Elsbeth. "We lived there until I was two," and she twisted to watch the building as it disappeared. "I still remember that apartment," she said. "I remember sitting on the floor under the piano, and I remember what the windows across the street looked like at night through my crib . . ." She could also remember shaking the bars and yelling like a tiny gorilla, with all her might, and nobody coming to her call.

"My dad's first restaurant was near here, too," she said. "The very famous one. Masha's. Did you ever go there?" But of course Julian hadn't; Elsbeth knew from reading articles about him at the Glenwood library that Julian had arrived in the city long after Masha's had closed. Elsbeth herself would have given anything to see Masha's as it had been, just once, but every time she had walked past the building, scanning it for signs of former glory, she saw only what it now housed: a ladies' shoe emporium.

"What's your earliest memory?" she asked Julian.

"Ha," said Julian. "You don't want to know."

"*Au contraire!* I do."

Julian drained his coffee, then crumpled the cup and tossed it into the back seat. They were crossing the Queensboro Bridge now, and stripes from the girders flicked rapidly over his face. "It's pretty bad. Honestly, I'm not sure I should tell you."

"Why?" Elsbeth said. "That's not fair; I told you about my half sisters."

"True," said Julian, merging off the bridge into Queens. The skyscrapers had been replaced by rows and rows of two- and three-story houses and apartment buildings huddled together; there was graffiti everywhere. Julian lit a cigarette. "I didn't grow up in a nice home like you, Charlie. I was a foster kid."

"So?"

"So," said Julian. He exhaled through his nose. "So I have no idea who my mom and dad were. So somebody left me in a shoe-box on a church step when I was eight hours old. So I was in an orphanage for a while—I don't remember that at all—but then I went to several different placements until they put me with Peg."

"So," Elsbeth said. She was scrambling to keep up, mentally

shuffling through the images as Julian described them. "So, Peg.
Was that your mom? Did she adopt you?"

Julian smiled, but Elsbeth thought it was the meanest smile
she'd ever seen; he looked like the Grinch. "Oh, no," he said. "She
didn't. But she had other ways of showing her love," and he flipped
his right forearm to expose the underside. It was peppered with
silvery dots, as if acid rain had fallen on the tender skin there.

"What is that?" Elsbeth asked.

"Burns," said Julian. "From her Swisher Sweets—you know,
those little cigarillos you can buy at gas stations? Yeah. Peg was
classy like that. She liked to play connect-the-dots on me when she
was drunk."

Elsbeth gasped. She could hardly imagine anything so horrible happening to anyone, let alone to Julian. Julian, who was so
kind and thoughtful; Julian, who all the art magazines said was
a genius—*Photoplay* had called him the best portrait photographer
since Eisenstaedt.

Julian reached for his Camel pack on the dashboard and lit a
new cigarette from the end of the first. "Amazing I still smoke,
isn't it?" he said. "The triumph of bad habit over memory." He
laughed.

"Where did this *happen*?" Elsbeth asked, as if geography would
explain the brutality.

"Wisconsin," said Julian. "That's where I was born, in a city
called La Crosse."

"I know La Crosse!" said Elsbeth, sitting up in her seat in excitement. "It's right across the river from where my grandma Ida lives.
We used to go to this department store called, called—"

"Doerflinger's," said Julian.

"Yes, Doerflinger's!" said Elsbeth. "It had an old-fashioned
lunch counter and chocolate malts—"

"It was a shithole," said Julian, "like everything else there."

"Oh," said Elsbeth. She sat back, feeling a little bad on behalf of the store and La Crosse, too; she had always liked it. But of course, Julian would know it better than she did.

Julian's mouth crimped. "Forgive me, Charlie," he said. "My memories of Wisconsin are not the best."

Elsbeth nodded. She felt like a fool for having brought it up. "How did you get out of there?" she asked, trying to steer him to happier recollections.

"As quickly as I could," said Julian and laughed. As with his smile, there wasn't a trace of humor in it; if it had been an object, Elsbeth thought, that laugh would have been tinfoil. "By the time I was sixteen, I decided I'd had enough of Peg's maternal love and hit the road. I took money from her purse and what I'd saved working odd jobs and started hitching. All I wanted was to get to New York—I'd read an article about it in a doctor's office, and I was obsessed with it. It just seemed like the kind of place where you could be whoever you wanted."

Elsbeth nodded again; she had heard much the same from her mother. "So you got to New York when you were sixteen?"

"Not exactly," said Julian. "I had to work my way there. I started out in Milwaukee, then Indiana—"

"Doing what?" said Elsbeth.

Julian's Grinch smile spread. "That," he said, "I am not going to tell you." He tossed his cigarette out the window; they were on 495 now, in a cement maze of liquor depots, carpet wholesalers, used car lots. "Let's just say it was rather unsavory. Until I got to Pittsburgh, and then I managed to snag a job at Sears."

"As . . . a salesman?" said Elsbeth, picturing Julian in a plaid suit, hawking washing machines.

"As a janitor. But one day they had an opening in the photo department, and I jumped on it. I loved it. I loved developing the film and seeing other people's lives, even if the images were really boring, like of a birthday party or a new grill or lawn mower. I started saving up to buy my own camera, and I found one at a garage sale, a beat-to-shit old Nikon—pardon my French."

"That's okay. I've heard it a time or two before," said Elsbeth.

"I taught myself to shoot with that thing," he said. "Black-and-white portraits, mostly. The guys in the stockroom. The bums in my neighborhood. My roommates. Very Gordon Parks, very derivative. Though of course I didn't know that at the time. All I knew was I loved it, and I could develop the film at night, at work, for free. And one night the manager, Al, came in for something and caught me and I thought he was going to fire me, but instead he said, These are good, kid. You've really got an eye. And that was the beginning." He shrugged and lit another Camel. "First he told me to submit to contests, even offered to pay the entrance fees, so I did. I won a prize in *Art Forum*—first prize, which meant money, and a show in Chicago. At the Klein Gallery, on Michigan Avenue— I had to borrow a suit from Al." He laughed. "It was four sizes too big for me, but there you go. Then I started shooting kids, and then nudes, and a couple more prizes later . . . I was in New York."

"Wow," said Elsbeth. She was awed, both by the story—which no articles had covered—and by Julian's disclosing so much. She had never heard an adult talk so much about himself, ever.

"Wow is right," said Julian. "Nobody was more surprised than me. Sometimes when I wake up I think I'm still in Peg's rat-trap by the Mississippi, with blue plastic on the windows." He turned to Elsbeth, talking around his cigarette. "Do you think less of me, Charlie, knowing I wasn't always the magnificent creature you see today?"

"Hardly," said Elsbeth. "I think you're even more amazing."

Julian grinned. "You're a pip, Charlie, you know that?" he said, and then the cigarette dropped from his lips and disappeared. "Fuck," said Julian and stamped around under the steering wheel; the car swerved. There was a scorched smell.

"I think it's under the clutch," he said. "Take over a sec, would you?"

"What—" said Elsbeth, but she didn't have time to say anything else, because Julian let go of the wheel. Elsbeth grabbed it as he bent down to fish around in the foot well. The car edged into the left lane, and Elsbeth jerked her arm back just as an eighteen-wheeler barreled past, blasting them with its air horn. She stared at the highway, terrified. She had done this sometimes with Liza when Liza wanted to fix her hair or put in earrings, but on suburban roads only; this was a whole different ball game.

"There!" said Julian, surfacing with the smoldering butt; he flicked it out the window. "So that happened. Thanks, Charlie."

"No sweat," said Elsbeth, although her armpits prickled and she had an awful taste of metal in her mouth. "I've done it before."

Julian laughed his deep, happy laugh. "Of course you have," he said, "there seems to be nothing you can't do." He took the right fork in the highway, beneath a sign that read HAMPTONS. "You're a marvel, Charlie," he said. "That's you being you."

*

The house Julian brought Elsbeth to was in Montauk and belonged to another friend—Julian had more friends than anyone in the world, apparently. Elsbeth climbed from the non–General Lee and shouldered a backpack of camera lenses Julian asked her if she'd mind carrying. This house reminded her a bit of a Nantucket cottage her family had rented the year Elsbeth was four: gray-shingled and covered in trellised beach roses, hydrangea bushes beneath the windows. The proportions were different, however; this place was the size of an airplane hangar, and inside just as stark and chilly. They entered a vast three-story room built of chrome and glass and white marble, full of the kind of art Elsbeth knew was art because one wondered, exactly, what made it art. Sculptures like melting bronze skeletons, woven mats, and sieves; a Lichtenstein woman mourned that she had left her baby on the bus, and one whole wall was taken up by what Elsbeth knew, from a private showing with Sol, was a Pollock. In the center of the room, bisecting the panoramic window featuring the Atlantic, a single strand of green gum stretched from the ceiling to a white pedestal. Julian's naked children were there too—boy and girl, holding hands, blown up to billboard size so their glowering eyes were as big as hubcaps.

Julian was encumbered by several tripod bags and another backpack with his cameras; he began to divest them now, sloughing them onto the marble foyer floor. "Rosa?" he called. "Anyone home? Got a drink for a thirsty man?"

"Jules," growled a voice, "you reprobate," and a man arose from what Elsbeth now realized was a couch, though she had mistaken it for another installation—it looked like a clump of oversize sugar cubes. The man was wearing a pinstripe oxford with the collar turned up and salmon-colored shorts, and his feet were bare; he had a flip of blond hair and looked like every preppy boy who had ever scared Elsbeth at school, especially when he came over to Julian and punched him in the shoulder.

"Ow," said Julian, rubbing it.

"You wuss," said the man, "you're supposed to fight back."

"Can't," said Julian, "slow reflexes. Late night," and the man gripped him around the neck and rubbed his knuckles in Julian's hair.

"Who's this?" he drawled, releasing Julian and turning to Elsbeth. "Let me guess, dear, you're the cage dancer from Limelight?"

"This is Charlie," said Julian, "my new model. Charlie, Richard; Richard, Charlie. Remember, I told you we were coming out to shoot today?"

"Riiiiiiight, right," said Richard. He squinted. "Wait, did you?"

"I said Saturday."

"Riiiiiiiight," said Richard again. "Except is it Saturday? I guess it's Saturday. Hey," he called, "Brie, it's Saturday."

"You don't have to shout," said another voice from the couch, and a woman uncoiled from it like a snake charmed from a basket by a flute. She was the most beautiful woman Elsbeth had ever seen besides her mother: short black hair cut in a bi-level like a boy's; ice-chip eyes; cheekbones that rivaled the sculptures in the room. She wore a skintight hot-pink dress with a cutout over one breast that almost but not quite exposed her nipple, and she too was barefoot, a diamond band on one toe.

"Since this jerk won't introduce me properly, I'm Brianna," she said to Elsbeth. She undulated to Julian and kissed him a little too long on the mouth. "Juuuules," she said. "Sooooooooooo good to see you, you beautiful genius. Did you just looooove that review in the *Times*? Did you just *die*?"

"I did," said Julian. "But then I came back to life."

Brianna hung on Richard's shoulder and swung back and forth as if he were a garden gate. "I'm sooooooo destroyed," she said. "We were up all night, or was it two? We had *people*," and she pushed at Richard's face. He batted her hand away.

"Get them some mimosas," he said, "or Bloodies."

"Get them yourself," said Brianna, "I'm not the maid. Speaking of, where is she?"

"I think I sent her to the store, three or four days ago," said Richard. He lit a cigarette and held it between thumb and forefinger in a way Elsbeth had seen French exchange students do. "You coming on the yacht?" he asked Julian. "Get some sun on that pitifully wasted body?"

"Thanks, but no," said Julian. "We're going to shoot out back."

Richard looked Elsbeth up and down. "You could shoot on deck," he suggested. "Plenty of room."

"Ohhhhhhhhh, dooooooooooooooo," said Brianna, pouring herself a Diet Coke.

"Can't," said Julian, "I get seasick," and he winked at Elsbeth. "Besides, you know I like organic settings. There's never anything better than when your subject synthesizes with nature, right, Charlie?"

"Right," said Elsbeth.

Brianna redraped herself on Richard. "Your name is Charlie? You're named after a boy?"

"That's her work name," said Julian. "It's going to be her supermodel name."

To Elsbeth's surprise Brianna didn't laugh soda out of her perfect nose at this, nor did Richard scoff—though he wasn't really paying attention; he had wandered to the counter and was chopping something on it with a credit card. Jesus, thought Elsbeth, was that coke? She didn't know anyone who had actually done it, but she'd seen it in movies, and some seniors at school had just been suspended for dealing.

Brianna tipped her head and peered at Elsbeth. "I guess you do have a look," she said. "Doesn't she have a look, honey?"

"Sure, absolutely," said Richard. "If Jules thinks she has a look, she has a look."

"You are soooo lucky," Brianna told Elsbeth. "Jules is going to *immortalize* you."

"Come on," said Julian.

"It's true," said Richard. "If she's your muse, she'll be preserved for posterity: shown in galleries, hung in museums, studied in art history courses throughout the millennia. You are the maestro, it's beyond dispute." He hoovered up one of the lines on the counter with a rolled-up bill. "Who wants a bump?"

"I don't think you need any more," said Brianna.

"I wasn't talking to you," said Richard.

"We're good," said Julian. "I'm on the clock."

"God, you're boring," said Richard. "I don't know why I hang out with you." He slapped Brianna on the rump. "Go get ready," he drawled, "debauchery awaits."

"I am ready," said Brianna.

"You're not going to change?"

"I'll just take this off," she said, drawing her hands down her hot-pink body.

"Charlie," said Julian, "why don't you meet me out back? I'll just see these guys on their way and get us a couple of drinks."

"Okay," said Elsbeth and tried to thank them, but she was so flustered that instead of saying "Thank you" or "Thanks" she said both: Thanksou. Luckily nobody noticed; Richard and Brianna were arguing, and Julian was pressing a button that allowed the far glass wall to slide up. Elsbeth crossed the white marble and exited onto the lawn.

The grounds, like the house, were punctuated with oversize sculpture: a melting dolphin, a giant spoon. There was an expanse of grass and a pool, which seemed redundant: Why would anyone want chlorinated water with the ocean just beyond the dunes? Elsbeth yearned toward the beach, but she wasn't sure where Julian wanted her, so she sat on a lounge chair next to some bushes clipped to look like big rabbits. She hugged her knees to her face and closed her eyes. The sun was hot on her face.

Inside, Julian and Richard and Brianna were talking; there was a burst of laughter, and a sound like a slap. Then they must have been coming closer, because Elsbeth heard Richard drawl, "Little older than your usual jailbait, isn't she, Jules?" and Julian saying, "Lay off, you pervert," and Richard saying, "I didn't mean it like *that*; I just meant you've graduated from grade-school to pubescent." "I'm trying something new," said Julian, and Richard said, "Just don't try anything in my house that'll get you arrested. That'll get *me* arrested. And promise me the first decent photo of the series," and Julian said, "Done," and there was the whap of footsteps, deck shoes or flip-flops, over patio flagstones and *crunch-crunch-crunch*ing on shells. Then Elsbeth heard Brianna asking, "Do you think he actually *fucks* those little girls he brings here?" and Richard saying, "Why, would that get you hot?" and Brianna saying, "You are officially filth," and

Richard saying, "You brought it up, you hussy," and the car doors went *chunk, chunk*, and there was the pop of crushed shells and purr of motor as they drove away.

Elsbeth sat paralyzed. Did Julian—do that to his models? She didn't think so; he had never made the slightest move toward her. Had he? Elsbeth wasn't very experienced; the farthest she'd ever gone was second base, in the back row of a movie theater with the guy who'd also given her her first kiss: Paulie T, who had a cute face but also a tongue like a reptile, darting in and out of her mouth. Elsbeth had gotten rid of him as soon as possible. What if Julian did hit on her? What was wrong with Elsbeth if he didn't? She and Liza and Very had discussed these scenarios at length: they didn't want anyone in their school to take their virginity, the guys were all so immature. Until they met the right one, they would be the queens of Everything But. Julian might be the one: tender-hearted, synesthetic, world-famous, and a genius. Yes, Elsbeth decided, he was definitely it—and if he wasn't interested, it was because, despite Elsbeth's self-improvement program, she was deficient, ungainly, still too fat.

As if she had called him over, there was the sound of ice cubes, and Julian pulled over a chair. "Mind if I join you?" he said, handing her a glass of club soda. He lit a cigarette.

"So *that*," he said, "was Richard and Brianna. I've known Richard my whole time in New York. He's a Wall Street dude, a serious collector. Exceedingly wealthy. Extremely. Obscenely." Julian exhaled and watched the smoke twist off over the dunes. "He's kind of an asshole, isn't he," he said.

"*Yes*," Elsbeth said with relief. "A total asshole."

Julian laughed, a deep happy sound of appreciation. "Oh, Charlie," he said. "I'm glad you're here. I'm sorry to have exposed you to them, but they can be kind of fun. And they do have a great house." He stood up and stretched. "Isn't it magnificent?" he said to the beach, the ocean. "Isn't it?"

"It is," said Elsbeth, pushing herself up to stand beside him. He was sweating; she could smell the rich scent of it on the breeze.

"This is it, Charlie," said Julian. "This is my cathedral, right here. This is God." He turned his face to the sun. "You know what? I'm hot. Let's go for a swim before we get to work, what do you say?"

He started unbuttoning his tuxedo shirt, then just pulled it off over his head and threw it onto the grass. Elsbeth felt him hopping up and down next to her, taking off his shoes. What next? His shorts, his underwear? Was he even wearing any, or had he gone, as Liza said, commando? Elsbeth bolted off across the lawn for the water.

"Are we racing?" Julian called behind her. "Fine, I'll give you a head start!"

Elsbeth plunged down through sharp grass, slipping in the sand, until she reached the waterline. Then she jogged alongside it, stopping when she got a stitch in her ribs. She slowed and looked up and down the beach: it was deserted, only surf and screaming gulls. Maybe Richard owned the whole thing.

She kicked away her Capezios, stripped off her skirt, tank top, bra, and panties—quickly, before she could change her mind—and waded in. The cold made her gasp. "That's my girl," Peter had said during that long-ago Nantucket vacation; "it's not so bad once you get used to it!" "Once you go numb, you mean," June had called from the picnic blanket. June had imported an umbrella, her cartwheel-size straw hat, a gauzy long-sleeved shift, and SPF 50 along with her cigarettes and Tab; Elsbeth had often wondered why her mother came to the beach at all. "That's it, Ellie, a little deeper," said Peter; "we don't mind the cold, do we? We are North Sea seals. Now we dive . . . no? Very well. I will go first." Elsbeth remembered Peter standing in the shallows with his arms folded like a general, assessing the best place to penetrate the waves; a four-foot comber rolled toward them, curling viciously; Peter plunged in and vanished from view. Elsbeth had held her breath until he finally reappeared on the other side, laughing, his shirt plastered to his body and his hair to his head. "You see?" he called. "You can do it! The only way in is through—there's my brave girl."

Now Elsbeth charged into the water, hollering. She turned sideways when a wave broke, then dove into it; it was excruciating for a moment, but once her head got wet, her dad was right: it wasn't so bad. She jumped one wave, then another, letting them lift her feet off the sand. The horizon bobbed; straight on from where Elsbeth was looking was England, and nearby, Germany. Had her dad ever taken her sisters swimming? Had Vivian and Ginger, too, been North Sea seal pups? Probably not; they were too young when the Nazis got them. Elsbeth burst into a vigorous crawl, churning back and forth. That was the last time she had been on vacation with her dad; the next summer he'd had his heart attack, and ocean swimming was considered too strenuous for him. Elsbeth slowed and floated, her back freezing, her face and bare breasts warmed by the sun.

Then: "Helloooo out there," a man's voice called from the shore. Elsbeth flipped upright and shaded her eyes. Julian, merely a silhouette from this distance, bending over a tripod. He straightened and waved—Elsbeth couldn't see whether he had any clothes on or not. She squinted.

"How's the water?" he shouted.

"It's beautiful!" Elsbeth yelled. She swam forward a few yards, until her toes touched the bottom, then did a handstand and waved her feet at him; when she surfaced, Julian was laughing.

"Come in," she called.

"I'd rather watch you. You're like a mermaid!" He bent to his camera.

Elsbeth dove. She did some somersaults, a butterfly, a backstroke. She glided on her back, breasts bare to the sky, and spewed water like a porpoise—luxuriating in Julian's laughter, his attention trained on her, although the *clickclick vssh click* of his camera was inaudible over the surf. Julian would never shout "Thar she blows!" or liken Elsbeth to a whale; he saw her as she truly was, her best self that came out in the water, not fat nor clumsy but buoyant and joyous. Julian shouted; a huge wave was swelling toward Elsbeth, much larger than the rest, foaming at its peak, the seventh in the series. Elsbeth flipped upright to meet it head-on as it rolled and roared, and as it lifted her high and higher and higher still, she spun to face the shore. Julian was clapping, applauding her bravery, and as Elsbeth flung up her arms in victory she felt, for the first time in such a long time, that everything from now on might really turn out all right.

15

QUELLE HORREUR

A nd then what happened?" Liza asked.

"I told you," said Elsbeth. "Nothing."

"Come on."

"That's it. We got in the car, and Julian drove us back to the city. Like always. End of story."

Liza had been leaning forward so far that she was practically dipping her nipples in her leftover gravy fries—a distinct possibility, since Liza's off-the-shoulder T-shirt was designed to expose as much of what she called her bodacious tatas as possible. Now Liza sat back, lit a Parliament Light, and regarded Elsbeth through the smoke.

"Elsbeth Viola Rashkin," Liza said—Elsbeth didn't have a middle name, but Liza always gave her one, a different one each time. "That is the lamest thing I've ever heard."

"Well, I'm sorry," said Elsbeth, "but that's what happened. Nothing."

"And he's not gay," said Liza.

"Nope," said Elsbeth.

Liza narrowed her eyes. She was wearing electric-green mascara today, which she'd just swiped from CVS. "What ear did you say the earring was in again?"

"Right," said Elsbeth.

"Huh," said Liza. "Not gay." She exhaled a series of smoke rings, indicating she was thinking. "*Très bizarre.* You seriously mean to tell me you've been naked in front of this guy multiple times, and he hasn't tried to slip you the hot beef injection."

"No. And it's five times."

"He didn't even go for the tatas? Or kiss you—French or no tongue?"

"I said," Elsbeth hissed, "no." She was mortified, and not just because the woman behind Liza had turned to scowl at them. No doubt if Julian had been shooting Liza, he would have made a move—or she would; Julian wouldn't have stood a chance. All guys loved Liza; she was tall and rangy, with ashy blond Madonna hair that she ratted every morning and tied up with a stocking; she wore spike-heeled boots and thigh-highs and a handcuff belt and fishnet tank tops over nothing but bras. She was sex on a stick, whereas Elsbeth was more of a corn dog on a stick—something she'd once eaten at the New Heidelberg county fair. Five shoots with Julian: his apartment, the Hamptons, Bear Mountain, the woods near Rhinebeck, and the beach again, but every time Julian only photographed Elsbeth, nothing more. If anyone would know what Elsbeth was doing wrong, it was Liza.

"It's me, isn't it?" Elsbeth said. "I'm still too fat."

"No, that's not it," said Liza contemplatively. "You're looking pretty fly. You've lost a lot of weight."

"Thanks. I'm down to one seventeen," said Elsbeth. Was that the problem? She had plateaued, even though she'd increased her jogging—five miles a day around Glenwood Park Lake, where she used to feed the ducks with her dad. Maybe she'd start smoking.

"Are you . . ." Liza pantomimed sticking her finger down her throat.

"Sometimes."

"Well, cut it out. It's supposed to be for emergencies, not a life-style." Liza pointed her cigarette at Elsbeth's barely touched side salad, no dressing. "Don't even think about throwing that up. I paid for it. Besides, if you hurl too much, you get chipmunk cheeks. And you can burst the blood vessels under your eyes."

"Great," said Elsbeth. She didn't tell Liza this had happened once already. After their shoot at Bear Mountain, when Julian hadn't so much as tried to kiss her, Elsbeth had been so despondent she'd ordered a Domino's pizza and eaten the whole thing, even though she knew better. Anything bread-based was hard to bring up, and she'd worked for half an hour to choke up the doughy balls that had already formed in her stomach. She'd been horrified by the mask of red pinpricks around her eyes—terrified they were permanent, she'd stayed in her room for two days, faking a summer flu. Eventually, though, the marks had faded, and Elsbeth had stuck to easy food, like June's nonfat cottage cheese, after that.

Liza gave a businesslike exhale and mashed her cigarette in the ashtray. "Could it be a religious thing? Is Julian Catholic?"

"That's beaucoup *Thorn Birds*," said Elsbeth, "but no."

"And you really like this guy. Do you love him?"

Elsbeth looked away, at the sunlight coming in the front window and highlighting the candy counter. She thought of Julian clicking away at her as she stood atop a slab of rock at Bear Mountain, calling, "You're queen of the mountain!"; murmuring, "Very nice, very nice, Charlie"; throwing his head back to laugh under a green canopy of leaves; tapping his hands on the wheel of the non–General Lee in time to music on Z100. Her throat constricted and ached.

"You do," said Liza. "You looooooooovvvvve him," and she drew the word out with a gargle that made it sound like something caught in a garbage disposal.

"Stop it!" said Elsbeth.

"Oh boy, you've got it bad. What did I tell you? No love. Just sex. Love leads to trouble, every time." Liza lit another cigarette.

"I can't help it," Elsbeth said miserably.

"Okay. Don't worry, kid. It happens. So you love him. Does he love you?"

"I don't know," Elsbeth said.

"I bet he does," Liza said. "Think about it. He's a big-time famous photographer, right? There're a zillion girls he could take nudie pics of. But he chose you."

Elsbeth shrugged, but she felt a little better.

"Now you gotta show him how *you* feel. Don't give it all away, but be a little more aggressive."

Elsbeth nodded. This was exactly the advice she'd come to Liza for. "How?"

"Well," said Liza. "For instance. Next time you're driving to a shoot, tell him you're dying for ice cream. Or a Popsicle. You say . . ." She tipped her head back and closed her eyes, drawing a hand down over her clavicle. "Ooooohhhhh, I'm so hot . . ."

"Hey," called Louie, the owner. "What'd I tell you about that behavior in here?"

"Sorry, Louie-Louie." Liza blew him a kiss, and then, when he'd turned to fill a coffee cup, she made a jerking-off gesture. "Then, when you get the ice cream, eat it like . . . Hold on."

She went to the counter and leaned over it to get Louie's attention, so far that a red strap showed above the waist of her painter pants—Liza was the only person Elsbeth knew who wore a G-string on a daily basis. She returned with a chocolate-dipped banana.

"You lick it," she said, "like this," and she swirled her pierced tongue around the top, then darted it at the tip. "Mmmmmmm," she moaned to the imaginary Julian, "I just love to make things melt in my mouth . . ."

"*Hey,*" said Louie again. "I mean it, Liza. I'll kick you outta here!"

Liza snapped her teeth over the top of the banana, chewed, stuck her tongue out at Louie. He slapped his rag on the counter.

"You know you love me," called Liza. "He loves me. Here, wanna try?" She handed the bitten banana to Elsbeth.

"I'll practice at home," said Elsbeth.

"Also," said Liza, "maybe he's not hitting on you because he's working. He's in his genius zone. So we need to find him off-hours. You said he goes clubbing, right?"

"Yes—he mentioned Limelight once. And Nell's."

"Awesome, we'll go in this weekend. You think that'll help?"

"Most definitely," Elsbeth said, and was about to ask about logistical matters, like her not having fake ID, when Liza craned at something over Elsbeth's shoulder.

"Don't look now," she said, "but is that *June?* Playing footsie with some guy? Do not look!" But Elsbeth was horrible at this; if someone was staring at something, she had to see it too. She turned, and at the very last table near the restrooms, there was the back of June's head, her pyramid of curls brushing the huge shoulders of the leopard-print suit jacket Elsbeth had seen her pull on that morning.

"Wow," said Liza, "nice power pads. She could play defense with those things."

"Let's go," said Elsbeth.

"Who's the dude?"

Elsbeth didn't have to look again to know. Seersucker suit, blow-dried gray hair, more teeth than any human mouth should have. "That's Harrison, her boss."

"He looks like a vampire," said Liza, tipping out of the booth for a better view. "Hey, where are your hands, buddy?"

"Liza," hissed Elsbeth, "don't."

"I seriously think he's going to third right there at the table. His fingers have gotta be all up in her—"

"Shut up!" Elsbeth said. She concentrated very hard on a straw wrapper that was uncoiling, snakelike, in some spilled water. She felt sick—the irony being that although she didn't mind throwing up meals, she couldn't tolerate nausea. She had sometimes had feelings about June and certain men, a kind of attention from June like a sparkling lasso from her to them. It happened with Peter when June was feeling loving toward him, which was nice but mostly consigned to the past. It had been there with June's tennis coach from long ago, the giant guy who'd brought Elsbeth a watermelon sherbet and her Lite-Brite, which she still used as a night-light. And now with June's boss, Harrison. Elsbeth despised these men, but she never said anything to June or, God forbid, Peter. She had no concrete proof, and she didn't want any.

"Dude, she's stone-cold busted," said Liza, "there's a real opportunity for blackmail here," but finally she saw how Elsbeth was frozen in the booth, hunching to make herself as small as possible. Liza dropped her voice. "Pas de problème, kid, it's no biggie your mom's a skank. Mine is too. They get that way in middle age, it's hormones," and she got up and yawned elaborately. "C'mon, let's go check out the record store." She propelled Elsbeth through the restaurant, walking behind her so June wouldn't see Elsbeth if she turned. But once the revolving door had ejected them into the hot and glaring afternoon, Liza yelled, "Sayonara, slut mom!" and raced off down the sidewalk to make Elsbeth laugh, yelling *yip yip yip!* like Wile E. Coyote, the handcuffs clanking on her belt.

*

Elsbeth's birthday that year was her supposedly golden birthday: she would be sixteen on July 16. She would have been perfectly happy if her parents had forgotten; all she wanted was to go to the Chinese diner on Bloomfield Avenue with Liza and Very, to drink tea and open fortune cookies in the boxcar, then catch the 66 bus to New York with Liza. But unfortunately her parents remembered, and June managed to tear herself away from the Motherfucker, as Liza now called Harrison—"Because that's what he's doing, you know," Liza had said and cackled. Even Peter managed to get up at a decent hour of the evening and put on dress slacks and a cardigan. So now here Elsbeth was, sandwiched between her parents at the Glenwood Bath and Tennis Club, trying to figure out what on the menu was the least fattening and not glance too often at her Swatch under the table. *Quelle horreur.*

"Isn't this nice," said Peter, taking his bifocals out of his breast pocket and sliding them on, then holding the menu at arm's length anyway.

"Yes, it's peachy," Elsbeth muttered.

"What, darling?" June said, scanning the table for an ashtray.

"I was agreeing with Dad," said Elsbeth, "it's so nice to be with the whole family unit." She looked pointedly at June's gold cigarette case. "That's new, isn't it? Where's it from?"

June shrugged and her scarf fell away, exposing her coat-hanger shoulders; she was starting to get age spots, just the faintest spreading freckles, like a giraffe. "It must have been a gift from a client," she said, "or from a store somewhere, I don't remember."

"Uh-huh," said Elsbeth. "*Sure.*"

"What's with the attitude?" said June. "I know you're still a teenager, but don't you think you're overdoing it a little?"

"It's not me who's overdoing him," said Elsbeth. "I mean *it.*"

"*Excuse* me?" said June, but Elsbeth had opened her heavy leather menu and was studying it intently.

"Okay, not-so-sweet sixteen," said June, "have it your way, it's your night," and she playfully bumped Elsbeth's elbow with her own.

"Ow!" said Elsbeth.

June sighed. "Pete, what're you going to have?"

Peter was sitting with his head tipped far back, all the better to see the italicized print in the low light. The club's restaurant was new—at least, people still called it that, "the new lounge," even though it had been operational since 1982. Like the mountaintop pool, it was for adults only; the minimum age was sixteen, so this was Elsbeth's first time dining in the big hexagonal room with its trellis wallpaper, its green rug and pink tablecloths with napkins to match. It was cushy, Elsbeth had to admit, but the menu was strictly paint-by-numbers, almost exactly like the one at Sol and Ruth's club, the Briar Rose. And the Glenwood Lounge had been built on top of the snack bar, to take advantage of the city view, so despite the fancy decor and classical Muzak, Elsbeth could smell chlorine and broiling burgers and hear kids splashing and shouting outside.

"Pete," said June.

"Yes?" said Peter, glancing up. He was so pale Elsbeth could see the veins in his forehead—of course he was, since he spent all the daylight hours asleep.

"I asked what you were going to eat."

"Oh, I don't know," said Peter. "It's standard country-club fare. Probably safest to go with the scallops."

"Dad," said Elsbeth, "you know you're not supposed to have shellfish."

Peter wiggled his eyebrows at her. "Saysh who?" he said in his gangster voice.

"Says your cardiologist."

"Cardiologist, schmardiologist," said Peter. "Tonight I'm living on the edge."

"Dad," said Elsbeth again and was about to argue further when their waiter finally showed up. To Elsbeth's surprise she recognized him: Michael Dermont, or Mikey D, the kids called him at school, a basketball and football player she'd had a mild crush on pre-Julian. He was tall—about six-four—with nice round green eyes, brown feathered hair, a pillowy lower lip. "Don't even bother,"

Liza had reported, after a failed attempt with Mikey D at a pool party; "he doesn't fool around. He says it's because he's Catholic, but clearly, if he turned down the tatas, he's gay."

"How are you folks this evening?" he said, setting a basket of rolls and breadsticks on the table. "'Sup," he added to Elsbeth.

"Hey, Mike," she said. "I didn't know you worked here."

"Just started this summer. Saving up for Holy Cross." He took out his pen and pad. "What can I get you folks?"

The Rashkins chose their drinks: gin and tonic for Peter, white wine spritzer for June, Diet Coke with lemon for Elsbeth. "I'm ready to order, too," she announced—all the better to hasten this evening along. Her parents looked startled, but Peter requested his scallops, compensating with no butter or sour cream on his baked potato, and June a chef's salad. Elsbeth smirked: for all the pin-wheels of meat and cheese in that dish, not to mention hard-boiled eggs, June might as well have ordered a hoagie.

"I'll have . . ." Elsbeth paused, running a long nail down the menu. She was wearing a hot-pink tank dress and rhinestone ban-gles on both arms; she had bleached her hair nearly white with Sun-In, and Liza had French-braided it, teasing the bangs into a pouf. Elsbeth could feel Mike watching her as she pretended to consider her dinner; he was nothing compared to Julian, of course, but it was nice to get some practice. "Green salad," she said finally, "dressing on the side."

"That's it?" said Peter.

"I had a big lunch."

"Ha," said June, as Mike took their menus and loped away. "I know the real reason." She nudged Elsbeth and nodded toward the bar, where Mike was placing their orders. "He's pretty cute."

"Are you for real?" said Elsbeth. "He's a total Clydesdale."

June glanced at Peter, but he didn't appear to have heard; he was gazing out the panorama window toward the city. "A horse?"

"A big galoot."

"A what?"

"A dork. An oily bohunk. All he does is play football and study."

"Are you hearing this, Pete?" said June to Peter, who cleared his throat and knocked his knuckles on the table. "A little more studying wouldn't hurt you, young lady," June added.

"Mother. It's *July*."

"Yes, and next year it's either summer school for you or a job."

"Whatever," said Elsbeth. "Excellent birthday conversation. Thanks. It's been real."

June put her cigarette to her mouth, then lowered it. "Shoot, I forgot to ask for an ashtray," she said and turned toward the bar, but Mike had gone into the kitchen now. "Anyway, he seems perfectly adorable to me."

"Everyone seems adorable to you."

"What?"

"Nothing."

"Is there something you want to say to me, Elsbeth?"

"There's nothing I want to say to you, *Mother*."

"Elsbeth," said Peter, deciding suddenly to rejoin the world, "be nice to your mom."

If only you knew, Elsbeth wanted to tell him. Wake up, Dad, wake the fuck up! But she prayed he'd never find out; if Peter discovered the truth about June, it might literally kill him. When Elsbeth thought about the Peter of her childhood—her impossibly tall, golden dad—she wanted simultaneously to shake him and to throw herself in front of him, arms spread, so nothing terrible could happen to him ever again.

They fell silent as Mike returned with their drinks and Elsbeth's salad. Elsbeth sipped her Diet Coke and shook out her napkin. "Oh no," she cried.

"What is it?" said Peter.

"They put dressing on it. I asked for it on the side."

"Waiter," called Peter.

"No, that's okay, Dad, don't worry about it," said Elsbeth.

"Are you sure? It is their job to fix it."

"It's fine," said Elsbeth. "Seriously."

She pushed the croutons and Thousand Island aside and began cutting the lettuce, cucumber, shredded carrot, and sole cherry tomato into ribbons. "Aha!" said June. "Now I get how you've lost so much weight. You look terrific."

"Thanks," said Elsbeth. She speared one sliver of carrot on the tines of her fork.

Peter peered at her over his bifocals. "You do look different," he agreed. "I like how you have done your hair. But you are a little too thin."

There was nothing more reassuring Elsbeth could hear. "Thanks, Dad."

Peter frowned. "You are maybe overdoing your diet," he said. "Here, have some bread." He pushed the basket toward her.

"Leave her alone, Pete," said June. "It never hurts a girl to have lost a few extra pounds. Insurance, right?" She winked at Elsbeth. It was so unfair—no matter how old June got, whether she had age spots or crow's-feet, her eyes were so blue; she was still so cataclysmically beautiful. "So, it's not the waiter. Who is it?"

"Who's what?"

"The guy," said June. "There must be somebody."

"There isn't."

"Ah, come on," said Peter, "you must have to fight them off with a stick."

"Hardly."

"Who gave you that, then?" said June, leaning over and lifting the medallion off Elsbeth's breastbone. Elsbeth jerked away before June could see what it was: her birthday present from Liza and Very, a love charm they had purchased at the witchcraft store on Bloomfield Avenue. "See," said Liza, tracing the spiraling tiny letters, "it says 'meat of my meat, flesh of my flesh, love of my heart'—or something like that. It's Latin. But anyway, if you wear this all the time, even in the shower, and think about Julian—he'll be yours. He won't stand a chance."

"Get off," said Elsbeth. "Don't touch me!"

June recoiled. She looked away across the dining room. "All right," she said, and her voice was quiet, without the teasing tone she had adopted all evening. "I'm sorry."

Elsbeth glared at her salad. She had gone too far, she could tell by how June's lips were pressed as she opened her cigarette case, and she knew she should apologize. But then June lit a Marlboro, and it was as though she had thrown a cherry bomb into the room: "Hey," the bartender called, "you can't do that in here," and he pointed to the large plaque over the door—NO SMOKING—and the only other diners, a couple near the far window, started flapping and yelling, "Put it out, put it out!" and Elsbeth saw that the man was attached to an oxygen tank. "For God's sake, June," said Peter, and June said, "For God's sake yourself, this is ridiculous," and Mikey D was hurrying toward them with a clean saucer, saying, "Here, ma'am, use this," and June was saying, "Is *everywhere* a police state nowadays?" Elsbeth took advantage of the situation to slip away to the ladies' room. She didn't have to throw up, she'd barely eaten anything, but she sat on a wicker chaise and counted off minutes on her Swatch, for which June and Peter had given her a new white band with rhinestones. It was seven thirty now, and with luck her parents' meals would have arrived by the time Elsbeth got back to the table, in the magic way of food appearing when you went to the ladies' room; by the time this charade was over and they were home and June had either gone out again or shut herself in her bedroom and Peter was occupied in the kitchen so Elsbeth could sneak out, through the front door which nobody ever used, and called Liza to meet her at the bus stop, it would be about ten. The night would be just starting in the city, the preparties cranking up in the places they would hunt for Julian, where they might run into him accidentally on purpose, at Nell's or Limelight, Odeon or MK.

*

But it wasn't until August that Elsbeth saw Julian again, during their next shoot—which Julian decided should be in the city. He gave Elsbeth an address in the East Village, where she had never been; she took the subway from the Port Authority, although June had always told her this was how nice suburban girls got drugged and kidnapped for the slave trade. At West Fourth Street Elsbeth walked across Washington Square, where she then left familiar territory and promptly got lost. She had to ask a punk with safety pins through his eyebrows how to find St. Mark's Place.

Julian was sitting on the stoop of a decrepit green-painted building, slumped on the top step as if he was asleep; his head was down, and a cigarette burned unnoticed between his fingers. Was he sick—or drunk? But as Elsbeth approached, he glanced over and smiled. He looked terrible, his hair lank, dark smudges beneath his eyes. "Hey, Charlie," he said, "you made it." He stood, hauling himself up on the railing; he was wearing a paisley shirt and shorts today. "Do you mind if we get started right away? I don't want to lose the sunset."

"Sure," said Elsbeth, following him into the building. It looked condemned from the outside, and it wasn't much better within; there was a freight elevator, which Julian ignored in favor of the stairs, and the walls were patched and the lightbulbs in little cages. Elsbeth watched Julian's calves working as they climbed and noticed for the first time that the backs of his knees were also studded with the silver burn dots. She shivered despite the dank uriney heat in the stairwell. "Is this where your studio is?" she asked; "where are we going?" They reached the last landing and Julian pushed open the door and said, "Onto the roof."

They were meeting later than usual, almost eight; Julian had said he wanted to take advantage of something he called Magic Hour. The magical Mr. Mistoffelees, thought Elsbeth. She looked around. Some city rooftops had decks or gardens—there was a whole other life going on in the sky—but this one had just sticky tar underfoot, an air duct, and one of those circular water tanks with a conical hat. All around them were windows, and Elsbeth felt the weight of eyes.

"Should I do the usual?" she asked, meaning take off her clothes, and Julian, who was attaching weighted bags to the legs of a tripod, said, "Sure—just put your clothes in the stairwell if you don't want to get them dirty." He returned to flipping levers on his Nikon, and Elsbeth crouched behind the water tank, taking off her new silk blazer and bustier and white stirrup pants.

She looked to Julian for direction. He was fumbling with a small canister he'd taken from an Igloo cooler. His hands were shaking; he dropped the film and said "Fuck!" Elsbeth stood and waited, hoping Julian would notice her hair, which she'd crimped again and pulled back on either side with jeweled combs, and also that she'd lost more weight since their last shoot. A couple of times in July, he'd mentioned it, saying, "Charlie, are you dieting on me?" and, once, "You're getting positively skinny, girl! Whatever kick you're on, you might want to dial it back a little."

Now he said, "Okay, I think we're good to go." Elsbeth leaned back against the water tank, hooking her elbows over its ladder rungs and arcing her back so her ribs would be on display. She didn't have much left in the way of breasts, which was too bad, but there wasn't any jelly on the belly either. She barely had a single stomach, let alone a double one.

"That's actually a little stiff, Charlie," Julian called. "You don't have to pose, remember? Just do your thing."

Elsbeth walked to the edge of the roof, holding her breath out of habit. She propped herself against the cement wall, peered over one shoulder at Julian, and said, "I went to Limelight last weekend. You go there sometimes, right?"

"What?" Julian said. He sounded irritable. "Hang on, Charlie. I've got to make a couple of adjustments here."

Elsbeth looked down into the East Village to give him a little time. This was not her parents' New York—Broadway plays, the bandleader nightclubs, and Masha's; nor was it Sol and Ruth's New York of fund-raisers, galleries, and museums. This was the city Elsbeth was coming to know: punks with mohawks, drag queens, clubs. The last time Elsbeth and Liza had gone to Limelight, using the fake IDs Liza had gotten, they'd worn lace-up stiletto boots and petticoats like lampshades; Liza's hair was spiked to new heights and she'd drawn an upside-down cross in black eyeliner by one eye. The bouncer had moved the rope aside immediately to let them into the old church. Inside, from the chalk-smelling mist from the smoke machines, a guy in a bomber jacket had materialized and shouted to Liza, Wan' dance? Sure, Liza had yelled back, inaudible over the stomach-throbbing base of hip-hop, and disappeared. Elsbeth had pushed to the bar, where she nursed a gin and tonic and watched bodies flickering in the strobe lights. At one point she thought she saw Julian, in a black leather blazer and with a scruff of beard, but it turned out to be George Michael. That was cool but also beside the point, and when by midnight Liza had still not reappeared, Elsbeth had left and taken the last bus home.

"Can you turn toward me, Charlie?" said Julian. "I want to see your face." *Click. Clickclickclick vsssh.* "Okay, walk toward me a little ways," he said, "I'm losing the light on your skin." He bent over his camera. "I don't know why the fuck they call it Magic Hour," he muttered. "Nothing magic about it." He moved the tripod a couple of inches. *Clickclickclickclick.*

"Fuck," he said. *Click. Click.* He yanked his hair, then pegged the film canister into the corner of the roof as if skipping a stone.

"Fuck!" he yelled. "Fuckity fuck fuck. Fuck it. I'm fucked." He lit a cigarette and removed his camera from its tripod; he was packing that away too, screwing down and folding in its legs, when he glanced up at Elsbeth.

"Oh, Charlie," he said. "I'm sorry. I'm just ruined. They've ruined me," and Elsbeth was about to ask, Who? when he added, "Let's go get a drink."

*

Julian marched back through the East Village and Washington Square Park, walking quickly, head down, a man on a mission. Elsbeth had difficulty keeping up, since she was wearing Liza's gladiator sandals and the black leather thongs kept slipping down her calves. They passed the Pink Pussycat, where Elsbeth and Liza had purchased their bustiers; she was about to point this out to Julian when he buttonhooked right and all but dove into a tiny unmarked restaurant, its windows and doorway obscured with thick red velvet curtains. She hurried in after him.

Inside the place had brick walls, plain white cloths, only about six tables. Elsbeth was disappointed; she had fantasized a first real date with Julian somewhere fancier, like Windows on the World or at least the Plaza. The maître d' scurried toward them, a pigeon-shaped man in black trousers, white shirt, black vest.

"Mr. Wilton," he was saying, "so good to see you again, sir! What a pleasure." He kissed his fingers and shook them at the ceiling. "That *Times* review of *Luminous Beings*! It is an honor to say I know you."

"Thanks, Luigi," said Julian, who was possibly surveying the room, though it was hard to tell because he was wearing his Wayfarers. Luigi started to lead them to what Elsbeth recognized as the best table in the house: near the front door but not next to it, so they could see and be seen. But Julian headed toward the back.

"I think something more secluded tonight, Luigi," he said, "if you don't mind."

"No, of course, Mr. Wilton, naturally you would want privacy, dining with such a charming companion," said Luigi. He smiled at Elsbeth as he held her chair for her, but his expression changed to a kind of surprise, and Elsbeth wondered whether she was over-dressed for this tiny place in her bustier and stirrup pants or had tar on her arms from the roof or what.

Julian slid into the booth side of the table, a two-top where Peter would not have seated anyone but his worst enemy: in the rear of the restaurant, near the hallway to the bathrooms. "Vodka, Luigi," said Julian. "Double. On the rocks."

"Of course, Mr. Wilton. For you, Miss? Would you like menus?"

"Jesus, Luigi, just bring drinks," Julian said. "She'll have what I'm having."

Luigi's eyebrows climbed his forehead at this, but he said, "Very good, Mr. Wilton," and bustled away.

Julian scanned the room, then whipped his sunglasses off and tossed them on the tablecloth. Elsbeth could see the whole restaurant in the mirror behind his head; there wasn't much to look at, only two other couples, even older than her parents, dressed for theater.

Luigi returned with their drinks and a breadbasket, and Elsbeth's stomach gurgled; the rolls were still warm, the butter flecked with sea salt. She pushed it away with two fingers and looked at Julian, who had already emptied his first glass. He shook the cubes in it: "Keep 'em coming, Luigi," he said.

Julian lowered his head into his hands. He needed a haircut; Elsbeth loved his long, dark curls, but it was getting out of control. Tentatively, she touched his arm. Julian jumped a mile. "What!" he said, bug-eyed.

"Are you all right?" said Elsbeth. "You seem, no offense, a little freaked out."

"Ha!" said Julian. "Freaked out, yes, you could say that. I am definitely freaking the fuck out." Another drink arrived, and he drained it and tapped the rim.

"Is it them?" Elsbeth asked.

"Who?" said Julian.

"The 'them' from the roof," said Elsbeth.

Julian stared wildly around the restaurant. "Are they here? Did they follow us?" He gripped the sides of the table.

"Who?" said Elsbeth.

"You said them," said Julian.

"Because you did," said Elsbeth; "you mentioned 'them' earlier, during our shoot."

"Did you see anyone who looked suspicious?" Julian barked. "While we were walking over here? Anyone who looked like they didn't belong? Clean-cut, too normal?"

"No," said Elsbeth. "Only drag queens and dealers and punks—I swear."

This seemed to relax Julian a little. He reached for his cigarettes as another vodka appeared.

"Thank God," he said. "I guess they've stopped tailing me—for now. But they've been following me for weeks."

"Who?" said Elsbeth again.

Julian cupped his smoke to light it. "The Feds," he said, barely moving his lips.

"Okay," said Elsbeth. The Feds? What was he talking about? She looked a little nervously at Julian's third empty glass; would he start babbling about aliens next?

"They're after me, Charlie," said Julian. "They raided my studio this morning," and then he sat back as Luigi set a platter of antipasto on the table.

"Compliments of the chef," he said. "May I bring you anything else?"

"Yes, vodka," said Julian. "And whatever my model wants."

Elsbeth sat up straighter; it was the first time since they'd been out in public together that Julian had called her this. She flipped her crimped hair over her shoulders and gave Luigi a nod.

"I'm fine for now," she said and turned back to Julian, who was shaking pills out of a prescription bottle and tossing them into his mouth.

"Why would the Feds raid your studio?" she whispered.

"That's what I wanted to know!" said Julian, so loudly now that the two other couples in the room glanced over. He slapped the table. "I was like, What is this? Is this America or the USSR? I was in my underwear, Charlie. In my *boxers*. I was *working*. I thought it was the delivery guy from the deli. But noooooooooo, it was the fucking FBI, there on, get this, a child pornography charge."

Elsbeth's stomach jumped. She said, "But that's ridiculous."

"Isn't it?" said Julian. "Isn't it though?" He started in on another vodka; there was quite a forest of highball glasses in front of him. Elsbeth knew her dad would never have allowed a server to leave the table uncleared, but probably Luigi was giving Julian a little space. "Pornography!" he burst out. "Purportedly the super was in my place to put out a small fire, and he saw my images and called the cops. The fucking NYPD. The child protection hotline!" Elsbeth saw with alarm that Julian had tears in his eyes. "They took my negatives," he said. "*All* of them. They took my contact sheets, my cameras, they *smashed* my best wide-angle lens. They *ruined* two batches of film. I'll never get those images back, never!"

"That's terrible," said Elsbeth.

"It's fucking un-American is what it is," said Julian. His voice was shaking. "I said, Where's your warrant? Show me your warrant. You know what they said? They said, We don't need one, Mr. Wilton. Not when we have reason to believe the suspect might remove incriminating evidence from the premises. Suspect. I'm a suspect!" He popped two more pills in his mouth like peanuts. His hands were shaking.

"You should have seen their beady little eyes," he said. "You could tell they were *hoping* to find porn. Drooling for it. As if those troglodytes would know the difference between art and porn if it bit them on the ass. Me! A pornographer! When *all* I aspire to do is capture innocence. Purity. Unself-consciousness. *Joy*. All the things only kids have, that utter lack of shame before the adult world gets to them and screws them over. Pornography, my ass—I'm the antiporn!"

Luigi trundled up then, and Elsbeth expected him to ask Julian to lower his voice or maybe suggest Julian might be more comfortable in the manager's office. Instead he said, "Mr. Wilton, so sorry to interrupt, but there is a lady here who is one of your biggest fans," and from behind him popped a woman with a silvery bob and what looked like a melted fork securing a Frank Lloyd Wright–patterned scarf around her throat. Ah, Elsbeth thought, art lover.

"Mr. Wilton," she said, "*such* an admirer, an acolyte really." She held out a cocktail napkin and pen. "Forgive the intrusion, but would you mind?"

"Not at all," said Julian graciously. "S'fine." He picked up the last glass on the table and emptied it, then scrawled his signature on the napkin. He drew a smiley face next to it, finishing with a grand flourish.

"Oh, thank you," said the woman, "*such* an honor to meet you. Your *Luminous Beings* changed my life!"

Julian smiled at her and lurched to his feet. "S'very kind," he said. "'Scuse me—I have to make a call," and he pushed past the woman and pinballed into the hallway with the restrooms.

The woman tucked her signed napkin into her purse with reverence. She looked at Elsbeth, and like Luigi's, her expression changed; she seemed about to say something, then forced a smile and went back to her table.

Elsbeth sat—and sat and sat. The ice cubes melted and shifted in the glasses. She sipped her vodka, then remembered how many calories were in it and set it back down. Her stomach felt hot. She watched in the mirror as more patrons arrived and sat, the waiters lighting their candles. The antipasto perspired before her: marinated red peppers, artichoke hearts dotted with oregano and oil; prosciutto, salami, thick wedges of Parmesan and asiago. Elsbeth's mouth watered uncontrollably. She lifted the plate and set it, as well as the full bread basket, on the neighboring table.

"Is anything wrong, miss?" asked Luigi, hovering; "may I bring you some other dish? We have gnocchi tonight, made in-house with browned butter and rosemary."

Elsbeth wondered whether the rosemary was candied, dipped in sugar water and roasted, the way Peter did it. She had started to tell Luigi she was fine—and could he remove the food?—when Julian came crashing back down the hallway. He had some trouble with the velvet curtain at its entrance, getting entangled in it and giving it a few karate chops before he got clear; then he staggered toward the table.

"'Scuse me," he said again, "hadda make a call. Hadda call Gene—my lawyer," and he lurched forward. Luigi caught him, bracing Julian under the arms.

"Alley-oop!" he said, "watch your step there, Mr. Wilton."

"Yessir," said Julian, weaving, "thank you, Luigi, 's very kind." He groped in the pocket of his shorts and brought out a wad of bills, which he dropped onto the table amid the glasses. Luigi and Elsbeth looked at it; it was all twenties, and Elsbeth wondered if Julian would regret, when he woke the next day, leaving Luigi a thousand-percent tip.

"It is all right, miss," said Luigi quietly, "I will hold it for him. Now you had better go," for Julian was now bee-lining for the front door at a severe diagonal, as though he were on the deck of the sinking *Titanic*.

"Thank you," he said to the room at large, "excellent as always, service 's always good here," and he blinked owlishly around. "Charlie?" he said, "less blow this clambake," and Elsbeth grabbed her purse and followed him. She felt triumphant as well as concerned, because their evening was not over; even if Julian hadn't expressly said what they were going to do next, somebody had to get the poor guy home.

*

Elsbeth had never been in Julian's apartment at night, although she had visited it in her imagination many times. There it looked like the after-midnight cable shows she sometimes watched at Liza's or in her own house until Peter wandered downstairs, whereupon Elsbeth quickly changed the channel. There would be stripes of light coming through the blinds, flashing on and off with a neon sign's rhythm across the street; Julian would lie in his underwear on the black sheets in his bedroom as Elsbeth advanced in a Victoria's Secret ensemble, a breeze blowing her hair back, Chinese flutes playing . . . In reality, the apartment was much messier than when she'd last seen it, clothes and ashtrays and equipment everywhere, and it reeked of smoke.

Julian went straight to the sink and gulped from the tap. This represented a recovery of sorts from the cab ride uptown, during which he'd passed out on Elsbeth's shoulder and had to be prodded awake to pay the driver. Elsbeth had propped him up in the elevator, but now he staggered off down the hall under his own power, flapping one hand behind him in what Elsbeth took to be a make-yourself-comfortable gesture. She got herself some water as well, pouring it into a MoMA coffee mug with a Magritte streetscape on it, and wandered around the apartment. Squares of light from cars passing below waxed and waned across the ceiling.

On the architect's table was a jigsaw of scattered images. Elsbeth pulled one of the contact sheets over with a finger pressed to the white margin. Would the Feds confiscate these too? "Pornography: pôr'nägrefē/ noun: printed or visual material containing the explicit description or display of sexual organs or activity, intended to stimulate erotic rather than aesthetic or emotional feelings"——Elsbeth had looked up the definition in *Webster's*. She used a magnifying cube to peer at images of her naked body: Elsbeth crossing a brook; Elsbeth walking up a wooded hill; Elsbeth sitting Indian-style on a picnic table. She was so much thinner now; in the photos, her breasts were conical, her stomach still had rolls. Elsbeth touched, on the slick paper, the light brown triangle between her legs. This wasn't an explicit display, and she didn't feel particularly aroused. The sight of her formerly chubby body naked in Bear Mountain State Park was just incongruous, dreamlike and weird.

She pushed the contact sheet back in place and looked at the clock over the stove. It was 10:15. She'd left a note that she and Liza and Very were going to the movies at the Willowbrook Cineplex, so she had until midnight——if either of her parents had even noticed the Post-it at all. She still had about forty-five minutes before she had to leave for the Port Authority. She ventured to the hall and listened. Nothing except bass pounding up from an apartment below and sirens on Riverside Drive, a city cacophony that Elsbeth, born to it, found comforting.

"Julian?"

Elsbeth checked the bathroom first, in case he'd passed out in the tub——or on the porcelain throne, like Elvis. But it was empty.

"Julian?"

There was only one place, really, he could be. In the bedroom Julian was spread-eagled on his back, one arm slung over his face. The wondrous clock cast its colors over him: aqua, fuchsia, periwinkle, pink.

Elsbeth tiptoed to the side of the bed. His shirt had fallen away from his shorts to reveal a slice of stomach, bisected by the dark line of hair Liza called the goodie trail. Julian had drunk so much vodka and taken all those pills; he could asphyxiate in the night and die, like that senior girl at the prom last year. Elsbeth should turn him on his side; she should at least make sure he was all right.

She eased onto the bed next to him, first sitting, then lying backward very slowly until finally her head was in the crook of his shoulder. She held her breath. Julian! Julian was holding her. Sort of. The air around his face was humid with alcohol; he was snuffling noisily. Elsbeth rolled up onto one elbow and looked at him, then lowered her face until his breath stirred her hair. She put her lips on his—they were as warm as she'd imagined they'd be, and much softer, if a little slack. She was kissing Julian!

He shifted and murmured, and Elsbeth drew back.

"What?" she said. "What, Julian?"

She eased a hand under the thin fabric of his shirt; the hair there was much crisper than she'd thought it would be.

"Julian," she whispered. "It's me, Charlie."

No response. Elsbeth laid her head on his chest, his breastbone hard as a halved walnut, the thump of his heart beneath that. She slid her hand down onto his stomach—she could feel it gurgling. The skin above his shorts was smooth as the inside of a shell. Elsbeth's fingers dipped beneath his waistband.

He wasn't wearing any underwear.

She pulled her hand back, and Julian's hips moved upward, as though seeking her. He was hard beneath his zipper.

"Julian," she said. "What do you want me to do?"

No response. Elsbeth waited. She thought of Liza saying there was one thing men loved above all others. Elsbeth slid down farther. Julian's fly was half open, and the zipper clicked down tooth by tooth. Elsbeth reached into the nest of hair—he was so warm, if a little soft. She took a deep breath, then dipped her head forward and took him in her mouth.

He pulsed once, twice. Elsbeth gripped him, wishing she'd practiced on something other than popsicles. She moved her mouth up and down; in this warm darkness, the shifting kaleidoscope pastels of the clock, nothing felt quite real. Elsbeth glanced up at Julian, his face watermelon, lime, lavender, pink. Was Elsbeth doing something wrong? Julian remained only half hard; it was like having the world's biggest mouthful of gum. Elsbeth tried to recall what Liza had said: "Use your hand; they like that. And don't give up—one time I had a guy take thirty-seven minutes!" Elsbeth didn't think she could last that long, but she kept trying. There was a chance, if she did this right, that Julian's eyes would flutter open, and he would say Hey, Charlie, where'd you learn to do that? and pull her up to him and say, I was awake the whole time. And then he would roll on top of her and make love to her, even though Elsbeth would confess she was still a virgin; it doesn't matter, he'd say, and after that they would be inseparable. Elsbeth would attend the opening of their show with him, and all the others after, and he would shoot her and nobody else from then on; when she was eighteen they'd get married and leave the city to start over on a farm Julian would buy in, maybe, Vermont. They would shun the press, Julian's reclusiveness only enhancing his fame, but every once in a while reporters would seek them out and Julian would receive them graciously in his barn, where he had his studio, and Elsbeth would bring out wine and cheese. She would sit next to him on a hay bale as he put an arm around her and say how she had saved him from himself, how she was his one and only muse; Elsbeth would be thin and wear her hair in a braid and smoke Gauloises, and Julian would have a rollneck sweater. And maybe a beard.

Finally, something did seem to be happening—Julian was moving!—but then he subsided again, and Elsbeth heard a sound she could not mistake: a snore. She sat up, disbelieving, and wiped her mouth. Sure enough, Julian was snoring—the whites of his eyes just showing between the lids. As quietly as she could, Elsbeth pulled his shirt down over his belly and slid from the bed.

Oh, God, she was mortified! The one thing men loved more than anything, and she had failed at it. What was she supposed to do?

In the main room she located her purse, then stood for a moment. She used a grease pencil to write a note on the back of a manila envelope:

> *Dear Julian, thanks for a wonderful evening! I'll look forward to the next shoot. Love, your Muse, Elsbeth. XOXO*

She was staring at this, debating whether to tear it up and start again, when another snore from Julian's room decided her. She didn't want him to wake now and find her here; she didn't want him to remember a thing. Do-over! they used to call as kids on the playground, and Elsbeth badly wanted one. She needed another night when Julian was less frantic, when this business with the Feds had blown over and things were back to normal, so the two of them could drive out to the country in the non–General Lee and have a shoot and laugh together, and Julian would not be drunk out of his mind nor doped up on pills. Then Elsbeth could try again; she would tell him how she felt, and Julian would make love to her and they would be on their way. She fled.

*

The New York Times—August 15, 1986

A special antipornography task force of the FBI, accompanied by members of the Child Protection Unit of the NYPD, searched the Greenwich Village studio of renowned fine art photographer Julian Wilton yesterday in what some say is a blow against child exploitation and others call a campaign against artistic expression.

The superintendent of Mr. Wilton's studio building, Rob Laubach, noticed photographs of "nude children in compromising positions" in Wilton's studio while helping put out a cigarette-caused fire there earlier this month, NYPD spokesman Thomas Champoux said.

Mr. Laubach, believing Wilton's photographs to be child pornography, contacted the police, who then notified the FBI.

No charges have yet been brought against Wilton, 27, whose brightly saturated, large-scale photographs of prepubescent and adolescent nudes are exhibited in the Metropolitan Museum of Art, the Musée d'Orsay in Paris, and the Corcoran Gallery in Washington, D.C., among others, and have garnered international acclaim and controversy since 1983, when Wilton's first show, "Unadorned," opened in Chicago's prestigious Roget Gallery.

"My client is doing what artists have done since cave drawings, which is to celebrate the human form," said Wilton's lawyer, Eugene Rubin of Rubin and Homonoff, Esq. "His models and their parents love working with him. They consider it a privilege. And he photographs not a single eyelash without proper consent."

Rubin maintains that the real criminal is "the FBI, who invaded my client's studio without a warrant and destroyed his property, his photos and his creative peace of mind."

The FBI confirmed it entered Wilton's studio without a warrant, but according to Special Anti-Pornography Unit spokesperson Jocelyn Martin, "We don't require one for the search of a premises from which the suspect is almost certain to remove incriminating materials, given the opportunity."

Among the possessions Martin said the FBI took from Wilton's studio were several rolls of undeveloped film, Polaroids, Wilton's personal journals and books, and some of his cameras.

Martin said the FBI couldn't comment more specifically because of a pending grand jury investigation into whether Wilton's work consists of pornography, in which case Wilton will face several charges of possession and trafficking. But she added, "We believe some of Mr. Wilton's work to be of a highly questionable nature."

Pornography as applied to art is notoriously hard to define. Legally categorized as "the portrayal of sexual acts solely for the purpose of sexual arousal," child pornography is specified by the Federal and New York penal code to be "any visual depiction of sexually explicit conduct involving a minor."

Although Wilton's subjects are all unclothed and under 18, his portraits feature them in solitary settings and poses, and Wilton's supporters fiercely deny his work is pornographic.

"To say that Mr. Wilton's photography is pornographic demonstrates a poor understanding of both pornography and art," says Henry Papel, curator of the Guggenheim, which currently features seven Wilton photographs. "His work is intended not to sexually titillate but to showcase personality in its most unfettered form."

Jean-Francis Krantz of MoMA agrees: "People who see pornography in Julian's sensitive portraits of children need to ask themselves what's in the eye of the beholder."

Wilton's critics are equally vehement in their dissent. "This man's so-called work not only criminally exploits our society's weakest members, children, but runs counter to the very morals this country is founded upon," said Alec Reagan, spokesperson for the National Center for American Values, which has organized antipornography demonstrations outside Wilton's exhibits in Chicago, New York and Los Angeles.

The National Endowment for the Arts, which has funded Wilton's work, agrees the controversy has reached a national level but calls it "a witch hunt."

"In the past year, we've seen the right wing start to persecute artists in the name of so-called family values," says Kate Woodward, chairperson for the NEA. "Mr. Wilton is its first target. He has our full sympathy and support."

Wilton, who resides in New York City, could not be reached for comment.

16

SHAMELESS

The gallery was in SoHo, and as Elsbeth stood in front of it, checking and rechecking the slip of paper in her hand and wondering whether she was in the right place, it occurred to her that she had never been in this neighborhood before. The Twin Towers once, Windows on the World with her parents for brunch— Elsbeth still remembered the eggs Benedict. And the Village, yes, obviously: before crossing Houston Street Elsbeth had detoured past the little Italian restaurant where she had been with Julian, shuttered at this hour of the afternoon, and looked at its closed red curtains with longing. In front of the Pink Pussycat she had indulged in a fantasy about how she had brought Julian in here after all, and he had helped her pick out a new bustier, and he had not gotten quite so wasted and there had been no blow-job disaster, and subsequently things went on as normal, a couple of shoots a month, and Julian had not then disappeared.

The gallery, like the Italian eatery, was closed. It was two in the afternoon on a Monday; maybe for galleries, like restaurants, this was their slowest day. What was more confusing to Elsbeth was that the floor-to-ceiling windows were sheathed in brown paper, as if the place were out of business. There was no sign announcing Julian's new show, no display to entice passersby; if not for the tiny brass-plated name beneath the bell—HAZAAN GALLERY—Elsbeth would have given up and gone home.

But she had called Julian's manager and pretended to be a collector—which was easy; Elsbeth had just channeled the imperious tones of one of Sol's art brunch ladies. So Elsbeth knew that the Hazaan Gallery was where the debut of Julian's new exhibit would be. And Elsbeth had read in several of Julian's biographies that although he rarely attended any showing of his work, he often oversaw the mounting of the photos. He was a perfectionist; he wanted to make sure the placement, the lighting, was just right. Elsbeth took out her Parliament Lights, which she had started smoking in September in lieu of eating—she was down to 102. She smoked a cigarette, pacing in the cold wind off the Hudson, her fingertips going numb in her fingerless gloves, then rapped on the gallery's window, once, twice, again.

A bike messenger with a Mohawk pedaled by. This was such a weird neighborhood; the brick streets potholed and deserted, the buildings graffiti-covered and derelict, and then there were brightly gleaming storefronts showcasing heaps of rugs, Japanese prints, African masks and statues. A tiny lady in a wide-brimmed black hat and an explosion of red dreadlocks dragged a lizard down the sidewalk on a leash—"Hurry the fuck up, Piccolo, Mummy's freezing." Elsbeth knocked and knocked, *taptaptaptaptap*, until finally the door opened a crack and an irritable Rasputin face peered out.

"Yes," he said, "what is it? All deliveries go to the back."

"I'm looking for Julian Wilton," said Elsbeth.

The man's eyebrows, silver triangles, flew up, then came together over his nose. "Mr. Wilton is not here."

"When do you expect him?"

"The opening is not until next week, young lady. Please come back then."

"I know that," said Elsbeth patiently, "but Julian rarely attends his openings. He's too shy. He only oversees the hangings."

The man's mouth twitched in his pointed beard. "You mean the mountings."

"Yes, the mountings," said Elsbeth. "May I come in?"

The man looked her over, the door opening a bit more to reveal his impeccably tailored suit and shining shoes. Elsbeth thought he must be the owner, Mr. Hazaan.

"We are quite a scholar of Mr. Wilton, I see," he said.

"We are Mr. Wilton's model," Elsbeth said.

Now the door did open fully, the man looking Elsbeth up and down. Elsbeth drew herself up to her full height, which, with the addition of spike-heeled boots, was five-nine—an inch taller than Mr. Hazaan. She tried not to tremble in the wind, although it was strong enough to whip her lace petticoats and crimped hair off to one side and drag tears from her eyes. Mr. Hazaan was frowning.

"Seriously," said Elsbeth, "please. It's frigid out here."

"Of course, of course," said Mr. Hazaan. "Come in, Miss—"

"Rashkin. Elsbeth Rashkin."

He stepped aside with a little bow.

Elsbeth walked past him into the gallery. The warmth was welcome after the raw wind, the honeyed hardwood floors and white walls an antidote to the gray and trashy streets. But what stunned Elsbeth were the images of—herself, everywhere. It was one thing to read about Julian's developing technique in *Photoplay* and *Aperture*, something called dye process that produced supersaturated colors, and the unusually bold size of his prints; it was another to be confronted with photos of her naked body blown up to five by seven feet and matted and framed so they were even bigger, much larger than life. Here Elsbeth was spouting water in the blue surf of Montauk, head thrown back and hands over her head, her skin a glistening peach; here she was wandering through a green forest, the dimple above her tailbone the size of a quarter. Here, there, and everywhere were her armpits, her curls, her thighs and chubby knees and her hated belly—all of it transformed by Julian's camera and vision into something . . . not comfortable for Elsbeth to look at, exactly, but so bright, so exuberant and full of movement, that she felt tears rising. He had caught exactly how she looked at him, how she had felt all along.

Mr. Hazaan was standing beside her now, watching a pair of assistants—it was hard to tell if they were male or female; they were both all in black, with short slicked-back hair and white gloves, like mimes—struggle to hang another of the photos on the far wall, beneath a sharply focused spotlight. Giant Elsbeth crouching at a stream, laughing back at Julian over her shoulder—the photo didn't show it, but there were iridescent dragonflies on the brook's surface that they had marveled at together. Next to the mimes, awaiting its turn to be mounted, was a small framed sign:

JULIAN WILTON

shameless

31 oct—5 nov

and another print of Elsbeth leaping into the air. Julian had caught her silhouetted against the sky, feet far above the hill, suspended against a billowing cloud. *You're queen of the mountain!*

"I think two inches to the left," Mr. Hazaan said, and the mimes readjusted the photo. He walked over to them and said something, and they climbed down off their stepstools and disappeared behind a black curtain.

"They will bring tea," he said. He took Elsbeth's elbow to guide her across the room, where there were two folding chairs. "Please, sit."

"Thank you," said Elsbeth. She had once in kindergarten fallen off the monkey bars onto her back; the surprised tears, the stupid breathless way she'd felt then, that was how she felt now.

"They are remarkable, the images, are they not?" said Mr. Hazaan.

Elsbeth nodded. One of the mimes reappeared, pushing a tea cart laden with cups, saucers, a pot and spoons. Mr. Hazaan poured.

"Extraordinary, even for Julian," he continued. "I expect most favorable reviews. And sales." He paused with tongs above the sugar bowl, his eyebrows a question, but Elsbeth shook her head. It had been months since she'd used anything but Sweet'n Low.

"Forgive me for not recognizing you sooner," said Mr. Hazaan. "The transformation is astonishing."

"Thank you," said Elsbeth again. If she had been shocked by what the images evoked, the memories of moments only she and Julian knew about, she felt safely detached from the big body displayed in most of the photos—in which, Elsbeth thought, she looked like a rubber bath toy. She had worked hard the past several months; by now she even had cheekbones. If Elsbeth came to the opening next week, nobody would identify her as the fat child in the photos. She was proud of that fact. But Mr. Hazaan looked inexplicably sad.

"Why are your windows covered?" she asked.

"For the big reveal, my dear," said Mr. Hazaan. "We wouldn't want anybody to get a sneak peek, would we?"

"I guess not," said Elsbeth and accepted her tea. "So when will Julian be here?"

Mr. Hazaan blew into his cup. "Miss Rashkin," he said, "I'm sorry to tell you this, but I haven't had direct contact with Julian in months."

Elsbeth sipped her tea. It was too hot, and she scalded the roof of her mouth. She set it down on the cart.

"But you're his friend," she said. "You gave him his first big break back in '83—I read about it."

"That is true," said Mr. Hazaan, "but I suspect Julian believes it to be kinder to his friends to stay away just now."

"What? Why?"

Mr. Hazaan drank deeply of his tea and set his cup deliberately back in its saucer.

"Miss Rashkin," he said, "since you seem to know much of Julian's affairs, I assume you are aware of his legal troubles?"

"Of course."

"Then you know he has gone underground until the investigation is over."

"Yes," said Elsbeth. She knew this all too well; how many times had she called Julian's number, letting the phone ring and ring and ring? How many afternoons and evenings had she stood outside his apartment, waiting for a shade to be raised, a light to be switched on, only for the windows to remain dark? She had even called his attorney—*Mr. Wilton is not available for comment at this time.*

"I understand," Elsbeth told Mr. Hazaan, "why he wouldn't want to talk to the press or FBI. Or anyone but people he knows really well. People he trusts. But that's you, right? And me—he knows me better than anyone." She waved around at the photos. "I mean, this is *ours*. We made it together."

Mr. Hazaan looked sadder than ever. "I see."

"So if you hear from him, if he comes here, would you please tell him Charlie's been trying to get in touch with him? I really just want to talk to him. I'll assume the risk."

"Miss Rashkin," Mr. Hazaan said, "may I speak freely?"

"Sure."

"I have teenage daughters myself," said Mr. Hazaan, "so I know what scorn I am inviting by giving you advice. You will not take kindly to it. But as you said, I have known Julian for years. I am his friend as well as colleague and ardent admirer. And even so, I will tell you this."

He put his fingertips together and touched them to his mouth. It seemed a long time before he spoke.

"Julian is a genius," he said. "You know this. I know this. The world knows this. One need only look at his work to see it."

He gestured around at the gallery of Elsbeths. She nodded, impatient now.

"And he means well," Mr. Hazaan continued. "His heart is in the right place. He has good intentions. And sometimes those people are the most dangerous of all."

He looked significantly at her. Elsbeth said, "Sorry, I don't get what you mean."

Now Mr. Hazaan did smile, for the first time since Elsbeth had entered the gallery. She thought it the most sorrowful expression she'd ever seen.

"Miss Rashkin," he said, "go home. Wash your face. Attend school. Be a girl again. You may think Julian cruel in disappearing, but in fact he has done you a great favor. You must forget him. You must pretend he never existed."

*

But she did see Julian again.

It was Halloween, and Elsbeth was staking out his apartment, in black cat ears and a tail. It was the night of Julian's opening, and if he was here, he had to come out sometime; Elsbeth would catch him when he did. She was alone, although at first she'd brought Liza with her—saying they'd wait at Julian's until the show, then check out the gallery, and then, if he wasn't there, they'd go to the costume ball at Limelight. Liza had acquiesced, dressing as her mother in an attorney's skirt suit and pearls. But once in the city she'd changed her mind—"I'm tired of hanging around that guy's apartment like a hooker," she'd said. "Why don't we go to happy hour instead, find us some new squeezes?" "I don't want a new squeeze," said Elsbeth, "I want Julian," and Liza said, "I don't know how to break it to you, kid, but he's gone." They were in Port

Authority, by the escalator amid exhaust fumes so thick they were visible. Elsbeth stood stupidly while Liza continued, *"Hasta la vista, baby, good-bye.* Forget him! Let it go," and Elsbeth had said, "I can't go to the gallery without you," and Liza said, "I'm not going." Elsbeth said, "You're seriously not?" and Liza said, "I'm seriously not," and Elsbeth said, "I'll never forgive you. You don't know what being in love is like," and Liza said, "If you're what it's like, thank God for that." She stepped backward onto the escalator and added, "I'll be at Limelight if you want to find me. See ya around, kid—and stop doing you-know-what! You'll grow fur!" and she pantomimed sticking her finger down her throat as she descended out of sight.

So here Elsbeth was, by herself. She lit her last cigarette, shivering—it really wasn't that cold out, pleasantly Halloweenish, in the forties. But Elsbeth was cold all the time now. Traitor Liza was right about one thing: if you got too skinny, your body could grow a thin protective layer of hair. Elsbeth had read about it. But she hadn't quite reached that point. Her periods hadn't stopped, either—just grown a little irregular. There was no way she was giving up her self-improvement program now; when Julian resurfaced, Elsbeth didn't want him to think she was a blimp.

She pulled her denim jacket closed over her black turtleneck and looked at Julian's windows. Still no movement up there. She decided to go to the newsstand by the subway for more cigarettes. If the first Parliament she lit only half burned, Elsbeth would know Julian was thinking about her—everyone said that was true. If that happened and she smoked it while holding the love charm Liza had given her, by the time she got back to his block, he'd be there.

Elsbeth had tried these rituals so many times without success that she was astonished to see, when she returned to her stakeout bench, that there actually was a light on in Julian's loft. Elsbeth squinted. The glow remained. He was home! She darted across the street, narrowly avoiding being hit by a cab, tossing her cigarette behind her as she went.

She burst into the lobby and pressed Julian's buzzer; when nobody answered, she mashed all the buttons with both palms until the vestibule door opened and she plunged in. She took the stairs up, forsaking the slow elevator. When she reached the top, panting and dizzy, Julian's door was closed, and for a moment Elsbeth was sure she had imagined the light after all. But the lock wasn't latched.

Into the loft she walked, cautiously now. What if it was a burglar? Crime was epidemic in the city, muggings in the subways, rapes in Central Park, thieves creeping over the rooftops and through air shafts. Elsbeth looked around: there was a record on the turntable, revolving quietly. "We've got magic to do," it sang, "just for you!" The room was just as disarrayed as it had been when she'd seen it last, only dustier, and there were clothes scattered near the hallway, as if somebody had just shucked them off. Elsbeth pounced on a shirt she recognized, with light blue lines on it like graph paper. Julian! She held it to her face: cotton, smoke. Then she heard noises from down the hall, a groan, a thud. What if somebody had broken in to find Julian asleep? What if they had him tied up in there?

Elsbeth seized a tripod and crept down the hall. Behind her the record started to hiccup: "Magic to do! . . . Magic to do! . . . Magic to do!" and from Julian's bedroom the sounds grew louder—a *thwack!*, a low male voice, sinister, not Julian's; a moan, definitely somebody in pain. The door was open an inch, and Elsbeth kicked it open—it was important to take them by surprise.

What she saw in the bedroom was so strange that at first she didn't comprehend it; the only thing she could think of was a Klee painting at one of Sol's fund-raising exhibits, called *Twittering Machine*. The painting should have been innocuous enough; it was just of some birds shackled together with wire and chained to a hand

crank. But looking at it had produced in Elsbeth terrible discom-
bobulation, vertigo, dread. The people on the bed were arranged
in a similarly nonsensical tableau. There was a man lying on his
back, wearing a Lone Ranger mask; there was Julian on all fours,
crouching over the man and doing to him what Elsbeth had tried
to do to Julian in this very bed a few months ago; behind Julian
was a woman with eggplant-colored skin and a huge Afro. She was
wearing a belt, and whatever was attached to it was connecting her
to Julian from behind. The sounds were coming from the Lone
Ranger and the woman smacking Julian, rhythmically and hard,
on one buttock. Julian wasn't making any noise at all, since his
mouth was full.

Elsbeth dropped the tripod—she'd forgotten she was holding
it. The Afro woman looked over; she was wearing a mask as well,
a bird beak with silver sequins. "Who the hell are you?" she said.

"Who the hell are *you*?" said Elsbeth.

Julian lifted his head and squinted—the hall light being much
brighter than that in the bedroom, which was provided only by
the colors of the wondrous clock. "Who is that," he said, "Who's
there?" and then: "Oh my God—Charlie? Is that you?"

"Who the fuck is Charlie?" said the Afro woman, but Julian
ignored her and tried to leap off the bed. He didn't get very far,
however, as the woman was still attached to him from behind.

"Ow!" he yelled, "get the hell off me," and he shoved away from
her and scrambled.

"Charlie!" he said, "Charlie, wait!"

But Elsbeth didn't wait. She backed away until her shoulders
bumped the wall, then turned and ran. She bolted without looking
back at the apartment she had loved so much, through the room
where they'd had their first shoot, where Julian had first told her
she would be beautiful. She sprinted out the front door and down
the staircase, her breath painful in her throat, her lungs hurting,
jumping down the stairs two, three at a time, and all the while Ju-

lian's voice, calling, "Charlie, wait up! Charlie, please!" grew fainter and fainter behind her.

٭

She started with the easy things: a plate of deviled eggs, tomato halves filled with crabmeat salad, June's cottage cheese with the Post-it attached to it: "Do not eat all of this—Elsbeth, this means you!" A tub of vichyssoise. Sour cream, scooped from the container. Then on to the cheese drawer: Brie, Jarlsberg, Gruyère, Roquefort. She wrapped hunks of it in prosciutto and roast beef and crammed it into her mouth. She dipped Peter's garlic dills into Thousand Island dressing, mayonnaise. She wolfed a whole platter of profiteroles and drank the chocolate sauce that went with them; she gobbled grapes by the fistful. When she got to the back of the refrigerator, she devoured the food Peter was supposed to eat but didn't: nonfat cream cheese, fake sausage links, heart-healthy bread with margarine. She moved on to the freezer: Häagen Dazs, coffee and vanilla and rum raisin; Popsicles; orange sherbet. Frozen lemonade and grape juice from the can. She even ate a half-open carton of Eggo waffles with ice crystals in their indented squares—and then she scrambled to the powder room off the kitchen.

She jammed her three middle fingers into her mouth, shuddering and crying. She had sobbed all the way home from the city on the bus, trying to hide her face behind the collar of her denim jacket so nobody would see; luckily, there had been only a few other passengers, some witches and a devil and the Stay Puft Marshmallow Man, and they were drunk and nobody cared. "Hey, little kitty," the Stay Puft had said as Elsbeth stumbled down the aisle at her stop, "want to come out and play?" but Elsbeth had said "Fuck you" and hopped off. All she could think about was getting home so she could do what she was doing now; she had thought it would be a relief. It was not.

She managed to get the ice cream up—that was easy. The rest

stayed down. Elsbeth crammed her hand in to the knuckles, drooling; over the past two months it had gotten harder and harder to do this, her gag reflex used to it, her throat as wide as the Lincoln Tunnel. She choked up something that had probably been profiteroles, maybe waffles, but a clump of dough lodged, burning, in her esophagus. Not for the first time, Elsbeth wondered whether she could choke to death doing this, or give herself a stroke. She pushed harder, gagging. Little lights danced in front of her eyes.

Then—*bam bam bam!* on the bathroom door, and her mother saying, "Elsbeth?"

Elsbeth froze, her fist in her mouth. What was June doing home? Why wasn't she out with the Motherfucker?

"I hear you in there," said June, "I know what you're doing," and Elsbeth swore—she'd forgotten to turn on the faucets to mask the sound. At least she'd remembered to lock the door.

"Go away," she called, but there was food stuck in her throat. She coughed and added, "I'm sick!"

"You're not sick," said June, "you're purging," and she rattled the doorknob. "Elsbeth Rashkin, come out right now."

"No," Elsbeth said.

"You need help. Let me help you. If you don't open this door—"

"Fuck off!" Elsbeth yelled, hurting her raw throat.

There was a pause, and then June said, "I'm getting your father."

Good luck with that, thought Elsbeth. She flushed the toilet, then stood and washed her hands. She glared at herself in the mirror: eyes streaming, the blood mask back around the sockets, a vomit beard dripping from mouth to chin. She was still wearing the stupid Pink Pussycat ears. She took them off and hurled them into the corner. "Fuck you too," she said to them and crouched over the toilet again.

She had choked up the grapes, or at least their skins, when she heard her dad say, "Ellie? What is happening? Your mother says you are throwing up?"

Oh, God, Elsbeth thought. "I'm fine, Dad. Go back to bed."

"She says she is fine," Elsbeth heard Peter reporting, and June said, "She's not fine, Pete. I told you, she's binged on everything in the kitchen and now she's vomiting it up. I saw it all the time when I was modeling." She pounded on the door. "Elsbeth! Come out, now!"

"No," said Elsbeth, as Peter said, "But why would she do such a thing?"

"Because she thinks she's fat," said June, "or to impress some dopey boy like that waiter at the club, who knows!"

"But she is not fat," said Peter. "If anything she is too thin."

"Well, she is now," said June. "I did notice she was losing a lot lately, and now we know why. Elsbeth!"

"Ellie," said her dad. "Is this true? What your mother is saying?" Elsbeth slammed the toilet lid down, hot tears leaking from her eyes. "Ellie, please. Open the door. We just want to help you."

"Yes, darling, we'll take you to a doctor," said June. "Or an eating disorder center, there are good places for these things—"

"Surely you don't mean a sanitarium," said Peter.

"No, I mean a treatment center, like I said," said June.

"As in a hospital? She is not sick, June."

"She is, Pete, she's sick in her mind, and you don't want to see it because you made her this way."

"I? I did this to her? How can you say such a thing?"

"Because it's true. Her whole life, you've related to her only through food, your little *commis*, you stuffed her like a foie gras goose—"

"And you, you should talk, you are the one who told her always she is too heavy. Not a single day went by that you did not comment on her weight. Telling her not to fill her plate. Telling her not to take seconds. I've heard you, June. It's you who've given her a complex!"

"Okay, Pete, whatever you say. I was only trying to help her— and none of this is getting her out of there. I'm calling the cops."

"And telling them what? Our daughter is vomiting?" Peter banged on the door. "Elsbeth Rashkin, come out this instant. Or I will break the door down."

"Good luck," said June, "it's solid maple."

"Stand back," said Peter. There was some scuffling while Elsbeth buried her head in her arms and sobbed, and then her dad said, "Three . . . two . . ." The door shook in its frame. "Goddamn it," he said.

"Surprise," said June.

"I suppose you have a better idea?"

"I told you, I'm calling nine-one-one."

"And I told you—"

"Stop it!" Elsbeth screamed. She leaped up, unlocked the door, and shouted right into her parents' faces. She had never done this before. "The door's open, you happy now? Now go away and leave me the fuck alone!"

She hurled herself back into the little room and slid down the wall while her parents looked in, frozen, aghast. Elsbeth put her face in her hands. She heard her dad come in, the pop of his knees as he knelt.

"Ellie, Ellie," he said. "The worst is over now. You opened the door, that's my brave girl. Now we can help—"

"You don't understand," Elsbeth sobbed. "It's all over. Everything's ruined."

"That's rather dramatic," said June from the doorway, and Elsbeth shouted at her, "What do you know? And why are you wearing that *stupid* outfit?" for June was also in a cat costume, although she was a sexy tiger.

"Work party," said June, "and watch your mouth, young lady."

"Fine," said Elsbeth, "whatever, do whatever you want with me, my life is over anyway. I'll never see him again, never," and she put her face in her hands and wailed.

"Who, Ellie?" her dad said; he was still kneeling next to her, in his khaki pants and button-down shirt, on the bathroom rug. "Is it a young man? on whom you have a crush?" and June said, "See, I knew it was a boy."

"It's *not* a boy, *Mother*," shouted Elsbeth. "It's Julian, Julian Wilton. I've been his model for months now. There, now you know!"

"Julian?" said Peter, still confused, but Elsbeth could tell from her mother's face, suddenly stricken beneath makeup whiskers, that June knew exactly who she meant.

"Oh God," said June. "Please tell me we're not talking about the same person."

"Will somebody explain to me what is going on here?" said Peter, and June said, "The guy from the party, Pete, from Sol and Ruth's, remember? The photographer, or pornographer, depending how you look at it—the one who takes pictures of nude kids."

"The—," said Peter, and suddenly he was gripping Elsbeth's chin.

"Look at me, Elsbeth," he said. "Is this true?"

Elsbeth was suddenly and horribly aware of how she must smell. She tried to pull away, but Peter's grasp was strong. She stared defiantly back at him, two green-blue stares locked and blazing.

"Did he touch you?" Peter said.

"Let go," Elsbeth managed to say, and Peter did and she rubbed her jaw.

"Did he?" Peter repeated. "Tell me this instant!"

"No, Dad, it wasn't like that!" said Elsbeth. "It was totally platonic. An artistic collaboration. I was his muse—"

"In the nude. He took photos of you in the nude."

"Well, yeah, but that's what he does. He's a genius, don't you remember? Even the *New York Times* said— *Dad?* Where are you going?"

For Peter had jumped up and pushed out of the bathroom. "That son of a bitch!"

"Pete," said June, "calm down, let's talk about this. Pete!" Peter was pawing through the key rack next to the back door. Some fell off their pegs and jingled musically to the floor. "Where are you going?"

"Where do you think?" said Peter, seizing the Volvo key tab. "That cocksucker Wilton laid his hands on our daughter!"

"Dad, no, he didn't," said Elsbeth; she stood with June, who had put one arm around her waist, and they watched Peter charge down the back steps.

"Don't do this, Pete," called June, "you'll regret it." She went to the doorway. "At least take your nitroglycerin!"

*

Special to *The Village Voice*, November 1, 1985

In the seemingly never-ending controversy surrounding fine-art photographer Julian Wilton, what was supposed to be the opening night of Wilton's new exhibit, *Shameless*, at SoHo's Hazaan Gallery last night turned into something more akin to a Halloween bar brawl.

Costumed guests, hors d'oeuvres and champagne had just begun circulating when the viewing of Wilton's latest series, portraits of an exuberantly awkward teenager, anonymous and unclothed per Wilton's tradition, was interrupted by the arrival of the model's father.

Restaurateur Peter Rashkin, retired owner of the once-iconic Masha's on the Upper East Side and more recently the Claremont in Glenwood, New Jersey, made a more dramatic entrance than the artist himself when he stormed in and demanded of gallery owner Mr. Alfred Hazaan to point out Wilton immediately.

Had this been a more typical Wilton opening, the photographer would not have been in attendance. Notoriously reclusive, Wilton has been all but invisible since this summer's FBI investigation, still ongoing, into whether Wilton's art constitutes child pornography.

However, luck was with onlookers who like a side of soap opera with their art, since because Hazaan gave Wilton his first Manhattan show in 1982, Wilton honored the friendship by appearing at the opening.

"Rashkin marched right in yelling, 'Wilton, you sonofabitch!'" said Dell Smith, art critic for the *Jersey City Tribune*. "He was shouting when he came through the door."

Rashkin, incensed by the 5-by-

7-foot nude portraits of his underage daughter adorning the walls, stormed up to the artist and punched him in the mouth.

"It was chaos for a while," says Bernadette Lee of SoHo's Lee & Childs Gallery. "[Julian] didn't know what hit him. He just lay there on the floor like, Wha?, and Rashkin was like a madman, circling him, kicking him, yelling, 'Get up, you child-molesting bastard, so I can hit you again.'"

Onlookers became concerned about Rashkin himself when the former restaurateur then grabbed his chest and asked for medical aid.

"I don't know who was in worse shape," said Whitney Scharer of *Art Now! Magazine.* "It was a toss-up between Julian and the father."

Hazaan had summoned the NYPD when Rashkin dealt the first blow, and police and paramedics escorted both Rashkin and Wilton to the emergency room at St. Vincent's Hospital.

"It was an absolute debacle," said Hazaan. "All Julian's pieces sold out within minutes. His prices were already escalated this summer thanks to the ridiculous pornography charges. Now they're through the roof.

"It was our best opening to date," he added, "Not to mention Halloween gala."

Wilton's attorney, Gene Rubin of Rubin and Homonoff, Esq., said, "My client did nothing wrong. He never once touched Rashkin's daughter. He had signed model release forms to photograph her. Rashkin assaulted Julian Wilton without cause, pure and simple."

When presented with the model release forms, Rashkin said he had never seen them before. Upon being questioned by the NYPD Child Exploitation Unit, Rashkin's daughter, the 16-year-old model, confessed to forging her parents' signatures in order to be able to pose for Wilton. She further insisted Wilton had never touched her.

"She considered it an honor to pose for him," said Rubin. "She's immortalized in art."

Wilton, who could not be contacted for comment, is still under investigation by the grand jury. Many art communities in New York and nationwide have made Wilton their reluctant poster boy for freedom of expression. His remaining photos in the SHAMELESS series are fetching upwards of $50,000.00 apiece.

17

ED

The eating disorder clinic was in the Berkshires, and the girls called it ED in a deep, dull foghorn voice, as if it were the name of a particularly dimwitted boyfriend. It was surrounded by forest and ringed by mountains, so even if one of them ran away, there was nowhere to go. They were not allowed outside much anyway, exercise being forbidden; once a week they were taken on a supervised nature hike, as if, Elsbeth thought, they were in third grade and traipsing through the woods to draw pictures of chipmunks. But most of their time was spent indoors: not in the reception area, which had nice couches and a TV to fool visitors into thinking this was a normal place, but in group, family, or individual therapy in back, which was a warren of rooms with industrial carpet, break-proof windows, twin beds, and not a single mirror.

Today, January 6, 1986, was Elsbeth's second ED birthday—she had been here for two months, huzzah! This had been fêted in group not with a cake, since they had to learn to celebrate without using food, but by all the members telling Elsbeth one trait they liked about her. It couldn't be appearance-related; if a girl was new to the group or forgot and said something like "You have nice hair," or "Pretty eyes," the rest would yell, "WAH!" Instead they had all said things like Elsbeth was smart, and funny, and determined. Nobody had mentioned her synesthesia, which was no coincidence because Elsbeth herself had forgotten about it anyway. The ability seemed to have deserted her, to have dwindled along with her weight. That was sad, like losing a favorite pet. "Do you have anything to say to Elsbeth, Tiffani?" Dr. Linda had asked Elsbeth's brand-new roommate, who had come in the previous day from the hospital wing, fresh off the IV, and was so anemic she looked like a fingernail moon. Tiffani had been shearing off her split ends; their hair was one of the few parts of their bodies they were allowed to control. Finally she said, "She doesn't snore?"

After this rather lackluster occasion they were released for the misnamed hour of "free time," which Elsbeth thought should be called "Big Brother time," since there were cameras in every room, including the bathrooms. She didn't mind being left to her own devices, however, since this was when she wrote to Julian. Not letters, of course, which would be confiscated and read before they were out the door, in case they contained pleas to family members for food, diet pills, or laxatives. Elsbeth wrote to Julian in her journal, which with any luck she would be able to share with him in person, someday, when she got out of this godawful place.

She was scribbling away when one of the nurses tapped on her door and said, "Elsbeth, you have a visitor." Elsbeth jumped up, tucked the journal back in her pillowcase, and followed the nurse down the hall. The nurse was smiling as if this were good news, but in fact Elsbeth was nervous. She doubted it was either of her parents, not after the disastrous family session they'd had yesterday; an improvement on the first one, according to Dr. Linda, during which Elsbeth had refused to say anything at all, just summoned an interior static that sounded like the ocean in a shell and watched her parents' mouths move, then Dr. Linda's, until finally she saw June say, *This is useless*, and get up and flounce into the hall.

Three more sessions had gone this way, until yesterday, when June and Peter filed in and Elsbeth had been dialing up her seashell noise when Dr. Linda said, "We have good news, Mom and Dad: Elsbeth has reached her target weight of one twenty-five," and Elsbeth, who had come in feeling like a glutinous blob anyway, had snapped, "They're not *your* mom and dad." "Good, Elsbeth," said Dr. Linda, "you're vocalizing! Do you have anything else you'd like to say?" and Elsbeth had shaken her head, and Dr. Linda had said, "All right. Peter, let's start with you. Any thoughts about what we discussed last week, how your profession as a chef might have influenced Elsbeth's behavior?" and again Elsbeth couldn't control herself; she'd burst out, "Lay off him, it's not his fault, it's *hers.*" "Me!" said June; "what did *I* do? You should be thanking me," and Elsbeth said, "For what, telling me I'm fat my whole life and then shipping me off to this dungeon?" and June had started to cry. "You needed *treatment*," she said, "and if we hadn't put you here you'd be dead of malnutrition or heart arrhythmia like Karen Carpenter, and don't you forget it," and Elsbeth said, "Well, fuck you very much."

"*Hey*," said both parents, and Peter said, "Don't talk to your mother that way," and when June got up to leave, Peter rose too. Something in Elsbeth's chest had felt like it was heaving, thrashing around. She yelled, "Fine, go with her! Take her side. You always do. Even though she's sleeping with her boss, she's been cheating on you for years!" Both Peter and June stopped, and Dr. Linda said into the terrible silence, "June? Peter? Is this true?" June was fumbling in her purse, taking out a cigarette although she couldn't smoke in Dr. Linda's office; holding it, she finally said, "Yes." "I'm sorry," said Elsbeth, "I'm so sorry, Dad, I didn't mean to just say it like that, but it's true. And you'd know it if you weren't half asleep all the time anyway." She was crying so hard she could barely get the words out. "I'm sorry," she said over and over, "I'm sorry," and June had walked out while Peter stood with his head down and his fists in his pockets. Finally Dr. Linda had said, "Elsbeth, why are you sorry? Do you feel responsible for your dad's feelings? For his well-being?" and Elsbeth had snapped, "Of course," and Dr. Linda had sat back. "Ah," she said, "now we're getting somewhere."

So Elsbeth highly doubted her visitor was either parent. June would never speak to her again, and Peter—Elsbeth could hardly stand to think about Peter. He had given her a cursory hug before he'd walked off yesterday, down the long hall; she hadn't even been able to watch him go. She prayed he wasn't in intensive care somewhere. But the staff here would have let Elsbeth know—and maybe it was Julian! Maybe he'd reemerged and found her. Not through Elsbeth's parents, obviously, since Julian was persona non grata at the Rashkin household, and anyway his lawyer had filed a restraining order against Peter after Peter had crashed his exhibit and assaulted him. But there were ways. Maybe Julian had hired a private detective.

"Here you go," said the nurse, pushing open the door to the visitors' room, and there, at the conference table, was Liza. Elsbeth shrieked, and Liza threw herself at Elsbeth and the two collided. Elsbeth teared up because Liza smelled so familiar, of menthol cigarettes and knock-off Obsession.

"Yo yo yo yo, baby pop," said Liza, when they separated. "Damn, it's good to see you. Elsbeth Olivia Rashkin, in the flesh."

"Too much of it," said Elsbeth. "Tell me the truth, do I look"— and, glancing at the monitor in the corner, she mouthed, *Fat?*

"Are you for real? No! You look so much better. You were starting to look like Skeletor. Plus, that color's good on you. Not everyone can carry off mint green."

"Thanks," said Elsbeth, looking down at her scrubs. "They won't let us wear anything else." She wiped her eyes. "Sorry, I cry all the time now. This place is like an emotional lobotomy."

"That sounds kinda rad," said Liza. She sat cross-legged on the conference table; she was wearing a cowl-necked purple sweater dress over black ripped tights, and her ashy hair was longer, to her shoulders. Elsbeth wasn't sure what she missed more, being able to eat unmonitored or wear civilian clothes.

"Can we smoke in here?" said Liza, taking out a cigarette.

"Hardly. I'd offer you some food, but—you know."

"Yeah," said Liza. She stuck the cigarette behind her ear and patted the table. Elsbeth hopped up, and Liza moved so they were sitting facing each other.

"How is it?" she asked. "Really?"

"It's hell."

Liza laughed. "But they're letting you out soon, right? Springing you on an unsuspecting world?"

"Not soon enough," said Elsbeth. She murmured, "So, did you get any more information for my . . . art project?"

Liza shook her head, and her sword earrings clanked. "That's what I came to tell you. I think that project's officially kaput. Over."

"Did you go to the sites?"

"I did," said Liza. "At his studio there's still police tape up, and it doesn't look like anyone's been there for ages. And uptown—well, kid, I hate to tell you this, but there's some woman living there."

"A woman!" said Elsbeth.

"Yeah, but don't get your panties in a bunch. Not *with* him. He's not there. Her name's on his mailbox in masking tape. It's probably a sublet."

Elsbeth thought about a woman living in Julian's loft and wanted to kill her, whoever it was. She hoped the woman was at least eighty, with a gray wig and wheeled shopping cart and lots of cats.

"How about the papers?" she asked. "Or his manager? His lawyer? Anybody?"

"Nothing new in the papers. His manager hung up on me— that guy needs a serious attitude adjustment—and his lawyer keeps saying he can't comment while the case is still open."

Elsbeth sighed. "Okay. Thanks for trying."

"Pas de problème."

"Will you keep looking for me? Until I get out?"

"Of course," said Liza, squeezing Elsbeth's knee.

"Thanks," said Elsbeth. "So, what else is going on?"

Liza hopped off the table. "Come with me, I'll show you!" she said. "Wait, are you allowed to leave the room?" She looked at the black camera in the corner. "Can Elsbeth come out to play?" she yelled.

"Stop," said Elsbeth, but she was laughing. "Yes, I can move freely within the gulag—I just can't go beyond reception."

"Come on, then," said Liza and tugged Elsbeth out of the room and down the hall.

At the door to the reception area they stopped and looked through its window at a man sitting on one of the couches. "There he is," said Liza, *"mon amour.* Ron!"

"What?" said Elsbeth.

"Yup," said Liza. "This is it, kid. I'm in loooooooove," and she gave it her special trademark gargle.

"Wow," said Elsbeth. The man had fluffy brown hair, jeans, bomber jacket; he seemed utterly unremarkable, except—

"Isn't he kind of . . . old?" said Elsbeth.

"Thirty-eight," said Liza cheerfully. "Divorced. Owns a bunch of condos down the Shore. I met him at Limelight on Halloween—when I was dressed as my mom, remember? Isn't that a scream?"

"It sure is," said Elsbeth.

Liza tapped on the window with a long red nail, and Ron looked up. "Isn't he to die for?" Liza said. "Isn't he a stone-cold fox?" She pushed the door open and skipped out. "Say hi to my best friend," she said, planting a smacking kiss on Ron's cheek.

Ron waved. "Hi, best friend," he said, in a slightly nasal voice.

"We've got to book," said Liza, "long drive back, and Ron has the kids tomorrow, don't you, honey."

"Bye, best friend," said Ron, and they started toward the front door with their arms slung around each other like competitors in a three-legged race. Liza turned and pointed at Ron's head, mouthing, *He's the one!* "Catch you on the flip side," she called, and then they were gone.

When the door had wheezed closed behind them, Elsbeth sagged against the wall. She felt sorrier for herself than ever: What was left for her out there? Her mom hated her; she had destroyed her dad; Liza would probably marry that geriatric dweeb as soon as she graduated, Very's parents were sending her to boarding school, and Julian was gone. Elsbeth would have nobody. Again Elsbeth replayed the moment she'd last seen Julian, backing away from his bedroom door: *Charlie, wait! Charlie, please!* He'd chased after her, and she'd bolted. She had been so stupid! She should have stayed; she should have let him catch her, persuade her to come back, shoo those other people out of his apartment, get dressed. Lead her to the deli. Explain. She'd been an idiot to leave. Of course those people didn't mean anything to him. It was just sex—everybody knew geniuses did things a little differently. But he'd cared about Elsbeth. He had. *There aren't many synesthetes, Charlie. We're two of a kind.* Elsbeth would give anything to have that moment in Julian's hallway back, to do over again.

Dr. Linda stuck her head out of a doorway and looked around. "There you are, Elsbeth," she said. "Coming to group?"

"Sure, I'll be right there," said Elsbeth. She waited until Dr. Linda withdrew, then went to the cafeteria—another misnomer, since there was no food in it, except at mealtimes. But it was where they ate then, three times a day, with knife, fork, and spoon, not fingers; in full bites, not tiny pieces; they were not allowed to engage with their food, to change its appearance or carve it up or push it around or do anything except put it in their mouths, chew, and swallow; they had to stay in their seats until everything on their plates, the caloric, carbohydrate- and fat-laden mashed potatoes and chicken breasts and peas and corn and salad with industrial dressing was all gone.

There was also a pay phone in the cafeteria, and although they were supposed to use it only during the hour before bed, it wasn't Elsbeth's fault nobody was supervising her, was it? She picked up the receiver and punched in the digits, using the number of the calling card she'd swiped from June's purse.

On the other end, Julian's phone rang and rang. And rang. *If you'd like to make a call, please hang up and try again.* Elsbeth did. "You know this isn't really about Julian, don't you?" Dr. Linda had said kindly, earlier this week, looking at Elsbeth with her big blue eyes. She was pretty, Dr. Linda, in a round doll-faced kind of way, except for that spare tire at her waist; didn't she want to get rid of that? "I know your feelings for Julian are very strong, but they're what we call transference. Are you starting to see how they're really about Mom, the love you feel she never gave you, and Dad and the love you tried to give him? And his sadness, and your half sisters, the ones who died in the war?" Elsbeth had nodded and said Yes, she saw it now—but she'd agreed only so Dr. Linda would write her a good report and let Elsbeth out of this hellhole. Privately Elsbeth thought it was the stupidest thing she'd ever heard. Of course her love for Julian wasn't about June, or Peter, or Masha and Vivian and Ginger or President Reagan or anyone else; it was about Julian. Oh, Julian! He was the only one who had understood her, who had really seen her, who was like her; Elsbeth had loved him the moment she first saw him, and she always would; she would go on loving Julian until the day she died.

When Peter came outside, into the backyard of the Glenwood house, Elsbeth was sitting on the swing set. It was an old metal structure he had put together for her when she was four, using a set of instructions only a little less complicated than the blueprint for the A-bomb, so the mission took a week and a lot of swearing. Peter had never been good at recipes for anything—his dishes he assembled by instinct, not by measurement—and mechanics were beyond him. The swing set therefore represented a triumph of determination over ability, a physical manifestation of his great love for his daughter. Peter had always secretly feared it might one day collapse, the one screw he had inserted incorrectly, the widget he'd put in backward giving way just when Elsbeth was at the top of the slide or sailing through the air. Somehow the contraption had held together, though its candy-striped poles were now rusty, the carousel horse's eyes whitened by seasons of sun and rain. Elsbeth was sitting on one of the two middle swings, not moving, her head drooping. She hadn't been on the thing in years.

Peter started across the grass toward her. It was April, just past Easter, and the ground squelched underfoot. The Glenwood backyard was awakening after the winter, gearing up to be at its most enchanting: the buds on the big oaks, now furled, would burst open; the wildflowers in Elsbeth's childhood fairy circle, a mysterious ring by the brook, would fill with small white stars. The forsythia hedge was just starting to turn yellow and the weeping willow to fuzz with tiny leaves. The grass was greening and the air smelled of mud and ice thawing in the stream; Peter had to wear what June called his Archie Bunker jacket, a heavy plaid flannel, because the sun's warmth was more an optimistic idea than any real heat. But it would get stronger.

Elsbeth looked up at Peter's approach. She gave him a little wave but didn't smile, and then she looked down at her feet again, in the dirt beneath the swing, in aqua basketball sneakers. They had scribbling all over them, mysterious sayings and drawings Elsbeth and her friends at the eating disorder center had done on her last day. June had told Peter this; the analyst there had told her. Elsbeth herself had not said much of anything since they had picked her up at the beginning of the month. She was respectful and polite but quiet, eating her measured amounts of food at the table with her parents three times a day, using a knife and fork, the door to her bedroom and bathroom left open at all times. She had stabilized, according to her analyst, and she no longer looked like a refugee from a DP camp. To anyone else, she would appear just an ordinary girl. But Peter would never absolve himself for not having seen it, how Elsbeth had grown thinner and thinner still, how her makeup had grown darker and her nails longer and her skirts shorter and her heels higher and all the while she was melting herself away, his Ellie, all to pose for that bastard, that soulless predatory cocksucker Wilton, he should burn in hell. "You have to forgive yourself," Elsbeth's analyst had told Peter, "for everything, for what's happened here and for your first wife and daughters. Because it hurts Elsbeth, you see? She senses your pain and internalizes it. When you forgive yourself, you help her." Peter had nodded and said he would try, but he didn't think he would ever be able to do it.

"Hey, Dad," said Elsbeth when Peter got to the swings. She looked at him, again unsmiling, and he saw how hollow her cheeks still were within her cloud of hair.

"Hi, Ellie," Peter said. He stood with his hands in his pockets, unsure how to approach her; he was a little scared of her, of saying or doing the wrong thing, something that might set her off again—his Ellie! It broke his heart.

"May I join you?" he asked.

"Sure," she said, and Peter sat in the swing next to hers. The red plastic seat, meant for a child, wasn't big enough, and the chains bowed out comically around his hips; there was an ominous crack. Elsbeth laughed.

"Don't worry," she said. "Mine did the same to me. At first I thought it was because I was—you know, fat. But that's what Dr. Linda called a false belief."

"Yes," said Peter. "You are just fine the way you are." They had told him to say this, but also it was true. Didn't Elsbeth know, how could she not know? She could weigh a hundred pounds or four hundred, and he would still love her.

"It's because the seat's too small for me," continued Elsbeth. "It was designed for a little kid, and I'm not anymore."

"No," agreed Peter, "you're not."

He smiled at her, sitting in the sun in her denim jacket and denim jeans, not warm enough for the day, her ghastly makeup washed off, her nails clipped and clean, the only sign of her earlier venture into premature womanhood being the big hoops in her ears. Peter wanted to tuck her light-brown curls back behind them and dared not. Where had it come from, her hair? It must have been somebody on June's side of the family, some throwback. Where had Ellie herself come from? She was a blessing, a gift from the God Peter did not believe in; a surprise after

June's miscarriage, one Peter had not been prepared for. He had thought after his girls and the lost baby there would never be another, that he was destined to be childless and that was exactly as it should be. And then there had come Ellie, wrenched from her mother red-faced and squalling with indignation, a person utterly unto herself, melting Peter as completely and easily as butter in the pan. He had never fully understood Ellie—there was too much June in her. But he was so grateful for that. In this American child her mother's genes had dominated her father's, so Elsbeth had more of June's stubbornness and determination and zest than Peter's timidity and formality. He feared for her, as any father would. To have a child was indeed to have one's stomach, one's heart, walking around outside one's body. But in Elsbeth the best of Peter and June was combined, and Peter thought this made her stronger than them both.

Elsbeth put the toe of one sneaker in the depression beneath the swing and pushed. "So what's the verdict?" she asked.

Peter looked away across the yard, at the big willow behind the garage, the forsythia lining the driveway.

"We're going to sell the house," he said. "Your mother is."

Elsbeth nodded. "And?"

"And," said Peter. There was such a pain in his throat he could hardly speak. He said, "Your mother and I will be getting a divorce. You and she will be going to Minneapolis to live. You will be closer to your grandmother Ida, and your mother has friends there who will help her get established as a real estate agent."

"No," said Elsbeth.

"Yes, Ellie," said Peter. "I am sorry. I know that's not what you want to hear."

"No, it sure isn't," she said, and began to cry. "Why?" she wept. "Why do I have to go? Why does she have to move? Why do I have to go with her? Why can't I stay here with you?"

"Ellie," said Peter.

"I don't want to! I won't go with her. She hates me! She always has."

"She doesn't," said Peter. "I know you and your mother have had your differences, but she loves you very much. And a girl needs her mother."

"I won't do it," Elsbeth repeated. Her face was fiercely red from crying. "I won't! I'll run away. I'll start purging again!"

"Elsbeth Rashkin," said Peter, "that will not solve a thing. If you run away, we will find you. If you make yourself sick, we will send you back to the center. We will keep you safe whether you like it or not. Now, the decision has been made. You must respect it. We are your parents, and there's nothing for you to do."

Elsbeth lowered her head and cried and cried, and Peter nudged his swing over toward hers and put his arm around her. He rocked them back and forth. Elsbeth's hair smelled unfamiliar, adult, of perfume, but her face was hot and wet against his shoulder, and this he remembered from a hundred girlhood hurts and consolations, from her early feedings. Thank God, there was still some child in her. He let her sob, listening to the rill of water in the brook, the swings creaking, the high sweet songs of birds.

"Why, Dad," she said finally, muffled. "Why?"

She detached herself and sat up. Peter handed her his handkerchief from his pocket, and she laughed a little, wiping her eyes.

"What am I going to do without your handkerchiefs?" she asked.

"I will send you with a whole package of them," said Peter, "and if you use them up, I will send you more."

"Why do I have to go with her?" Elsbeth said. Her face was swollen, her eyes—Peter's eyes, his mother's eyes, gray-green—bloodshot from weeping. "Why can't I stay here with you?"

"I would like nothing better, Ellie. But after the house is sold, I'll likely be staying with Sol and Ruth for a while. And then I'll probably move back into the city."

"That's all right," said Elsbeth. "I like the city."

"I am aware of that," Peter said dryly, remembering the giant images of his child's naked body in lurid Technicolor, hanging by the dozen beneath gallery lights in SoHo. Like a creature from a storybook, a centaur who was half child, half woman. It was something no father should ever have to see, not to mention have exposed to other adults. Peter had stared around at the well-dressed, ultracivilized art lovers, holding their plastic cups of wine, eating cubes of cheese and discussing his daughter's nudity in terms of "lighting," "brilliance," "saturation," "composition," and he had wished them all struck instantly and permanently blind.

Elsbeth had the good grace to look embarrassed.

"Sorry," she muttered. "But seriously, why can't I stay with you? I like apartments. I don't need a lot of space."

"What, and cramp my style?" said Peter. "I'm getting a swinging bachelor pad." He wiggled his eyebrows at her, but she glowered at him.

"A bad joke," he said. "Apologies. But Ellie, whether you think so or not, you do need more space. A house. A good school. A fresh start, where you can focus on what's next." He almost said *Like a culinary program!, and then perhaps our restaurant*, but stopped himself in time; the analyst had been insistent that Peter let Elsbeth form her own ambitions, ones that might not revolve around food. Goodbye to the Fabulous Rashkins—perhaps.

Elsbeth scowled. "So this is a punishment," she said. "Sending me off to the land of Minnesota Nice with Mom, to keep me away from the big, bad city and people like. . . . *him*. Well, it doesn't work that way, Dad. I can get into just as much trouble in Minneapolis. There are guys there too, you know."

Peter felt terror and despair in the pit of his stomach, but he said, "I'm aware of that as well, Ellie. That will be your choice. You can choose to do things that will hurt you, or you can choose things that won't. Your mother and I can't affect that. But we can help you, and we are always here for you, whatever happens."

"How can you say that, when you'll be half a country away?"

"You may have heard of a device called the telephone," said Peter. "I'll call you every night."

"*Every* night?"

"I'll call you as much as you like," amended Peter. "And I hear there are modern conveyances called airplanes. I will come see you, once a month. And you'll come to me. And we'll have holidays, and you may spend the whole summer with me, if you wish." He almost added, *Cooking!*

Elsbeth dug her sneakers into the dirt. "I'd like that."

"Then it shall happen."

"Dad?"

"Yes, Ellie."

She looked over at him, her face full of fear. "What will happen to you?"

"Oh, Ellie," said Peter. He had been so unable to understand a child feeling responsible for a parent; it was such a complete reversal of the natural order of things that the analyst had had to work hard to persuade him. She is very protective of you, Peter, the doctor had said. You must reassure her you'll be all right.

"I've got big plans," said Peter. "I'm going to finish my cookbook, for one thing."

Elsbeth looked dubious. "Okay, and?"

"And . . . after we sell the house and I get my own place, I'll probably start working again. In a kitchen."

"But Daddy, your heart," she whispered.

"My heart will be fine," said Peter. "I won't be running a restaurant; I'll be a lowly chef. Just the way I like it. I diet. I exercise. I have medication. And most importantly, I've got you, Ellie. You are my heart. Don't you know that?"

"Daaaad," she said. But she smiled, and her eyes filled with tears, and she scooted her swing over to put her head on Peter's shoulder again. Peter kissed the top of it.

"Don't you worry about your old man, Ellie," he said. "I will be fine."

He felt her sigh. A cardinal sang overhead and was answered by its mate, and Peter remembered Hilde, his family cook, teaching him how to identify birdsong long ago.

"Daddy?" Elsbeth said.

"Yes, Ellie."

"Would you tell me about them?"

"About whom?"

"Masha," said Elsbeth. "And the girls."

Peter sat still. Elsbeth did too. He felt her breathing against him, the breeze pushing strands of her hair against his face.

"My sisters," she said. "I do know a little about them. Ruth told me. And I saw their picture. But Dr. Linda said I should ask you. She said it would help me to know."

Her voice was small and getting softer, as if someone were turning down a radio.

"I don't know," she went on. "Maybe it's stupid. It won't really change anything. But I've thought about them my whole life. I want to know them. I just want to know."

Peter looked over Elsbeth's head across the yard, at the mist rising from the forsythia in the sun. So long ago. So far away. Another life altogether. And here it was, here they were still, on this gentle spring morning. Masha. The girls.

Elsbeth stirred, separating from Peter, sitting up. "Sorry. I knew I shouldn't have asked . . ."

"No," said Peter. "You should have. You should, Ellie. And you are brave to ask."

He felt her glance doubtfully at him, but he couldn't look at her. Not right now. He focused on the shrubs with their new leaves, the yellow flowers. He stilled his swing so he and his daughter sat together.

"Well," he said. "I met Masha when I was seventeen, only a year older than you are now . . ."

And somehow, whether from some inner source or this child beside him, Peter Rashkin, who had long ago thought he was past making any fresh start of his own, found the strength to begin.

ACKNOWLEDGMENTS

The author would like to thank multitudes of people but will try to keep this shorter than an Oscars speech and get offstage before the music plays.

Booksellers, librarians, dear readers: whether you've hosted me at an event or in your home, kept me company on social media, or read my novels in blissful solitude, thank you for reading my books and inspiring me so greatly.

My amazing team at HarperCollins, especially Amy Baker, Daniel Vazquez, my girl Katherine Beitner, Christine Choe, Leah Wasielewski, Nathaniel Knaebel, Milan Bozic, Adalis Martinez, copy editor Miranda Ottewell, and my phenomenal editor, the iconic Sara Nelson, whose warmth and wisdom I'm so grateful for and whose first reaction to this novel is my screensaver.

My foreign publishers: Verlagsgruppe Random House GmbH; Cappelen Damm; de Boekerij—*dankeschoen, takk, bedankt.* Maaike le Noble, Jorien de Vries, Suzanne Plug—huge XXX to you!

The exceptional MMQ crew, particularly Lexi Wangler, who make a writer's life not only possible but smoothly functional.

Grub Street Writers, best writing school in the world: thank you for employing me for twenty years, thereby allowing me to teach such talented, fierce, funny writers. Love to my Council.

Literary fairy godmothers Robin Kall Homonoff of *Reading with*

Robin and Susan E. McBeth of *Adventures by the Book*: thank you for everything you do to connect writers and readers—which is everything. SaraJane Giddings, you are my secret weapon.

My first *Lost Family* readers: Cecile Corona, Tracy Hahn-Burkett, Henriette Lazaridus, Mari Passananti, Becky Tuch; Julie Hirsch, my one and only Puppet; Stephanie "Goodie" Ebbert, who delivered her suggestions over whiskey; and Kirsten Liston, who scrolled through the whole novel on her iPhone: thank you for your encouragement and feedback. *Geliebte* Christiane Alsop, *danke* for your childhood recipes. Kirsten Beck and Bernadette Lee, who will recognize way too much in this novel. Tom Champoux, for lockdown nourishment. Maddie Houpt, for Woodrow care. Edmond Manning, for the dueling-laptops writing session and eating chocolate cake from the floor (unbeknownst to you). Necee Regis, for the *Betty Crocker New Pictures Cookbook*. Claudete Rizzotto, for influencing captive audiences. Dr. Glenda Lawless and Dr. Lydia Baumrind, for listening and advice. Eric Grunwald and Jean Charbonneau, my mainstays.

Above & Beyond Awards go to my writer girls Kate Woodworth and Whitney Scharer, whose empathy, cheerleading, and simultaneous labor sustained me every day.

My *Grand Central* sisters, who keep WWII stories alive, and especially Kristina McMorris, who invited inspiration without which this book would not exist. Every writer who supports others; deep curtseys to Caroline Leavitt, Sarah McCoy, Jane Green.

My family: Joey Blum, Lesley MM Blume & Co., Judy Blum, and the Joergs. My indefatigable mother, Frances Blum McCarthy—love you, Mama.

There are not enough words in any language to express my gratitude to my superagent, Stéphanie Abou, to whom I owe my books and my whole literary life. I treasure every conversation we had about *The Lost Family*, from ideation to Masha's menus to post-midnight Bitmojis. Dearest Stéphanie, *merci bien*. I'm so thankful for you.

Finally, to my beloveds, Woodrow and Jim "Book Daddy" Reed. Jim, love, thank you for the countless breakfasts during which you patiently listened to ideas for scenes, scraps of dialogue, and utter non sequiturs, then issued excellent advice. For not talking to me or kissing me until I had written that day's scene. For you and Woodrow, for your stamina, company, laughter, and love, I am eternally grateful.

ABOUT THE AUTHOR

Jenna Blum is the *New York Times* and number one international bestselling author of the novels *Those Who Save Us* and *The Stormchasers*. She was also voted one of the favorite contemporary women writers by Oprah.com readers. Jenna is based in Boston, where she earned her MA from Boston University and has taught fiction and novel workshops for Grub Street Writers for twenty years.

READING GUIDE

INTRODUCTION

The *New York Times* bestselling author of *Those Who Save Us* creates a vivid portrait of marriage, family and the haunting grief of World War II in this emotionally charged, beautifully rendered story that spans a generation, from the 1960s to the 1980s.

In 1965 Manhattan, patrons flock to Masha's to savour its brisket bourguignon and impeccable service and to admire its dashing owner and head chef Peter Rashkin. With his movie star good looks and tragic past, Peter, a survivor of Auschwitz, is the most eligible bachelor in town. But Peter does not care for the parade of eligible women who come to the restaurant hoping to catch his eye. He has resigned himself to a solitary life. Running Masha's consumes him, as does his terrible guilt over surviving the horrors of the Nazi death camp while his wife, Masha — the restaurant's namesake — and two young daughters perished.

Then exquisitely beautiful June Bouquet, an up-and-coming young model, appears at the restaurant, piercing Peter's guard. Though she is twenty years his junior, the two begin a passionate, whirlwind courtship. When June unexpectedly becomes pregnant, Peter proposes, believing that beginning a new family with the woman he loves will allow him to let go of the horror of the past. But over the next twenty years, the indelible sadness of those memories will overshadow Peter, June and their daughter Elsbeth, transforming them in shocking, heartbreaking and unexpected ways.

QUESTIONS FOR DISCUSSION

1. Consider Masha's restaurant. How is running the restaurant important to Peter? In what ways does it help or hinder his attempt to bear his loss and grief and live a fuller life?

2. When Peter and June first meet at Masha's, what draws them to each other? Despite their very different personal experiences, what do they have in common?

3. Consider the various relationships different characters have with food. What's revealed by what and how each person eats? Which approach seems particularly healthy or not?

4. To 'blot out unwelcome thoughts,' Peter 'took inventory, cataloguing what the restaurant had in its storeroom.' What are these thoughts? How does this activity help him? To what extent can work or distraction help with emotional difficulty? What are the limits of such an approach?

5. Note the many allusions to art and music throughout the novel. What does each add to the layers of meaning in the story? What's the value of art and music in one's personal life? How, in particular, might it serve in times of grief and suffering? Why did Peter try 'not to listen to music at all'?

6. 'If Peter's insides had matched his outsides, he would have looked like a Picasso. Like *Guernica*.' What does this mean? In what other ways does Peter conceal elements of himself? To what extent is this normal and when might it become unhealthy?

7. Compare and contrast how Peter and June each feel about and present their physical selves, their bodies. In what ways does each change or not as they age? What factors determine how a person feels about his or her body? How is Elsbeth's relationship to her body influenced by her parents?

8. In what ways have Sol and Ruth been good for Peter or not?

9. In what ways do the memories of Masha and Vivian and Ginger influence Peter, for better or worse? Is his adamant decision to never speak of them helpful or hurtful? What are the best ways to heal from such profound grief and loss?

10. When June had finally seen Peter's scars, 'the braille of [his] humiliation and helplessness,' he thinks that 'happiness . . . had made him careless.' What does he mean? What is 'the blessing of scars'?

11. After talking to June of his scars and the suffering that caused them, Peter's 'heartened' that 'she had handled it well.' What is it in her response that is so effective and helpful? How is it that she could understand some of his profound experience? What's important in any response to another's suffering or grief?

12. Peter becomes concerned that his growing love for June 'had punctured the sealed chamber into which [he] had put Masha and the girls.' What is he afraid of? To what extent should these two loves be kept separate or not?

13. Sitting in Carl Schurz Park, Peter experiences the 'calming effects of being near water.' His daughter Elsbeth also 'loved the water.' What is it for each of them that is so valuable about water? Where else in the novel does water seem significant?

14. Peter realizes that 'his worst, most damning trait . . . that defined him, the secret at his core . . . was his inability to act, his paralysis in crucial situations.' Where has this demonstrated itself in his life? What might explain this behaviour?

15. What is the 'magnitude of discrepancy' June experiences with Peter as their relationship progresses? Consider her various responses to frustrations and unhappiness, from rearranging the furniture to being unfaithful. What does each reveal about what she wants and needs?

16. June believes herself to lack 'natural maternal instinct' for Elsbeth and to simply 'want other things.' What does she desire in her life? Is this incompatible with having a child?

17. Regarding food – its preparation, presentation, flavour, etc. – Peter's 'passion consumed him.' Why is this? What might this reveal about his profound emotional experiences and burdens?

18. What kinds of difficulties does Elsbeth struggle with as she becomes a teenager? What particular emotional difficulties

does she have with her mother? What is attractive to her about Julian? For what various reasons might she be so drawn to being photographed by him?

19. Are Julian's photographs justified as art? How does such subject matter connect to the theme of the body — in injury and health, shame and pride, ugliness and beauty — throughout the novel? To what extent is the body personal or public? Where do these lines blur?

20. How is it that Peter is eventually able to open emotionally to Elsbeth, to begin to share the story of his deep love and loss of Masha and the girls? What are the risks of such sharing? How does it work to heal?

EVERYTHING I
NEVER TOLD YOU

CELESTE NG

'Lydia is dead. But they don't know this yet.'

So begins this exquisite novel about a Chinese-American
family living in 1970s small-town Ohio. Lydia is the
favourite child of Marilyn and James Lee, and her parents
are determined that she will fulfill the dreams they were
unable to pursue. But when Lydia's body is found in the local
lake, the delicate balancing act that has been keeping the Lee
family together is destroyed, tumbling them all into chaos.

A profoundly moving story of secrets and longing,
Everything I Never Told You is both a gripping page-turner
and a sensitive family portrait, about love, lies and race.

'If we know this story, we haven't seen it yet in American
fiction, not until now' **New York Times Book Review**

'This ghostly debut novel calls to mind
The Lovely Bones' **Marie Claire**

B
BLACKFRIARS

THE SISTERS CHASE

SARAH HEALY

The hardscrabble Chase women – Mary, Hannah and their mother Diane – have been eking out a living running a tiny seaside motel that has been in the family for generations, inviting trouble into their lives for just as long. Where eighteen-year-old Mary Chase is a force of nature, her much younger sister, Hannah, is imaginative, her head full of the stories of princesses and adventures that Mary tells to give her a safe emotional place in the middle of their troubled world.

When Diane dies in a car accident, Mary's finely tuned instincts for survival kick in. As the sisters begin a cross-country journey in search of a better life, she will stop at nothing to protect Hannah. But Mary wants to protect herself too, for the secrets she promised she would never tell hold the weight of unbearable loss. Vivid and suspenseful, *The Sisters Chase* is a whirlwind page-turner about the extreme lengths one family will go to find – and hold onto – love.

B
BLACKFRIARS